I0558868

Living Dead
in Delaware

An Undead-Earth Novel
Book 2

M.P. Esham

Revision 4

ISBN-10: 0982762321
ISBN-13: 9780982762325

10 9 8 7 6 5 4 3 2 1

Undead-Earth Series:

Book 1…Getting Out of Jersey
Book 2…Living Dead in Delaware

Contents

Chapter 2 15
Chapter 3 30
Chapter 4 43
Chapter 5 59
Chapter 6 96
Chapter 7 110
Chapter 8 131
Chapter 9 141
Chapter 10 162
Chapter 11 179
Chapter 12 187
Chapter 13 197
Chapter 14 199
Chapter 15 208
Chapter 16 213
Chapter 17 225
Chapter 18 230
Chapter 19 236
Epilogue 257

Chapter 1

The Buick rode like a tank, floating on its suspension as the shocks struggled against the weight of the Park Avenue chassis. A blanket covered the backseat, but I could still feel the edges of split vinyl beneath my head as I lay across the backseat, my feet on the driver's side door and my arms over my head to brace myself as Justine weaved her way through abandoned cars and other random debris on the road.

In too much pain to sit up and look, I could only listen as she cursed and named random objects as she worked her way around them. Grills, dressers, and every piece of furniture ever made fell from her lips in muted anger. All the things people abandoned when their evacuation turned to an outright flight littered our path.

I tried to stay awake, but the gentle rocking of the car and the constant hum of Justine's cursing lulled me half to sleep. I opened my eyes, stared at the back of the driver's seat, and frowned. Something was different. The car was too quiet, and we seemed to be slowly coasting.

I pulled myself up until I could get my feet on the floor and push with my left leg, struggling into a sitting position. I winced as my right hip screamed at me, but it was worth the pain to see out the window.

We were cruising slowly away from the Delaware River along 273, moving at no more than ten miles an hour. "How far have we made it?" I asked Justine, running my hands through my hair.

When she didn't answer, I put my hands on the back of her seat and pulled myself up. Her head rested against the back of the headrest. When I grabbed her shoulder, her head tilted toward me, eyes closed.

"Justine, wake up!"

I shook her shoulder more forcefully, but she didn't respond. Instead, she slid down in her seat until her knees lodged against the dash. I reached over the seat and grabbed her chin so I could see her face. Her eyes fluttered open for a half second when I shook her head gently, long enough to see that the deep brown of her irises was fading, a cloudy slate color taking its place.

I started to pull myself over the seat back, but the moment my lower back flexed, pain shot up and down my spine. I fell back into the rear seat as my back spasmed. Just as I tried to get a hold of the seat to pull myself back up, the car's right tires rolled off the road onto the grass, jostling me around.

I looked up just in time to see the telephone pole looming ahead. We hit doing about three miles an hour. It felt like sixty. I braced myself as my butt slid forward, pain shooting up and down my back. I watched helplessly as Justine tilted forward, hitting her head on the steering wheel with a solid *thunk*. The engine turned over roughly and died as we came to a halt against the pole.

"Are you OK?" I asked, hugging the headrest and panting through the fiery pain in my back.

Justine, now draped over the steering wheel, did not reply. I let go of the headrest and reached forward to touch her, my fingers stretching until I could just brush the back of her shirt. Ignoring the pain shooting down my right leg, I lifted myself just enough to get a handful of her shirt and pull her off the steering wheel.

She flopped back and then fell sideways toward the passenger door, but at least she was close enough for me to get my hands on her. Her chest rose and fell gently, but her skin was cool to the touch.

Cursing as I tried to climb into the front seat, I winced as my lower back throbbed every time I tried to lever myself up. I uttered a low scream when my legs gave out, dropping me back onto the rear seat. There was just no way I was climbing over the seat in my current condition.

I scanned the ground around the car. I was going to have to get out, but the idea of leaving the artificial safety of the Buick scared me. Justine was unconscious, and I was so beat up I could barely move. I looked around the car, staring at abandoned vehicles with apprehension.

I steadied myself with several long breaths before I unlocked my door, analyzing every movement before I made it. With my courage gathered, getting out of the car and staying on my feet was another matter entirely. I strained the muscles in my arms as I used my upper body to stabilize myself.

The climb around the back door toward the front left me with sweat running down my face, stinging my eyes and torturing me with the temptation to take my hands off the car to wipe my brow. I resisted, shaking my head so the sweat sprinkled onto the window.

I yanked the driver's door open and let myself fall sideways onto the edge of the seat, my hips colliding with Justine's, sliding her smaller form into the middle of the bench seat. I grabbed her by her shirt, the fabric tearing as I dragged her onto my lap. She didn't react as I manhandled her; her body remained limp.

I said her name, desperate for her to show some sign of life. Her chest moved as she breathed, but the rest of her lay flaccid, her skin growing colder.

I said her name over and over as I grabbed her head and lifted one of her eyelids. Her pupils and the whites of her eyes were gone, replaced by pools of dull, molten lead. I grabbed her arm, pulling her hand up so I could see her fingers. Black, inch-long claws had taken the place of her short, stubby nails.

I took her pointer finger and touched the tip of her nail, wincing and pulling back suddenly as it bit through my skin with ease. A drop of blood flew off my finger to land on the pavement outside the door as I pulled back. I put my finger in my mouth as I stared at Justine, my heart racing.

My chest ached. I'd never felt so much need in my life. From the first moment I'd talked to her, she'd slipped past all my defenses. Her deep brown eyes had pulled me in every time I looked into them. Even now, as I stroked the hair around her ear, I felt as if I couldn't breathe.

Cardboard skittered across the road, startling me. I craned my head around as far as I could and checked the mirrors to make sure something wasn't coming up on us from behind.

I turned back to Justine, the raw emotion inside me shifting and consolidating. Looking at her, even with her strange eyes and her fingers tipped with deadly claws, I felt completely connected. She was my mirror half. I didn't know what she was, and it didn't matter. When I looked at her, all I saw was the girl who'd snuck into my heart without even trying.

"I love you," I told her, touching her face with dirty fingers. Nothing else in the world mattered.

The scraping noise came again, then suddenly stopped. I rechecked the mirrors—still nothing. I looked at the open car door and my one leg still resting on the pavement feeling very exposed. I slowly pulled my leg into the car, a small sense of relief overcoming me.

The sound came again, lighter, different—but definitely much closer. I had the feeling I was being stalked. I let myself have two deep breaths as I scanned the rearview mirror. The road behind me was unchanged, but that only made my unease grow. Something was out there, and the driver's door was wide open.

I reached out, holding onto the steering wheel for support. The tips of my fingers brushed against the armrest then slipped free. My shoulders creaked as I stretched again, my fingers finally sliding into the gap on the armrest. I tightened my grip on the steering wheel, pulling the door closed just enough to get a better grip on it.

Just as I was about to slam the door shut, a shaggy mass of long brown hair came into view from under the car. I froze, looking down at the back of a woman's head.

Thin arms stretched out, palms slapping onto the ground as the thrall hauled itself forward. Its shoulders and upper back came into view, revealing a stained yellow sundress. Cuts and bloodless wounds covered its skin and bits of dead flesh hung here and there.

The thing put its head down and licked the surface of the road, lapping up the single drop of blood with a sound like sandpaper on concrete. The woman's hair fell around her face, hiding it from view.

I eased the door closed, trying not to breathe. It was a third of the way shut when my shifting weight made the seat groan. The thrall's head twitched slightly to the side at the noise, listening as I froze in place.

Sweat trickled down my face, falling from my chin to splash on the door sill. The thrall sucked in a deep breath and then went mad, slamming into the bottom of the car as it tried to lift itself on its arms.

I pulled the door closed as hard as I could.

I desperately wanted to hear the door slam shut, but the thrall lifted her head at the last moment. The door handle flew out of my fingers as the door whipped back open.

The thrall thrashed about, writhing beneath the car in violent spasms. I grabbed the car keys, pumping the gas as I frantically turned the ignition. The car turned over but refused to start, the noise accomplishing little more than to drive the thrall into a fit of rage. It beat against the underside of the car as it rolled over.

I let go of the key, leaning over Justine to grab for the hilt of my machete, ignoring the pain in my lower back as I worked the blade free. I turned back to the thrall to see dead hands reaching up.

The woman's hair had fallen away from her face—or what was left of it—as she rolled over. Her eye sockets were angry red pits sinking into her head, and her nose and lips were gone, making her teeth seem long and vicious.

Her arms flailed about as she searched, her teeth clacking together as she sucked in breaths through open sinuses, moving quicker now that she was certain something was close by. Her hand thudded against the car seat several times before she clamped down on the vinyl, pulling herself upright as her head moved spastically from side to side, searching.

I pushed against Justine, trying to get away from the hand feeling its way across the seat. The thrall's teeth continued to open and shut as I pushed against the steering wheel, sliding Justine farther across the seat as I fled the thrall's searching hands.

The thrall dragged itself up until its head was level with the bottom of the seat. It reached for another handhold, getting ready to pull itself into the car.

I pulled the machete back as far as I could in the confines of the car and struck. I hit her with all the strength I had, sinking the blade into her skull.

Two hands jumped up to grab the blade, and her head twisted about as she tried to free herself. For a moment, her legs kicked and fluttered, banging into the bottom of the car. Her knuckles crackled as she clamped down on the blade, and one of her thumbs fell into her lap, the force of her own grip severing it.

I held onto the machete as every muscle in her body went rigid, fighting to hold on as she bucked. Pain shot through my lower back and down my right leg as she yanked me about. I braced myself against the foot well, trying to straighten my body and pull the machete free. As I did, I caught a glimpse of the rearview mirror.

More thralls were climbing out of the abandoned cars behind us, and several were already walking toward the rear of the car, their path mildly erratic as they struggled against the sun in their eyes. I screamed in pain and anger as I drove the machete handle down, levering the blade up and out of the female thrall's head. As soon as the blade was free, she stopped jerking about and fell limp to the road.

The driver's side door stood wide open—too far away for me to grab it easily without getting out, which wasn't going to happen. Instead I pushed the accelerator a third of the way down and prayed the engine would start when I turned the ignition.

The thralls were getting closer, their actions becoming spastic as they smelled their fallen comrade and saw me in the car. The pack broke into a jerky run as I let up on the gas and turned the key. The engine turned over, the starter motor whining as the big eight-cylinder refused to catch. I stole a glance in the mirror. The thralls were even with the rear bumper.

I let up on the ignition, afraid I'd burn out the starter, pausing a moment before giving it another go. I feathered the gas and turned the ignition, trying to get the engine to catch. The thralls were parting, coming around the car on either side. One had run into the back of the car and was punching the trunk in confusion, rocking the vehicle as it dented the sheet metal.

The engine coughed. I let up on the gas ever so slightly as it turned over then gave it just a little more as it caught and rumbled to life. A thrall in a business suit stood at my door, hands reaching into the car as his upper body banged into the roof.

Gears slipped and squealed as I slid the shifter into reverse, feathering the gas as the engine started to struggle against the inertia of the vehicle. I pegged the accelerator and the transmission caught with a loud bang, sending the Buick jolting into reverse.

The open driver's side door slammed into the thrall in the business suit, carrying him with us as the front tires rolled over the dead female, giving us a nice bounce and causing him down to slip under the door. The thrall punching the trunk disappeared under the car as we accelerated over him.

Car doors opened all around us—thralls hesitantly creeping out into the light as the sound of the engine stirred them from their daytime slumber. I wanted to throw the car into drive and get out of there as fast as I could, but the Buick's transmission hung by a thread.

We were rolling backward at ten or fifteen miles an hour, directly toward a minivan T-boned by a Cadillac. I took my foot off the accelerator and hit the brakes. As soon as the car started to slow, the engine began to cough and sputter, threatening to stall, forcing me to give it gas.

I looked behind me in the rearview. I didn't have much room left, and there was no way I was going to be able to weave between the abandoned cars and the thralls in the road in reverse.

The gear shifter shook in my palm as I gently pulled it down, wiggling it into neutral so I could get my foot on the gas and the brake at the same time. As the car came to a stop, the driver's door slammed shut, scaring the piss out of me.

Justine's head popped off my lap at the sound. She looked around in puzzlement as I pulled the shifter into drive and let up on the brake so I didn't destroy the transmission.

"What's going on?" she asked, gripping my thigh with one hand as she braced the other on the center of the dash. I gasped, expecting a sharp pain in my leg as her claws dug in, but her fingers were her own again, her nails chewed down to nubs. I looked at her face, lingering on her beautiful brown eyes.

"I don't know," I told her, grabbing her hand for just a second to feel the warmth returning to her skin.

I pressed the accelerator down steadily, picking up speed as we blew by the telephone pole we ran into earlier, topping out at twenty—which, in the Buick, felt like eighty. I got my first taste of driving in the new world as wrecks littered the road.

A hand slammed into the passenger side window as we rolled past a school bus, making me jerk the steering wheel hard to the right in surprise. The car rocked from side to side as I sawed at the wheel, fighting to regain control. Justine braced herself in the passenger seat until we were stable again.

"What happened to you?" I asked her, my head darting about as I scanning the road and my mirrors while trying to watch her at the same time. She looked at me and then into the backseat, not sure. She had no idea how I'd gotten into the driver's seat.

"I don't know. I started to feel weird, and then I felt like someone else was here, and then everything went dark."

"OK, but you changed," I blurted out, not meaning for it to sound like an accusation.

"I'm sorry; I know. I felt it for just a second when I woke up, like a tide going out, pulling away." She shivered next to me and tried to move as far from me as she could. I clamped a hand around her shoulder to keep her near.

We drove on for a little while, both of us watching the deserted landscape, trying to come to terms with what was happening. The whole time we were in Jersey, the goal had been to get across the river to Delaware. Now we   were here, and things were just as bad. We'd actually thought we'd be sleeping in a Holiday Inn once we got out of Pennsville.

Normal life seemed like a long-lost dream, not something we'd known just a week ago. The mood in the car grew darker as we drove on, not really knowing where we were going, what to do, or what lay ahead. Our entire plan had been to get across the river into Delaware; now we were just wandering.

I'd been driving for an hour when our speed began meandering up and down as the pain in my leg made it hard to keep uniform pressure on the accelerator. "Time to switch,"

Justine announced when she started getting car sick.

"OK," I agreed. "Let's find a less cluttered area." We came upon a cluster of vehicles. Several cars were backed up behind a church van and a station wagon, which had played tag.

I slowed down a bit more as I rode the shoulder to get around the wrecks. As we passed the van, a hand landed on the glass from the inside, leaving a dark handprint where it struck. Pale faces popped into view as we rolled by, pressed to the glass as their jaws worked up and down.

"Yeah, let's wait until we find a clear section of road," Justine agreed.

From a distance, everything around us looked abandoned, but I steered as far away from the knots of cars in the road as I could. The thralls preferred to be still during the day, but that wouldn't stop them from coming out into the light if we disturbed them.

When we reached a stretch of open road, I took my foot off the gas and worked the gear shifter into neutral as we slowed so the Buick wouldn't stall. We coasted to a stop, and turned to look at each other.

We were both dirty, and I saw the same fatigue around her eyes that I felt. I smiled weakly at her. I wanted to tell her it was going to be OK, but I just couldn't get the words out. She wasn't the type of person to be comforted by worthless promises.

"OK, let's do this," I said, grabbing the back of her headrest and pulling myself toward the center of the bench seat. Justine crawled on top of me, straddling my waist as I pulled myself inch by inch into the passenger seat. It would have been damn sexy if the little bit of weight she was putting on my right thigh wasn't sending pain shooting up and down my lower back.

"You have your license, right?" I asked as she got the Buick into gear. She shot me her go-fuck-yourself look and goosed the gas, rocking the car as it surged forward. I stared at her until she let a smile curl the corners of her lips and settled back into my seat, taking it as a victory.

After two hours, I began fidgeting. No matter how I positioned myself, my back would start to ache and send shots of electricity up and down my right thigh and into my lower back. I'd taken a good fall onto a concrete floor in the process of escaping Jersey.

"You OK?" Justine asked, listening to me complain but not taking her eyes off the road. She was leaning forward, paying such acute attention to the road that her knuckles were white.

"Yeah, just sore. What's up?"

"Think you can get my pack?" she asked.

I tried to turn around, but there was no way I was going to be able to get to it. "Not a chance...sorry," I said.

"Time for a break then," she said. She brought us to a halt, almost stalling the Buick until she remembered to slip it into neutral as we slowed.

She climbed halfway into the backseat and grabbed her bag, throwing it between us. As soon as she sat behind the wheel again, she worked the car back into drive, scanning the mirrors.

"Something there?" I asked her, trying to look in the rearview.

"Nothing I can see," she said, putting me on edge with the way she said it. She realized she was freaking me out as I struggled to see the road behind us. "I'm sorry; I just feel strange," she said, trying to make me feel better.

"Strange?" I said, my voice betraying how much that *didn't* make me feel better.

"I have that feeling like something is watching me, but I think I'm just tired and burnt out," she told me. I put a hand on her leg and squeezed her knee. "I'm starving," she said, putting her hand over mine as she changed the subject.

I rustled through her pack, spilling things onto the seat as I searched for edibles. "Peanut butter crackers or vanilla wafers?"

"Peanut butter crackers," she said, not sounding too thrilled with her choices. I tore the edge of the wrapper with my teeth and handed her a cracker.

I rooted around for something to drink as she finished the first pack. We ate three packs of crackers between us, enjoying the peanut butter as it gummed our mouths shut, forcing us to drink sips of water between bites.

"I was saving this for after you had something in your belly," Justine said, handing me a small square of plastic. I held it up, happier than I'd ever been to be holding a dose of ibuprofen.

That spark of happiness turned to cursing frustration as I struggled to open the package. The heavy plastic just wouldn't tear. Justine asked me if I needed help, but, refusing to let the wrapper win, I folded it back and forth until it finally weakened enough to split open.

I washed the two pills down with the last bit of water in the bottle, imagining I could feel my back loosening up as the medicine made its way down my esophagus. It's amazing what the mind can do—and how short lived such happiness can be.

"It's almost four in the afternoon, and we aren't going to make it to the highway before dark," Justine said solemnly. She rubbed her eyes with one hand, trying to stay frosty. Route 273 stretched out in front of us, dotted with cars and wrecks here and there but mostly deserted. At least while it was daylight.

"Can you make it over to the airport?" I asked her. We'd spent too much time getting free of the residential areas along the river; there was no way we were going to make it away from the population centers before nightfall.

"Hmmm, yeah," she said, giving the car some gas now that she had a destination. "I can muddle my way through driving a boat, Daniel, but there is no way it's going to work on a plane," she muttered.

"I promise, no flying," I said. As she turned north onto Route 13, the airport's control tower appeared in the distance.

"You sure this is a good idea?" she asked as we drove north. She had a point. The southbound lanes were one long traffic jam of wreckage, forming a barricade between us and the airport, which would be on the left.

"It's all I have at the moment," I admitted wearily.

We continued north, our way mostly clear. Police and fire rescue vehicles dotted the grassy strip between the north and south lanes, keeping the traffic mostly on the other side of the grassy divider. They must have been trying to keep the northbound lanes clear for the military.

"Do you think any of them made it?" Justine asked, mostly to herself, as we rolled past strip malls and car dealerships. Smoke poured out of several stores, and furniture and other office supplies stood piled high against the windows of others where people had tried to barricade themselves in.

"I don't think so," I said hoarsely. If we'd seen a green Buick rolling down Main Street on the other side of the river, there was no way we wouldn't have been flagging it down. If there were any survivors, we hadn't seen them.

The imposed order on the road failed the closer we came to the airport. Cars had tried to make it across the grass median to use the northbound lanes, but the ground had been wet and soggy from a few solid days of rain the week before. As more and more cars churned up the ground, those behind got bogged down, sinking up to their axles. Cars that would never move again filled big sections of the grass divider.

In other sections of the road, miniature destruction derbies appeared to have taken place as cars had been smashed and destroyed trying to break free of the traffic jam. I tried not to think about where the vehicles' occupants might be now.

Justine worked the Buick through the wreckage, cursing under her breath as she spun the wheel this way and that. She drove up onto sidewalks and through strip mall parking lots when the spillover from the southbound lanes blocked our way, but she kept us heading north.

She worked the gear shifter into neutral and let us coast to a stop when we were even with the airfield. The stream of southbound cars and a high fence stood between us and the runways.

"I'm not walking," Justine said as she looked at the runway longingly. We had to get across to the airfield, and the light was beginning to fade.

"No shit," I agreed. A lot of the cars looked abandoned, their doors standing open as clothes, bags, and everything else imaginable littered the ground. But other vehicles showed overt signs of violence with smashed out windows and doors torn off their hinges. The people hadn't simply walked away—at least, not while they were still alive. The bodies were too fresh to smell yet, but I was sure thralls lurked out there.

And worse.

Chapter 2

"There," I told her, pointing to a gap in the traffic. A flood of cars had spilled through at the intersection, ignoring the cop car parked at the light. They'd left a narrow alley, cutting diagonally across the southbound lanes toward the airfield.

Justine slowed to a stop, looking down the path warily.

The cars on the right side of the alley had been engulfed in flames so intense that some of the vehicles were nothing but metal husks in the road.

"I really don't like this," Justine informed me as she worked the Buick back into drive. "What if we get stuck?"

"Drive carefully," I told her, grabbing the machete and resting its tip on the floor between my legs.

"Thanks," she muttered under her breath as she eased us into the narrow alley. "Mind telling me why we are going to the airport anyway?"

"During World War II, this used to be an army air base. Female pilots used it to ferry new aircraft over to Europe," I told her, remembering some history as Justine knocked the mirrors off my side of the car with a wince.

"That was Motrin, not Percocet I gave you earlier," she interjected, assuming I was rambling.

"Relax," I said, looking behind us as she continued to thread her way through the cars. The sun was setting, and car doors slowly began opening as the sound of our passing drew thralls from their daytime resting places. "The army was afraid the Axis powers might try to attack the air base."

I tilted the rearview toward me, pretending to pick something out of my teeth before continuing. She was already on edge; if she saw the thralls, she might try to floor it. Then we really would get stuck.

"You know, they built forts and gun emplacements all over Cape Henlopen not an hour from here, at Fort Miles. It was supposed to keep the German subs from getting into the Delaware River, where they would be able to attack Wilmington and the shipyards in Philly."

Justine shot me a look of annoyance as we slowed

down, metal scraping on metal as we squeezed between the cars boxing us in on either side.

I glanced behind us and swallowed, hoping I could keep my voice from cracking. Thralls were quickly filling the alley behind us, and more were getting out of cars every moment.

"Shit," Justine muttered.

In front of us, a hatchback half blocked our way. Justine started to slow down. We were almost clear of the alley; the fence around the airfield stood just twenty feet ahead.

"No, no, no," I told her rapidly. "Hit it going slow, and then throttle through it."

She heard the urgency in my voice and glanced at the rearview, which I'd angled away from her. The mirror on my side of the car was already gone, but she glimpsed what was behind us in the driver's side mirror and started cursing again.

We hit the hatchback with a small crunch, the Buick's engine revving louder as Justine gave it gas. The smaller car squealed as we shoved it out of our way.

"Nice," I told her as we broke through to the other side of the traffic jam.

"Kiss up later," she said, grabbing the rearview and adjusting it so she could see behind her again. We bumped up over the curb, driving with one wheel on the road the other on the sidewalk, hugging the fence as we made our way to a service gate.

The wave of thralls grew behind us as bodies poured out of the traffic jam. It looked like every car in the southbound lane was hiding something inside or under it. The thralls stumbled after us in a low-speed chase.

Justine made contact with the gate at ten miles an hour, shattering the cheap padlock to send the gates flying open with a crash. A piece of the lock spiraled into the air and came down on the windshield right in front of me, making me jump in my seat. The sudden movement twisted my back the wrong way, sending a dagger into my spine. I yelped, digging my fingers into the seat as the muscles in my lower back twisted and knotted, my eyes watering from pain.

"It wasn't *that* scary," Justine snarked at me.

"My back," I hissed at her.

"Sorry," she apologized, realizing I was in real pain. She picked up speed as she got onto the runway, and I relaxed in my seat, my back muscles slowly releasing. She gave me a moment as we put some distance between the thralls and us before she asked me where exactly we were going.

"Do you see a large hangar with a red band across its top?" I asked as I straightened my right leg in the foot well with gritted teeth.

"Yes," she said, increasing speed as she made a hard left onto the east-west runway. The gentle thumping as we crossed over sections of concrete picked up as Justine increased speed, the car swaying back and forth as its suspension struggled to keep up. We hit the blistering speed of forty miles an hour.

"The doors to the hangar are open, but there's nothing in it," she said, sounding worried and angry at the same time.

"Head around it to the right; there should be a section of runway leading to three domes," I told her.

I hoped my memory wasn't playing tricks on me. I'd come here with my dad as a kid, and he'd shown me the statue honoring the Women Air Force Service Pilots who had ferried fresh planes across the Atlantic to fight the Axis powers in WWII.

"Got them," she said. "What are they?"

"Reinforced shelters for fighters," I told her. "Find an open one, and get the car inside."

"Yessa, Master," she said, distracted by the view in her mirrors. Passing the terminal and mechanics' hangar had awakened another wave of undead, now flooding out behind us.

The shelters, designed to hold P-47 Thunderbolts safely until they could be ferried to Europe, were remnants of another time. Justine drove up to the first shelter housing a replica of one of the old fighters and spun us around without stopping.

"They welded the hanger doors open," she said, her voice short and clipped. She drove us back down the feeder runway and turned onto the paving leading to the second dome.

"Motherfucker," she blurted as we got close enough to

see chains holding the second set of doors closed with a heavy-duty padlock. She continued to curse as we spun around again, heading back out to the last shelter.

The tires squealed and the car tilted heavily as she cut the corner as close as she could, clipping a group of thrall mechanics who'd been catching up to us. She shot me an ugly look as we went down the last path, a horde of undead ready to block the way behind us.

When she slammed on the brakes at the front of the last shelter, the engine paused as if it were going to stall, causing her to hit the gas. We lurched forward and then halted as she slammed the car into neutral and got her foot on the brake at the same time. It was my turn to curse as she jumped out of the car.

She put her shoulder against the partially open door and gave me a thumbs-up. I positioned the rearview so I could see the thralls coming down the runway behind us, shifting my eyes between them and Justine laboring in front of the car.

She bent over, using her legs to get the door rolling. Her face turned red with exertion. Once she had it rolling, she put her back to it and continued to push. With the door two-thirds of the way open, she ran to the car and jumped into the driver's seat.

"You're so damn lucky," she said breathlessly as she rammed the shifter into drive and punched it. The thralls were twenty paces off our rear bumper.

"Yeah. That is exactly how I feel," I told her, grunting as the car thumped roughly over the rail embedded in the concrete. I braced myself as she slammed on the brakes once we were inside.

She made a weary noise as she killed the engine, then jumped out of the Buick to run back to the rolling door. She grabbed the large steel handle, the muscles in her arms and neck standing out. Her feet rasped across the ground as she struggled to get the door moving in the opposite direction. I watched in the rearview as the door started to roll shut.

Thralls shambled down the runway as I turned away from the rearview to quickly study the inside of the shelter as the closing door cut off the light. It had been turned into a storage area for the landscaping and maintenance crews. Shelving units stood off to my left, and a wooden platform rose off the floor in front of me. They appeared to have built their break room on top of the platform.

My attention returned to the rearview as I heard Justine chanting the *f* word over and over. The light streaming through the opening was superimposed with the shadowy outline of thralls.

Depth was hard to determine in the fading light. The door was still open just wide enough for a human to slip through sideways, but I could see arms stretching out, trying to reach Justine. I swallowed hard as the shadows and Justine appeared to merge, the door just inches from closing. Justine screamed as she called upon her last reserves of strength.

A beautiful metallic sound filled the inside of the shelter as the door slammed closed, followed by multiple thuds as thralls rammed the other side. A second, smaller clang echoed through the interior as Justine slammed the locking bolt into place.

Darkness filled the inside of the hangar—highlighting a rectangle of light in the back left corner of the structure. "Shit!" Justine yelled as she sprinted toward the rear of the hangar.

I pushed open my door, trying to lift myself onto my good leg with my arms while being careful not to stab myself with the machete clutched awkwardly in my left hand.

There was a loud bang as that unseen door slammed shut, engulfing the space in complete blackness. The Buick's interior lights didn't work. I wanted to call out, to scream for Justine, but I couldn't be sure what had happened or who was where.

I tried to take a step away from the car but had to keep one hand on the door for support. The machete started to slip from my hand, and I overcompensated, cutting myself as I grabbed the blade, not wanting to risk losing it in the dark.

I stifled my curse and listened, expecting to hear the shuffling of feet or snapping teeth. As blood dripped from my hand in a soft patter onto the concrete floor, my imagination went wild. In my mind, I saw Justine creeping in the dark, trying to keep away from the searching hands of the dead while I stood there, helpless.

"Shit!" Justine cursed loudly as something danced metal-lically across the floor. "Mother fucker!" she yelped angrily as she thudded into something else. I sighed, releasing my grip slightly on the machete, its stippled handle now sticky with the blood oozing from my hand. She uttered more curses, and then a sudden brightness bloomed around Justine, blinding me.

"What's going on?" I asked, my voice betraying my anxiety. She came back to the car, an electric lantern illuminating her pale face.

"I'd just got the hangar door shut when I saw shadows moving at the back of the building. The side door was wide open. Thralls were just walking by it."

She paused to set the lantern on the roof and help me sit back down. Electricity shot along my lower back and right leg.

She stood in front of me, putting her arms on top of the car so she could rest her head on them. "I'm so tired, Daniel."

"I know. It's been a rough couple of days."

She laughed, and I smiled. It was an understatement.

As I hugged her waist, my head nestled on her chest, she lowered an arm and put it around my shoulders, hugging me back. I wanted to ask her how she felt after what had happened while we were driving, but I just couldn't find the words. She stiffened up a little, as though reading my mind, and pulled away.

"I'm going to look around. Are you OK in the dark?" she asked me, holding the lantern high to see as much of the building as possible. I nodded and sat there, the machete spanning my lap as I watched her wander around the inside of the shelter in the wash of lamplight.

She picked through several shelving units, but I couldn't quite see what she was scavenging until she came back. She'd found another heavy-duty flashlight and a pair of beat-up but functional aluminum crutches.

"No wheelchair?" I complained.

Justine gave me the finger and helped pull me to my feet,

giving me my first good look around.

The floor of the concrete dome was a fifty-foot circle, which had been divided into three general sections. In front of us was what looked like a rundown apartment living room set up on a wooden platform. Off to our left stood rows of shelving units full of lawn chemicals and spare parts to mowers and weed trimmers.

The Buick sat in the space left vacant by missing riding mowers. Grass clippings had stained the concrete under the car green. The smell of old grass filled the building with an oddly comforting smell.

I followed Justine to the wooden platform and hobbled up the two wooden steps made out of sections of two-by-eights. The makeshift break room for the maintenance crew looked like a palace after the last couple of days of sleeping in a bathtub or huddled together against the rain out in the woods.

A card table stood in the center of the platform, surrounded by old plastic chairs. A beat up, overstuffed couch in a lovely maroon color sat against the railing on my right. On the far side, its top scraping the down-sloping edge of the dome, stood an old GE fridge. I saw the door Justine had slammed closed off to the left in an alcove.

As soon as I was stable on my crutches, she let go of me and went to check the door again. It looked as if it had been stolen from a submarine. The inside had a large lever, which moved four steel bars at the corners to lock it in place. She pulled it to make sure it was snug. I went to the fridge and was shocked to see light spill from inside it when I opened the door.

"Shiiit," Justine said, drawing it out as she hit the light switch by the back door. Rows of fluorescent lights buzzed overhead and snapped on. "Power's still on," she said as she stood there holding the lantern, smiling in dumbfounded amazement.

"There's beer in here…and cold cuts!" I said excitedly, my stomach growling.

"Beer," she said longingly, rushing over to the fridge. She turned to me in mock accusation as I handed her a beer. "Are you going to try and get me drunk?"

"If you're a light weight," I said, letting her grab the food and beer as I went to the card table and sat down heavily.

Justine hugged everything to her chest, bringing it all to the table in a single trip. My crutches clattered sideways to the ground as they slid off the back of my chair, but I didn't care. Justine was putting a feast on the table.

We sat there and wrapped cold cuts in cheese, eating a pound and a half of meat and almost as much cheese between us. I outweighed Justine two to one, but she kept up with me as we chowed down. When the food was gone, she opened us both another beer and we sat at the table, enjoying the feeling of full stomachs.

"To surviving," Justine said to me, putting her beer up for a toast.

"To getting out of Jersey," I replied, tapping the edge of my can against hers. I drank three more beers as she sipped number two. I'd had a lot more training than she had.

The alcohol and fatigue turned into a powerful buzz, and I almost fell on my face when I reached for my toppled crutches.

"Time to get you to bed," she said, coming over to stand in front of me. I threw my arm around her and pulled her close so I could hug her. She stroked my hair and kissed the top of my head. "OK, big boy, let's get you settled for the night," she said gently.

I barely remember her helping me to the couch, but I had a brief moment of full awareness when she settled in next to me, her body snuggling close to mine. I put my arm over her and fell asleep.

We slept with the lights on—a dreamless, heavy sleep. Sometime after midnight, the sounds of fighting woke me. Justine's hand tightened on mine as an explosion popped loudly somewhere outside; she was awake as well. I figured it must have been something big for us to hear it so forcefully through a foot and a half of concrete and steel.

Neither of us said anything; we just lay there and listened.

What was left of New Castle and South Wilmington had looked deserted when we drove through, but we knew we were hearing survivors fighting their last desperate battles outside.

Halfway through the night, we heard a crackling from the fuse box and the fluorescents died. We were back in the dark. "Think the beer will still be cold in the morning?" Justine asked.

"Better not risk it," I said, letting my hand slide across her hip and rear end as she slipped away from me and flipped on the lantern to make her way to the fridge. She came back with the last two beers and we drank them on the couch in the dark, ignoring the sounds outside. There was nothing we could do for anyone out there.

We napped on and off after that, neither of us able to fall back into a deep sleep. We didn't talk, but the way Justine twitched whenever a noise invaded from outside told me she was awake too. It was hard to tell what time it was inside the confines of the shelter, but eventually, a thin line of growing light from the bottom of the rolling door told us we'd lived through another night.

I relaxed back into the couch, relieved, and fell back into a light sleep without meaning to. Justine was gone when I woke up, but I heard her nearby. I worked myself into a sitting position and saw the lantern on top of the Buick.

Justine finished emptying a red five-gallon gas can into the Buick she must have found among the mowing supplies and threw it into the darkness. The sliver of light from beneath the rolling door shone bright and strong.

"Where to today?" Justine asked as she walked back to the platform.

"Let's try to get to the main highway, get as far south as we can," I said, taking her offered hand to help me sit up.

"And from there?" she asked. She wasn't being pessimistic; her tone was more curious than anything.

"Not sure, but either way, let's head south, get away from Philadelphia and Wilmington, and try to go west. Maybe head up into the Blue Ridge Mountains."

"Car's gassed up and ready to go whenever you're ready, gimpy," she said, holding my crutches out for me. She saw me take notice of my machete strapped to her thigh. "Do you want it back?" she asked.

"No. I'll use my crutches if I have to," I said, making a

chopping motion in the air with a crutch. She smiled and patted me on the shoulder as if I were nuts, her face lighting up as she did so.

"You feel up to driving a little?" Justine asked, throwing our lanterns into the backseat.

"Sure thing," I told her, slipping my crutches into the backseat before sliding behind the wheel and grabbing the keys off the dash.

"Whenever you're ready," she called out, lifting the locking bolt from the rolling door.

I gave the Buick some gas and slid the key into the ignition, turning it as I worked the accelerator, trying to give it just enough to turn over without flooding the engine.

Justine watched me, one foot braced against the massive steel door frame, ready to push. The moment the engine caught, she braced her foot on the bumper of the car and started to muscle the door open.

Beautiful sunlight spilled in from outside, and I had to scramble to put my shades on as the burning light consumed the interior of the shelter. Justine had her back pressed to the door as she pushed with her legs.

Once she got the door was six or seven feet open, I popped the car into drive, giving it gas with one foot to keep the engine running as I pressed the brake with the other. It definitely would not have gotten me a good grade in Driver's Ed, but it was the only way to keep the engine spinning and creep forward at the same time.

Justine shot me a look as the front bumper edged closer to her. I glared back and yelled at her to get her ass in the car. Justine let go of the door and slipped into the passenger seat, slamming the door as she climbed in.

I took my foot off the brake and let the car roll forward, the Buick just clearing the opening on both sides thanks to the absence of the passenger's side mirror. I accelerated to twenty and made it onto the main runway.

The airport had looked deserted when we drove in, but even after a single night, things looked different—worse. The terminal and control tower off to our right were on fire. Hazy smoke hung in the air, making everything look drab and washed out, and a car had been driven halfway through the wall of one of the other hangars.

I steered the Buick away from Route 13, leaving the air-field on the opposite side from where we'd come in. The fa-miliar signs of death and destruction filled the streets, but, with a little steering effort, the roads were passable.

Justine stared out the window as we made our way south toward Route 1, staying silent until the smell of burn-ing rubber invaded the car. "Someone burning tires as a de-fense?" she asked.

"No," I said and kept driving until it came into view: a huge black scar running parallel to the road, the ground still smoldering. The stench of burned rubber and petrol from the napalm was so strong it made our eyes water as we drove past.

The field of black was interspersed with lumps of varying sizes, some of them too large to be human forms. Score one point for the good guys.

Once we passed the napalm strike, the going got easier. Cars littered the road, but a passage had been cut right down the center of the traffic. Something had pushed vehi-cles out of the way, crushing them against each other or forcing them off the road to leave a clear path.

Little chunks of pavement flew up around us as we mo-tored on, the car vibrating as we drove over rumble strips created by the tracks of M1 Abrams tanks. The road looked intact, but the heavy vehicles had ground the asphalt to bits as they rolled past. I pegged the speedometer at thirty and rolled my window up all the way up to keep the dust out.

Justine slid into the middle of the bench, leaning into my shoulder and resting her hand on my leg as we drove along. She glanced up, catching me as I watched her in the mirror. She smiled at me, her face glowing.

"God, you're beautiful," I told her.

"You're biased," she replied, her expression rapidly shift-ing back and forth between pleasure and pain.

"Would you have it any other way?" I asked more quietly, not sure I wanted to hear the answer.

She thought about it for a while before responding. "No," she said, and then put her head on my shoulder again. We drove that way for quite a while.

"Something big is burning," she said, lifting her head to look around.

"What?" I asked, caught off guard by the comment.

"Something big is burning," she repeated. She was right. Ahead of us, large, billowing clouds of smoke rose toward the sky. I'd probably been looking at them for a few minutes, thinking they were clouds when they were still on the horizon.

Several miles farther south, we crested a rise and were able to see the broad base of the fire. The city of Townsend was burning in a single, massive blaze.

Both of us stared at the burning city as we drove past. I'd seen buildings burn and oil fields spraying liquid fire into the air during the Gulf Wars, but those memories didn't compare to seeing a city on my home soil devoured by flames.

Two miles after we put the burning city behind us, we drove through a massive pileup on the highway. Cars were folded together and stacked one on top of the other. It felt eerie to be driving through a ravine made of shattered vehicles. I kept waiting for something bad to block off the far end and attack, and I was relieved when we broke out onto open highway on the other side.

We followed the tank tracks down the road for another mile before they cut across open ground to the east. Our road clearing crew had decided to go another direction, one we couldn't follow. We stayed on the highway and headed south.

As I sat behind the wheel, lulled into a false sense of security by an hour of clear sailing, we climbed a rise to go over a county road—only to find the overpass gone, fallen onto the street below. I stomped on the brakes, locking the wheels up as the car dove forward, the front bumper trying to turn into a snowplow. I stood on the brake, fighting the wheel as the car shimmied and shook, sliding sideways.

Justine screamed, wedging herself in the passenger seat as we slid sideways to a halt. The edge of the broken overpass lay just two feet past the hubcaps of the car.

"That was close," Justine said, lifting herself in her seat to look over the drop and whistling appreciatively. I scooted next to her to see.

I was expecting to see the fallen overpass below us and was surprised to be looking down at what must have been the site of a serious fight. Military and civilian vehicles had been crushed beneath the concrete and steel of the fallen overpass, but a ring of secondary vehicles, mostly Humvees, stood fifty meters out. Little bits of brass glittered in the sunlight below us.

The boys who'd fought and died under the overpass had gone down swinging. It looked like they'd backed into the overpass and then fought until the outer perimeter had been overrun, falling back to a smaller defensive position directly under the bridge.

I could see the flow of the battle from the destruction on the ground, watching it play out in my head. The only part I couldn't figure out was how the overpass had been taken out. Had it been the last act of desperate survivors or something less intentional? I would never know.

"Maybe I should drive?" Justine offered as I put the car into gear.

"Can you see over hills?" I shot back roughly. "Let's backtrack and get down onto the county road. You can drive when I get tired."

She didn't say anything, just stared out the window as I pulled away.

We backtracked, looking for a path down onto the local road that tracked its course. Route 1 had been built to federal highway standards and was anywhere from level to twenty feet above the land around it, depending on where you were.

We had to drive back almost a mile before we found a break in the guardrail that didn't have too steep of a slope leading down onto the local road. I stopped the Buick at the lip, wondering if I should backtrack even further, maybe even look for an actual exit.

"Drive the fucking car down the slope and let's get going," Justine said to me sweetly, bracing her hands against the dash as she gave me a no-nonsense look. I couldn't help but smile at her. She was right: I was going to have to drive the fucking car down the slope.

I eased the Buick off the road and into the grass, slipping the transmission into neutral as we reached the point of no return. Justine screamed in joy as we tilted forward. I screamed with her, holding onto the steering wheel as I used the front tires as rudders to keep us straight.

The ground, soft from rain the week before, made the brakes useless as we slid down the hill. The bottom of the slope was coming up fast, but there was nothing I could do but hang on. The bumper dug into the ground as we reached the bottom, digging up a furrow before we straightened out and thumped over the curb, coming to a stop with a jarring impact.

We sat there, my face white and coated in sweat as Justine hooted in excitement, her fingertips digging into the dash. Literally.

"Dan-*yel*," she spit out in a voice between a lisp and a slur as she turned to look at me. The whites of her eyes were the color of an angry sky about to storm, her irises lost in the depths of their clouds. I slammed the gear selector into park and tried to get closer to her, but my seatbelt caught me.

I thumbed the release and slid across the seat so I could ease up next to her. Her arms were shaking and her eyes had turned a solid steel color in the moment it took me to get to her. Her mouth hung open just wide enough for me to see the length of her incisors and how they extended down into sharp points—a good centimeter longer than they should've been.

She whispered my name again, tears sliding from her eyes to race across her fair cheeks. My hands hovered just off of her skin, afraid to make contact. She pulled her fingertips from the vinyl dash, revealing black claws that would have looked at home on a mountain lion.

Her face was locked forward, but I could see the battle raging within her as she fought to push back whatever was trying to take over. The pain slowly faded from her expression as her face went slack. She was losing the fight. Her right hand moved slowly toward the door latch.

"Justine," I whispered, filling the word with all the love and longing I felt for her. Her hand paused for a second, but it was a short-lived victory. She continued reaching for the door latch a moment later.

Panic gripped me. I didn't know what to do. I was afraid that if she made it out of the car, I'd never see her again.

Chapter 3

I grabbed Justine's shoulders as she shifted toward the door. She carried me with her easily, my added weight no hindrance to her. I pulled myself onto her lap, but still she ignored me. The door lock clicked open as she pulled the release, her body rotating to climb out of the car.

I shifted my hold on her, grabbing her neck and pulling my head up to her, putting my mouth roughly over hers in desperation. I kissed her violently, wrapping my arms around her body to hold her down. I felt her sliding farther and farther away, both physically and mentally.

The tip of my tongue darted against the razor-sharp points of her incisors, cutting me as I kissed her, smearing traces of blood over our lips as I struggled to hold her against the seat.

Her right foot was on the ground. I held onto her and kissed her with everything I had. She was on the verge of pulling away from me, about to stand up and go when I felt her mouth start to mold against mine, her tongue moving ever so lightly, carefully sucking in sweet little kisses as I dripped blood into her mouth.

There is a professor at MIT named Dan Ariely—or there was—who performed a study on young men using a series of provocative questions about sex while the male subjects were in two states: a normal state he called cold and the aroused state, which he referred to as hot.

The results showed how the simple act of being aroused not only changed a person's answers to the same high-risk questions but also increased their likelihood of having sex with partners (or animals) they did not find attractive in the cold state. Basically, when we're hot, we make decisions we ourselves are surprised at once the heat of the moment is over.

The way I figured it, at that moment, I should have been either freaked out (cold) or about to cum in my pants (hot), but I was neither. I wasn't aroused, and I wasn't turned off or even scared. I was coldly rational, my only thought being to keep her in my arms. I could not let her get out of the car.

Justine shifted, trying to get her other foot out of the car, and I speared my tongue on one of her incisors. For a moment nothing happened, and then her sucking little kisses turned into hard suction on my tongue. Something transformed inside her. She ran her hands over my back, shredding my shirt and making me cry out as her clawed fingers raked across my flesh as she continued to suck on my tongue, her motions growing in urgency.

As tears slid down my face, I held on, ignoring the pain as she slowly twisted away from me, both of her feet now on the ground. Blood ran down the inside of my shirt from the long cuts in my back. Despite her reaction to me, she kept moving ever so slowly out of the car. I was on the verge of losing her. She was breaking away.

I bit her lower lip as she turned her face away, trying in vain to keep her focused on me. I loosened my grip on her to grab her face, needing her to see me. She reacted so quickly that I wasn't sure what had happened. One moment I was against her; the next, I was pinned to the dash, my head at an uncomfortable angle as it pressed into the roof. Justine's gripped the front of my shirt in tight balls.

I ignored the fiery cuts on my back as she let go of my shirt, sliding out of the car in a smooth motion. I grabbed her wrists, clamping down with all the strength I had left. She turned her head slowly toward me and looked at me, her face vacant, and pulled me back to her so quickly my head whipped about.

For a moment, terror washed over me as she wrapped her arms around me, her face going to my neck. I should have tried to push her away. Instead, I wrapped my arms around her and held her tightly, relaxing, giving in.

Her breath washed over my neck and the tips of her teeth brushed against my flesh, giving me goose bumps. For a very long moment, her incisors rested on my neck, two razor sharp points ready to pierce my flesh. I waited for the stabbing pain, for her jaws to shut, but instead she pulled back from me. Her chest started to hitch, and I couldn't tell if she was laughing or crying until she spoke.

"Daniel, I'm so sorry," she said, her voice thick with emotion. Her claws now gone, she touched my back, trying to hold my shirt together to stop the bleeding.

"I'm OK," I lied. "I was afraid you were going to make a run for it."

"What happened?" she asked, afraid to meet my eyes.

"We were going down the hill, and you were yelling like you were on a roller coaster. Then, when we got to the bottom...you were." I struggled to find the right words. "You were like you were back at the power plant."

Justine let go of my flayed shirt, leaning back so she could get her hands in front of her. Blood stained her fingers.

"You're not safe with me," she said, her voice full of pain and self-hatred.

I looked into the beautiful deep brown of her eyes. "Shut up," I said, gently but firmly, gripping her waist in case she tried to run.

"OK," she said, smiling weakly.

"Think you can drive?" I asked, trying not to let the pain reach my face as I shifted on her lap. She turned to get out of the car, but I told her to slide under me. It hurt to climb over her and fall onto the passenger seat, but I still didn't want her to get out of the car.

I got a finger around the open door handle and slammed it shut as Justine put the car back into gear and headed south. Thankfully the dark vinyl hid the dark smears of blood on the seats as I sat there, trying not to shiver as I leaked.

We moved south on the old local road, passing deserted gas stations and convenience stores. The fallen overpass was just coming into sight when our surroundings changed.

Evidence of the fight was everywhere. Some buildings were so riddled with bullet holes you could see through them. Others had been simply torn apart, leaving huge pieces of wall lying on the ground with their windows and doors still intact.

The closer we got to the fallen overpass, the worse the damage became. All the buildings nearest the overpass had been devastated. Most of them looked like they'd been put through a massive shredder, and a few had burned down completely, exposing their basements.

Most surprising, the bodies of the dead laced the innermost ring of destruction—the not-moving-for-good dead, which was unusual. By now, we'd seen the aftermath of many fights, and the undead rarely left any meat behind.

"Crap," Justine said, tapping the window to point at the body of a headless brute leaning against a pile of cinder blocks, a ring of destroyed thralls surrounding him.

His body was at least nine feet tall from feet to shoulders, and his arms rested too far down on his legs, giving him the appearance of an ape. The rough-hewn clothing the creature wore was tattered and ripped all over, and the thralls had torn handfuls of meat from his thick body wherever they could get purchase.

"Maybe they got lucky and took out a gray," I said as we crept forward, examining the scene.

Thralls wouldn't normally attack a brute. The gray men had some control over the humans they turned into their undead thralls, but when you killed the master, the thralls went berserk, attacking whatever was closest to them. If the soldiers had managed to take out a gray, his thralls would have turned on whatever was closest to them.

"I've never seen a thrall use a blade before," she said as we passed the brute. The stump of his neck appeared to have been cut in two or three hacks: definitely not the action of enraged thralls.

"Maybe it was a gray," I offered, studying the scene.

"What would make a gray attack a brute?" she pondered. The car thumped over the detached lower body of a thrall, reminding her to focus on her driving. "Sorry," she offered as I grunted.

We got as close to the fallen overpass as we could, stopping when we reached the outer ring of vehicles. Chunks of the destroyed overpass littered the ground even this far out, some sections of the concrete large enough to crush vehicles.

A Hummer not far off demonstrated how automotive steel stood up to concrete. A huge section of overpass had crushed its hood, and spikes of rebar jutted from the concrete, pinning the roof gunner in place. His machine gun lay in pieces all around the Hummer. Something had ripped it off the mount and smashed it.

I yanked up the lock on my door and grabbed the latch.

"What are you doing?" Justine asked me, looking around at the destruction with wide eyes.

"We need guns, and by tonight, I don't think anything will be left here," I said, pushing the door open and climbing out.

"OK," Justine said quietly, her voice full of emotion as she stared at the bloody streaks I'd left on the seat. I banged a hand on the roof, jolting her into action. She threw the car into park and climbed out after me, grabbing my crutches from the rear seat.

We threaded our way between two destroyed Hummers to make it into the inner defensive ring, searching for anything useful. The aftermath of the battles we'd come across in Jersey had all been very similar. In all those battles, we'd only seen one body left behind, and it had been hidden in a downed helicopter. I hoped that since the fallen still littered the area under the overpass, we might get lucky and find a weapon or two.

My hopes sank as we moved closer to the epicenter of the collapsed overpass. While there was no shortage of bodies, both thralls and men who'd died before they could be turned, the few weapons we found lay scattered across the ground, their barrels bent and distorted.

"Maybe over there," Justine said, pointing to a pickup filled with duffel bags. I let her lead the way.

Red coated the inside of the windshield and multiple holes dotted the roof where weapon fire from the cab had punched through from the inside, but the duffels in the back appeared undisturbed.

Justine pulled a few to the ground and started pawing through them: clothes, personal items, but no weapons. I grabbed a fatigue shirt from one of the bags and pulled it on so Justine would stop staring at my back every time I got half a pace in front of her.

"Nothing," she said, disappointed after emptying two more duffels. She'd found us some spare clothes, but that was about it. She stuffed them in one of the duffels she'd emptied and ran the bag back to the Buick.

As she was putting the duffel in the car, I inspected a black government Lincoln that had caught my attention. The rear of the car was buried, and chunks of concrete had fallen onto the roof and windshield. What caught my attention was the way the windshield had turned opaque but not shattered. The bulletproof glass had really done its job.

I hobbled closer to the Lincoln as Justine made her way back to me. Chunks of stone blocked the driver's side of the vehicle, but the passenger door stood open, the ground outside it littered with empty shell casings.

"Armored car," Justine said as she stopped next to me. I nodded. "I've always wanted to rob an armored car." She smiled as she said it.

The rear doors were either locked or held closed by the weight of the concrete across the back of the car. Justine cursed as she poked her head inside and pulled it out quickly. I wanted to tell her how cute she looked with her nose all wrinkled up, but she read my mind, shooting me the finger as she told me she'd found half of someone on the backseat.

Before I could say anything, she was climbed back into the car, her legs kicking as she maneuvered into the backseat. She squealed a moment later when she put her hand in something wet.

"Motherfucker!" she said in one long shout as she kicked open the rear door from inside, climbing out as fast as she could. She threw a black plastic case the size of a flight bag onto the road and then scraped her hands clean against the nearest piece of concrete.

"There are intestines all over the back seat," she said with a shiver as she sucked in fresh air. "This better be good."

The heavy-duty clasps snapped loudly as she opened the case. I whistled as the lid fell open. An MP5K lay nestled in black foam, a row of spare magazines resting in cut outs beside it.

Justine pried it out of the foam and felt its weight. She took it in both hands, using the forward grip to stabilize the weapon as she tracked an imaginary target.

"Merry Christmas," I told her.

"You still owe me a shotgun," she said, smiling. I'd dropped her shotgun and lost it back in Jersey.

"Some girls are just never happy no matter what they get," I teased her.

She told me to fuck off with a smile as she loaded the weapon and pulled the charging handle back until it cocked with a satisfying click.

"Do you hear that?" she asked, coming to full attention, the weapon tracing a slow path in front of her as she scanned the mountain of rubble blocking the road behind the Lincoln.

"Yes," I whispered back, looking around at the piles of fallen concrete, suddenly feeling very exposed. She gave me the quiet sign, and used the blade of her hand to point toward the fallen overpass before darting up the slope.

I watched in appreciation as she climbed, not a single stone falling or rolling behind her as she ran. She climbed easily, moving from cover to cover without thinking about it. I couldn't help but feel I'd found the perfect girl.

The going was a little rougher for me. I had to fumble my way over fallen concrete and rebar on crutches until I found a long section of the concrete median still intact, giving me a slightly easier path up the slope.

Justine cut across from where she was to help me, looking annoyed that I was bothering to make the climb, but I wanted to see who was making the noise.

We hid behind a jutting fragment of paving at the top of the pile, overlooking an artificial valley on the other side, and listened. The chemical smell of explosives hung heavy in the air, mixing with the sweet odor of rotting meat.

We heard two people talking, arguing in hushed tones. Bodies littered the bottom of the hill. It took me a moment to figure out where the voices were coming from, and then I spotted him: a massive brute lying half crushed under a slab of concrete, his chest rising laboriously. Every time he struggled to breathe, I could hear wet sucking noises. A gray knelt at the brute's head, a long, shining bowie knife dangling between his knees.

"Is Ravi coming?" the gray man asked, his voice annoyed and bored at the same time. He'd clearly asked the question more than once.

The brute sucked in another breath, and then paused as it slowly bubbled out a hole in his side around a piece of rebar.

The gray waited patiently as the brute struggled to breathe, spinning his bowie knife around on its point in the concrete dust as he crouched. He started to ask the question again and then stopped, chopping down with lightening speed on the brute's hand, sending a spark flying.

The brute's breath hitched, but the beast didn't speak. The gray used the knife like a spatula to pick up the two fingers he'd just severed, waving them slowly in front of the larger creature's face like plump sausages.

The brute tried to raise his bloodied hand to grab his fingers, but the gray swatted it away. I once saw a brute stop a police cruiser with a punch—while I was in it—but the gray seemed to have no respect for the injured creature at all.

"Is Ravi coming?" the gray repeated, growing less patient.

"Tell Han-su he's dead," the brute said. He tried to laugh, but could only cough.

"I would remember, my friend, we stopped you cold, even after you attacked us from behind while we were finishing our work here." The tone of the gray man's voice was sharp and cold. The brute did manage to laugh then, but it was weak. The gray didn't get another chance to ask his questions. The brute's laughter faded and then stopped. Small bubbles of blood foamed at his side, popping slowly as his life ended.

Justine was looking down the sites of the MP5K, her eyes locked onto the gray's back as he stood and poked at the dead brute with the tip of his foot.

"I'd be careful if I were you," he said easily, and it took me a moment to realize he was talking to us, his back still turned our way.

"Fuck," Justine whispered, gripping her weapon tighter.

"It's daylight, so why don't we call it a draw," he said, turning slowly as he scanned the concrete hill.

"Why don't you just keep your eyes facing the other way," Justine called back, giving away our position if he didn't already know where we were.

"Don't worry. I don't have any powers of sight," he said, as if we knew what that would mean. "I am amazed you've made it this far," he continued, turning slowly and stopping when he faced us.

Justine stood up, the MP5K locked on the gray's chest, her arms shaking ever so slightly as she gripped the weapon with all her strength.

"Stay calm," I whispered. She had a submachine gun, but where there was one gray, there were likely to be more, maybe even another brute, and I wasn't going to be running back to the car very fast if the shit hit the fan.

"Like I said: let's call it a draw. But you should be careful; my master is very displeased you destroyed his portal. It has made him weak in the eyes of his peers. Once he discovers you're alive, you will be hunted."

"And why are you being so helpful?" I called down. The gray kept his eyes locked on Justine's as she watched him from behind her iron sights.

"I've fought all night, and the sun is high in the sky. I could maybe reach you, but maybe you'd put a few holes in me before I did...and there are other enemies around today. I can be patient."

His voice replayed in my head. I'd heard it before. "He was at Mr. Deringer's house," I said as images flooded my mind. The memory was so powerful I could almost feel the rain pounding on me again as I hid, watching as Mr. Deringer and his sister were pulled out of their home. They murdered Millie on the front lawn, and this gray had stolen Mr. Deringer's memories as he drank his life.

Justine's finger tensed on the trigger, her face flushing red with anger at the mention of Mr. Deringer. The old man had deserved better. The gray held up a hand in supplication, sensing how close he was to being sprayed with nine millimeter rounds.

"I'm a soldier, just like your Daniel," he said to Justine. "I do what I am ordered to do." He paused, waiting for Justine's finger to ease off the trigger just a fraction. "Now, I would advise you to get moving. There are still bodies lying about here, and that always brings out the hungry."

"He's right; it's time to go," I said to Justine, looking behind us. I didn't like talking to this thing and wanted to get back to the car.

Justine turned her head for just a second to follow my

gaze behind us. When she looked back into the ravine, she began cursing. The gray was gone.

I just put my finger to my lips and motioned back down the hill. It was time to get moving.

Getting down the hill was surprisingly harder than getting up. I tried to rush, and both of us were on edge. Every time I'd slide and start to fall, Justine would grab me roughly and give me a dirty look, as though I were trying to get us killed on purpose.

I hobbled as fast as I could on the crutches, taking long strides as we raced to the car. I actually got ahead of Justine for a second when she stopped to grab the gun case, but she caught up easily, pacing me to the car.

Justine sprinted ahead when we got close and opened the passenger door, urging me to move faster with her eyes. The gray had made us both nervous, and now that we were almost away, a feeling of impending doom filled us.

I threw the crutches at her and practically dove into the car as she shut the door on my heels. She nearly took my head off a moment later as she whipped my crutches into the backseat from the driver's door, jumping in and setting the gun down on the seat between us as she searched for the car keys.

She was cursing as she grabbed them off the dash and slammed them into the steering column, mad at herself for forgetting where she'd put them.

Off to our right, half of a cinder block wall tilted and fell over with a crash, revealing several thralls in the midst of a tug of war, fighting over a petite, naked body.

We both watched the thralls as Justine turned the key. As soon as the engine started to crank, they froze, searching for the source of the noise. In unison, they dropped the body and began to trot toward the car.

The engine shook the Buick as it started and then rumbled some more when Justine slipped it into gear. The car lurched forward, picking up speed as fast as Justine could make it go.

"Who the hell are Ravi and Han-su?" Justine asked, breathless.

"Got me, but hopefully they'll keep fighting each other," I

said, biting back the pain as fire crawled up and down the nerves of my right leg, punishing me for pushing myself.

We weaved our way south, trying to ignore the destruction around us as we paralleled Route 1. Seeing the stillness was like staring at a fresh wound. It hurt to see. I kept waiting for another car to pull up at an intersection, or for a group of people barricaded on a building roof to flag us down, but there were no signs of life.

When we reached the next on-ramp to Route 1, Justine flipped an imaginary coin in the air and I called heads. She nodded and headed back up onto highway.

By two in the afternoon, we were talking about finding a place to hide out for the night, discussing what type of bolt-hole we should be looking for. We ate more of our dwindling supplies and drank a two-liter bottle of lemonade, passing it back and forth as Justine drove.

When we reached Garrisons Lake, we stopped in the middle of a long, low bridge over the water, getting out to stretch our legs and go to the bathroom. I peed over the low wall into the water as Justine squatted against the rear bumper, complaining that guys had it much easier.

I kept my mouth shut.

As we got back into the car, she gave me back my machete, patting her new MP5K as I strapped the blade against my thigh. I hoped I wasn't going to have to use it while hobbling along on crutches.

"Let's get off at the next exit and look for a bank," she suggested when we were moving again.

I groaned as she picked up the topic again. I kept telling her I didn't think bank vaults had controls to get out from the inside, but she wouldn't listen. She groaned back at me when I told her we should head for a mall in retribution for her insistence on a bank.

We talked about trying to drive through the night using some insane logic based on staying on the move, but the decision to get off the highway was made for us when we made it to the next exit. On the outskirts of Dover, we hit a blockade of concrete road barriers set across the highway. Empty tents stood along the divider and papers blew around aimlessly.

We stopped in front of two sandbag walls forming a choke point for any vehicle trying to take the exit. Cars sat neatly parked down the highway divider to our left, their doors and trunks open as if someone had rifled through them for valuables.

"Not much choice," Justine said, looking down the exit ramp leading into Dover.

"Don't really like the idea of being stuck in the city at night," I thought out loud.

"Dover is hardly a city," Justine replied.

"It may not be New York, but it has three times the people in half the space of Pennsville." I'd been amazed to learn what data could be found on a few old maps in a glove box.

"Turning around feels like utter failure," she said.

I nodded, understanding exactly what she meant.

She put the car back into gear, and we headed down the ramp into Dover. I rested my head on the back of the seat, watching her as she concentrated on driving.

Her face was long and narrow but gently rounded, framed by shoulder length brown hair pulled back into a ponytail. When you first looked at her, she seemed a bit too young, but that first impression faded quickly when she opened her mouth. She could curse with the best of them.

"You're a beautiful woman," I said, thinking it in my head, the sound of my voice registering in my ears only after I'd said the words.

The car wavered for a second before she looked at me with hard eyes. "Your back is covered in cuts, and I was sucking your blood off your tongue this morning," she said, full of disgust and self-hatred. "How do you know I won't kill you next time?"

"Letting you go would have killed me just the same," I said as lightly as I could.

"Maybe I'd rather risk that," she replied, the fire in her voice fading. I scooted toward her so I could touch her.

"I need to kiss you," I said, putting my arm around her and accidentally grabbing her left breast in the process. I cringed as she slammed on the brakes, fearing I'd pushed too hard, but she grabbed me and pulled me to her tenderly as the car rolled to a stop at the bottom of the exit ramp.

"I need you to kiss me too," she said in a hushed voice, kissing me slowly before I could open my mouth and ruin it.

My heart swelled, and my body felt light. I was so afraid she was going to shut me out. And yet, there I was, slipping through the cracks in her armor.

"Oh shit," Justine said, pulling her lips away, forcing me to open my eyes midkiss. I looked out her window and came face to face with the business end of an M16.

Chapter 4

"Get out of the car, love birds," a middle-aged soldier said affably, although he kept his rifle pointed at our heads.

"Just stay calm," Justine whispered, as if I was the one who had the habit of getting excited and cursing like a sailor—or growing claws.

She held up her hands and then lowered one to the door handle before putting it back up in a very good imitation of abject uncertainty.

The soldier laughed under his breath and motioned for her to open the door.

As Justine moved around, she knocked the MP5K off the seat and pushed it up against the fire wall with her feet. She did it so smoothly I barely noticed.

"Please, help us! He was thrown through the windshield," she said as she climbed out of the car, stuttering in horror as if remembering the wreck. She took my hand and helped me slide across the seat, pulling me to my feet.

Several rifles wavered and fell to the ground or rose to point into the sky, but the majority of the soldiers just looked at me with steely eyes. One soldier gently pulled her away as they looked me over, closing around her as if I might hurt her. They pulled her directly into their midst as I held onto the car door for balance.

"Was he bit, ma'am?" a soldier asked Justine quietly, not taking his eyes off me.

"No. He drove into them to save me. I've been trying to get him somewhere safe since yesterday," she said, looking from me to them. It looked like a nervous gesture, but I saw her mind working. I locked eyes with her and shook my head very slowly. There were too many for her to try anything.

"He's been hurt for a day?" an older man asked, breaking through the ring of soldiers.

"Yes. It was late the night before, when he saved me," Justine said, her face lighting up as she gave her biggest smile to the newcomer.

"No one lasts twenty-four hours," the newcomer said to his men.

Justine slipped between several soldiers to get back to my side, one of her arms snaking under my armpit to help steady me.

One of the soldiers griped that he wished *he'd* saved her as he stalked off, but I couldn't see which one, I was doing my best to look helpless.

"I'm Captain Jones," the newcomer introduced himself, putting his hand on the back of Justine's shoulder as he called for a medic. He stayed just long enough to make sure we were being looked after before allowing two soldiers to pull him away. We had apparently driven into their midst just as they were pulling up stakes.

The medic had me sit on the hood of the Buick, asking me if I'd been bit as he pulled on a pair of latex gloves. All the soldiers except for an overweight reservist had gone back to work, packing up everything of value as they abandoned their checkpoint. The reservist leaned on the concrete barrier, watching us without much interest.

"This is going to hurt," the medic said, pulling at the shirt glued to my back with dried blood. He used a bottle of saline to wet the cloth down as he peeled. Justine bit her fingers, pacing a short path back and forth as she watched.

"Why don't you take a walk?" I suggested to her as the medic opened a second bottle of saline.

She just shook her head.

"This could have been a lot worse," the medic said. "Most of these are pretty shallow." Justine ignored us both and kept pacing. Luckily I was so dirty and cut up from head to toe that he never saw my other, half-healed wounds.

With my shirt completely cut off, he examined the deeper cuts to make sure there was no glass or dirt in them and then used one more bottle of saline to rinse away the fresh blood that had started to run down my back as he worked.

A tube of antiseptic gel later, the medic wrapped me in gauze from my belly button to my armpits. "Keep that dry for at least a few days, and no rough stuff," he said, looking at Justine in envy.

The overweight reservist came over as the medic finished up and tossed me a fresh BDU shirt, probably hoping it would help the smell some. I was pretty gross. No one paid any attention to the machete strapped to my thigh. I guess a wounded man on crutches just didn't look like much to be worried about.

Justine helped me button the BDU, smoothing the fabric out across my chest. "They wouldn't even know if I slipped away. You could be safe with them," she said, not meeting my eyes.

"How far do you think I'll get chasing you on crutches?" I asked her. When her eyes rose to meet mine, I held her gaze, letting her see just how serious I was.

"Time to go find out what the captain wants to do with you," the reservist said, interrupting our moment. He led us one block over to a one-story house surrounded by an equal numbers of Hummers and pickup trucks. Soldiers were everywhere, loading equipment and moving about. It was the most people I'd seen since the end began.

On the outside of the house, they'd stacked sandbags up to the windows. Justine put a hand on my shoulder as we made our way up the walkway to the front door, her grip tightening as we approached. Three steps from the entrance, she stopped cold.

Just as the reservist turned to see what was wrong, something inside the house battered at a wall before rebounding into what sounded like chain-link fence.

"Yeah. We got one of them," the reservist said warily, clearly not thrilled to have one of the undead was on the other side of the wall. He didn't realize Justine had reacted before the thing made any noise.

I looked at her, my eyes moving from her to the door, not sure what to do. She motioned for me to keep moving with her chin, but she stayed close by my side, keeping her chin almost on her chest.

"Don't be scared," the chubby soldier said, pushing open the door for us.

The interior of the rancher was sparse, a large table covered in communications gear and a large dog kennel bolted into the corner of the room were its only remaining furniture.

A soldier sat inside the cage. His fingers, caught in the cyclone fencing, made a rattling noise as he moved it back and forth. A second soldier sat on an upturned packing crate guarding him, an M9 service pistol in his hand.

Justine stayed on my right, keeping close to my machete as she hid behind me. The thrall scanned the room with exaggerated sweeps of its head. Captain Jones stood on the other side of the table yelling into a radio and then listening carefully, trying to decipher the garbled transmission coming back to him.

He started to curse but stopped when he saw us, pausing to regain his composure. A steady stream of soldiers moved in and out the back and side doors, emptying the house of the last of its supplies.

"You were coming south?" Captain Jones asked, tracing a line on a map with his finger.

I nodded, easing up to the table to look at the maps and papers casually, Justine glued to my side.

"What's it like further north?" he asked.

"Bad," I told him, looking at the troop allocations. There appeared to be two battalions on the maps, one of which had the captain's name next to it. "We didn't see anyone else alive."

"And how exactly did you make it through the night?" Although the captain was trying to sound casual, something about his tone revealed an edge.

"We were in New Castle when it happened," I told him, looking to Justine hesitantly before continuing. "I'm a little older than her, and her dad really doesn't like me," I began. It's always good to mix some truth with a lie. It makes it harder for the listener to sift the bullshit from the facts. "We were…hmm…camping out in White Clay Creek State Park for a few days when the shit hit the fan."

Justine shot me an angry look. I was clearly implying we'd been out in the woods bumping the nasty.

"You're not twelve, right?" Jones asked, his eyes narrowing as he looked Justine over.

"I'll be eighteen soon," she shot at Captain Jones defensively. She hated to be told she looked younger than she was.

The thrall shook the fencing more vigorously, reacting to her voice. The guard brought his M9 up defensively, looking uncomfortable.

"Then I don't care what you were doing in the woods. It probably saved your lives."

I liked the man already. The world was falling apart, and he still wanted to make sure I wasn't taking advantage of a teeny bopper.

"Yeah," I agreed sheepishly.

"I wish I could tell you we had our shit together," the captain said, catching my eyes as they scanned the table. "But they've chewed us up at every turn and almost overran our outposts last night." He lowered his voice when he talked, as though the soldiers milling about didn't know the score. "Our sister battalion decided to make a run south. They left at first light this morning, but we've already lost contact with them. The undead bastards seem to know what we're going to do before we do."

"Kill that," Justine said, pulling my machete out so fast and smooth I didn't even feel it and pointing it at the thrall in the cage.

The room froze and fell silent. All eyes were on us.

The captain looked at Justine and then me, his eyes squinting as he reevaluated us. "Kill it," he said to the guard without taking his eyes off us.

The guard stood, pointing his M9 at the thrall but unable to pull the trigger. He looked around the room to see everyone frozen, watching him. One of the other soldiers nodded, telling him it was OK, and he pulled the trigger.

I winced at the sound of the gunshot as it hit my ears, the noise magnified inside the building. The room emptied slowly as the dead thrall slid to the floor, its head gone from the jaw up. Everyone suddenly had someplace else to be.

"Now tell me why?" the captain said to Justine.

"It scared me," she said, sliding the machete back into the sheath at my leg.

"Bullshit," Captain Jones said quietly, a hint of anger in his voice.

"We saw some of them fighting at a supermarket," she said. "The thralls aren't just dead; the other things, the grays, they have some control over them."

"You saw a fight like that and survived?"

"Not up close," I assured him. "We had a monocle and watched from a good ways off. The thralls seemed to do what the grays wanted them to do."

"They seem to know what we're going to do before we do," he repeated quietly, the words full of self-reproach. He put his hands on the table and hung his head as he let out a long sigh.

"You had no way of knowing," I told him gently.

"I should have," he replied, lifting his head to stare at me. He'd aged ten years in the space of a few minutes. "We have to keep going, moving forward," he said tiredly as he stood up. "So where were you two heading?"

"We were hoping to run south and get in front of them," I said, glancing down at the map on the table. More than three-quarters of the unit positions had been scratched out in pencil, and the radio on the end of the table was hissing quietly—no traffic getting through from any quarter.

"Too late for that," Jones said, dropping a thick finger on the map and running it along two sets of defensive lines south and north of the Delaware Memorial Bridge. Every unit and position on the line had been crossed out in pencil.

"Can't give up," I whispered to him.

"No, not that," he whispered back before continuing. "We are pulling back into Dover. What's left of my battalion and the survivors we've found are going to make a stand. I'd suggest you do the same."

"We're going to continue heading south," I said—as Justine agreed to take him up on his offer. It brought a little smile to the corners of the soldier's mouth.

"OK, here's the deal," he said. "We're pulling out of this checkpoint today, so you're pretty lucky we found you. There are a few hundred of us still alive, and we are holding onto downtown Dover. We've lost all contact on the radios, so we don't know where or how many other survivors there are. You can join us there, but everyone works," he said, nodding at my crutches.

"I can do his work until he heals up," Justine said quickly. I started to say something, but she put a finger over my mouth and said, "Shut up. You need someplace to heal—someplace safe."

"We've decided to take you up on your offer," I informed the captain. Jones smiled wryly before calling for the chubby reservist and telling him to take us back to our car and escort us to downtown.

We left Captain Jones packing up his maps, looking tired and worn.

I expected the soldier to get in the car with us, but he sat on the hood and told us to go slow. I warned him Justine was not the best driver, but he just slapped the hood twice with the flat of his hand and said, "Get moving."

"Thanks," Justine muttered, punching me on the shoulder.

"Anytime."

We trundled down empty streets, watching the buildings as we passed. Now I understood why the soldier rode on the hood. They might control parts of the city, but he wanted to be able to use his rifle if the need arose.

It was easy to see where they were making their stand. We turned a corner and found the road at the next intersection blocked by two city buses. The soldier waved his rifle in the air, and several shapes waved back from near the bus and atop the surrounding buildings.

As we got closer, I was surprised to see so many people working. It was the most living, breathing people we'd seen since the night everything went sideways back in Jersey. A constant stream of people filed into the buses, dropping sandbags and then walking out of sight, presumably to make another trip. The buses, their tires slashed and their interiors half filled with sandbags, rested almost on their bellies. The workers threw more sandbags against the windows from inside as we watched.

"Park the car there," the soldier said, pointing to a half-empty lot on the corner opposite the stationary buses. "Take the important stuff, and hope the rest will be here when you come back for it." He slid off the hood and lit a cigarette while he waited for us, sucking in the smoke and nicotine like only a truly stressed-out addict can.

Justine parked the car and grabbed our duffel, stuffing the MP5K in with what other meager supplies we had as I put on a show for the soldier, struggling to get out of the car and onto my crutches in the narrow space Justine had left me between the Buick and the car next to us.

When we were ready, the soldier guided us through the narrow gap between the buses, pounding on the large steel plate resting against the bodies of the buses as we passed. Several men with acetylene torches and welding equipment were making a rail for the huge piece of steel to slide on.

"Good luck," the soldier said before abandoning us, disappearing into the throng of people before I could even ask him a question. We stood there, watching the controlled madness as everyone worked to fortify their new home. A stream of wheelbarrows ferried sandbags from somewhere down the street while a smaller group cut lumber with handsaws. The sounds of construction filled the air.

It would have looked like the rebuilding effort after a natural disaster if it weren't for the guns. Half the people in sight carried hunting rifles or shotguns and were clearly not military. The other half were soldiers carrying M16s, but they had already started to go native, half in and half out of uniform.

"You fresh?" a young male voice with an urban twang asked. It took me a moment to identify the little white teen a few feet away as the source of the question.

I started to smile but hid it behind my hand as I rubbed my nose like I might sneeze, which was very possible: I could smell his Italian shower across the ten feet separating us.

"Yes," Justine said after looking to me for support. I could only give her a half-hidden smile in return.

"I'm Dubya-C, or at least I was until all this shit went down," he said. I wanted to tell him to watch his mouth but decided it didn't really matter if the kid cursed.

"WC." I said the letters out loud. "You know which rooms are OK to take?"

"Sure, sure," he said, coming a little closer. "Can I carry that for you?" he asked, pointing to Justine's duffle.

"I got it, but thanks," she said, pulling the duffle higher onto her shoulder.

"OK," WC said, his eyes spending just a little too much time looking Justine over. I glared at him, but he was already turning away, leading us down the street. It surprised me how I was overwhelmed with the instant urge to punch WC when he looked at Justine's ass. I picked up the pace on my crutches to stay close enough to hear what he was saying.

"So we have about four square blocks. The greens picked out the spot because we only have the outside walls of the buildings and four intersections to protect."

"The greens?" Justine asked.

"The GI Joe guys," WC responded.

I couldn't help but smile.

"There were a lot more yesterday, but about half of them left." WC clearly thought leaving was a crazy idea.

As WC talked, we made our way further into downtown. I noticed that everyone was packing, and I mean everyone. Even teenagers who wouldn't be allowed to get their driving permits in the old world had shotguns slung over their shoulders. WC's weapon of choice was a large chrome semiautomatic. He kept it tucked into his waistband but pulled it out to show Justine.

"You know how to use that?" I asked, nodding at his gun.

"Well enough," he said confidently.

"If you're interested in proving it, I'd be more than happy to give you some constructive feedback," I told him. I doubted the kid had even shot a gun before last week—maybe not since then either.

WC nodded, trying to hide his excitement. I figured it was the least I could do for the kid since he was showing us a little kindness, even if it was motivated more by Justine's ass than anything else.

"Social or nonsocial?" he asked when we reached the next corner. The buildings off to our right, formerly dorms for the state college, bustled with activity. They were clearly the center of life for a lot of people. Grills had been lined up along the front for cooking, and various articles of clothing hung on makeshift clotheslines on what used to be the front lawn.

"Nonsocial?" Justine said tentatively, not wanting to insult anyone.

"No worries; the rooms are almost all spoken for anyway," WC said, leading us away.

"Where to then?" I asked, trying to wedge myself between WC and Justine as we walked; not an easy task on crutches.

"There are a lot of open buildings around, but I'd stay closer to the center of town. There are lots of second-floor apartments over the stores, and you won't be too far away from everyone," he explained, pointing to the row of storefronts on our left as we approached them.

"How do we tell if the rooms are taken?" Justine asked.

"You knock," WC said bluntly.

"How about this one?" I asked, looking at the corner building. A set of pressure-treated stairs led up to the entrance on the second floor.

"I'm pretty sure it's open. Most everyone else is sticking to the other side of the street for now. Some of the greens like to hit the gym next door, but I don't think anyone lives there."

"We'll take it," Justine said, putting her arm awkwardly around me and my crutches like we'd just bought our first house.

"Once you're settled in, you need to go see Big John. He runs the work teams." He took out a piece of construction paper with a stamp on it. "If you don't work, you don't get to eat from the public kitchen. You can also hand in tickets for other supplies."

"Thanks," I said and started up the stairs, putting my crutches down and lifting myself up each step carefully. WC stood there fiddling with something as he watched us climb the stairs—or, more likely, watched Justine climb the stairs.

We found the door locked, but Justine was able to kick it open without doing too much damage. Thankfully, the deadbolt remained intact so we could still lock it behind us.

Justine dropped the duffel in the hallway and knelt to get her MP5K out. It was still light outside, but the blinds were drawn, leaving the interior of the apartment half lit. She found the lantern and turned it on, just to be safe.

The apartment had a simple layout. On our right, just off the entrance, stood the door to the master bedroom and attached bath. A sliding glass door in the smaller bedroom to our left lead to a balcony just big enough to put a grill on. It had a lovely view of the gym roof next door.

The living room and kitchen were very open, divided only by a counter. A couch and matching love seat sat beneath the windows along the front of the apartment.

We threw back every curtain and raised the blinds as we surveyed our new home, letting the late afternoon sun flood in. The apartment gave me a strange feeling that it took me a few minutes to identify: I felt secure. It was an exhilarating feeling—right up until my body told me to sit before I fell.

The fatigue I'd been holding at bay for days crashed down on me. I collapsed onto the couch, and Justine followed with a sigh. It felt so good to sink into the cushions. We lay there, letting the sun wash over us through the open blinds as we did absolutely nothing.

I was drifting toward sleep when I felt her get up. When I forced my eyes open, she had the duffel on the floor in front of the couch and was busy organizing the contents into two piles: food and not food. I reached for my crutches, but she pushed them out of reach.

"You need to rest," she said. "Take a nap."

I wanted to argue, but the softness of the couch drained all the fight out of me.

I dreamed of a different place. Justine was still my neighbor, but in my dream, I was still a Marine and she was not a tortured teen who cut her arms to deal with the stress of living with an insane foster father. As we walked along the river in the sunlight, she wore a long, flowing dress, rather than hiding herself in an oversized hoodie. She was smiling, our hands linked together and swinging back and forth as we walked.

Even in the dream, I was aware of my need for her—an alien feeling to me. I was so used to being alone—a byproduct of my eye disorder from childhood, my father would say. I know he would have liked Justine. He always wanted me to be happy.

The desire to be close to Justine was so strong. I turned to her in my dream, bending down to kiss her lips, my hands on her narrow waist. She stroked my neck with her hand as she kissed me...

And I woke with a start. The sun sat low in the sky, and

the apartment was turning dark. I called to Justine and waited to hear her voice, but she didn't reply. Clothes lay strewn about the floor in disarray. Could I have slept through a struggle?

I jumped to my feet, ignoring the pain in my right leg, my machete rasping out of its sheath as I started for the front door. I tripped over some of the crap on the floor and caught myself on the wall via the machete, the blade easily going through the drywall to make a convenient handhold.

The bathroom door shot open, sending an arc of light out into the living room as Justine barreled out. I don't know what was the more stunning sight: the tight boxer briefs hugging her pelvis or the MP5K held low and tight to her pink cami, all illuminated by our electric lantern sitting on the bathroom counter.

"It's all good," I said, trying to lean nonchalantly against the wall, my face turning red as she determined nothing was wrong but me.

"Your turn, babe," she said, turning to put the MP5K on the bathroom counter before coming back to help me. I left the blade sticking in the wall.

I was so pleased by the way she'd called me babe, I didn't even realize she was cutting my pants off until she'd almost reached my groin. "What the hell?" I blurted out.

"I'm burning our old clothes," she said, ignoring my protests as she continued to cut my pants off. I'd been in them since we made it out of Jersey.

Justine told me not to be a baby as she worked the scissors up the fabric of my jeans, complaining that she should have put some gloves on before she got started. Bits of dried mud and blood flaked off the stiff fabric as she cut through it.

"You don't have to go through this much effort just to get my clothes off," I told her, cringing as she stripped the front of my pants away, including my boxers. I grabbed a washcloth off the towel rack to keep some dignity and was relieved to see her getting just as red in the face as I was.

"Keep dreaming," she muttered as she pulled me off my butt just far enough to slide the other half of my soiled pants from under me. I sat there bare assed as she unbuttoned my new BDU shirt and put it aside. That could be washed.

"I think it's good for a few more days," I told her as she started to cut the gauze off my chest.

"I promise I'll put fresh bandages on after you're clean," she said, crinkling her nose at me. "Think you can climb in?" she asked, looking at the tub.

I nodded.

I was more confident than I should have been. I almost took us both down as I stepped over the edge of the tub. Once safely inside, I clutched the washcloth over my junk as she poured a liter of water in a bucket and squirted some liquid soap into the mix. She took her time, starting at the top of my head and working her way down. I would have enjoyed it more had my scrapes and cuts not stung from the attention—and if I wasn't so aware of being essentially nude while she was fully clothed.

"Time to let go of the wubby," she said in mock baby voice, pulling at the wash cloth. It had turned a suspicious rusty brown color as the dirty water ran down my body.

"I could have managed a bit of this myself," I told her, letting her pull the wash cloth away with two fingers before she threw it into the pile with my cut-up pants. I held my hands over my groin, trying not to turn a deeper shade of red.

"Yeah, you can barely stand up on your own. At least this way I don't have to pick you up off the floor," she said, rinsing me off with another liter bottle of water. "I think you lost a few pounds in dirt," Justine said as she wrapped a towel around my waist and helped me out of the tub, its bottom now full of grime.

She patted me dry with a second towel, being very careful when she reached my back, and then draped the towel over my shoulders, wrapping her arms around me and hugging me from behind. It took me a minute to realize she was crying. When I tried to turn around, she tightened her grip and told me to be still.

"I'm sorry," she said into the towel.

"I'm not. If you hadn't broken my window that night, I'd be dead," I reminded her.

"That's not what I'm talking about."

"I know. I'm just trying to keep you grounded. I *need*

you."

"What am I?"

"You're a beautiful girl."

"Am I?"

"I won't let you do this."

"I don't know what you mean, Daniel," she said. But she did. Her arms tightened around me a little more.

"You are what you are. I won't let you run away from me. I need you."

"Even if I'm bad for you?"

"Don't say that," I said. Not letting her hold me still this time, I turned around, grabbing her and pulling her against my bare chest. There was nothing sexual about it. I just held on to her, breathing in the clean, wet scent of her hair.

Justine stiffened, wanting to resist, but gradually relaxed until we were clutching each other in equal measure. My heart was racing. "I love you," I breathed heavily into her ear.

"I love you too," she told me, but she pulled away, not looking me in the eye as she said it. I took a breath in, trying to ignore the way she'd said it, like it hurt her. She was still scared she might do something bad to me.

"Sit on the toilet," she said more gently. "We have to put fresh dressings on." She disappeared into the living room and brought back a first-aid kit the size of a small backpack. She pulled supplies out of it onto the bathroom counter as I watched.

I couldn't help but laugh. What I'd thought was the aftermath of a fight in the living room had just been Justine unpacking. "Where did you get all this stuff?" I asked as she pawed through the kit.

"I ran back to the Buick to get the rest of our things while it was still light out. I found a plastic bag in the trunk full of cigarette cartons and almost left them." She laughed a little. "Then a few of the men on top of the buses started calling down, offering me this or that for the cartons."

"Prison currency," I said.

"Yeah. Six cartons of cheap cigarettes were worth two cases of water, food, and the first-aid kit."

"My little shopper," I muttered, turning away from her so she could get to my back more easily.

She was actually a lot more thorough than the army medic. She swabbed the cuts with betadine and used a package of butterfly stitches to span the worst of the wounds on my back.

"Man up," she said, kissing the back of my head when I shivered from the combination of pain and cold as she applied the betadine. Satisfied with her work, she fanned the reddish orange stains covering my back until they were dry and wrapped me back up in gauze.

I shooed her out so I could put shorts on but had to call her back in defeat to help me stand up. My body seemed to know we were out of immediate danger and refused to be pushed any further when a soft couch lay just a few feet away.

We walked out into the living room, light from the lantern spilling from the bathroom behind us as we looked out our front windows onto the little settlement taking shape in downtown Dover. Flashlights and fires dotted the darkness. Farther out, spotlights scanned the roofline of our external border. It felt surreal.

"Do you think it's safe here?" she asked.

"It will have to be for tonight." It was the best answer I had.

We ate cold beans and beef sticks for dinner before finding our way into the master bedroom. Neither of us wanted to sleep in the room facing the gym. It would be too easy for something to jump down from the building's roof and get onto our balcony. The living room felt just as exposed. I'm sure we were the first "tenants" to ever be excited that the master bedroom had no windows.

"Take these," Justine said, handing me two oblong white pills and a bottle of water as I sat on the bed. I raised an eyebrow at her. "Motrin, to help with your aches," she said as I gulped them down. "And a muscle relaxer for your back," she added as I swallowed another mouthful of water.

"Thanks," I said drowsily, the soft bed and sheets pulling me under faster than any sedative.

"No problem, babe," she answered.

We fell asleep with the dresser jammed between the door and the bed frame, spooning under the sheets, my fingers entwined with hers as I tried to hold on to her.

Chapter 5

We slept like babies on a mattress that may as well have been made of clouds. I woke up with Justine half lying on top of me, one of her legs nestled comfortably into my groin—all the strife, fear, and anxiety of the last week gone. That we were lying in a dark bedroom with a dresser pinning the door closed made no difference.

But everything in life has to balance out. I lifted my head, sending shots of pain down my spine and leaving me struggling to breathe. Justine heard me and woke up, leaning away to find the lantern in the darkness.

"Oh my God," she said as the light switched on, adding painful dancing stars to my torment. She grabbed my face, trying to get a finger into my mouth. "Are you choking?"

I pushed her hand back, finally able to take a breath. "My back," I whimpered. She had to lower her ear to my mouth to hear me.

"You scared the shit out of me," she said, as if the lava burning down my spine wasn't a concern.

She stood up and slipped on a heavier shirt as I took inventory. I was able to move my arms fine and could wiggle my toes, thankfully, but my whole body hurt. I eased myself around so my legs could fall to the floor, lifting my upper body with my arms while trying to keep my hips and waist relatively immobile.

Justine moved to the door, putting the tip of her MP5K to the wood at head height as she listened for anything outside. Satisfied it was safe, she slid the dresser clear and stalked out into the living room, leaving me washed in natural light from outside, my eyes watering. I was about to call out to her when she came back. I couldn't see the bright smile on her face until she was almost on top of me.

"It's light outside, and people are moving on the street!" She was giddy with excitement. She took my hands and pulled me the rest of the way to my feet.

"Yay," I said feebly, trying not to grimace as I hobbled down the hall. I picked up a shirt off the couch as I looked out on downtown with squinted eyes. "I guess we should go earn our keep." I didn't feel so bad once I was standing.

"You're not going anywhere," she said, sliding a pair of sunglasses onto my face. As I started to protest, she pushed me into the couch and grimaced as I yelped. "I'm sorry," she offered as I leaned back into the couch, trying to straighten my midsection. "I don't think you should be left alone," she said, helping me lift my legs onto the couch so I could lie flat.

"I'll be fine. Leave me some water and the machete."

"Yeah," she replied, drawing the word out. Clearly she didn't think much of my chances in my current state. "We have enough supplies for a day or two."

"It's daylight," I said. "Go outside and get the lay of the land. Figure out what these people are doing and whether we're likely to be overrun tonight. Better you get some idea of what's going on out there now than if we have to make a run for it in the dark."

"OK, OK," she agreed in frustration after I argued with her for ten more minutes.

It ended up being the first of several hard days for me. My body crashed that morning, calling in debts I'd racked up when I wasn't sure I was going to live through the hour. That first day was the worst. The combination of being alone in a new place and feeling so helpless left me jumping at every noise. Justine checked on me sometime in the afternoon before heading out again. I didn't tell her how freaked out I'd been all morning or she'd have never left.

Boredom mixed with fear is the worst. Fortunately, Justine brought me a couple of boxes of remote control car parts she'd salvaged from a hobby shop on the second day. I didn't have a way to charge the batteries yet, but building the cars from the ground up kept me busy for a few days.

She kissed me on the forehead when she gave me the boxes, telling me she remembered seeing the toys on the shelves in my parents' house. My dad had pretty much left my boyhood room the way I left it when I joined the Marines after high school.

While my right leg and lower back slowly recovered, Justine went out each day to work a detail the de-facto mayor, Big John, had assigned her to. She'd come back dirty and tired and tell me what was going on and who was doing what.

It was my favorite part of the day. She'd come out of the bathroom with wet hair, her T-shirt clinging to her (I don't think she knew how to use a towel real well) and sit down next to me.

Life in downtown Dover revolved around little orange raffle tickets with Big John's stamp on them—the currency used to pay each person for their day's work. The work mostly consisted of boarding up windows and blocking off every way in and out of the fortified zone. Men with rifles earned tickets for standing watch overnight while others brought in as many supplies as they could to earn theirs.

The townspeople broke down into three basic groups: the militants, the Fort people, and the religious wackos. They all played nice for the most part, united by a common goal, but it took a while for the boundaries to settle out.

The militants took care of organizing the town watch and making sure a nightly guard always kept watch. Mostly made up of the soldiers left over from Captain Jones's battalion, with handfuls of other reserve units thrown in, they spent their nights in shifts on the roofs of the outer ring of buildings, clutching their rifles.

Most of the families lived among the Fort people: a loose-knit group of survivors who'd turned one of the old dorm buildings into a walled-up fort and guarded it like a bank vault. Someone had started a rumor that the things outside hunted children. The Fort people kept to themselves. They were a distrustful lot, looking at everyone else like they might turn at any moment. They wouldn't even allow anyone they didn't know in a work group with them, much less into their building.

The third group consisted of what I would call the end-of-the-world religious nuts. They met every morning when the sun came up outside the church near the center of downtown to listen to the man who was largely responsible for pulling the whole thing together. The religious nuts swallowed what Big John spouted with total belief. The other groups relied on him because he was driving the town's overall organization, but the religious nuts thought he was the second coming.

Big John had been a truck driver in the before. He'd

been hauling building supplies when the shit hit the fan, and it was his load of lumber and plywood that boarded up most of the exterior doors and walls. He'd been the one to talk Captain Jones into making a stand in Dover. Big John was convinced there was nowhere left to run. Where could you hide from God's wrath?

So the huge black truck driver had turned into a bit of a prophet. He'd been the one to organize the work groups, making lists of what needed to be done and making sure it happened with the help of his foremen. In the early days, he would head out at noon and come back with a tractor trailer full of supplies before dark fell. He wasn't afraid to go out into the dead city, and that made him a sort of folk hero for a lot of the regular people.

He'd showed a lot of scared and frightened people that they could survive, and he'd enforced some form of order when everything else was falling apart. I'd listen to Justine tell me about his "people" and get a little scared, even in the early days. Big John wielded a lot of influence and I'm a firm believer in Lord Acton: Power corrupts, and absolute power corrupts absolutely.

Captain Jones didn't seem to care, which surprised me. He worried about the walls and the guns. After that, the only thing he worried about was vodka. I think Big John's status actually relieved him in a way. He didn't want to be responsible for feeding or organizing a town of frightened people.

I could get around fairly well with crutches by the fifth day, but my lower back still sent shots of pain down my right leg if I did too much. If I stood, my back would ache until I sat down. After sitting for a while, it would ache until I got back on my feet. The pain would start out dull and then get sharper and sharper until I moved, but the relief only lasted a few minutes after I shifted positions.

While Justine filled sandbags and nailed doors shut on work crews, I wandered around the streets, the MP5K slung to my chest. Once I became slightly mobile, she wouldn't let me go out without the gun, figuring I needed it more than she did.

Most people ignored me as I wandered about. The work crews concentrated on earning their tickets, and the soldiers generally focused outward. Except for Captain Jones; he saw me but didn't seem to remember who I was. Every time I saw him, he looked a little worse, eventually appearing to have stopped eating, sleeping, and brushing his hair.

As I made my rounds a few days later, exercising my legs as I worked to take more weight off the crutches, I came across Captain Jones and Big John sitting on a bench on a deserted street. I hung back out of sight and listened.

"Come back to the church with me. You need to get something to eat," John said to him.

"I just wanted to tell you what a good job you're doing," the captain said, sounding truly relieved, his voice thick and slurred from too much drink.

"You're responsible for these people being alive just as much as me."

It was the first time I'd really gotten a chance to experience Big John from closer than a hundred feet. I understood why people were flocking to him. He possessed a quiet intensity—a strength of character that his large physical size could just barely contain.

I moved on before they saw me. Only an hour later, as I stood watching a bunch of army engineers trying to get a large diesel generator running, I heard the news: the captain had gone back to his bunk and hung himself.

The town fell quiet for the rest of the day, everyone sticking to their designated groups as the news spread through New Dover. I went back to our place, not liking the eyes watching me from inside locked-up buildings as I passed.

Captain Jones wasn't the first to go out like that, but, like Justine and myself, a lot of the nonmilitary people in downtown had been pulled in by his checkpoints. That put him in the same category as Big John—someone who was supposed to protect them.

Justine made me promise not to go out the next day. People were talking about something bad happening. They thought the thralls were coming and whispered that it was the reason Jones had hung himself. He didn't want to be there when they came.

It was clear most of the survivors hadn't actually ever seen a gray. Thralls were everywhere, but the grays were boogie men: ten times scarier because they were the un-known. A few of the soldiers may have been telling the truth when they claimed to have seen a gray, or even a brute, but their stories didn't help put anyone at ease. They always ended with lots of dead soldiers.

Justine had heard people saying the grays were like sharks: they could smell blood from miles away, and the sick and the weak attracted them. Some of the Fort people talked quietly about wanting to cull the herd before the weak ani-mals brought in the predators. Not exactly a good time to be out walking around on crutches.

People held their breath through the night, but no attack came. The next night, when the generator rumbled to life, powering a set of mobile light towers around downtown, the mood shifted as people yelled and cheered from behind locked doors.

The next day, Justine hauled cable up and down the block while other work crews hung lines. They started string-ing lights in the small square at the center of town first, which was good for us. Several of the lights hung just out-side our front windows.

Everyone was happy as a clam the first time they left the generator running through the night, but I made Justine sleep with her pants on. She told me to wake her if anyone started shooting and fell into bed, worn out from spending all day filling and hauling sandbags. She slept while I sat propped up on pillows, listening for something bad to start outside. I knew the grays weren't stupid, and if we'd been passed over in the chaos during the first days, there was no way they could miss us now.

I sat with the MP5K in my lap, listening and waiting while Justine slept next to me. At first I watched the door, but as the night wore on and didn't erupt in gunfire and screams, I found myself watching her more and more.

Midway through the night, she grew restless, twisting and turning, the sheets getting all tangled up in her legs as she struggled against something in her dreams. I was debat-ing trying to wake her when she quieted down, her body stretched out in a funny position on the bed.

When the sun came up, she denied remembering any

nightmares, but something in the way she said it made me wonder. I watched her more closely. Sometimes she looked worse than others, but it never seemed to slow her down. She swore she'd tell me if she felt something pulling at her again.

As the days passed, Justine, who was already thin, turned what little softness she had on her into muscle. Men twice her size were sitting by the end of the day, but she would keep going until the end, earning the double ticket more than anyone else.

Every day, one member of the work teams would get two tickets for their work instead of one—a cheap and easy way to keep the work teams motivated. The tickets were the only currency Big John allowed in town. Dollars were worthless, but a raffle ticket with Big John's stamp was what you got paid to scavenge or work on a detail, and what you used to buy everything in the town store.

Of course, tickets weren't his only way to keep order; he had more direct methods as well. His foremen made sure what Big John said happened. His followers had the scary tone of fanatics when they talked about him, which kept me pushing to get back on my feet and back to full strength.

I'd healed enough that my back no longer sent stabs of pain down right leg when I walked, but I still paid a price if I pushed too hard. I could walk without the crutches, but if I didn't use at least one to take some of the weight by the end of the day, I really suffered the next morning.

I wasn't fit enough to join a work detail, but I pushed a little harder every day. As I returned from a walk one day, I came across a group of people pushing and shoving two men to the ground in front of the church. I got close enough to see and hear a little better but not so close as to become part of the mob.

The two men were young, their bodies fully grown but their faces still showing a bit of their baby fat. The crowd kept herding them until they were in front of the door to the church. One of the foremen outside leveled his shotgun on the boys while the other went inside to get Big John.

A screaming match between the two boys and the mob continued until Big John's deep voice cut through it all, commanding silence.

"First, what are they accused of?" he asked, looking first at the man-boys and then the crowd. A middle-aged woman stepped forward, her face streaked with tears.

"These monsters," she spit at them, "were about to rape my fifteen-year-old baby."

"That's not true," one of the man-boys protested, but Big John silenced him with a look.

"Where were you when this happened?" Big John asked the woman.

She didn't seem ready to answer the question; her lips moved for a moment before she finally put a sentence together. "I went to get a drink, and when I got back, they was both in my daughter's room, pawing at her. She was yelling and screaming."

"She didn't..." one of the young men tried to butt in.

"You'll get your turn." Big John cut him off, holding his hand up again for them to be quiet. As the foreman with the shotgun took a step closer, the look of potential job satisfaction on his face gave me a chill.

"She's a good girl," the mother hissed.

"I'm sure she is. Where is your daughter now?"

"She's back in our rooms crying, with the door locked."

"Do you have anything else to say?" Big John asked her. She shook her head, confident she'd made her case. Big John turned his attention to the young men. "What happened?"

They looked at each other and then at the mob surrounding them. Their clothes were ripped, and bruises were already appearing on their faces and arms. The taller of the two accused spoke for both of them.

"We live down the hall from Robyn. She came down for a pop and a cigarette when her mom left. She told us she didn't want to be alone, so we came back to her room with her."

"And you just gave her a can of soda and a cigarette for nothing?"

"She was all flirty and nice to us," the kid said.

The mother was stamping her feet in anger, but it only took a glance from Big John to keep her quiet.

"And flirty means you get to pull your dick out?" Big John's words might have garnered a snicker on another day, but the intensity of his voice kept everyone quiet.

"She didn't start to scream until her mom came in," the shorter boy pleaded, falling forward to try and put his hands on Big John's feet. The foreman stopped him with a kick.

"How old are you?" Big John asked, kneeling down to look the boy in the face.

"Seventeen," the shorter boy replied.

"Nineteen," the other said.

Big John stood up, his eyes looking over the crowd. I hugged the tree that hid me, trying to fade into it as his eyes swept past me. The two boys clutched the ground, one of them blubbering, spit hanging from his lips as he begged for forgiveness in a run-on stream of barely intelligible speech.

"I find you guilty," Big John said, his voice booming out over the thirty or so people there. They erupted in cheers and began moving in on the two boys until he bellowed for them to halt. Both the boys were crying, begging for mercy.

"They are guilty, but, like all men, they deserve a chance to redeem themselves."

The crowd pulled back, their sudden energy sucked away. One of the boys tried to stand, swearing he'd never do anything ever again. Big John ignored him.

"They will be put out with enough water and food for two days. If they can make it to the water tower to the east and hang a lantern, they will be forgiven, and allowed back in."

The crowd regained their enthusiasm, cheering loudly.

I shook my head in disgust. Big John was killing the two boys more cruelly than the mob ever could. The water tower was just visible to the east. To get to it, you had to cross the bridges over the Silver River and move to within a mile of Route 13. The scavengers never headed east. Those who did didn't come back. It was one of the heaviest areas of undead activity. Everything east of the highway was a no-man's-land. People didn't go there, even in daylight, and expect to return.

I watched Big John as his foremen escorted the two convicted men away. The mob wouldn't go against Big John openly, but without the foremen there, they might just put the boys out without any supplies or a lantern.

I wasn't interested in the boys. It was an unfortunate situation, but they were already dead. I watched John as he rubbed his chin and went back into the church.

The mob had wanted blood. That was clear. And as much power as Big John had, I wasn't sure what would have happened if he'd done anything that hadn't resulted in a very bad outcome for the boys. What I wanted to know was whether he'd put the boys out to try and keep his hands free of blood, which was a joke, or whether it was the only punishment he thought he could get away with that gave the boys some small hope of survival.

Or was it worse than that? Did he really believe he was giving them a chance to prove their salvation by living through the night and hanging a lantern on a water tower? The religious undertones and the power he exerted over the town made me more uneasy than ever.

I headed back to the gym next to our place, intent on pushing myself a little harder. The faster I was fully healed, the sooner Justine and I would be able to plan our next step.

Treadmills, elliptical machines, and stair climbers filled the first floor of the gym. The weights were on the second floor, so I walked through the empty gym with the electric lantern I kept inside the door and slowly made my way upstairs.

I tried to forget the scene by the church, working up a sweat as I ran through my workout. The tinted windows limited the light coming in from outside, and the lantern light cast shadows everywhere as I worked out, making it hard to focus. Every time my concentration slipped, I would think about the kids—and Big John. I wasn't in a proper state of mind to sit in the shadows working out.

So instead I hobbled next door to the apartment to get the bag of tools I'd found in the closet. I'd thought about it for a few days: I was going to take apart one of the large, four-station weight machines and move it. Between the physical effort of turning a wrench and the thought process that went into figuring out how it came apart, I managed to lose myself in the work.

I realized how late it was growing with just enough time

left to make it back to the apartment before Justine. She was tired and hungry as usual, and I felt the same. We cleaned up, ate a quick meal of canned goods and locked down for the night, neither of us talking much. She kissed me lightly before rolling over and going to sleep.

I spent the next several days breaking the workout machine down into its smallest pieces and carrying them up the stairs to pile them on the flat roof of the gym in the open air and sunlight.

I thought carrying the larger frame sections up onto the roof of the gym would be the hard part. I was wrong. The hard part was trying to figure out how everything bolted back together and how the cables were routed after I had everything moved. In the end, I was forced to walk downstairs and study its twin with a flashlight multiple times before finally getting it right.

The cabling looks straightforward once it's all together, but try and take it apart and get it back together without cursing a little. I got so uncomfortable sitting on the roof that I took a huge square of green plastic indoor/outdoor carpeting from the smoothie bar and dragged it up the stairs, giving myself something other than hot tar and stone roofing to sit on while I puzzled the equipment back together.

Life fell into a routine. Justine would leave at first light to labor on a work crew and come back with whatever supplies she could buy. I'd work out and continue adding décor to my rooftop gym as I slowly regained my strength.

As I started feeling better, I tried to talk to Justine about the future, but she made it clear she didn't want to go there. She'd let me hug her close as we slept, but if I tried anything more than a kiss, she would pull away. I tried to tell her how I felt, but it seemed to hurt her to hear me say it.

I wanted to push her, to make her understand, but I thought she'd come around if I just gave her more time. Once I was fully healed, we'd get away and things would be different. I had to believe that.

In some ways, those days were bittersweet. Justine would get pissed and brood if I said the wrong thing, but she was so tired and sore at night that she couldn't refuse my offers to rub her shoulders and back. She would fall asleep topless with me sitting on her butt, working the kinks out of her muscles.

She either slept through me taking care of myself after or pretended to be. I tried to be quiet. I wasn't trying to be gross, but there is only so much a guy can take.

The rooftop of the gym became my hideout during the day. I pushed myself, knowing that last extra ounce of strength I might be what saved me—or her. The gym roof became my secret, my second home. I added some vinyl lounge chairs and other deck furniture, but my most genius move was hanging a clear plastic water jug on the end of a pull-up bar. After sitting in the sun all day, it actually felt like a hot shower.

I completed my personal gym with a ladder, lag screws, and some rope. Any Boy Scout master would have been proud of what I'd built.

The gap between our apartment building and the gym was just wide enough for a walk to fit between them. If I'd been willing to risk it, I could have easily jumped from the gym roof to the balcony off our second bedroom. As it was, I used a ladder, some rope, and a fair bit of upper body strength to set a gang plank between them.

Making half-decent hand rails on either side actually took more time than anything else, but I figured it out. The last thing I did was use the lag screws to permanently seal the door that opened onto the stairwell leading to the gym's second floor. The only way on or off the roof would be through our apartment.

The day I finished up, I could barely wait for Justine to come home. I'd been keeping my little hideout secret from her, mostly so she wouldn't realize how hard I was pushing myself, but it was time to share.

She came through the door like she always did, hungry, tired, and ready to collapse, and just a little grouchy to keep me from trying to get too chatty. She snapped at me when I told her not to go into the bathroom, but I wouldn't accept anything less than surrender as I blindfolded her, spun her about and marched her through the apartment.

"What the fuck?" she sighed as she stumbled up the plastic chair I was using to get over the balcony railing. "Are you pushing me off the edge?" she asked, a tremor of fear, or maybe excitement, in her voice. It hurt me equally no matter which way I took it, but I didn't let it ruin my mood.

"Will you be serious," I scolded her, my hands around her back, the tips of my fingers on the sides of her bra. She used her hands on the rope guardrail to help pull herself up the incline until she stumbled down off the lip around the roof with a curse.

"Can I look now?" she asked, a hint of a smile sneaking onto her face as curiosity got the better of her. I was winning, or at least starting too.

"Not yet," I told her, leading her over to the pull-up bar. I positioned her under my homemade shower and pulled the blindfold off. She looked around, dumbfounded, trying to orient herself.

When she saw the jug of water and soap resting on a cross brace, her face lit up with a smile that only got brighter when she reached up to feel the warmth of the sun still inside the jug. She actually bubbled with excitement as she hugged me and then commanded me off the roof so she could shower.

I wanted to tease her and tell her she would need help scrubbing her back. Afraid of ruining her good mood though, I gave her some privacy instead and went to make our dinner. I used the cutting board in the kitchen as a tray and emptied our MRE meals into bowls. It was the equivalent of using the good china after eating our meals directly out of their containers for days.

If Justine used the whole bag of water, she would have about a five-minute shower. I timed my dinner prep so I was coming back up the ramp just as she was getting dressed. The military taught me excellent tactical skills. She was pulling on a pair of boxers when I made it onto the roof, giving me a great shot of her ass.

"Really?" she asked as she stood there, her eyebrows raised. The nipples on her small breasts stood straight in the rapidly cooling night air. I was too stunned to speak and didn't regain my senses until she pulled on a shirt with a laugh.

"Dinner is served," I said, clearing my throat. I put the

food down on the plastic table as she combed her hair with her fingers. "Lady's choice," I informed her with a wave of my hand over the cutting board. She took the beef stew, leaving me the chicken and vegetables.

We ate as the sun set, the streets emptying as everyone took refuge for the night. We sat through a few minutes of muddy darkness before the generator kicked in and the lights strung along the buildings hummed to life, lighting up the center of town.

When we were done eating, she wiped her mouth with the paper towel included in the MRE and gave me a funny smile. Then she jumped up, told me to sit tight, and ran back to the apartment. She returned carrying a decent-sized box, its flaps folded crudely shut. I saw something reflective inside and some wires poking out here and there.

"I'm sorry I've been such a pain lately," she said, putting the box down and pulling open the flaps. "I was going to find the right time to give this to you, and it's definitely now."

She stood beaming as I took a rectangular solar panel out of the box along with various bits and pieces of electrical components. Under the solar panel lay a security camera and several other pieces of electronics.

"Where did you get this?" I asked her, turning the solar panel over in my hands.

"You'll have to guess. I figured it was kinda not fair to give you some electronic toys with no way to charge them." Just like everything else, the electricity was metered out by Big John and his crew. The penalty for tapping into the power line was expulsion, and the only building in Dover with inside lights was the church, which happened to house Big John's office.

I turned the solar cell over in my hands, looking at the thick plastic protecting it. At four inches wide by two feet long, it definitely wasn't a full-size panel. What cinched it for me was the piece of black plastic molding stuck to one corner.

"Expensive German car?"

"Damn, you *are* a geek," she mused, her face lighting up with another smile. "I figured you could use a piece from a big car to power the little ones."

I grabbed her and pulled her into my lap, kissing her.

She stiffened at first but gradually relaxed, melting into me.

"I'm sorry I've been kinda rough around the edges lately," she said into my neck. She paused and I waited, hoping she was going to say something else. Something was bothering her, but she wasn't sharing.

"No worries," I said finally. "I know it's not easy being stuck here, but we're almost ready to get moving again."

The comment clearly surprised her. "Moving again?"

"Sure. I'm almost good as new, and after we stock up on some supplies, we are getting out of here."

"I thought you might be putting down roots," she said, admiring my handiwork on the roof.

"Just keeping busy."

"OK," she said, her tone and face completely unreadable.

"Tomorrow you are going to throttle back, and I'm going to join a work crew with you."

She gave me an odd look, but I still couldn't read what was going through her mind.

"You ready? I still hear you groan when you roll over at night," she said, her voice touched with concern.

"Don't worry about me."

"Think you can walk and run?" she asked, picking up a stray pea from her stew and eating it.

"Did I miss the announcement for the work crew Olympics?" I asked.

"No, but scavengers get a ticket for every cart they bring in," she said enticingly. The scavengers went out into the undead city and brought back everything from bottles of water to toilet paper, and what had turned out to be the most precious commodity of all: cat litter. Without flushing toilets, bags of kitty litter were quite valuable.

"It's gotta be better than nailing plywood or filling manholes with rocks," I said, nodding my head. Big John's foremen would either accept or reject what the scavengers brought back, giving tickets for each cart they accepted. Anything rejected you got to keep, but you didn't get a ticket for it. Generally, if it was worth hauling back, it was accepted.

"Good. I have another present I was saving for you," she purred, sitting back in my lap. She must have felt the thrill run through me because she shook her head in exasperation as my eyes traced the line from her neck down to her chest, locking on the hard protrusions of her nipples.

"Pig," she said lovingly as she jumped off my lap and went back to the gang plank to grab something she'd left just out of sight. Clearly we had different thoughts about what my second present should be.

This time she returned carrying a hard plastic case. She handed it to me and pulled her deck chair over so she could watch me open the latches, excited to see my reaction. Not sure what to expect, I was surprised to find a pair of Glock Model 22 .40 caliber pistols resting inside.

I got up and gave her a huge hug. You have to love a girl who gets you a pair of hand guns as a present. It's a rule.

"I have a shoulder rig for them, but you only have one spare clip for each and I could only afford a single box of rounds," she said, peeling one of the weapons free as I did the same with the other. The action was clean and smooth as I pulled back the slide and let it go.

I slept that night with the shoulder rig hanging off the closet door. As we went to bed, Justine chuckled and said it was OK if I wanted to put one under the pillow, but I ignored her.

The next morning we headed over to the church to get in line for a scavenging slot. Big John wanted to keep track of who was going in and out of the gates, and his foremen wanted to give some direction as to what they needed brought back, so we had to stand in line to be "approved" before going out.

Justine told me there had been some competition for slots in the beginning, but things were starting to go the other way—fewer and fewer people were willing to go outside. The excellent pay was a draw, but some never made it back. Just the week before, a large scavenging party had disappeared entirely while raiding a grocery store.

Big John paid several soldiers to go look for the party the day after they failed to return. The patrol went to the grocery store the scavengers were supposed to hit but found no sign of them. It didn't look like the scavengers had even made it that far. The doors and windows to the store were still intact.

The line moved quickly once the foreman sat down with his notebook and map. The parties in front of us listed out their members, and the foreman told them what types of supplies were needed and gave them a rough idea of where they might want to look.

A partially unfolded street map of Dover rested under the foreman's notebook. Red circles highlighted the areas where other teams had gone missing, and little marks crossed out stores that had already been picked clean.

The foreman took our names and motioned another fellow to come over when it was our turn. The second foreman spit a long stream of brown saliva into a bush and came over. He was short and stocky but had the look of a man who'd spent a good part of his life doing heavy construction. You don't get arms banded with muscles like that working at a dentist's office.

Justine gave him a big smile when he came over to the desk, which he returned, revealing teeth stained permanently brown by chew. I tried to ignore the little flame of jealously stirring in me.

He looked us both over and nodded at Justine with approval, clearly recognizing her. "You sure you want to do this?" he asked in a deep baritone, mostly to her but looking at me as he said it.

"Don't worry. We'll be coming back, Jim," she said, her voice absolutely positive. Jim didn't look convinced. He eyed the machete on my right thigh and the two pistols under my arms skeptically. The little flame of jealousy turned to anger. I could protect my own. I felt my face reddening.

"We're good," she promised Jim, rubbing my upper arm as she said it. Her touch was like heroine to a junky. My heart rate immediately fell and the anger ebbed, eased away by her touch.

"They're good," Jim said, waving two fingers good-bye to us as he started to turn around, directly into Big John.

"Everything OK?" the big man asked. You could feel his voice in your chest when he talked.

It was the closest I'd ever been to him, and I couldn't help but look him over from head to toe. He was at least six foot three and close to three hundred pounds—something that seeing him from a distance didn't fully impart.

I'd known big guys before and could generally tell the ones who used it to bully from the ones who knew what real violence was. For all the quiet confidence Big John exuded, he also had the air of a man who'd used his fists before, and would again if you gave him a reason.

"New scavengers," Jim said to his boss.

"You should bring more firepower," Big John said in his bass rumble, then walked into the church without another word.

Everyone's a critic.

Jim followed Big John, leaving us with the first foreman. He gave us several nearby sites to choose from. "I've been saving them for a bunch of noobs," he said with a smile.

Justine had to haggle over two carts—an activity I wasn't prepared for. They were like the square metal shopping carts old ladies used, but with bicycle tires in place of the smaller ones used when the world was civilized. The fore-man took a while as he weighed her promise of payment on return against the likelihood of us actually making it back. In the end, he accepted after she told him Jim would vouch for her.

The foreman gave us our carts, and we made our way to the closest gate. I was surprised to see two groups of na-tional guardsmen fueling Humvee's from jerry cans on the opposite corner when we made it outside.

One of the soldiers came over and smiled very broadly at Justine, chatting her up. He seemed to think that his uni-form and the Humvee would impress her. She kept smiling, and he kept talking. He said the radios had been nothing but static since the day the other battalion headed to Washing-ton, but yesterday, intervals of clicking had followed a brief moment of chatter. It wasn't quite Morse code, but it did sound like someone was thumbing the mic.

Justine kept nodding, and the soldier kept talking. The two Humvees were going to make a run south and see if they couldn't find the source of the radio transmission. They weren't sure what they'd heard, but if the radios were picking it up, it had to be within a ten-mile range.

Justine let the soldier talk until his buddies harassed him

into packing it up. He finally spared me a glance as he was walking back to his Hummer, telling me with his eyes that he planned to continue his conversation with Justine when he returned. I shot him a stern look, but it's hard to look tough pushing a shopping cart.

We wheeled our empty carts down the road, looking at the world with new eyes. Grass grew up through the cracks in the street, and stores stood empty, their windows broken and everything of value cleaned out. The only sounds we heard were our own footsteps.

Our moods grew more somber the further we made it into the city. Leftover bits of other peoples' lives littered the streets, and every block bore the signs of some last, desperate battle. Shattered windows were either covered in dark brown stains or boarded up. At one corner, three police cars and a truck were circled bumper to bumper, shotgun shells and empty casings littering the ground.

The worst was a burnt-out three-story apartment. A sheet blew in the wind over the roof's edge. Multiple burn marks covered the sheet, but the word "Help" remained clearly legible. It took me a moment to realize what hung next to the sign.

A blackened, mummified corpse had been hung upside down by a foot, the bottom of its head about level with the second floor. The concrete under the body was stained black. The fire had burned out before reaching the third floor, but the heat rising from below had smoked the body, liquefying its fat and letting it drip down to the concrete below to be consumed like a candle dripping wax. What was left was a dried-out body left to swing in the breeze.

"Let's keep moving," Justine said, nudging me to get me walking again. "Are we close?" she asked after we'd gone a bit farther in silence.

"Just a few more blocks," I told her. Walking through the dead city reminded me of the posts Elena Filatova had shared of Prypiat after Chernobyl.

"Good. That means we'll have time to make two runs," she said. I picked up my pace.

Our quickie mart came into view not long after. We stood across the street from it, looking at the traffic jam clogging the road between us and our target.

Justine covered me with the MP5K as I jumped up onto the trunk lid of a sedan and scanned its interior, a Glock in either hand as I stepped from car to car as lightly as I could. I made it to the far side without incident and then retraced my steps to help Justine roll the carts between the cars once I was reasonably sure it was clear. We were both breathing heavily when we got to the quickie mart.

"That was fun," she said with a wan smile. Slipping between the cars pushing shopping carts had left us both feeling exposed and on edge.

"Let's finish this up," I said quietly, pulling out a flashlight to peer through the windows of the store, trying to get a good look around the signs advertising slushies and hotdogs.

Of course the doors were locked.

"We should have brought a hammer," she said, tapping the glass with the butt of her flashlight.

Shooting it was out of the question. I didn't want to bring every thrall for blocks around down on us.

"A window punch would be better," I said, trying to remember the last time I'd seen a fire truck. It had been a while. Not about to let the locked store put an end to our first day of scavenging, I went over to the traffic jam, found an unlocked sedan, and popped the trunk release.

I had to wonder what the owner of the car had been doing when all this started as I emptied the contents of his trunk onto the road. Who has a game of Twister, a gallon bottle of baby oil, a bag of clothespins, and a badminton set strewn about their trunk? I imagined some odd scenarios where they were all used together as I pulled the carpet out to get to the jack.

Justine tapped her imaginary wrist watch as I brought the scissor jack back and looked around for the last thing I needed. I found it in the back of a plumbing truck on the other side of the street: a short length of galvanized pipe.

"Hold this in place," I told Justine, kneeling to position the pipe under the middle hinge of the quickie mart door. I set the jack on the lower hinge and turned it by hand until I had the jack and the pipe holding themselves between the two hinges with tension.

"You think that up on your own?" she asked as I used the lug wrench to keep expanding the jack.

"Nah. A kid in the Sudan showed me this trick," I told her. The life I'd spent in the service almost seemed as if it belonged to someone else.

I turned the jack until the glass in the door exploded with a pop, startling me.

Justine was chuckling. "You jumped," she said with satisfaction.

"Startled me," I admitted, breaking a few last pieces of glass out of the door frame with the piece of pipe.

We climbed in and cleared the front of the store, relieved to find ourselves alone in the quickie mart. We filled our carts with cases of water and batteries before topping them off with lighter dried goods and bags of chips. Everyone was craving salt. We had to laugh when we found the rear door unlocked at the back of the store.

The full carts slowed us down a little, but the closer we got to New Dover, the lighter they got. The foreman was happy to see us and happier to take the first tickets we'd earned as payment for the carts.

We turned right around and headed back for the gate. The guards let us out without a word. We bypassed the burnt-out apartment building with its hanging ornament—a detour well worth the extra few blocks of walking it cost us. The quickie mart looked just as we'd left it, but we cleared it again anyway, making sure nothing had crept in in our absence.

We took the last three cases of bottled water in the store and then loaded up with canned goods. I still had some room left in my cart when we were done loading, so I ran back inside to grab a few boxes of trail bars. I came back out to find Justine standing at attention, looking around warily. I dropped the food and drew a Glock, scanning the surrounding buildings.

"Did you see something?" I whispered, trying to scan a thousand possible hiding places at once.

"No…o." She struggled to get the word out, her eyes fluttering as she strained against something. "I *feel* something," she said slowly, carefully squeezing the grips of her MP5K, the muscles in her arms straining as she struggled against an unseen foe.

I slid closer to her, worry and fear mixing. It had been weeks since she'd changed against her will.

"Kiss me, and I'll deck you," she promised, gritting her teeth. I didn't care what she said: if her eyes started to turn slate, I was going to kiss her. She seemed to know what I was thinking and turned away.

"Can you walk?" I asked. We had to get back to New Dover.

She nodded mechanically, and I grabbed her arm, trying to lead her off. "We are not leaving the carts," she said, shaking loose.

"OK," I said, putting my gun on top of the supplies to keep it close at hand. I let her lead the way so I could watch her.

We made it two blocks before a high-pitched keening hit us like a siren, blasting through the streets and bouncing off the buildings to hit us from every direction.

Justine let go of her cart. "Are you OK?" I asked her. She didn't answer. I made it to her side just as the shriek ended with a loud *pop*. A concussion wave swept down the street, hitting us in the face with grit and dirt as it passed.

Justine jerked her shoulder away from my hand and took off running before I could stop her. I chased her, pumping my legs as hard as I could, struggling to keep up with her as she flew down the street. She was fast, and the distance between us slowly grew, putting a knot in my stomach until she stopped as suddenly as she'd begun at the next corner.

"Jus…tine?" I panted, out of breath.

"Something is in there," she said, pointing the tip of her MP5K at the construction site in front of us.

A large steel frame had been in the process of going up. Supports and rigging were everywhere. It looked like the workers were in the middle of pouring the second floor decking when the world was turned on its side. A concrete truck and pumper were partially visible on the far side of the property. Piles of sand and other building materials stood along the front of the structure, just beyond the open gates. Plastic tarps flapped around the edges of the first two stories of the building, hiding most of the interior of the steel structure.

"Sounds like a good reason not to be here," I said, trying to turn her to face me. I thought I was being completely reasonable.

She disagreed, slipping my hand off her shoulder and darting across the street and through the open gate. She turned to see if I was coming—and got blindsided by a gray. He hit her like a linebacker before I could say a word, doubling her over his shoulder as he caught her in the gut. The gray straightened and turned to me with a toothy smile.

He didn't see Justine straighten in the air or stretch out her hand to take part of the force of impact as she slammed into the plastic body of a Port-O-John, landing on her feet. A normal person would have been hurt. Justine was mad.

The gray had his eyes on me, unafraid of the pistol I was aiming at him, when the burst of fire from Justine's MP5K tore into his side in a tight group, punching holes through his ribcage and puncturing his right lung.

He turned on Justine, his face full of rage. She was supposed to be down, and she certainly wasn't supposed to be shooting at him. I got two shots off, both of them cutting through empty air as the wounded gray charged back at Justine.

She put another burst directly into his sternum at near point-blank range, spraying dark blood onto his pale face just before he tackled her. They rolled to a stop with the gray was on top, his arm pulled back to slam a punch into her face. I fired, but I was already running and the shot went high, over his head. Just as his fist was coming down, Justine's palm closed over it.

The gray looked at his fist wrapped in her small hand in disbelief. Before he could comes to grips with his astonishment, she was lashing out with her free hand, punching him twice in the jaw as she bucked under him, trying to throw him off.

I crossed the remaining distance at a run, putting the tip of my Glock against his head as my shoes slid through the sand covering the ground and pulling the trigger just as I came to a stop. Blood and brains splattered the ground.

Justine spit and cursed as she pushed the body off her

chest, wiping bits of brain off her arm. "Fuck!" she said thickly as I pulled her to her feet. The moment she was standing, she let go of my hand and snapped the MP5K to her shoulder.

She was firing before I could ask her what she was doing, the tip of the submachine gun spurting fire. I stepped back, away from the wash of heat from the gun's discharge, and looked across the yard.

Three more grays were running at us, coming from the back of the construction site like quiet ghosts. I started to bring my Glock up but froze as I got a look at their faces. I thought they were thralls for a moment, but they moved too smoothly.

The tissue around their eyes was bruised and swollen, like some madman had taken a razor to their faces trying to remove a chunk of flesh in the shape of a sleeping mask. They crossed half the distance between us in the moment it took their oddness to register, then I opened fire.

I heard Justine cursing in staccato between bursts from the MP5K. The lead gray fell face first into the ground in a short slide just as she reached the end of her clip, blood soaking into the sand beneath him.

I stepped in front of Justine as the last two grays closed, a pistol in each hand, firing one then the other in a rapid back-and-forth action. I'm right dominant, and the gray on that side fared worse than the other. The .40 caliber rounds punched neat little holes into the gray to my right, sending chunks of meat flying from his back. A lucky shot to his neck felled him. Meanwhile, I only hit the gray on my left with a single shot.

Justine flipped her selector to full auto, screaming as she unleashed two long bursts into a fourth gray I hadn't even seen. It had apparently jumped from the steel skeleton of the building to come down on us from above. He didn't have much ability to dodge or move in the air and took both bursts right up his middle from his groin to his chest.

He landed on his feet, but the shock of the impact finished what the bullets had started. His pelvis separated and his abdomen ruptured, spilling a mess of bloody organs onto the ground. The gray lived just long enough to look down at his insides before he crumpled.

The remaining gray had only taken a shot in the arm and was still moving fast, using the distraction his airborne comrade had supplied to dart behind a stack of wooden forms, coming out on our flank.

I dropped my pistols to the ground as I ducked under the gray's first swipe, dodging low as I brought my knee up hard into his gut, keeping him from slipping past me as I drew my machete from its sheath. One step behind me and to my left, Justine reloaded.

The gray snarled at me, throwing up an arm to shield his head as my machete came down on him. His hand fell to the ground as the blade passed cleanly through his forearm and bit into his shoulder. His snarl turned to a scream as dark red blood pumped from the stump of his arm.

Justine had her MP5K on her shoulder ready to fire, but I was in the way. I should have stepped back and let her finish him, but pent-up rage and anger blinded me. Our world was never going to be the same, and there was nothing I could do about that. The sense of helplessness turned to boiling steam in my veins. I bullied the gray over, hacking off his remaining arm at the shoulder as he fell. I fell on him, hacking away with my blade.

"I think he's dead," Justine said, trying to pull me off the gray by my shirt. "Come on," she barked, choking me as she pulled harder.

I stopped swinging and looked at the yard around us. "I'm sorry," I said as I stood, tugging my shirt free of her grasp.

"Do you see this?" Justine asked, looking at the first gray we'd killed as I searched the ground for my pistols. She stood over him, tilting his head from side to side with the tip of her shoe. I blew as much sand off my pistols as I could before slipping them into their holsters.

"Looks like a drunk surgeon went to town on him," I offered, using my own foot to push down on the thing's thigh. The meat of his leg opened up to the bone. Something had cut him deep.

"You sure you didn't get a whack at him?" Justine asked, thinking the same thing I was.

"No. I still had bullets left when we came through the gate," I said, looking around. "Let's get our carts and get out of here," I suggested, feeling like we were begging for trouble the longer we stayed put.

A metallic ring of metal on metal came from inside the building's skeleton just as I finished speaking. Justine looked at me and then toward the interior of the building, cocking her head as she did so.

"I don't think an enemy of my enemy is my friend this time," I warned as she darted closer to the building. I sighed as I followed her, wanting desperately to be running in the opposite direction.

The sounds of fighting grew louder as we reached a gap in the tarps stretched across the steel girders. I wanted to caution Justine, to argue with her to run, but there would be no stopping her.

We moved as quietly as we could, darting from beam to beam and looking all around, trying to make sure nothing was coming up on us from any direction—including above. My neck was hurting and the old injury to my back was sending twinges of pain down my right thigh, warning me I wasn't fully healed yet. Halfway through the building, we saw flashes of movement.

Justine darted behind a contractor's storage box, waving at me to stay low. I followed her, peeking around the side of the box.

We saw a huge brute grunting and swinging his arms in wide arcs as he fought off five grays. Beams of light filtered through the building from above us, casting shafts of brightness down onto the battlefield. Claw marks covered the brute's arms, and drops of fresh blood hit the girders each time he took a swing.

A sixth gray moved around the brute like a dancer, and I didn't understand what was going on at first. The brute and a single gray appeared to be fighting the five attackers, who all had the same markings around their eyes as the grays outside. The "normal" gray moved about the brute, covering his back.

The fighting moved in blurs as the cut-eyed grays circled the pair, grinding them down. The brute was holding them back but took a constant stream of small wounds, slowly but surely being bled out. I thought it was going to be a slow, drawn-out end, but the cut eyes were impatient. One of them launched forward in a headlong attack, leaping at the brute.

The four others surged in as their comrade flew forward, thinking to overwhelm their enemy, but the brute caught the leaping figure in mid air, grabbing him by his skull and using his body like a club to sweep back the onrush. The brute dropped his club to the floor as a horrible shriek filled the air.

We couldn't see where the scream had come from.

The four remaining cut eyes picked themselves up, snarling and snapping with renewed energy as they circled the brute, their anger driving them to attack. They were either blind with rage or just didn't care that the brute now stood alone. The gray that had been guarding his back had vanished.

They realized their mistake too late. The gray darted out from behind a support column as one of the cut eyes spun past, chrome lightening flashing as he pulled back the cut eye's head, muscling his blade across his target's throat with enough force to nearly behead him.

As the body fell to the ground, the wailing scream repeated itself, sending a chill down my spine. There was something else close by, and it did not sound happy.

The three remaining cut eyes were working the brute over, trying to take him down before the knife-wielding gray could come to his aid. The gray saw the brute struggling and darted in, snarling as he drove the others away with his knife.

It looked like it might be too late for the brute, however. The huge creature put his hands on his knees, blood dripping from every surface of his body as he panted. The cut eyes circled wide, well out of reach. With their numbers reduced, they were willing to wait while the brute bled.

"I'm sorry, old friend," the gray with the knife said to the brute as he stood between the large creature and the others. There was something familiar about his voice I couldn't quite place.

I pulled on Justine's arm, trying to get her to budge. Whatever was going on had nothing to do with us. She pulled me down roughly as the source of the screaming walked into view: the largest gray I'd ever seen.

"Kneel, and Ravi will give you a place of honor," the newcomer bellowed slowly; each word seemed an effort.

"This would be new, honor among the Ravens," the knife wielder said, his eyes darting among his enemies, his body tense as if he expected to be rushed at any moment.

"My master understands the value of your gifts," the huge gray said, his voice stretching out each word. "We would not waste you on the front lines like Han-su seems intent on doing." The bulging gray tilted his neck to each shoulder until it cracked loudly.

"And Ravi would have me in a gilded prison, taking what truth he could from his enemies," the gray replied. Behind him, the brute stood up slowly, groaning as fresh sheets of blood washed down his skin. The knife wielder turned to him, giving him a solemn nod.

The brute put down his hands, forming a step for the knife wielder to jump from. The brute grunted as he pro-pelled the gray upward to disappear into the girders above.

The Ravens were too slow to stop the knife wielder from escaping, but they fell on the brute with a vengeance. Chunks of meat flew from his bones as the cut eyes sav-aged him. The brute screamed as he swung about blindly, pain driving him to madness. One gray underestimated the brute's remaining strength and was pulled in.

The brute tried to crush the gray he'd caught in a one-armed bear hug as he swung about wildly with his free arm, trying unsuccessfully to hold back the claws of the others. One of the grays darted about in front of him as the other tore into him from behind, cutting the tendons behind his knees so he crashed to the concrete floor.

Fresh screams of pain erupted from the brute as his captive got an arm free and drove a clawed finger deep into an eye socket, earning the gray his freedom as the brute swatted about in blind agony. The gray tried to hobble away, thinking it had escaped, but the brute caught his leg and flung him past our hiding place.

The Raven's body spun as it moved through the air, striking a girder and wrapping around the steel in a way that intact bones should not have allowed. The big gray stood watching the scene passively, his muscles twitching as his head fell back, a look of pure ecstasy on his face.

The two remaining cut eyes were on the brute the moment he released his projectile, immobilizing his arms as they slashed at his neck and chest with their claws. The brute struggled to free himself but was too weak. The grays tore away at his neck until they opened his arteries, sending blood spraying upward in huge geysers. The brute died with his head tilted back to stare at the girders above, watching as his heart pumped the last of his blood into the air.

The two surviving Ravens looked to their large brother for direction. The big gray had just opened his mouth when something dropped from the darkness above, landing directly behind the two smaller Ravens.

The cut eye on the right crumpled to the ground as if a switch had been thrown, sliding off the large knife that had been driven down into his spine where his neck met his body.

The remaining cut eye lashed out, but he was no match for the knife-wielding gray, who slipped beneath the sweeping strike, bringing his long blade up into his enemy's armpit. The blade speared upward, the tip popping out of the skin at the front of the Raven's neck.

As the cut eyes died, the massive gray started to pant and flex his arm and legs. He couldn't stand still. Something in the air popped, and the huge Raven tilted his head back, screaming in joy and anger at the sky.

The knife wielder didn't wait; he pushed the body of his last victim away and tossed his blade into the air, grabbing it by its point and whipping it at the huge gray in a flash. The blade flew end over end, whistling as it spun through the air.

I waited to see it sprout from the huge gray's chest, but the Raven was quick, twisting away so the blade struck him in the upper arm, piercing him through a massive bicep instead of the heart.

"First you reject my master, and then you dare use steel on me! You will regret this, *Haeslig*," the Raven said, pronouncing the name like it was a curse.

Haeslig circled away, coming ever closer to our hiding spot. I cursed under my breath as I realized who the knife wielding gray was.

"Not so much as you, I'rea," Haeslig said, darting forward as if he were about to make a frontal assault.

I'rea turned his body to present Haeslig with a smaller target, bringing his wounded right arm up as if there weren't a knife sticking from it. Haeslig came in with his left hand flying in a huge haymaker, telegraphing his attack. The big gray put up his forearm and blocked the blow with ease, not realizing until it was too late that it was exactly what Haeslig wanted him to do.

Haeslig pulled his punch as I'rea blocked, his right hand snaking forward to pull his knife free, stepping away just in time to avoid being hammered by a huge fist.

The two shuffled back and forth, twirling around the floor, striking and parrying. Haeslig moved with the grace of a dancer, always just ahead of the crushing blows I'rea tried to land. While I'rea tried to end the fight with a single hit, Haeslig was content slicing and stabbing the Raven with minor, irritating wounds in return.

The big gray grew impatient. Haeslig would dart and faint, but each time I'rea thought he was going to stand his ground and fight, he found himself chasing after his prey instead. I'rea began letting anger and frustration blind him and put all his strength behind every strike. Haeslig waited until I'rea overcommitted and slipped in close behind his opponent's attack. Silver flashed as Haeslig's knife darted for I'rea's throat.

I'rea pulled his head back, the tip of the blade just missing his neck. Haeslig tried to dart away, but I'rea lashed out with a vicious kick. The blow landed squarely on Haeslig's thigh, the impact taking his feet from under him as his upper body fell forward.

Haeslig landed hard on all fours and the big Raven used the moment to his advantage, punching Haeslig rapidly in the face as his smaller opponent tried to climb back to his feet. Haeslig was stunned, slashing about in front of him wildly as he tried to regain his senses. Ignoring the knife in Haeslig's hand, I'rea swatted it away to grab the smaller gray by the throat.

Haeslig tried to stab at I'rea's arm but couldn't find the mark before I'rea slammed him into a steel upright and the blade fell from his hand. I'rea pulled Haeslig close, wrapping a muscular arm around his neck. Haeslig panicked, clawing at the arm around his neck as his legs kicked about, his normally pale face turning dark. I'rea flexed his arm, laughing as he drove two short punches into Haeslig's side from behind. Haeslig's struggles slowed, growing weaker until his hands fell to his sides, his head now a deep shade of purple.

"You will regret not taking my offer. It would have been better for you to come willingly," I'rea said, reaching into a pouch at his belt for a length of braided silver cord. It looked like finely wrought sliver chain woven into a strand as thick around as my pinky finger. I'rea wrapped the cord about Haeslig's neck, a smug look on his face.

When I'rea let Haeslig loose, the smaller figure stood passively, his hands at his side, a blank look on his face. I'rea spit in Haeslig's face, laughing in contempt as he picked up the long end of the cord to loop it around his captive foe's throat again.

I was so enrapt by the show before me that I hadn't even seen Justine move from behind the contractor's box. I saw her stepping up behind the huge gray, her MP5K pointed at the back of his head. I wanted to scream at her; she was losing her mind.

Time blurred, lapsing into slow motion as I watched the side of I'rea's eyes crinkle, his nostrils flaring as though catching a scent. A brief moment of surprise crossed his face, and then he was in motion. Everything in my vision slowed, every detail becoming sharp and bright.

I'rea pushed Haeslig away, turning to face Justine as one of his clawed hands reaching out to swipe the gun away. The huge gray moved smoothly, fluidly, reacting as Justine pulled the trigger of her weapon.

The MP5K fires nine hundred rounds per minute, but I heard each round *pop*, *pop*, *pop* as it flew down the barrel, the shell casings spinning through the air like brass hummingbirds. Justine's mouth formed some curse word in slow motion as I'rea shifted sideways. What was meant to be a ten-round burst into his brain caught him in the cheek, sending pieces of meat and chips of jawbone flying.

Even with half his lower face missing, he didn't slow. He

grabbed the body of the MPK5 and jammed it flat to Justine's chest. His huge hand wrapped around the weapon and the front of her shirt balled up as he lifted her off the ground with ease. Time snapped into fast forward as I watched Justine get punched in the face.

I'rea was laughing as he lowered Justine to the ground, surprised when her legs wobbled but held beneath her. Not understanding how she was still upright, he pulled back his fist to hit her harder. I watched the muscles in his arm ripple, about to pulverize her face. Justine was tough, but everyone has their limit.

The contractor's storage box rolled as I jumped from it, landing on a pallet of cinder blocks. I took one step before leaping at I'rea with my machete, screaming to get his attention. As I leapt, I willed the distance between us to evaporate.

Blood dripped from the gaping wound in I'rea's cheek as he tried to bark something at me, his black tongue flopping about in his mouth as I came at him. I think he was trying to curse at me.

He threw up an arm to shield his head, and I cut him just above the wrist. The impact raced up my arms a moment before the blade kicked back at me, my hands tingling. Beneath his dark shirt, black plate vambraces protected his arms.

I jumped back as a booted foot struck out for my gut, just missing me. I'rea grabbed Justine by the front of her shirt, dragging her along as he followed me. She was conscious, but barely, her feet trying to find the ground as he dragged her.

I backpedaled as I looked at the thing in front of me, the machete in my hands feeling small and inadequate. I'rea followed a few paces before he stopped, watching me. His tongue wiggled in his ruined face, licking at the blood and shattered bone as he lifted Justine off her feet. He felt her weight and smiled at me as best he could as he took a step toward the nearest upright. Like most evil things, it knew what would drive me mad; he wanted to force me to attack.

I twirled my machete in my hand to make sure my arm had recovered from the shock of hitting his armor, closing the distance just enough to keep his focus on me.

With each step forward, I also shifted toward his side, putting Justine's body between the creature and myself for just a split second while he shuffled to keep me in front of him. I timed my strike, took a step, waited for her body to blind his view, and attacked. My blade was already coming down when he realized I was on the offensive.

My first strike hit his thigh, biting into the meat of his quadriceps. He tried to use Justine as a shield, but I was already shifting to his free side as he blinded himself behind her body. When his eyes found me again, my blade was already moving toward his head. He threw up his free arm to shield his face, steel ringing on steel.

The blow was checked—I hadn't put all my force behind it. Even so, the machete came bouncing back. Instead of fighting it, I used the energy to spin it about, turning the weapon around in a flash of steel to cut into the underside of his forearm.

I'rea's bracers consisted of fairly simple sections of curved black metal strapped to his arms, leaving the belly of his forearms completely exposed. My blade cut into his flesh, tasting bone before the edges of the bracer stopped it cold. I pulled the blade clear with a growl.

I'rea looked at me and then at his arm, turning it over to see the wound more clearly. In their swamp of scarred flesh, his eyes darted up to me every second or so as he tried to clench his fist, but the fingers were no longer his to control. I'd struck deep enough to sever the tendons.

Justine's body fell to the floor as he tried to force the fingers closed with his other hand. I'rea seemed in disbelief that I'd been able to strike such a blow. He hesitated as I continued to circle to the right, wanting to put myself against his wounded side and draw him away from Justine. He looked at me and snarled through the hole in his face. I smiled. He was big, but I'd drawn blood. He was no longer leading the dance, and he knew it.

I forced my breathing to slow and backed farther away, letting I'rea follow me step by step. I'd gotten a few blows in, but the fight wasn't over by far. I needed to keep him moving and reacting to me. I'rea looked at me with a bit more respect as he followed, his eyes watching the machete in my hand warily. We were almost to the exterior of the building when he struck, moving with surprising speed for such a bulky creature.

I barely had time to react. Metal twanged off metal as I struck twice in a crisscrossing pattern in front of me, fending off his first attack. Bloody spit sprayed out of I'rea's face as he continued to push forward. I slid behind a girder, trying to slow his charge. He jinked forward on one side of the column and then the other, making me jump from side to side. He was toying with me.

He jinked forward, and I grabbed the edge of the girder, using it to sling myself around to his damaged side. I chopped down into his thigh. Blood sprayed as I yanked the machete free, ducking back around the girder as he bellowed in pain. I don't like to be toyed with.

I'rea stumbled as he tried to put weight on his wounded leg, and I tried to take full advantage. I went for the head shot, but he straightened as I came in, catching my wrist in his good hand. I knew I'd made a mistake the moment I went for his head. He'd let me think he was off balance just to lure me in. I should have kept kiting him around the building.

I might have left one of his hands limp and useless, but that didn't stop him from using the limb like a club. He knocked the machete out of my hand with a vicious chop.

It was a sad return to reality for me. I'd begun to think I might actually carry the day. I was trying to pull myself out of his grip when he hit me again with his ruined hand. I doubled over his limp fist as he drove it into my gut, sending me flying back onto my ass.

Pain mingled with a dull cramping sensation as my abdomen and diaphragm spasmed. The urge to vomit and crap myself rolled over me in waves as I struggled to breathe. I tilted and fell onto my side as my abdomen convulsed.

His laughter sounded like uncooked steaks slapping together. I blinked away tears, straightening out on the concrete and forcing my body to uncurl from the fetal position it so desperately wanted to be in.

When my eyes focused, I saw the hilt of my machete three feet away. I crawled for it, but, still stunned, I moved slowly. I'rea laughed again, the sound closer. I turned my head to see him shuffling forward, half dragging his left leg. A sense of hopelessness swept over me. We'd made a ruin of him, but he kept coming.

My hand slapped down on empty concrete, just inches from my machete. It might as well have been a mile. I'rea was almost on top of me; I wasn't going to be able to reach the blade in time. I rolled onto my side, hoping to see Justine, hoping to see her backside one last time as she ran away.

She was gone, but I was so disoriented I couldn't even be sure I was looking in the right direction. I lay my head on the concrete, exhausted. I had nothing left. It was enough that Justine was gone. I chose to believe she was safe and away in that moment. I lay still, hoping it would be quick.

"Hey, motherfucker!" she called out. When I heard her voice, I wanted to curse. I should have known she wasn't going to be a smart girl and run, but I wasn't as upset as I thought I would have been. "Hey motherfu…" she started to repeat, the end of her statement washed out by the pro-longed roar of the MP5K chewing through a clip in a single burst.

I'rea threw up his arms to shield what was left of his face as she let loose on him. I crawled away as lead ricocheted off his armor and slapped into the concrete around me.

Justine continued to curse as I'rea stood his ground, looking from her to me, still unable to understand how the two of us were putting up such a fight. I'rea's shirt hung in tatters, and fresh blood poured from above and below the breastplate revealed beneath his chest. I got my hand on my machete and crawled away from him toward Justine.

She slid a fresh clip home and cursed as the bolt jammed, screaming in frustration as she struggled to clear the weapon. I'rea took two shambling steps forward, blood running over the front of his breastplate in thick streams.

"Time to run?" Justine asked as she gave up on clearing the charging handle to pull me to my feet.

"Hell yeah," I said, watching as I'rea took another step toward us. He was hurt and moving slowly, but the look in his eyes was nothing short of murder.

I'rea froze in place, his eyes going wide as an arm sud-denly snaked around his side, driving a shining blade between his ribs. I'rea's head twitched and he tried to say something, but the hand holding the blade twisted violently, taking away his breath. A wash of blood poured around the knife as the hand worked it from side to side, widening the wound. I'rea stiffened and stood on his tip toes before falling to the ground with a loud thud.

Haeslig was left standing after the huge gray fell, his blade and arm covered in blood. I leveled the tip of my machete at his throat.

"Mmm!" Justine said in alarm, pointing to the dead Raven with the tip of her MP5K. The flesh under I'rea's skin was writhing and expanding. The smell of ozone crept into the air.

"Run," Haeslig said, darting by us. Justine looked at me, then at the body, and then at the fleeing gray.

"Run!" she and I both said at the same time.

We made it out of the building and almost to the fence before the concussion hit us. The force of the shock wave picked us up and sent us flying. Justine sailed passed me and into Haeslig. They tumbled to the ground in a twisted pile of limbs. I hit the ground and rolled twice, coming up with my machete at the ready as the dust rolled by in a wave of hot air.

Justine kicked herself away from the gray, pointing her jammed weapon at him as he stood, brushing dust from his clothes. Haeslig looked at Justine on one side of him and me on the other as he wiped a blood-covered hand against his pants.

"I should move away so you don't accidently hit your friend," he said to Justine, his voice gritty and alien and yet full of amusement as he took a step to the side so I wasn't behind him.

I circled, keeping the machete between us until I could put out a hand and pull Justine to my side. She slammed the charging handle with her hand then pulled it back, an unspent round flying as she unjammed the weapon.

"Shoot," I urged.

Haeslig shook his head from side to side, putting his hands up in supplication, eying the nearest cover as he did so. "I could have left you back there," he said, pointing behind him with his thumb, "but I returned the favor for saving me. If he'd gotten another loop around my neck, I'd have been his for sure. So let's call it even…shall we?"

Justine started to lower her weapon, and I saw with fear that her eyes were the color of slate. "Fuck!" I cursed. I tried to reach for the gun, but she was still with it enough to elbow my hand out of the way.

"Very interesting," Haeslig said, a finger placed to his lips as he watched. "But…it is time to be moving on. The Ravens will know two of their circles are dead, and they will want to know what happened. It would be best if none of us were here when they arrived."

Justine turned and walked away, leaving me to either stand and face Haeslig blade for blade or follow her. It sucks being pussy whipped. I followed her, the fear of losing her in the city outweighing my desire to try my luck against the gray. It was starting to get annoying how he kept popping up.

I caught up to Justine at our carts and turned her gently toward me. I kissed her before she could stop me, happy to be alive, and happy to see the deep brown of her own eye color returning. She spun away from me with a strange smile on her face, grabbing her cart and practically running the whole way back to New Dover. I followed her, wanting nothing more than to get off the streets.

Chapter 6

Justine wouldn't talk to me on the way back to New Dover, not even once we were within a few blocks of the gate. She'd point to her eyes and then around us like we were being stalked and then push her cart hard to get in front of me again so I couldn't say anything else.

The guards barely even looked at us when they let us in. It was a different story when we went to turn in our supplies and exchange them for tickets. The foreman kept one hand under the table the whole time he was talking to us, keeping a grip on the sawed-off shotgun he didn't think anyone knew about.

Justine smiled at him and told him we'd fallen through a floor and gotten stuck in the basement of a half burnt-out house. He looked at her like he wasn't sure, but she kept smiling and talking while I unloaded the carts. He looked us over one last time when I was done unloading and handed us our tickets, telling us to go.

When we got back to the apartment, I tried to talk to her again. She pulled away, going into our bathroom and locking the door. I stood on the other side, struggling to find the right words. I kept telling her I was OK, repeating myself at least five times.

I thought I was getting through to her, but she proved me wrong a second later by slamming her fist into the wall. "I nearly got you killed again today," she said in a hoarse voice. "Just go away, Daniel. I need to think," she begged me.

I wanted to break down the door and take her in my arms, but I was so afraid she'd bolt. Instead, I wandered into the kitchen and sat down heavily. My pistols came apart easily in my hands as my mind and my body did two separate things. I could think of nothing but Justine.

Every now and then my mind would register what my hands were doing as they disassembled the weapons and cleaned them, but it was a distant thing, like watching someone else do the work. With the pistols cleaned, I slid rounds into their clips, each one bringing me a bit closer to the here and now.

I went to the door and listened, thinking I'd moved quietly until she told me to go away in a pitiful voice. I picked up her MP5K from the end of the bed where she'd thrown it and went back to the kitchen.

The MP5K took a little more time to clean. There was enough sand in the receiver that I wondered if the weapon would have even fired if she had pulled the trigger on Haeslig. I took my time cleaning and reassembling the weapon. When I was done, I worked the action by hand through a full clip of rounds to make sure it was back in working order.

Justine was still locked in the bathroom.

I sharpened my machete, putting a few drops of gun oil on the small whetstone I'd found and starting a series of long strokes, first on one edge of the blade and then the other. The blade had nicks here and there, but I smoothed them over and sharpened the two deeper divots with a small, round file. It was mildly anal, but it took my mind off what was bothering me. Besides, all of the nicks in the blade had been well earned. I believe in taking care of the tools that took care of you.

Justine was still in the bathroom when I finished. "Are you hungry?" I whispered to her.

"Go away," she said again, but at least it sounded as though she had calmed down some.

I peeled off my dirty clothes, went in our bedroom, and shut the door, wedging our security system (the dresser) in place before lying down. Justine would be able to squeeze out of the bathroom door, but just barely.

The longer she stayed locked in the bathroom, the more anxious I became. My heart rate slowly climbed, the thrumming impact of my ventricles filling my ears as I waited to hear the little click that would signal the bathroom door unlocking.

I could feel her pain and anguish like a tangible thing. I knew what she was thinking, and it scared me. She had it in her head that she was doing me more harm than good. She was terrified she was something like them and that she wasn't going to win the next time it gripped her.

I didn't have any doubts. Her eyes turned colors and her

fingernails became razor blades, but none of that mattered. She'd told me the three most important words I'd ever wanted to hear from her. She'd told me, "I love you." I could never be afraid of her.

My eyes had tired of staring at the dark ceiling when I heard the lock click and the bathroom door open. It was pitch black in the room, but she moved without making a sound.

My heart rate redoubled as she climbed into bed, pulling the sheet over her and settling in with minimal movement. I wanted to say something to her, but I couldn't get the first word out.

We both lay there, suffering until exhaustion pulled us under.

The next morning was strained. Justine woke up and made breakfast without a word. She was robotic, setting out our food without looking at me. When we finished eating, she asked me if I was well enough to get a work assignment. I nodded dumbly; it really wasn't what I'd been expecting to discuss.

I tried to begin a conversation with her, but she pretended not to hear me, heading into the bedroom to get dressed. Eventually we were going to have to talk about what had started at the power plant, but the time was never right. She couldn't ignore it forever; I couldn't let her.

She won the day, though. We were in line to get a work assignment before I resolved myself to say anything. I shuffled forward when our turn before the foreman came, equally pissed at Justine and myself.

It didn't help when the foreman said something with a smirk about us giving up on scavenging after just a day, but we both ignored him and he shut up, picking up on the tension between us. He gave us our assignment and moved on to the next in line.

We were tasked with clearing out the first floor of a fire house on the east side of downtown. The soldiers had requested the space be cleaned out so they could turn it into a mechanics' shop and a barracks. Some industrious souls had used cinder blocks and mortar to seal up the large rolling doors and filled the stairway to the second floor with dirt and rubble when the world fell apart.

The foreman had assigned three others to work at the firehouse with us. They took the job of cleaning out the stairwell while Justine and I started breaking down the cinder block wall blocking the garage doors. I think the three men working to clear the stairs were all brothers, or at least cousins, they all had the same sharp features, but they didn't talk to us beyond a few one-word exchanges. We dumped everything into a growing pile on the side of the firehouse.

Sometime after we took a lunch break, WC showed up with a foreman, slipping into our work team without a word. The foreman nodded to us, telling us we were doing a great job before he walked away.

I looked at WC suspiciously, but he just shrugged. I wondered how much it had cost him to bribe his way onto our work team. If I hadn't been in a bad mood, I might have found it amusing.

WC gave me one look and moved away from me, putting Justine between us as we worked. I tried to ignore him as I continued to hammer at the wall while he and Justine picked up the junk and put it in the wheelbarrow. My mood only worsened as the two of them started talking quietly, even laughing now and then. I gave WC a stern look as he put a hand on Justine's shoulder and spoke into her ear. He didn't seem to notice.

I swung my sledge through the next section of cinder blocks with too much force, sending chunks of concrete flying. Justine looked up at me, raising an eyebrow in question. I set the head of the sledge on the pavement between my feet and shrugged at her. WC looked at me and swallowed hard. Maybe he wasn't so oblivious after all.

Justine scowled at me and shook her head, warning me to be a good boy. I gave her a dark smile and pulled off my shirt. Scars covered my chest, neck, and abdomen. I'd been wounded several times in the military, but those scars were pale and old compared to the ones I'd earned more recently. The large bruise I'rea had given me dominated my abdomen.

I let WC stare before I picked up the sledge and went back to work. When he went back to picking up chunks of concrete, he did so a few feet from Justine. I was being childish, but Justine had put me off kilter, and WC wasn't helping himself by giggling and laughing with her when I was already off balance.

"Do you want me to take a turn with the sledge?" WC asked me when I stopped to wipe sweat from my face.

"It's OK. I'm good," I told him. When I threw the T-shirt down, I noticed he wasn't really paying any attention to me anymore. Three kids about his age were walking up the wide driveway to the firehouse.

"So that's where you ran to?" one of them said.

I heard WC say, "Oh, shit," under his breath as he smiled at the new arrivals in resignation.

"Our work team is short now," the shortest of the three newcomers said. He had a thin face with large front teeth and a mop of red hair. I'm sure he'd been teased in school. He looked like a rat.

"You mean you guys would rather come get me than do any work yourselves, right?" WC quipped back.

A pause followed as the three processed what he'd said, clearly not pleased with his reply. They'd expected WC to fold the moment they showed up. They clearly hadn't expected him to show any spine.

The tallest of the three teens scratched at the scraggly beard covering his face as he looked us over. "It looks crowded in there, like you have one too many guys," he said, trying to sound reasonable to us—the other people on WC's work team.

The three other guys we'd spent the morning with put their heads down and kept working. It wasn't any of their business, and they weren't getting involved.

Justine stood there, rubbing her fingertips, a slack look on her face. It might have looked like she didn't care what was going on, but I saw through her. She was wondering whether she'd be able to control herself if she had to get involved.

"What's your name?" I asked, my tone anything but friendly. I dropped the sledge and hopped over what was left of the wall in front of me.

"None of your fucking business," rat face replied.

"Well, you see, the kid was just asking me to pay up on

a promise I made to give him a shooting lesson, and now you guys are here disturbing us."

"Fuck off. This doesn't have anything to do with you," the tall boy said, trying to get control of the situation and assert his dominance. The third boy, the one who hadn't spoken yet, reached into his pocket and pulled out a folding buck knife. He opened it with a click, ready to enforce what his tall friend was saying.

"Well now, three on one," I said, putting a finger to my lower lip as if in thought. "Well, it won't be fair," I told them. The tall one smiled, thinking I was acknowledging defeat, oblivious to the sarcasm in my voice. "Maybe if all three of you had knives? Or maybe just one big one?"

Their eyes followed my hand as I drew my machete. The black scabbard had been lost to their eyes against the dark fabric of my pants. I flipped it in the air to hold it out to them hilt first.

The tall one snatched it away like he was expecting me to sucker punch him.

"There's something wrong with you," rat face said, urging his buddy with the buck knife forward.

"I'm unarmed, you pussies," I told them, holding my hands out, taunting them.

It was enough. The tall kid came in with a wild swing of my machete. The last thread of restraint left me as he started to move. I ducked under his swing easily, driving a punch into a kidney that would have him peeing blood for days.

He was sucking in a surprised breath when my elbow made contact with his face, crushing his nose. I caught his arm as it came down, grabbing his wrist and bending it with a swift jerk that made his hand open whether he wanted it to or not.

I caught my machete as it fell free, sliding the blade home into the scabbard in a smooth motion as the tall kid fell to the ground, crying and clutching his broken face.

Buck knife didn't hesitate or wait to see if his friend was OK. He came in low and quick, driving his arm forward in an attempt to punch a hole in my gut. I hit his wrist hard as he came in while stepping to the side, letting his momentum carry him past me. When he was even with me, I kicked out, making him scream as his knee was pushed to the verge of rupturing.

Anger and pain made him reckless. He came back at me hopping on one leg, slashing wildly. I let his second slash cut through the air just in front of me and hit him square in the jaw. He crumpled to the ground, the knife still clutched in his hand. Rat face looked at his two downed friends and ran.

I let the other two crawl away, leaking tears and blood as they went. They'd live, but they would be hurting bad for a few days. Justine was smirking at me when I came back into the firehouse and got back to work. The other three men loaded up their wheelbarrow as quickly as they could and took it outside to empty. They never came back from dumping their load.

WC looked like he wanted to run too, but he stuck around, picking up the cinder blocks as I knocked them down. "Thank you," he said to me quietly after we'd been working for a few minutes, never taking his eyes off the chunk of concrete in his hands.

"No worries," I told him, taking out the next section of wall with a swing of my sledge.

An hour after the altercation, one of Big John's foremen showed up cradling a shotgun. He came to the edge of the firehouse driveway and waited for me to come to him. He was short and stout but very solid, and tats covered his arms. He looked like he might have been a biker before it all started.

The foreman didn't beat around the bush. "Big John says it was a fair fight, and he's said as much to their families. The other three men on your work team came in and told him what happened." He waited for me to nod before continuing. "But that's about all he can do for you. He's not going to start a war with Building C over you. Watch your back." The foremen had to call it Building C because the crazies got mad if you called it the Fort.

Justine was on edge for the rest of the day, walking with me when I took my turn dumping the wheelbarrow. It was just around the corner, but she followed me anyway, which I thought was kind of sweet. When we were done for the day and walking back to the church, she held her MP5K loosely in her hands. Nearly everyone carried weapons, but she normally let the gun hang from its sling against her chest.

There were several hours of daylight left when we got back to our apartment. Justine told me she was going to go work out and asked me if I wouldn't mind making dinner. I prepped our food, listening to the steel plates of the workout equipment clapping together as she exercised.

She seemed almost herself when she came down to eat. She was chatty and engaged, asking me about my time in the Marines and telling me teasingly that I might want to keep my shirt on in the future. My scars were going to scare people.

She kept me talking as I cleaned up and then gave me a quick hug before telling me she was going to sleep early. She was tired. I let her go, but I didn't buy it for a second. She was still hiding from me—she was just using a different tactic.

I sat at the kitchen counter and played with the electronics she'd given me when I was still on crutches. I'd hooked the solar cell up on the roof a few days before, which gave me a source of power. Combined with a few old car batteries, it was enough to keep one or two light bulbs going and charge up some RC batteries. I tinkered as I thought about how I was going to deal with Justine.

She'd kept me talking after dinner, driving the conversation with questions about my time in the service and generally being mesmerizing. I was too easily distracted when she touched my arm and smiled at something I said, and she knew it.

My hands worked as my mind churned, bits and pieces of metal, gearing, and electronics slowly taking form. I wasn't really working from a grand plan, but I gradually finished one project and started the next. The first was a straightforward RC car I'd worked on when Justine had given me the parts several weeks earlier. Having the juice to run it gave me a reason to finish it.

The second project was in its early stages. I'd started it with a foggy idea to build a remote-controlled car to put a handgun on, but the parts could barely hold the weight of one of my Glocks, much less withstand the kick of one firing.

I gave up on the idea, ending up with a partially articulated arm I could move in the four primary directions. It wasn't pretty, but it kept me from storming into the bedroom and demanding Justine talk to me. I forced myself to wait until I was calm before going to bed.

Justine pretended to be asleep when I came in.

The next two days went much the same way. We worked at the firehouse. When we got home, she would go up to the gym roof and then hide behind a book before going to bed while I played with the RC car and tinkered with my gun mount.

The third day broke the tedium, although it started just about the same. We were almost done at the fire station: the rolling garage doors could be cranked up and down, and the staircase to the second floor was nearly cleaned out. Soldiers were already starting to roll equipment down the street, bringing in toolboxes and carts full of parts.

WC had actually made friends with several of the soldiers, which was good. I didn't like the fact that he was still living in the Fort after the way his mates had turned on him. I hoped he could get in with some of the soldiers and find a new place to sleep at night.

I was inside the firehouse shoveling the last load of dirt from the stairway when one of the soldiers whistled at me, pointing outside with a finger. A mob of ten or eleven men from the Fort were walking up the driveway.

Big John hustled up right behind them, four of his biggest foremen on his heels with shotguns. Justine peeked outside and then disappeared up the firehouse stairs like a rabbit, so quick and quiet she was almost a blur. WC saw what was coming outside and turned to say something to her, shaking his head when she was gone—and her MP5K with her.

"Maybe I should just go with them," he said, turning to me, beads of sweat breaking out on his forehead. I could tell he didn't really mean it. I think he thought that without Justine there, I might just let him do it.

I laughed at him and walked out into the open, watching Big John and wondering if I'd been found guilty of some crime after all. Maybe he was here to tell me I was required to take a trip to the water tower. In a way, I almost hoped that was it. It would put the decision to leave on someone else. I was starting to think we were getting too comfortable, and I didn't really think we were safe behind our walls.

I walked out into the sun, lowering my shades as I did so, to stand in front of them. I didn't have anything to say. I just kept a hand on the hilt of my machete. I left my .40 caliber pistols resting under my armpits. Some of the men from the Fort were carrying baseball bats and billy clubs, but no guns were visible among them—yet.

I stood there patiently, my eyes moving from Big John on one side to the rough-looking fellows from the Fort on the other. I expected to see the red-headed kid with the rat face in their midst, but they must have made the little ones stay at home.

"Well, Billy?" someone grumbled from the mob.

The men from the Fort were getting impatient. Billy stepped out of their midst, a lanky thirty-year-old who didn't look like he'd discovered that you could still bathe even if the water wasn't running. A patchwork beard covered his face.

Billy was clearly the big brother or older cousin of the tall kid from the other day. They both had the same lanky, awkward build and bad facial hair.

"You busted up my little brother," Billy said, jabbing a finger at me in the air.

"It was more than a fair fight," I told him, looking around at the number of men he'd brought with him.

"You pick on three kids and call it a fair fight?"

"Well, two of them had knives," I told him, drawing my machete. One of the foremen raised his shotgun as I did so, holding it low with the butt against his thigh but clearly in my direction.

"It was a fair fight," Big John said, looking at me and motioning for his foreman to put the gun down. I let the machete fall to my side. "These men have a grievance with you, Daniel, and I'm here to make sure that this doesn't get out of hand."

"You going to shoot us if we make him pay?" Billy asked, his mob full of energy at his back.

"Billy, there is some level of…social interaction…that will

happen," Big John said. "It's the way we're built. But there won't be any guns, or anything else," he said, eyeing my machete, "and this ends it. I won't tolerate anything more about this after today. Besides, let's not give his little lady any reason to use that fancy gun of hers on us."

Billy looked at Big John, not sure what he meant. One of his people whispered something in his ear, and he began looking around us, realizing Justine was nowhere to be seen.

"So you're just going to let this go down any way it falls?" I asked, turning around to take my shoulder holsters and machete off and hand them to WC.

"I heard you took down three men, two of them armed, in about twenty seconds. You didn't come in with the soldiers, and I'm not really sure who you are. That bothers me," Big John said before pausing. "I guess I want to see with my own eyes."

I gave Big John a hard stare. I didn't like being his entertainment, whatever he said his reasons were. Billy was looking around, saying something to his people before turning to me.

"Is that slut of yours going to shoot me from in there?" he yelled, pointing up to the second floor of the firehouse.

"You really shouldn't have said that," I told him. "So what makes this a fair fight? All of you versus me?" I asked, walking toward them.

Warmth flooded through me as the adrenaline hit my system. This was going to be ugly, regardless of what Big John thought. I was going to have to hit hard and take out as many as I could as fast as possible—and take a few hits myself. There's no way to fight a mob without getting pounded.

I'd never try to take on so many if they had the least bit of experience, but they were untrained louts who had probably worked at menial jobs until the world had shifted on its axis a few weeks earlier. Now they were displaying the typical pack mentality, thinking they would overwhelm the few with the many. I was sure they'd never picked a fight with a Marine Scout before, and equally confident that they never would again.

Billy was trash talking as I stepped up to him, expecting

me to just sit there and let him decide when they were going to attack. He started to say something else, but I shut him up with a quick shot to the neck with my open hand, clamping down hard. I felt his scream vibrating against my fingers as I grabbed him by his groin with my other hand and lifted him into the air.

It wasn't something I would have done if I hadn't been seeing red, but it got the job done as I threw him into the men on our right. He was tall but light. I got good air on him before he tumbled into his fellows.

They'd expected me to wait for them to start the fight and were still frozen in shock when I tore into the group on my left, moving as fast as I could. If I let them grapple, I'd be meat, no matter how untrained they were. I used short, powerful punches aimed at guts or heads—someplace that would take them out of the fight long enough for me to control the rest of them.

Men lay scattered on the ground, stunned at the speed and ferocity of my attack. They'd expected me to shy away from the fight, probably even thought they'd have to run me down. I had half of them on the ground before Billy was back on his feet, rallying the men around him as their morale wavered.

Billy was a fool, but he understood that I was going to beat him if he didn't do something. Five men were still standing, including him, and two of them were starting to back away, not wanting to push it any further. He snarled at them, calling them names and yelling that their bunks were going to be burned if they ran.

Then he got really smart: he told them to spread out. I backed up a little, catching my breath, and kneed one of their wounded friends in the face as he tried to get up. Billy was coaching them, telling them to close in on me from all sides. As much of an idiot as he was, he was catching on quick enough.

None of them stood a chance against me individually, but put enough flying fists and boots on me and it wasn't going to matter how much skill or experience I had.

I didn't let them fight on their terms. I darted to the right, taking on the leading flank so the men farthest from me had to take a few steps to get in the fight. The lead man on the right made up for his lack of size with toughness, standing through a shot to his face that should have dropped him.

I was trying to move past him before I realized he was still standing—too late. He wrapped an arm around me, delaying me just long enough for his buddies to get to me as I knocked him loose with an elbow to the face.

They pounded on me from two directions at once. One fist hit me on the side of the head, snapping my neck sideways as another blow connected painfully with my ribs. I lashed out blindly, making contact with somebody's flesh as I put my head down and tried to punch my way free.

They didn't give me a chance; more bodies were already piling on. Someone clung to my back, his fingers trying to get into my eyes. I twisted hard, trying to throw the bastard off. I wasn't able to shake him. I was, however, able to shift him far enough to my side to get an elbow into his groin. His fingers eased away from my eyes as he slid off my back.

It was a small victory. I still stood in the middle of a tangle of arms and legs, all trying to kick and punch me. I lashed out, keeping my arms close and using rabbit punches to strike out at anything in front of me as I stomped down on the tops of their feet. It wasn't my best work ever, but it got the job done.

The pile tipped over a moment later when someone dove into us, forcing me almost flat. I fought to my hands and knees, grabbing whatever flesh I could and pulling it down with me so I could drive an elbow or a fist into it before grabbing the next bit of squirming meat. The press of bodies around me lessened gradually, grown men crying as I laid into them.

Billy was the last one I got my hands on. I must have hit him a few times in the pile because blood ran from his nose down through his beard, staining his shirt.

"Motherfucker!" he sputtered.

"That was my line," I growled back, grabbing him and surging to my feet.

I cocked my arm, my fist covered in cuts and wet with blood. Some of it was mine; most of it belonged to the men littered around me. Billy shut his eyes, expecting the end.

Big John saved him. "I think you've proved your point," he said. Two of his foremen lifted their shotguns to make sure I was listening. I kept my arm cocked, looking at Billy. I wanted him to know how close he'd come to having the delicate bones around his nose and eye sockets fractured.

Shotguns crept higher as I held steady, not backing down.

"Be real careful with those shotguns!" Justine yelled from above us. She stood up slowly from her hiding place on the roof across the street. It took the foremen a moment to locate her, but once they did, they realized their danger. She was sighted in on them, her finger resting on the trigger.

"Like I said earlier, let's not give the lady any reason to use that fancy gun of hers," Big John said. "This is over. They won't be back or they won't be buying any food inside New Dover," Big John said. Billy nodded eagerly in agreement, desperate for me to release him.

I let go of Billy, stepping over bodies as I walked back up to the firehouse house to grab my gear. As I passed Big John, I spit a mouthful of bloody saliva onto the ground at his feet. He could have stopped it all before it began, but he got what he wanted. I was now on his list of people to be extremely cautious of, with Justine right next to me.

Chapter 7

I ached all over, but Justine was in a better mood than she had been in days. She led me to the gym roof and helped me pull my shirt off and then unbuckled my belt. I swallowed as her fingers brushed across my skin.

A strange mix of fear and excitement filled me. We'd gotten dressed in front of each other before and seen each other as we bathed, but this was different. She took her time as she scrubbed me down, a coy smile on her lips. The sensation of her fingertips as they brushed against my skin around the sponge drove me crazy. When she'd finished scrubbing me, she spun me slowly under the water nozzle, rinsing away the soap.

"You were very brave today," she said into my ear as she stood behind me.

I grunted, not really able to process her words around the other thoughts racing through my head.

"You're a good man," she said, wrapping a towel around my shoulders.

"I love you," I said, turning my head, wanting desperately to kiss her.

"I love you too," she said, nuzzling my back with her face. I wanted the moment to last forever.

The feeling of the towel wrapped around me was almost painful. Every nerve in my body was on fire. She led me down into the apartment by the towel, pushing me onto the bed. She disappeared into our bathroom and told me she'd be back in a minute.

I fell into a daze as I listened to her moving about, my skin tingling as it dried. She came out wearing one of my shirts, its hem hanging down to her thighs. She climbed into bed next to me, pulling a light sheet over us as our legs slid over each other.

"I'm sorry I've been so distant the last few days," she said, her voice a mixture of sadness and regret.

"You can't push me away," I said, kissing her face urgently until I found her lips. She met me with equal need, and I found myself pinned beneath her as she straddled my hips, our intimates straining to touch through the stretched cotton of her panties.

She moved against me in a slow grind as I fought the mixture of bliss and desire, trying to hold back. Justine seemed to sense my internal struggle and laughed into my ear as she moved a little quicker against me. I couldn't control myself. My breath hitched in my throat as I came, my semen spurting into the cotton of her panties, creating a warm wet spot between us. Justine arched her back, her hands on my shoulders as her legs squeezed tight against me.

I could feel her abdomen convulsing in little waves as she climaxed, her fingers digging into my shoulders as she moaned in pleasure. I'd never felt so close to anyone in my life. My heart thudded in my ears.

"I love you," I whispered hoarsely to her in the dark.

She started to say something, but it turned into a moan followed by a slightly louder cry, making me feel like a king.

I was *the man*.

Then I felt her fingertips bite into my shoulders as they elongated, piercing my skin like little razors. I whimpered, trying to press myself down into the mattress and away from her spiked fingertips. Her head snapped down, her eyes cloudy as she stared at me, fighting to stay in control.

Her little cry turned into a scream as she forced her fingers to unclench from my shoulders and looked at the blood staining the pale white skin of her fingers, trembling in self-hatred. She flew backwards off the bed and into the closet doors, breaking them with a splintering crunch.

I sat up and saw her standing there, her eyes pure slate and her fingertips ending in inch long black claws. She stared back at me for a moment and then disappeared, out the door and gone before I could get out of bed, tears streaming down her face as she darted through the spare bedroom and over the railing of the balcony.

I raced after her, begging her to stay, telling to her that it was OK—but she was gone. The sky had just begun to darken, but some people were still out on the streets. A few of them called up as I stood on the causeway between our apartment and the gym, asking if I needed help.

I mumbled something about my girlfriend and a fight and went back inside, slamming the sliding glass door to the balcony behind me with enough force to crack the glass. I ran into our room and hastily pulled on a set of fatigues as my head spun.

My life experience with women had been fairly limited. I'd had a single juvenile relationship as a teen, which had left a hole in my chest. It wasn't until I was an adult and in the service that a chance meeting threw me into my next relationship. In the end, it hadn't turned out much better. When she'd asked me to choose between her and the service, the only other place I'd ever felt accepted, things had fallen apart. The pain I'd felt then had been like a slow settling of concrete in my chest, weighing me down until all I could do was sleep and struggle for breath.

That horrible feeling rushed through me again, telling me to lie down and let myself be crushed under the sadness. Justine was gone, and the room spun around me. A crushing sense of failure forced me to my knees.

I stood on the brink, balancing on the edge, about to fall into the abyss, when I saw her face again as she ran. She had been crying. She didn't want to go. She thought she was protecting me.

The thought galvanized me. I had made a promise to her, told her she couldn't push me away. I wasn't going to break that promise. I had to find her. I strapped my gear on and picked up her MP5K, loading my cargo pockets with her spare clips.

She was out there, no doubt already past the outer wall, somewhere in the dead city, running. I had to catch up to her, but the lights were already on in New Dover. They wouldn't let me out through the gates once the lights were on. I'd have to make my own way out.

I slipped quietly along the streets, sticking to the darkness where I could, staying away from the few people who remained outside. I made my way to the outer ring of buildings, moving quietly and carefully as I watched men patrol along the roofs above me. I could see their lights moving, but they were concentrating on what was on the other side of the wall, at least as long as I kept quiet.

I used a Dumpster to climb up and reach the first-floor fire escape of one of the buildings, pulling myself up and hugging it as I listened. No one had heard me. I moved quickly, darting up to the roof while the foot patrol was at the other end of the building. As they turned to come back, I raced across the roof to a nest of air conditioners and ventilation equipment, squeezing into the shadows.

Two men with flashlights walked within three feet of me, but their eyes followed their lights as they searched the ground outside our border. I lay down and slid under a large section of duct work to a small opening left in the center of the hardware. The dark blue gym bag sat just where I'd left it weeks ago.

The bag contained fifty feet of coiled line and my home-made Swiss seat. I pulled it on, being careful to keep my nuts out from under the ropes wrapping around my legs. I locked the end of the line to the foot of the largest air handler and tested it with several long pulls.

The patrol passed by again, totally oblivious. When they reached the far end of the building, I rolled out from beneath the ventilation equipment, tossing the bag over the edge and following it a moment later.

For just a moment, the pain of losing Justine disappeared as my belly filled with the sensation of free fall. I tightened my right hand around the rope as my body straightened out, my right foot hitting the side of the building. I let my legs absorb the impact and took a giant stride, letting out rope and then clamping down just in time to slow myself as the ground came rushing up at me.

The moment I hit the ground, I grabbed the line and pulled it tight against the building, waiting for the guards to pass over it. I did my best to tuck it along a storm gutter running down the side of the building and took off into the night.

A section of rope still stretched from the tie-down to the edge of the roof, but unless they tripped over it, I doubted the patrol on the roof would find it until sunup. If I wasn't back with Justine by then, I doubted I'd need it anyway.

My heart beat steadily in my ears as I hit the corner of the next street, sweeping the path ahead with the MP5K. I needed to decide which way to go, and my internal compass was telling me to move north. Every time Justine started to change, she would look north. I had to follow some method, even if I was grasping at straws, so I headed north at a jog, listening for a change in the quiet as I ran.

Three blocks away, I found the first sign I was heading in the right direction. Pieces of several thralls lay spread across the street, their limbs ripped from their bodies in front of a consignment shop, along with half a rack of clothing spread out across the street. I hoped that meant she was not running around in just panties and my T-shirt. It made me feel oddly better to think she'd maintained enough awareness to want to put some clothes on. I was probably grasping at more straws.

I continued north, ignoring the sounds around me as thralls or worse moved inside the surrounding buildings. I stayed low, running in a crouch in the deepest shadows I could find, never sure if I was the predator or prey. I actually heard a gray talking as I ran by a storefront, asking, "Did you see that?"

It didn't matter. I kept moving, darting down the next alley and climbing over a low fence to continue north along a narrow street between two rows of townhouses. On either side of me were endless rows of empty carports and postage-stamp-sized backyards. Something yelled in protest behind me, and a general cry went up from multiple mouths as other harsh voices picked up the call and answered back.

My instincts told me to dart into one of the buildings and make a stand, but I fought them, forcing myself to keep moving. There wasn't any artillery to call in here, no predator flying at five thousand feet ready to pepper the ground with bomblets once I put my back to the wall. If I stood and fought, I'd eventually run out of bullets and strength to swing my machete.

Dark forms moved on the rooftops ahead of me, separating from the shadows as they leapt down to the ground. I was in trouble. I darted behind an old Suburban squeezed into a carport as more shapes moved over the rooftops ahead of me. The sounds of pursuit grew louder behind me, and I began to smell the rotting meat of thralls blowing on the wind.

Shambling undead appeared at the end of the alley I'd just traversed, and more were forcing their way through the interiors of the surrounding homes, breaking through doors and pushing through windows, tearing through walls bit by bit with the weight of numbers.

Grays ahead of me, thralls behind, and poor me stuck in the middle. What I needed were a few grenades and an M249 Squad Automatic Weapon—the light machine gun affectionately known as the SAW. In the narrow confines of the alley, the weapon would chew the undead to pieces. I thought of Justine as I prepared myself for the battle, hoping that maybe I was drawing some of the heat off of her and she would be able to slip away and regain herself. I'm an eternal optimist.

I moved to the front of the carport to put my back to the house. A cinder block wall separated me from the carport next door, and the big Suburban would limit their ability to swarm me. They'd eventually wear me down, but I was going to make them pay as dearly as I could for my life.

Thralls were closing from one end of the street, more of them crashing through the surrounding houses every moment as a row of grays came from the other end, sandwiching me in the middle. I was in big trouble. The thralls and grays met in the middle of the street, ready to descend on me.

I waited for them, my machete in one hand and a Glock in the other. I'd save bullets for the grays and for when I needed to rest my arm. I held my breath, waiting for the first wave of undead to make their way around the Suburban.

Then something strange happened. The thralls and the grays met in the road, and neither side stopped. Limbs went flying and bodies were tossed about as the grays tore into the horde of thralls like they were made of wet tissue. The ground around the knot of grays rapidly turned into a wasteland of broken bodies.

An arm ricocheted off the top of the Suburban and slid down the windshield to land at my feet. The hand twitched, tearing my focus away from the fight in the street. I sighed in relief. Whatever was going down had nothing to do with me.

I crept slowly to the door into the house and found it

locked. Wedging the tip of my machete into the wood just above the strike plate, I used my weight to drive it down, taking a chunk of the pine away. I repeated the process, struggling to cut enough wood away to free the bolt. The fighting on the street began to spill around the end of the Suburban. I didn't have much time before I would be noticed.

After the third cut, I was able to pull the door free, the bolt taking the strike plate out of the doorframe as I muscled it open. I slipped inside, pulling the door shut behind me. I stood there in the dark, my hand holding the door closed as I waited for my eyes to adjust.

The sounds of the chaos just outside grew, but I stood still and quiet. Outside in the open air, my night vision had been able to compensate for the darkness. Inside, it was pitch back, leaving me struggling to see.

I waited just long enough to realize my night vision wasn't going to get any better and took a tentative step forward. I moved in short, shuffling steps and held the machete out in front of me, moving it back and forth like a blind man's cane. I held a Glock in my free hand, keeping it tight to my body, afraid something might barrel into me at any moment.

The end of my machete pressed into something soft and before I could think, I was hacking away violently. Chunks of foam and upholstery flew before I realized I was being attacked by a couch. I took a deep breath to calm my nerves, and that's when I smelled it. The basement smelled musty and rotten—it was more than a spoiling fridge. I moved around the couch cautiously, hoping whatever I was smelling had suffered the final death.

As I circled the slain couch, I saw a faint circle of lighter darkness above me. I hit the first stair leading up and tripped, nailing my knees on the treads before I caught myself. The row of townhomes were all split-levels. I'd come in from the rear, essentially entering from the downstairs. I padded up the stairs, following the dim circle of light like a lost insect.

I slipped into the kitchen in a crouch, staying low as the faint circle of light in front of me broke through the blackness. The front door had a glass panel set at about head height, letting in the moonlight from outside. I crept toward the light.

The front door was closed but not locked. I turned the

handle slowly and pulled it open just enough to look outside, freezing as a stream of bodies ran down the street moving fast and quiet with an unnatural grace.

My gut tightened as they veered my way, but they weren't interested in me. I heard them crashing through the house next door, using it as a shortcut to get into the alley behind.

I put my head against the door for a second, relieved and sick to my stomach at the same time. If I'd chosen one house further down the street, I'd have been stampeded by a stream of grays.

The sound of the battle behind me got me moving again. I looked up and down the street and darted to the sidewalk, pausing for just a second before crossing. I ran hard, ducking behind the meager cover the cars lining the curb provided until I reached the next intersection.

If anything saw me, it either didn't recognize me for what I was or simply didn't care. The fight behind me escalated, spilling onto the street I'd just crossed.

I kept moving and didn't slow until the sounds of fighting grew faint and distant. When they did, I slowed to a walk, my legs burning from exertion as I moved cautiously down the street, staying out of the open whenever I could.

My sense of time was corrupted. I kept moving north, but I began to question how far I'd travelled. I was chasing a feeling, and as the minutes ticked by, I started to question my logic. I was arguing with myself, the fear of going further off track growing with each step. Should I stay on my current course? Should I head back to the fighting, figuring Justine would be heading in the general direction of trouble and not away from it?

I was almost relieved to trip over a leg sticking out from under a car. I stopped and kicked it, unsure whether the rest of the body might be under the car. It wasn't; the leg spun around and fell off the curb. I looked over the car's hood into the road and saw the rest of the thrall I'd just tripped over, along with several more.

Relief flooded through me. I was still on the right track. Several thralls had been torn apart in the middle of the street, and one had been thrown into the building across from me so hard its body was compressed against it like a rotten tomato.

My fear and anxiety were gone, my doubt wiped away. I was catching up to her. This was a fresh kill; the blood still dripped off the wall. I picked up my pace, my skin tingling. I could almost feel her as I ran. I came to the next intersection, not hesitating as I turned right. She was close.

The sharp cry that cut through the night wasn't human, but I knew it was hers. My heart rate spiked. I would know her voice anywhere. I moved faster, charging to the end of the street where the houses ended.

I stopped at the end of the block, looking across the road at a large public park. Cars packed the street in front of me for as far as I could see in both directions.

Movement caught my eye on the baseball diamond in the center of the park, but I was too far away to see more than shapes. I ran to the cars, the MP5K clutched in my hands as I moved between the vehicles as best I could, not caring if I stirred up sleeping thralls. Justine was almost in sight.

Another scream, half rage and half pain, came from the ball field. I used a bumper as a footstep, leaping up onto the hood of a car so I could run across their roofs. Nothing mattered except getting to Justine.

Something big popped in the air, like at the construction site, followed by a deep, long howl. I was almost across the street, but the ground sloped up to the park proper, making it hard for me to see what was going on. I jumped off the hood of the last car, landing with a grunt before running up the small slope and going belly down as I looked down my sights.

I'd found her. Justine was crouching inside the baseball diamond at home base, my T-shirt hanging off her thin frame and a pair of nursing scrubs cinched about her waist. Four grays circled her, edging forward and back as she growled and hissed, keeping her center of gravity low.

One of them ventured too close as I watched, allowing Justine to get a hold of his arm. She spun him about like a shot put, throwing him into another gray. They both went spinning across the dirt in a ball of arms and legs. They would be getting back up, but it left her with only two opponents in front of her.

She used it to her advantage, pushing off the ground like a cat and leaping eight feet in the air to land on the closest upright gray. She landed square on his shoulders with a crunching of bones, carrying him face forward into the dirt as his arms flopped around spastically, unable to reach her as she perched on his back.

The gray squealed like a stuck pig as she raked his back with her claws, exposing the white of his spine to the moonlight. I was already standing, digging into the hillside with my toes to propel me forward. The other gray was closing on Justine's back, and she was lost in the kill, tearing apart her downed prey.

I ran at half speed, unable to run full tilt and still aim effectively. I clutched the MP5K in both hands, its metal sights following the gray as he made his own leap at Justine. I let go with two bursts, catching him in the chest and the shoulder. He spun in the air, flying over Justine's head to roll into the batters cage, rattling the fencing.

Justine stood up, crushing the gray's skull into the dirt with the heel of her foot. She growled low and deep as she looked around, trying to figure out what just flew over her head. She flung out her arms, a fierce cry coming from her lips—a challenge to the night. The two grays she'd sent tumbling answered the call.

I continued to close the distance, rushing through the knee-high grass and crossing into the infield. The gray I'd shot was getting back up, coughing and sputtering in rage as he wiped blood from his chin. His eyes locked on me and he charged, almost tripping over his own feet as he ran. I'd wounded him, but he wasn't backing down.

I burnt the rest of my clip into his chest, screaming as we closed on each other across the infield. I tagged the clip release and drove another home in one clean motion as we closed to within a dozen paces. Bone and organs showed through the gray's chest, but he was still standing. I skidded to a halt, aiming a burst at each of his legs as he closed to within spitting distance.

The gray stumbled but continued to take awkward steps

forward, swinging his arms wildly for balance, desperate to reach me. I worked my way up his body with well placed bursts, but he refused to go down. I knew I was hitting him. I saw the rounds punching out chunks of meat as they went through him, but he refused to die. We met face to face, each of us bringing a hand up to strike.

I got the searing barrel of the gun against his head and fired my last three rounds. His clawed hand was coming around, but my rounds were already shattering his skull. His hand hit my shoulder weakly as he died and he fell backwards, hitting the orange dirt with a thud.

Justine spun around to face me. It was almost our undoing.

Her eyes were pure slate, her long incisors exposed in a growl of fury as she looked at me, shaking her head in anger and confusion. She was almost completely lost, but I saw her struggling to remember. She looked down at her hands, which were covered in blood to her elbows, and then back at me. The blazing anger behind her eyes shifted, her gaze no longer able to hold mine as they locked on the ground at my feet.

"Justine," I said desperately, the word, full of need, bringing her eyes tentatively back to mine.

One moment she was bristling with strength and vitality, and the next her shoulders were slumping forward, the slate in her eyes fading until I could see the whites of her eyes reflecting in the moonlight. Her petite form that had looked so huge as she fought shrank in on itself as her shoulders slumped. I ran to her, sliding another clip home, spraying bursts at the two grays charging us.

Then I did the only thing I could. I grabbed her and kissed her. "I love you; now please help me kick some ass," I begged her. The two grays were almost on top of us.

She smiled at me, a look of curious amazement lighting up her face. She was as pleased and surprised that I'd found her as I was. Her eyes shifted back to slate as I stared into them, the look on her face changing as her elongating incisors altered her facial features.

Time slowed as she touched the side of my face gently with the back of a bloody hand, being careful so her claws wouldn't cut me. She left a smear of sticky darkness on my skin as she caressed me, then turned and stepped away.

Her transition from gentle lover to deadly fighter was stark and sudden. The moment she stepped away, she cartwheeled onto her hands, propelling herself at the lead gray feet first. She hit him like a horseshoe, wrapping her legs around his neck before he knew what struck him. The moment she locked her ankles behind his head, she threw her body weight sideways, taking the gray off his feet.

They hit the ground with a wet snap as Justine's weight broke his neck, his legs twitching wildly in the dirt as she rolled away and came back to her feet. The last gray slowed, a horrible sound coming from his lips. It was a strange sound, pleasure and pain mixing all in one. The gray's skin rippled and bulged, his flesh pulsing as muscles writhed, growing. I looked at the dead gray in front of me. The eyes in his head were not his own.

They were Ravens. Haeslig had said something about circles at the construction site, but it hadn't really dawned on me with everything going on, not until I was standing there on the baseball field. The Ravens were linked.

"You're something special," the Raven intoned to Justine, the words all the creepier for being mixed with whatever pain and pleasure was rushing through him.

I didn't bother to say, "Fuck you," I just lifted the MP5K and pulled the trigger.

The Raven dodged to the left, most of my rounds flying to the right of his head as he moved. I tried to shift my aim, but he was quick, putting Justine between me and him before I could lock on. If any of my rounds hit him, he shrugged them off without reaction as he charged Justine.

She stood her ground, dropping sideways at the last moment and supporting her upper body with a hand on the ground as she kicked out, taking the Raven hard in the gut. His clawed hand passed through the air where her head had been a moment before as her kick struck home.

If the gray felt the blow, he didn't show it. He clamped down on Justine's leg with both hands and hurled her away, sending her sailing over my head and into the chain-link fence behind home base with a look of surprise on her face.

The fence caught her and bowed inward, wire ties flying like bits of shrapnel as her body tore the chain link free.

Justine screamed as the fence bit into her back, and the air filled with a metallic rattling and her cry. The fence stretched inward until her momentum was gone. She hung in the air, held by the depression she'd made in the fence until gravity got hold of her. She rolled over once and then fell to the dirt, shaking her head as she climbed to all fours.

The gray closed on me as I watched Justine fall to the ground. When I looked up, he was almost on top of me. He dove the last few feet, rolling head over heels once before coming to his feet in front of me, driving his hands into my chest. One moment I was standing, the machine pistol stuttering in my hands as I fired, and the next, I was flying through the air.

I landed on my ass and tumbled across the ground, my chest on fire. I came to a stop with a mouthful of dirt, my head still spinning, and grabbed my chest with both hands, making sure my sternum was still where it was supposed to be.

Tears blinded me as I sat up, trying to wipe the dirt away with one hand as I fumbled with the MP5K in the other. Before I could clear my eyes, the gray was on me, shoving my back to the ground. I tried to get my arms up to hold him off, but my strength was useless against him. A drop of saliva fell from his jaws, touching my cheek like liquid nitrogen, burning me with intense cold as he forced my head to the side.

I tried to turn to scream into his face, but his iron hand held my cheek to the dirt so he could get a solid bite into my carotid. His teeth had just touched my skin when Justine's bare foot blurred by, catching the gray on the chin and sending him flying off me with a grunt.

Justine yanked me off the ground and pulled me behind her protectively. The gray was already on his feet. He tried to say something, but his voice was unintelligible. It didn't sound like any language I'd ever heard.

Justine stood her ground, taking a defensive posture as she waited for the gray to move. The Raven kept his eye on her, but he was sniffing at the air and listening, distracted by something. Justine picked up on it too, the sound coming to her a moment before I could make out the tell-tale sounds of fighting drifting on the night air.

Something screamed in the distance, and the big gray called back. He looked at us and then in the direction the call had come from, weighing his desire to finish what he'd started against whatever duty called him.

He turned and loped off just as I got a new clip seated in the MP5K, but Justine pushed the tip of the weapon down with a clawed finger, shaking her head. The larger fight was spilling toward us, the noise and odor of thralls on the wind.

Justine turned to me, her eyes blazing silver in the darkness, and looked me over from head to toe, her nostrils flaring as she sniffed the air. She opened her mouth to speak but only seemed able to mouth a few words. One of them might have been my name; it was hard to tell.

"We have to get around the fighting and move south to New Dover," I told her, pointing in that direction. She looked to the north and back at me, frustration playing across her face as she struggled to express herself. "I know it's pulling at you, but I need you more," I said, inching closer, invading her personal space. She watched me with concern, tensing as her eyes darted to the north.

"I need you more," I repeated, pointing south.

She looked at me, struggling against whatever was trying to claim her and finally pointed south. I sighed in relief and then she was on top of me before I could get my hands up, knocking me to the ground. I tried to push her off, but her arms, a third the size of mine, were immovable bands of steel.

"Justine," I said, straining to push her away before giving up. I didn't know what she was doing, but having her squirm all over me wasn't horrible—until she rolled me over in the dirt, rubbing herself all over my back as I ate some more clay. Satisfied, she pulled me to my feet and sniffed at me, giving me a nod of approval.

I picked up my shirt to smell it. It smelled like sweat and dirt to me. I gave her a weak smile and a thumbs-up. I think she tried to smile back, but her elongated teeth marred it. She pushed my shoulder with the knuckles of one hand and motioned with her head toward the west. I gestured in front of us, telling her to lead the way. We'd have to get around the fighting before we could turn south.

Justine moved like a ghost.

Broken glass and other debris littered the ground, and I couldn't see where I was walking half the time because the grass and weeds had sprouted up to take over every crack and joint. Justine moved through it all without a sound—or any concern for her bare feet.

It wouldn't have been so bad following her, but she was pushing so hard I was panting for breath inside of thirty minutes. She would slow down as we came to corners, and I'd think we were going to take a break, but she'd just sniff the air and move off again before I could catch my breath. It wasn't until she was a hundred feet in front of me and disappearing around the next corner that she realized she was pulling too far ahead.

She waited for me, looking around uncomfortably, her eyes skimming the dark buildings around us impatiently. She slowed down a little, taking a position next to me and letting me pace her until she'd urge me to go faster by getting a step ahead. That step always became two and then three. I'd try to stay with her, but my legs just didn't have the stamina.

I don't know how many times we repeated the cycle. She'd slow down for a little while and then pick up the pace until I faltered. My Marine drill sergeant would've been proud of the way she ignored my physical pain, pushing me to burn through it.

It wasn't long before we began turning at every corner. Justine was becoming agitated, pushing me to go faster and constantly looking around us, but she wasn't letting me lag behind her anymore.

We were halfway down a residential street when she stopped, grabbing my shoulder and dragging me up the stairs of the nearest house. She put a hand over my mouth, her long, clawed fingertips resting gently against my cheek.

I breathed around her fingers, gagging as something coppery and acidic burned my lips. Before I could hurl, she let me go to grab the front door and pulled it open with a brittle crackling sound. The doorjamb creaked and popped as the deadbolt tore free and then she was yanking me through the open door.

She left me with my back against the door to hold it closed and went to the window to peek outside. I started to move to her, but as the floor creaked, she shot me a look that froze me in place. I settled for crouching and looking through the mail slot.

A knot of thralls were coming down the street. Two massive brutes walked in the center of their group, their waists equal to the top of the thralls' heads. I let my eyes close to slits as they passed by the front door, as though this would help hide me. Even with my eyes half closed, I noticed the gray.

The brutes stood on either side like an honor guard, dwarfing him between them. The thralls formed the outer ring, standing four and five deep around the gray, completing his guard. It made me wonder who he was, why he was being so well guarded.

What I couldn't see were his eyes. Was he one of the new players to the game? Or was he one of the grays we'd already encountered? So far we hadn't seen any of the cut-eyed Ravens with thralls or brutes, making me think he was the "classic" variety of gray, but I was guessing.

Justine stayed at the window long after they passed, moving her head slightly from one side to the other to see up and down the street. After being pushed so hard, it felt good to have a few minutes of rest.

The night continued to slip by, Justine frozen in place but for the small motions of her head. What had been a pleasant break turned into boredom after my legs recovered and I had nothing to do but peek out the mail slot at nothing. Waiting was beginning to grind on my nerves.

We weren't safe. My instincts were telling me to keep moving, but Justine was the one calling the shots. She was standing so still I started to worry she was frozen in place. When I started to move toward her, a clawed finger shot out, commanding me to stay put. My fifth grade teacher couldn't have done a better job.

I sank back on my haunches and peeked out the mail

slot again. Outside shadows danced across the street as clouds passed in front of the moon. It took me a moment to realize they weren't shadows. Seven or eight grays were moving from cover to cover down the street, following the larger party.

It was the largest group of grays I'd ever seen together. They moved in a loose but evenly spaced formation, and something seemed very predatory about the way they ran. If they were coming after me, I might surround myself with two brutes and a shitload of thralls too.

I put my head in the corner and rested my eyes, no longer so eager to head back out onto the street. Maybe it wouldn't be so bad to wait until daybreak.

I yelped when Justine's hand gripped my shoulder, waking me. I'd drifted off. Her nails were biting into my skin even though she was being careful. She tried to say something to me, mouthing words I couldn't understand. It didn't really matter; I knew what she wanted. It was time to follow her again.

We retreated down the road the way we'd come and turned west at the next street. Justine's pace had slowed; she seemed more cautious, watching and sniffing at the air more frequently as we tried to work our way south toward New Dover.

We were moving at a walk when she stumbled on a lip of raised concrete, a throaty growl escaping from her as she hopped on one foot. It would have looked comical if it wasn't scaring the crap out of me.

I wasn't an idiot. She was the one who was going to keep us alive if we ran into anything nasty. I'd been so afraid of seeing her like this, turned into something else, not even able to talk to me, but now, I was hoping she would stay changed for just a little longer.

She put her foot down, exhaling in pained frustration. Our pace was slower when she led the way off again, her footsteps more measured and careful. Two blocks later, she stumbled and caught herself on a telephone pole. She rubbed her temples, a grimace of pain on her face. She tried to take a step but swayed drunkenly. I took one of her arms and slipped it around my neck to steady her.

At the next street, I stopped on the railroad tracks cutting across the pavement, waiting for Justine to tell me to go one way or the other. She shrugged her shoulders, looking around like she wasn't sure where she was. More white was showing around her eyes by the moment.

I knew roughly where we were but had no idea what lay between us and New Dover. As I grabbed a handful of Justine's scrubs to help hold her up as her arm slid from around my shoulder, I decided the straightest path was the one I needed to take. I led us onto the tracks, planning on using them to cut through town to get us back to New Dover as quickly as possible.

It was a great plan—right up until Justine's legs gave out entirely. I grabbed her and scooped her up before she could fall. Her head flopped against my shoulder, her forehead resting on my neck. With cold, clammy skin, she felt like a corpse just pulled from an icy river.

I lifted her higher in my arms, stepping from wooden railroad tie to wooden railroad tie. The deeper pools of darkness seemed much more ominous now that Justine had become a wet noodle in my arms. In the distance, glass shattered and a small caliber weapon popped once, then twice. It wasn't any comfort to know we weren't the only ones out in the night, fighting for our lives. I lifted Justine so I could draw one of my pistols, holding it beneath her knees when I cradled her back to my chest.

I jogged, jumping over every other railroad tie until my thighs burned. A high fence blocked my view to the right, but I could hear shuffling feet off in that direction. Following the rail line began to feel like a bad idea. We were halfway through an industrial park, but warehouses and yards full of semi trailers surrounded us. I could hear things moving in the dark, but the sounds bounced off the warehouses and trailers, making it hard to tell which direction they came from.

A thrall stepped from between two trailers twenty feet away, freezing as it spotted me. Justine's knees rose as I centered the Glock on the thrall's chest, her knees draped over my wrist. It would have been easy to shoot the thrall, even from the hip, but it wasn't the one in front of me I was worried about. It was all the other things I'd heard in the dark.

Another gunshot popped, closer, and the thrall turned jerkily and disappeared back into the yard. I swallowed and hurried past as the sounds around me grew louder. The shooter was drawing unwanted attention down on us.

I froze when a stream of thralls crossed the tracks at the next intersection. A steady stream of bodies continued to stumble across as I stood, holding my breath. I breathed out slowly and stepped onto the gravel around the railroad ties, descending the small hill of stones to escape into the truck yard on my left. I hid behind a large steel cargo container, peering around it to make sure no thralls were coming down the tracks.

I moved along the container until I was at its far side, looking into the shipping yard. To our left stood more containers, some stacked five and six units high. The right side of the yard looked mostly empty in comparison. I saw the warehouse across the yard, its loading docks empty.

I cut across the yard to reach the warehouse. I was three-quarters of the way there when I saw the scavenger carts standing guard beside a shipping container. The door was cracked open, but the interior was nothing but a deep, inky black. Wet sloppy noises echoed from within its steel walls.

I moved as wide as I could around the container doors and continued for the warehouse, hiking Justine up onto my shoulder to free up my gun hand. Her hands hung down, touching the back of my thighs as I walked.

I climbed the stairs to get to the loading dock. The nearby door was locked, forcing me to walk farther down to where one of the rolling bay doors was open. I stood in front of the black square of darkness covered in heavy plastic drapes, feeling trapped by the shadows all around me. Something about walking through the square of darkness put me ill at ease. I pushed past the hanging strips of plastic and put my back to the wall once we got inside a few feet.

The warehouse had no ambient light at all. I was going to have to risk my flashlight. I edged further into the building so nothing outside would see the light, stuck my pistol in my front pocket to free my hand, and pulled my flashlight off my belt. It wasn't a great display of gun safety, but it did keep the weapon close at hand.

I held the flashlight up next to my head and hit the button with my thumb, looking down the interior of the building while holding one of my eyes closed. The moment I switched the light off, I started moving. Tall racks of pallets lined the interior of the warehouse, but at the end of the building, I had seen glass reflecting the light back at me.

I kept the wall to my left, stopping once to switch the flashlight on again before continuing. When I reached the far end of the building, I walked right into the glass. Justine's butt took most of the impact, but the quiet warehouse reverberated with a dull thud.

I pressed the flashlight against Justine's butt before turning it on, pulling one edge free just enough to look around. I was standing in front of a break room. The lower half of the wall was drywall, but the upper section up to the ceiling was constructed of thick safety glass. I scanned the interior. Several tables and chairs occupied the room, and a TV hung mounted to the ceiling in the corner. A fridge and a counter hugged the opposite wall near a door bearing a plaque reading "Office."

I slid around the outside of the break room until I found the entry. As soon as I opened the door, a rotten stench greeted me. It wasn't the smell of death, but it reminded me to be cautious. I scanned the room. The trash can had been turned over, its contents spread about; otherwise, the room was empty.

I locked the break room door behind me, went to the office door, and pushed against it lightly. It wasn't locked. I opened it the rest of the way with my foot, the beam from the flashlight revealing a long hallway. Office doors stood at regular intervals down the left side of the hall. An exit door stood at the far end, a fire placard screwed to the steel above the push bar.

I entered the hall and kicked open the first door on my left, clearing the room before dropping Justine into the heavily padded desk chair. I stood just outside the door, letting the flashlight shine down the hall, giving myself a moment to catch my breath and stretch my shoulders.

I cleared each office quickly. At the end of the hall, I

pushed on the exit door to make sure it was locked before making my way back down the hall, searching through each office for supplies.

There wasn't much to find. My take: a few light jackets with shipping company logos, a tin of Slim Jims off a bookshelf, two six-packs of no-frills orange soda hidden under a desk, and a bowl of hard candy off another.

Despite doing everything as quickly as I could, it still felt like too long before I made it back to Justine. Her skin still felt cool and clammy, but her heartbeat was strong. I wrapped her in the jackets and lowered her onto the floor. She curled into the fetal position but didn't react when I touched her hair and whispered her name.

I sat on the floor next to her and drank an orange soda, watching her. I was thirsty, but the soda was too sweet. I set the half-empty can on the floor under the desk and lay down next to Justine.

I left my flashlight under the edge of one of the jackets to bathe the room in a soft glow, remembering how Justine had begged me to let her have some light on those first nights stuck in the house by the river so long ago.

I fell asleep.

Chapter 8

Justine woke me up in the middle of the night begging for something to drink. I felt guilty pouring two cans of orange soda into her, but she didn't seem to mind. She drank them and went right back to sleep. I kissed the back of her head and followed her back under, never more happy to have been woken up in the middle of the night.

I fell into a deep sleep, fatigue and relief over Justine's improvement carrying me under quickly. I dreamed of Justine putting an arm around me, not quite sure if it was real or imagined, before another time and place took over.

I could feel my mother's arms around me, warmth and safety overwhelming me. I tried to open my eyes. I wanted to see her, but it was too dark. She died when I was very young, before I received the treatment that would give me functioning corneas again. I don't remember what she looked like, but in the dream, I was safe in her arms, the sweet smell of her hair locked in my memory forever.

I tried to hold on to the dream as the landscape changed. I was playing in our front yard with our neighbor's dog. My dad worked too much for us to get a dog as a kid, but my neighbor had a golden who loved to play. I would throw a tennis ball over and over until the dog would just lie down and chew on the ball, his big tongue hanging out as he panted happily.

Being a kid, I would sometimes tease the dog by pretending to throw the ball, watching as he took off looking for it. He'd come back and whine at me, pawing at the ground as he begged me to give him the object of his obsession.

The whining came with me as I woke up, drifting from the dream into reality as I heard the sound transition into a physical sensation: pulling at the collar of my shirt. I opened my eyes and came face to face with the black muzzle of a very thin dog.

He backed away as I put my elbow on the ground, supporting my head. It took him a good minute of staring at my outstretched hand before he would sniff at it and move forward enough for me to scratch his chin.

He was the first living dog I'd seen since the world ended. He was a medium sized mutt with brown fur, and by the way his tale was wagging I think he was just as happy to see me as I was surprised to see him.

Once we made friends, he grabbed my sleeve with his teeth and tried to drag me away. I pulled my hand back and we started the cycle over. He'd let me pet him, and then he'd grab my sleeve and pull at me.

The dog came to the conclusion that I wasn't quite understanding him and he needed to be more clear. He grabbed my sleeve and threw his body weight backwards, trying to pull me away. When his teeth tore through my sleeve, he fell onto his butt, a look of surprise on his doggy face.

He looked at me with a curious expression, his head tilted to the side, and then at Justine, showing his teeth in a low growl as his nostrils bunched up. I sat up, putting one hand out to calm him down, scratching the whiskers under his chin as I tore open a Slim Jim with my teeth. The moment the wrapper opened, he froze, eyes locked onto the beef snack, watery saliva running out of his mouth. I handed him half the stick and was lucky to keep all my fingers when he snatched it away.

Justine snored softly.

It took three Slim Jims and a few minutes, but I eventually lured him closer and closer with pieces of beef stick. He'd snap up the treat and swallow it whole before slinking back, watching Justine nervously. By the time I had him eating out of my hand, he was almost sitting in my lap, oblivious to her small form behind me. Slim Jims are powerful things.

"Your breath really reeks," Justine mumbled from behind me. "Oh, shit," she exclaimed in quiet amazement when she opened her eyes. The dog, which was just now getting used to Justine asleep, pushed painfully off me to skitter backwards into the wall with a bang.

"See if he will take this," I said, handing her a piece of Slim Jim as she sat up. She popped it into her mouth and ate it without a word, smiling at me when the dog whined. "Try again," I told her, giving her two more pieces, one for her and one for him.

The dog came within a foot of the food before stopping, looking at Justine warily—until she popped her piece of Slim Jim into her mouth and moved to eat his half as well. Then he slinked forward and took it, whining the whole time.

"Think he's been in here since it started?" she asked, taking another piece of meat to lure the dog back to her.

"He must have been in here for a while," I thought out loud, feeling his ribs through his fur as I ran a hand down his side. "He must have a good hiding spot; I missed him when I cleared the rest of the offices."

"Can we keep him?" she asked, leaning against me and putting her head on my shoulder. I would have given her anything in the world at that moment.

"Of course," I told her. That was when she broke down in tears.

"I don't want to be this thing," she sobbed softly, covering her eyes with her dirty hands, streaks of reddish brown running down her forearms as she cried.

"I was worried until I saw you at the baseball field," I told her, pulling her into my lap. She wrapped her arms around me hesitantly. "You stopped and touched my face, careful not to cut me. I knew you hadn't let me go at that moment." She laughed into my shoulder, still crying. "What do you remember?" I asked her.

"I remember the heat of being on top of you, and letting myself go. The moment I came, I was so relaxed, and that's when it grabbed me, pulling at me so hard I couldn't resist. I've never felt anything so strong before; it was like a burning thirst in my throat, but nothing I had would ever quench it. Whatever was reaching out for me was making me feel like it was the only thing that could ever stop the need."

"Do you think you can fight it if it comes back?"

"I think so. It doesn't feel like me…no, I'm not sure what I'm trying to say. It feels like it's coming from outside. I think I can fight it if I don't let it catch me unguarded."

"Were those other grays responsible?" If the cut eyes were involved, I'd hunt every last one down if it would put an end to this.

"No, I don't think so. They were fighting several of the normal grays when I ran into them. It was bad luck. Once they saw what I was, they tried to get one of those silver cords around me. It didn't go so well for them."

"You kicked ass," I said, tilting her tear-streaked face up so I could kiss her on the lips.

"Even the dog was smart enough to want to get away from me," she blubbered when I let our lips part, half crying and half laughing.

Dog was looking at us, trying to figure out what we were doing. He stepped closer and licked Justine across her face before she could do anything.

"See, you even won him over," I teased her. She smiled and hugged me, thanking me quietly as she rested her head in the crook of my neck.

We sat there for a little while longer, enjoying the moment, trying to pretend our little office sanctuary was the world. Dog ruined it when he disappeared, forcing me to get up and examine the interior of the office with the flashlight.

I missed it the second time around as well. A box fan sat next to a bookcase, hiding a hole in the wall that probably had a vent cover over it at some point. "I'll be right back. You OK for a minute?" I asked Justine, easing the desk away from the door.

"Go find your new friend," she told me, waving me away with a hand.

I slipped out into the hallway expecting to see Dog sitting there, but it was empty. I moved to the next door on the left, clearing the office again. No Dog. I found Dog in the last office, sitting on the floor, tongue hanging out. I put my hand out, but he didn't let me get within a foot of him before he barked and ran back into the vent at the back of the office.

When I went back to Justine, she was squatting behind the desk, Dog watching her with a cocked head. I slipped the box fan directly in front of the opening in the wall to trap him.

"Sorry, I had to pee," Justine said, sighing as she stood up and tied her scrubs around her waist again. I hadn't even realized what she was doing.

"No worries," I said as I pushed the MP5K across the desk to her. Dog sat on the floor between us, looking from me to her expectantly.

"You coming with us?" Justine asked, making the end of

his tail beat at the carpet. It was both heartwarming and sad at the same time.

I cut a length of power cord from the desk lamp and used it to make a leash for Dog. He didn't like me touching his collar, but I didn't want to risk him getting away. I handed Justine the makeshift leash and led the way down to the fire exit.

A large sliding bolt had been screwed to the interior of the fire exit door. I slid it open, a pistol in one hand as I depressed the door bar. Bright light spilled into the hall as the door started to open. I flicked my head forward so my shades fell into place, then the door came to a stop. Loops of chain had been wrapped around the exterior door handle and secured to a post supporting the awning over the door. The fire inspector would have been livid.

"I take it you didn't come in this way?" Justine asked, raising an eyebrow at me.

"Nope," I said, pointing past her into the dark. The emergency door shut slowly behind us as we walked back down the hallway to the break room.

I opened the door, the flashlight bathing the room in light. Dog began to growl as I leveled my pistol, sweeping the room. Bloody handprints were smeared along the glass walls. I could see where thralls had rested their hands on the safety glass and pressed their foreheads against the flat surface, leaving strange smears and imprints across the glass. Dog whined and barked as Justine dragged him into the room, her MPK5 gripped in one hand as she pulled him along with the other.

"I take it the artwork is new," Justine said quietly as I walked along the edge of the break room, shining the flashlight through the windows to look out into the warehouse.

"Anything?" she asked as I peered about. The smeared blood made it hard to see very far.

"Yeah," I said quietly, raising the flashlight over my head to shine down through a clear spot in the glass. Justine inched closer to the glass to take a look.

A pool of blood congealed on the concrete a few feet in front of the break room, a trail leading off down the aisle and out of sight. At least it was heading away from the loading dock entrance.

"It's not that far," Justine said, looking in the opposite direction of the blood trail. In the distance, we could clearly see the square of light coming in from the loading dock.

"What do you think, Dog?" I asked, pulling away from the glass and going to the door out of the break room. He stopped pulling when I talked to him, looking at me warily. "Do you want to stay here or come with us?" I asked him since he was looking at me so seriously.

Dog thought about it and walked forward to meet me at the door. I guess the urge for companionship was stronger than fear.

Justine checked her MP5K to make sure she was locked and loaded, and we slipped out into the warehouse, moving at double time toward the bright square of light at the other end of the building.

"Do you think you walked by it in the dark last night?" Justine asked, making me wonder how close I'd come to whatever had been hiding in the back of the warehouse.

"Thanks," I whispered to her, keeping the light pointed at our feet as we jogged for the loading bay door.

Dog was leading the way by the time we made it to the plastic flaps opening into the daylight, trying to trip me up on his makeshift leash. He slipped through the plastic curtain just in front of me, his tail wagging.

I flicked my shades back onto my eyes as I transitioned into the morning light, covering the loading yard with my pistol. I put one hand on Dog's head, scanning our surroundings. The yard looked deserted, but the warehouse behind us cast the yard in shadows, lending an ominous feeling to the air.

Justine handed me the leash, taking point without a word. She moved easily, her MP5K held to her chest as she led the way. She was still barefoot and wearing ragged nursing pants and a T-shirt, but I would have followed her anywhere.

I've heard professional athletes talk about that moment when they are on the field and everything is just gelling, as if they know what their teammates are thinking and everything just lines up perfectly. It's what well-trained military units strive for, spending millions of dollars on training and simulated warfare to pull together. I'd felt a similar if muted version of that synchrony with my scouting unit.

With Justine, it was like breathing. I didn't think about it; I just knew where she was and what she was doing. I knew she would cover her field of fire without me having to say anything. We moved swiftly, not wasting any words as we moved through enemy territory.

We both relaxed a little when we made it out of the industrial park, and more when we made it onto a street bathed in the bright morning sun. Justine walked with one hand on her MP5K, letting it rest across her chest on its sling. I stayed a few paces behind her and couldn't help but stare at her backside now and then. She caught me looking, but she just gave me a broad smile and a lift of her eyebrows. It was the same smile that had struck me back in Jersey, the one that made me fall in love with her when she was my crazy neighbor's kid.

I was almost sad to see how close we were to New Dover when Justine stopped at the next block.

"We look like we've been through the ringer," Justine said, looking at her pants and shirt and then at me.

"And smell worse," I agreed.

"Thank you," she said. "Do we sneak back in?"

"I really don't feel like climbing the wall with Dog."

"Yeah, I guess you're right." She sighed. "You think it will be a problem?"

"I think we look and smell like half the people living in the Fort," I said.

She nodded, not exactly encouraged.

I expected some trouble when we got to the gate, but we got lucky, coming in just as a group of scavengers was heading out. The gate guards ignored us in the shuffle of bodies moving past each other.

We made a beeline for our apartment, hoping to slip in before anyone saw us. I figured we had a good chance, as most people had been shifting their sleeping patterns later into the night as they stayed awake and alert through the night and then slept through the first half of the day.

Except, of course, the day we wanted everyone to be

sleeping. People filled the street—nervous people, carrying their guns and looking amped up. I'd been around firearms all my adult life, but seeing so many scared people with their fingers on triggers put a knot in my stomach.

We'd made it halfway to our apartment when WC saw Justine and made a beeline for us through the crowd. He talked so fast Justine had to tell him to slow down twice before we could understand him. He thanked us both again for saving his ass, rambling until Justine grabbed his chin and told him to calm down. He babbled for another thirty seconds until Justine pinched her fingers together a bit, helping him focus. He told us what everyone else in town apparently already knew.

The patrol sent out the previous morning looking for the other half of the battalion hadn't made it back intact. Of the nine men sent out, only one had returned, and he was so covered in bites and scratches he was almost shot on sight.

Big John had arrived just in time to keep the good townspeople from giving the soldier "mercy." With scratches and bites, even if the soldier was talking and in pain, he wouldn't be for long.

Rumors flew. Big John had the foremen chain the soldier to a bed in an empty apartment across the street from the church. WC told us the latest news was that the soldier was still talking, but his skin was getting paler and paler, and it was taking him longer to answer questions.

"Tell us from the beginning," Justine said, dragging him to the side of the street near our apartment when he started to repeat and jumble up what he'd already told us.

"They headed south, and the farther they went, the stronger the static on their radios became. Eventually they thought they heard something like Morse code, but they couldn't make out what was being transmitted.

"The smoke was the first thing they saw, then the tail end of the convoy came into view. It wasn't until they got closer that they saw the scope of the destruction. Thrall bodies surrounded the vehicles. The soldier said some of the vehicles sat on piles of bodies so deep their tires had lost traction."

It sent a chill down my back to hear the story, even third

hand. The soldiers in the convoy had fought until they ran out of ammo and were overrun. It was a soldier's worst nightmare. I felt guilty for wishing that Captain Jones was still alive to hear he'd done the right thing by sitting tight and not heading south with the other soldiers.

"They drove along the median next to the column until they saw a thrall sitting inside a Humvee, triggering the mic on the radio and gurgling. The one who made it back, no one knows his name, got out with another soldier, and they shot the thrall.

"It's not clear what happened after that. But the survivor said the thralls woke up. I don't think a lot of the bodies around them were dead dead. The soldier told one of the foremen that he got an old Chevy started after he broke free of the fighting, but it ran out of gas before he could make it back to Dover."

As we stood on the street with WC, the next wave of rumors swept down the street. The survivor was dead. They were telling people he died from his wounds, but everyone was saying one of the foremen crushed his head with a mallet so no one would panic when they heard a gunshot.

It wasn't until after the news of the soldier's death that WC noticed Dog crouching behind Justine's legs. "I haven't seen one of them alive since before," he said, his face growing concerned as he backed up a few steps. "I'm going to go get on a work crew before all the good slots are filled," he said, but the last look he gave Dog was one of uncertainty and fear. I guess we weren't the only ones who'd seen a dog ripped to pieces on the streets.

Shutting the door to the apartment felt like bliss. We were finally safe and alone. Rumors still weaved their way up and down the streets outside, but inside, it was just us.

Justine spent a long time in the bathroom getting cleaned up, staying locked inside while I tried not to fret on the couch. I was debating how angry she'd be if I kicked down the door when she finally opened it. She came over to hug me but realized I was still covered in dirt and grime. She settled for mussing up my hair with a tired smile before collapsing into our bed.

I took my turn in the bathroom, scrubbing myself clean

and putting on a pair of shorts. I called Dog into the bedroom and locked up, sliding our security dresser into place against the bedroom door. When I slipped under the covers and put a hand on her hip, she stiffened. I kept my hand where it was as she slowly relaxed.

"I don't want to turn again. I don't want to feel that pull on me," she said pleadingly, putting her hand over mine.

"I know," I told her, putting my forehead against the back of her head. I fell asleep thinking about how I was going to free her from whatever was tearing her apart.

Chapter 9

Justine woke me up a few hours later when she got up. I wasn't sure what time it was, but I knew it was sometime after dusk; the generator was running and the lights glowed outside. I was falling back to sleep, listening to Dog racing about when he decided he should make sure I knew they were up.

Dog ran back into the bedroom and jumped onto the bed, making mad circles on top of me. Paws and claws landed all over until I pushed him off long enough to sit up. That was just about when Justine made a noise from the living room and he decided he desperately needed to see her, taking off before I could get my hands on him.

There was nothing for it but to get up. I rolled out of bed and lifted myself up with a grunt, my back and abdomen reminding me to take it slow. I'd taken a couple solid blows over the last few days.

Dog was running back to me when he heard food hitting a bowl and somehow managed to turn around while continuing to move in my direction, his claws scrabbling at the floor the whole time. I followed him into the kitchen just in time to see him wolfing down cat food.

"That's just wrong," I told Justine. "You're going to give him an identity complex."

Justine gave me the finger with a smile as she replied, "I think he's just glad the previous occupants had pets."

Dog swallowed his food whole, his body shaking in excitement. He barked excitedly the moment his food was gone, his body wagging with his tail as he decided he'd made a mistake by not coming back over and saying high to me again.

He barreled into my knees, and I fell against the wall laughing as he attacked me with his tongue. I pushed him back by his chest only to have him rush forward again. He playfully bit at me, snarling as his tail wagged. I tried to put my arms around him, but the move spooked him. He ran back to Justine, hiding behind her legs.

"You're just so fearsome," I said to her, and for a moment, I thought it was the wrong thing to say as her face paused between serious and happy before she settled on a smile.

I was about to say something else when sirens blasted from outside, washing out my voice. I grabbed a pistol and rushed up to the gym roof, trying to see what was going on. All I was able to do was get a better sense of where the noise was coming from. Something was coming at the eastern gate.

When I got back into the apartment, Justine was pulling on her clothes as Dog tried his best to trip her up. I grabbed my fatigues and pulled them on, thinking better of making fun of the granny panties Justine was wearing as she wiggled into her pants.

Dog put up a fight at the door, trying to come with us. I had to throw him back and slam it closed to keep him from escaping. We left him scratching madly at the door as we rushed down the steps.

People rushing about in different directions filled the streets. Half of them were running away while the other half tried their best to make it to the east gate, causing havoc as everyone collided. I grabbed Justine's hand and pushed our way through the crowd.

As we got closer to the eastern gate, the staccato of our mismatched redneck arsenal drowned out the wailing of the sirens. Handguns popped, shotguns blasted, and automatics roared. We were close enough to the wall that the gunfire lit up the night like strobes.

"Smell that?" Justine asked, scrunching up her nose.

"No," I said, sniffing at the air. It took a few more steps for the smell to fill my nostrils. "Rotting meat," I said under my breath—thralls.

The street was nearly deserted just inside the gate. The militia had all filtered up through the buildings on either side of the street to provide fire support from above. In front of us, a single soldier in fatigues carried an ammo crate up the crude stairs built of dirt-filled tires. A pillbox had been built on top of the buses. The rear entrance and gun slits of the bunker flashed continuously as the men inside fired in long bursts.

We were about to take the stairs when something hit the gate, crushing it back into the aluminum bodies of the buses with a crunch. Another blow hit the steel plate, breaking the welds on the casters to send steel wheels flying. One of the casters landed on its edge and rolled down the road, escaping.

"Breach, breach!" I started to yell uselessly as another blow struck the gate.

Rain sprinkled across my face as I pulled Justine back just as a third massive strike brought the gate down in an earth-shaking slap. The steel plate hit the asphalt, sinking into the blacktop with the force of the impact.

"Up," Justine said, tapping me on the arm as more rain hit my face. A gray stood at the entrance to the pillbox, discarding the halves of a National Guardsman he'd just ripped in two.

"I'll cover the gate," I told Justine.

She nodded and took off up the stairs.

I positioned myself at the mouth of the opening between the buses, directly in the path of anything that wanted to get into New Dover. The first thing to step from the darkness into the space between the two buses was a massive, angry brute. I knew I should have taken the pillbox.

I don't think the brute even saw me as he moved through the space left between the fronts of the two buses, stepping out onto the street just in front of me. He lifted his chin to the sky, roaring in anger as he beat his chest. The part of my brain responsible for self-preservation was screaming at me to run.

Instead, I darted forward. The brute was still pounding his chest when I put the tip of the Glock against the side of one of his knees and fired two shots. His hands thudded on his chest one more time before he looked down, his eyes locking on me as I backed away slowly, suddenly feeling very small. The brute's face scrunching up in anger as he took his first step toward me. I wanted to scream at him. Two rounds to his knee had to slow him down.

As the brute put his weight down on the injured knee, I held my breath, watching as his expression slowly changed.

The brute's brow unfurrowed as he shifted his eyes off me to look down at his leg and shuffled to keep his balance. That was when the pain hit him. I let out my breath as the brute screamed a high-pitched cry.

The huge creature grabbed the rough material of his pants, ripping it away to reveal his knee. The bullets hadn't penetrated all the way through, but his kneecap was a funny shape. Bits of bone distended the skin over his knee in sharp, jutting points. He touched his knee with a finger, pieces of bone moving under his skin as his cry took on a disturbingly childlike quality.

The brute looked at his knee in confusion, tears welling up in his eyes as he tried to figure out what was wrong. He was in pain, and I was standing in front of him. He lunged at me, falling forward as his huge hands reached out. I slipped under his arm as he half dove, half fell at me, moving under his armpit with so little room to spare that the cloth of his shirt brushed across the top of my head. I'd dodged his arm, but he lashed out with his good leg, kicking madly about. I stepped onto the bumper of a bus to leap over his flailing leg, jumping into the narrow space between the two buses.

Thralls poured through the opening where the gate had once stood. With little choice, I stepped away from the brute's kicking feet to meet the thralls head on.

I stood with my back to the brute as he struggled to get up behind me, a pistol in each hand, not firing until the thralls were shoulder to shoulder in the short tunnel between the buses. I let them get within arm's reach before putting well-placed shots into their heads, firing one weapon and then the other, making every round count.

Bodies dropped, some bullets cutting two or three thralls down, but more were crowding against the front of the buses every moment. The fire support from the surrounding buildings had slackened.

At least one gray must have breached the rooftops of the surrounding buildings, tearing into the militia. A body hit the pavement next to the brute, splattering as it hit. The gunmen who had been thinning out the press of thralls were now focused on whatever was up on the rooftops with them. More thralls shouldered their way into the opening between the two buses, trying to force their way into New Dover.

The situation went from bad to worse as 5.56mm rounds began punching into the busses. Two national guardsmen stood on the side of the street spraying the brute with automatic fire. I ignored the sound of lead punching into the bus as I reloaded. There was nothing I could do about the idiots behind me. At least they were distracting the brute.

The space between the buses gradually filled with bodies, slowing the stream of thralls as they were forced to pull away their fallen to get to me. I slid my last two clips home, turning to check my back just in time to see the brute rip a parking meter out of the ground and hurl it at the two soldiers peppering him with rounds.

The parking meter hit them across their upper bodies, carrying them off their feet and sending them crashing through the large plate glass window behind them. A single boot rocked back and forth on the street where they'd both stood a moment before.

The brute snarled and hissed at me, standing like a gorilla on his knuckles and good leg as he turned to face me. I sighed, putting my back to the thralls as the brute slammed his knuckles into the ground and took a hobbling step my way.

I pointed my weapons at him, darting a glance behind me to make sure the pile of bodies jammed between the buses was still keeping the thralls busy. I was acutely aware that I was surrounded and almost out of ammunition.

I had a hard time waiting for the brute to take the second step. I wanted to turn, to see exactly how much progress the thralls were making at my back, but I forced myself to stay focused on the brute. Even wounded, he could kill me easily.

Thrall fingertips brushed against my back as the brute put his knuckles down again and I surged at him, taking two running steps and dropping to my knees, sliding across the fallen steel plate on a slick of blood.

The brute's face looked down to track me, his big, square teeth exposed in a snarl as I slid between his arms and legs. I tried to put a few rounds into his good knee as I went by, but my aim was off. The bullets plowed into his lower leg, punching holes into the meat at the back of his thigh.

I slid off the end of the steel plate and rolled away as the brute spun about, punching the ground I'd just occupied with a massive fist. I rolled to my knees, coming up to put two more rounds into him as I scrambled to my feet, steadying my aim as I put his head in my sights.

His eyes, full of rage, locked on mine as his arm muscles flexed, supporting his weight as he dragged his wounded legs behind him. I shifted my sights and put a round from each pistol into one of his thick forearms.

It was enough. For just a second, he tried to put weight on his shattered knee as his arms buckled. He lost his balance, falling sideways as his legs gave out. Thralls flooded between the buses behind him.

The brute fell onto his hands and lifted his head to bellow at me, his face so close I could see the veins pulsing in his forehead and the chip missing from one of his front teeth. Time slowed as I concentrated on the pistol in my right hand, sighting in and firing a round directly into his left eye.

Time passed as if I were watching the discrete frames of a film. The brute blinked reflexively as the weapon went off, his eyes shutting as the round traversed the distance between us. His eyelid had just finished closing when the tip of the .40 caliber round touched the surface of his skin. For a nanosecond, the tip of the round pushed against his flesh, compressing the eye behind it, and then time snapped back to normal, sending a spray of blood exploding from his eye socket.

The brute fell forward, his head thudding onto the pavement as a long, heavy sigh left his lips. His left arm scraped across the ground, struggling to reach his face. I put a boot on the back of his head and fired both my weapons into his neck until the pistols locked with open slides, their magazines empty.

The brute was dead, even if his feet wouldn't quite acknowledge it yet, his lower legs doing a spastic little dance as his blood pooled on the pavement. I holstered my pistols and drew my machete as I stood with his head between my feet, ready to face the wave of thralls coming at me.

It gave me a perfect view of Justine as she stepped back

along the length of the bus on my right. She was holding her MP5K high, aiming carefully as she put well-placed shots into a gray who was taking baby steps toward her, a pained look on his face. Every time a round hit him, he winced.

Still he kept coming, his feet dragging just a bit more with every step. I spun the machete in front of me as I watched with a smile. The gray was dead; he just didn't know it yet. Justine finished him with a head shot, and he fell off the top of the bus and out of sight. I waved at her like a moron when she looked my way. Then it was time to get to business.

The first thrall came right at me, hands outstretched to grab whatever he could. He lost both appendages as I chopped them away, followed by his head a moment later. Then things got a little crazy. The gray on top of the bus must have been linked to a good number of the thralls trying to make it through the gate. When he died, they went berserk, going crazy inside the crowded space between the buses, tearing into each other.

Rotting flesh and congealed clots of blood flew as maddened thralls fought, all the while the press from behind pushing them closer to me. I spread my feet, lashing out in broad strokes, cutting into whatever came within my reach. I was forced back one step, then two, trying to control the flood pouring through the gate.

My footing was getting slick, and I was forced back another two steps as I slipped and struggled to stay upright. I heard Justine's MP5K firing, but I couldn't see her. I cut down the three thralls in front of me, coming face to face with a second brute—or at least that's what I thought at first.

The man must have weighed over four hundred pounds and been six foot five when he was alive. His button-down shirt hung half open, his exposed stomach rolling in waves with each step he took. Scores of thralls surged around the big dude. I'd been pushed too far away from the opening between the buses to have any hope of holding them all back.

The big thrall rushed me as fast as he could, forcing me to backpedal as I slashed at him, cutting his belly open. Long, rotten strands of putrid intestines spilled to the ground, but that didn't slow him. I could see men coming down the street behind me, led by one of Big John's foremen. I slashed away, forced back step by step as more thralls crowded in, trying to get to me.

Several shotgun blasts tore into the thralls to my left, pellets whizzing by close enough to alarm me. I fled to the edge of the street, the big thrall following. I was taking chunks out of him with each swing, but he wore the equivalent of a suit of blubber armor. I just couldn't cut deep enough to do any real damage.

A relief force was forming a line across the street, their guns blazing as the thralls climbed over each other to get to them. I don't think the people fighting in the middle of the street had ever seen enraged thralls before. They slowed the rush down as they tried to hold their firing line, but they had underestimated how dangerous the maddened thralls would be.

I danced back and forth, cutting away at fatty as the leading edge of the thralls met the line of gunmen, pulling first one man down and then another, swarming over them. Three of the men tried to run but were taken from behind before they could get a dozen paces.

Gunfire began to rain down onto the thralls from above—too late to save the skirmish line. The men on the rooftops must have cleared the grays or pushed them back, because they were beginning to shift their fire into the street again.

I stepped in close to the fat thrall, trying to put my machete into the rolls of flesh around his neck. My blade sank into the meat between his neck and his shoulder and stuck. I was working the blade free when he caught me hard in the face with a sweeping blow from a forearm, slamming me back into the building behind me.

Fatty tried to hit me again with a flailing arm as I bounced off the wall. I ducked under the sags of flesh hanging off his arm and popped up at his side as I lashed out with my blade, feeling metal crunching through bone as the machete took the big thrall in the back of the neck. He collapsed to the ground as the press of thralls swept me back out into the street.

I took two steps, keeping up with the bodies around me—and then they stopped. Thralls who had been moving down the street turned, focusing on me. I was surrounded and all alone.

I whispered Justine's name under my breath, flexing my fingers on the machete's grip as the ring of thralls closed. I hoped she was still alive, but I hadn't seen her since she'd killed the gray on top of the bus. I swung with all my strength, whipping the blade about me hard and fast. Hands and arms fell as I fought, thralls from behind replacing the ones I killed as soon as they went down.

I screamed in rage, spinning about, my blade held in both hands as I cleared a small circle around me. I'd gained some room to fight, but my strength was fading, my arms burning from swinging the machete. There were just too many of them.

I rubbed my left hand on my pants, trying to scrub away the slickness that covered my arms from my elbows down. I readied myself as the thralls began to close again.

A window above me shattered, raining down glittering slivers of broken glass from the darkness above. I thought maybe some redneck was trying to give me some covering fire.

Then I saw it: a dark shape falling through the shards of glass, passing like a shadow made real into the floodlights strung along the street. The shadow resolved into a tightly balled body, slowly expanding as it fell into the light.

Justine's short hair hung suspended in the air as she fell, then snapped down as her boots hit the pavement. She landed behind me, putting her back to mine as she grabbed me with her free hand, keeping me close as she lifted her MP5K. I closed my eyes as she guided my body in a tight pirouette, knowing I wasn't going to die. She wasn't going to let them have me.

I felt the kick of the gun through Justine's body as each round flew free to strike its target. Our heels clicked together as we turned, Justine firing single rounds so fast it sounded like automatic fire.

We'd danced this dance once before, and just like then, my heart soared. Her hand snaked along my arm, pulling it to her until she could slide her hand over the machete's grip and take it. I opened my eyes as she stepped away from me, directly into the stream of undead pouring through the gap between the buses. A ring of fallen bodies surrounded us.

The thralls were charging through the gap, bearing down on Justine in an angry wave. She stepped forward to meet them.

Lifting her MP5K, she took out the three leading thralls in a heartbeat, their bodies taking half a step more before they collapsed. The next wave moved in to surround her but fell to the ground as she slid between them, the edge of the machete flashing as she flowed through them like water. Step by step, she pushed into the gap between the two buses.

She gained the front of the buses where the gate used to be, lifting her MP5K to empty her clip with careful shots. When the gun was empty, she let it fall against her chest on its sling, tapping the machete on the edge of the bus to shake a bit of gore from it. A fresh wave of thralls attacked the gate, trying to overwhelm her.

Several times it looked like they'd broken through, but the thralls would collapse within a step of moving past her, their bodies falling apart from multiple cuts. Sometimes the undead are stubborn.

She let the machete drop to her side as the last thrall collapsed to the ground and looked out into the darkness beyond the flood lights. The last of the maddened thralls were being torn to pieces by their brothers, giving us a short respite. We'd pushed them back, but the battle wasn't over.

"I'll keep them thinned out," Justine said as she walked back to me, handing me my machete. She ejected her empty clip, putting it into the cargo pocket on her thigh before sliding a fresh magazine home. I grabbed her shoulder as she tried to move away, looking into her eyes.

"You OK?" I asked her. Dark slate clouds washed over the deep brown of her irises.

"I'm controlling it," she said, swallowing hard. I handed her a pair of my sunglasses to hide her eyes, and she put them on with a smile, revealing teeth just a little too long. Then she ran up the makeshift stairs to get back to the top of the buses.

As long as she didn't smile at anyone too much or take off the sunglasses, we'd be OK. Besides, no one was coming down the street to help us anyway. Men were watching us from the corner, setting up a secondary position. I rubbed my bicep as I readied myself for the next attack.

It didn't take long for the push to come. The thralls moved slower compared to the flood of the enraged, but what they lacked in speed they made up for in sheer numbers. Justine's MP5K popped at regular intervals as she thinned out the thralls pushing in from the other side, taking just enough of them that I wasn't overwhelmed.

"One more left," Justine yelled down from above me, the regular intervals between her shots pausing as she loaded her last clip.

"Don't get too badass," I yelled up to her. She understood what I meant.

"You better get really badass in just a minute then," she called back, disappearing out of sight.

We did our thing, but the clip to her MP5K emptied all too soon. Thralls filled the gate entrance, the bodies of the fallen being pulled away as soon as they fell. Whatever gray was controlling them had watched and learned.

A mixture of rifles, shotguns, and M16s continued to fire from atop the closest buildings, but there were just too many thralls.

Justine and I were still all alone at the east gate.

"How many?" I asked Justine as she darted down the stairs while I continued my butcher's work.

"Standing room only for two blocks," she said grimly, holding her hand out for the machete. I tossed her the blade and stepped out of the way as she threw me two clips for my pistols.

"Very nice," I said, ejecting my empties and reloading.

"You got lucky. One of the men in the pillbox had them on his belt," she said, pausing. "Is it time to go the other direction?"

"Fuck," I said thoughtfully. We were planning on leaving eventually, but running in the middle of a battle wasn't the way I wanted to go. Most of the people in New Dover were screwed, and I knew that. It was a tough new world. Most of the people were struggling to survive after a few short weeks, but leaving the gate open and exposed while we ran for it felt like the worst kind of betrayal.

"Leave the cursing to me, OK?" Justine said with a big, evil smile as she grabbed my shirt and pulled me violently out of the way, dragging me out of the road and onto the sidewalk by the storefronts.

I was cursing anyway, not sure what was happening. Headlights barreled down the street, sweeping across us as tires squealed. I saw through the glaring headlights just enough to catch WC sliding an orange Nissan pickup 180 degrees, kicking up a wave of body parts as he skidded around directly in front of the east gate.

The truck tilted precariously as its heavy cargo almost took the pickup over sideways, then settled to rock back and forth on its struggling shocks. A green tarp covered the cargo area like a poorly constructed tent.

A soldier stuck his head up from under the tarp, peeling it back with one hand as he slammed the top of the cab in anger with the other. WC jumped out of the cab, ignoring the soldier's anger as he popped the hood and pushed a set of jumper cables into the man's hands, pointing at the gate and the thralls about to spill through it.

The soldier clamped the jumper cables down on terminals inside the truck bed and kicked open the rear hatch as WC got back into the cab and floored the engine in neutral. I looked at Justine, still not sure what was going on, but her eyes were locked on the gate, her lips smiling in anticipation. I understood why a moment later.

Gunfire erupted from the back of the pickup, rolling it forward until WC stomped on the brakes. The chain gun sitting in the truck bed slowed slightly when WC took his foot off the gas, but the kid was able to get one foot on the brake and one on the accelerator as soon as he realized what was happening.

The soldier in the truck bed swept the weapon back and forth, trying not to chew into the sides of the buses as he fired. The feed belt coming up from the bed of the truck supplied a constant stream of .30 caliber ammunition to the gun.

The after image of the flames was burned into my eyes

even after the chain gun stopped firing and was spinning down, its electric motors whirring until it came to a stop. WC waved to us from inside the cab and gave us a big "OK" sign with his thumb and forefinger, a huge smile on his face.

The barrels had just come to a stop when the solider spun them up again. He cycled on and off twice more, waiting for the thralls to file back into the middle of the street before he let loose.

I dragged Justine up the dirt and tire stairs so we could look out over the street. The chain gun was turning the center of the road into a blender, clearing the thralls in a five-foot path all the way down to the end of the street.

It's hard to describe what it looked like. The chain gun had evaporated everything in the core of its firing path, but the damage wasn't so contained. Bits and pieces of bone and body had been turned into secondary projectiles, widening the path of destruction. Fresh blood coated the walls of the buildings leading down the street up to the second floor.

The smell of weeks-old thrall was normally enough to make you vomit in your mouth, but the smell of a few hundred thralls thrown into a blender and poured onto the street was worse. It was as if someone had set fire to a garbage heap and tried to put it out with sewer water. Liquefied thrall covered the center of the road, gradually turning into larger chunks of meat and limbs closer to the curbs.

The chain gun had turned the tide. After the third long burst, the thralls didn't pour in to fill the middle of the street anymore. They were retreating back into the night.

WC got out of the truck and tiptoed over to us as we came down the stairs, ignoring the soldier who was yelling at him for driving like a maniac and putting them so close to the fight. Apparently the man was under the impression that WC could have gotten him killed.

"Nice driving," I told WC. He could barely contain the grin on his face.

"What's with the stripes?" Justine asked, looking at the truck. The sides of the orange vehicle were painted in faded white stripes.

WC shrugged. "It happened at a concert one night. The fans got a little crazy." WC nodded his head as he said it, very pleased with himself as he gave Justine a smug smile. It must have been his truck from before.

Justine smiled back at him, but she turned her head toward me as if to say something, biting her tongue and trying not to let WC see her turn red as she bit back laughter. I wanted to smack the kid for flirting with Justine but felt too sorry for him to do it.

"Nice, Justine. He's got a chain gun in his pickup and you notice the paintjob?" I said instead.

She shook her head at me, punching me hard in the arm, still trying not to laugh.

"I was one of the first people in New Dover. I had my truck in one of the allies before they planted the buses. When the soldier's moved into the firehouse, I started to help them a bit. I helped them move the gun from a destroyed APC to the firehouse so they could work on it. I think I might have one of the only running vehicles inside the walls at this point." He just kept on grinning. I patted him on the back, thanking him. He deserved it. He'd saved our asses.

As is often the case, the bulk of the reinforcements showed up after everything was over. The gate became a madhouse for a few minutes as a mixture of soldiers and armed rednecks "secured" everything.

We let ourselves get pushed to the side as several foremen started to order people about, telling them to be careful. The blood could turn you if you got it in a wound, or worse, got some in your eyes or mouth.

"I wouldn't mention the dog if I were you," WC said to us quietly as the foremen continued to order people about. There was going to be some gruesome cleanup on our side of the gate, but the work teams would be paid double.

"Not a bad idea," I said to him. "As a matter of fact, I think we are going to slip away. You're the one who brought in the heavy guns here." I patted him on the back again.

"Yeah, but I saw you take down that huge monster," WC said to me, not understanding how I might not want recognition for my part in the fight.

"Just keep quiet about the brute. And if anyone asks, I think the two soldiers in the pillbox put up a hell of a fight before they died."

WC was looking at me, his facial expressions rapidly shifting as he transitioned from confused to suspicious. "You're not bit, are you?" he asked, taking a step back, trying to look nonchalant as his hand drifted to the chromed automatic at his belt.

"Relax," Justine said. "We just don't want any attention. We're fine, I promise," she told him. WC looked around then back at us and nodded for us to go. We slipped away in the throng of people moving about, the foremen yelling about Clorox, trash bags, and welding equipment to fix the gate, all in one rapid stream of commands.

We made it back to our apartment without incident, at least until we walked in the door and discovered a bit of information about our new four-legged friend: Dog really hates being locked up.

Chunks of end table covered the entry hall. The damn dog had chewed a wooden table to bits and then moved on to shredding the comfy chair in the corner. Bits of cloth and stuffing gave the living room a nice holiday snowstorm feel.

"Your dog was really bad," Justine said, looking at the mess in the living room with quiet astonishment.

"Oh, now he's my dog," I shot back, looking for the mutt. I missed him the first time I scanned the room because he was sitting on the destroyed chair, covered in stuffing. What gave him away was his tail started to wag when he saw us.

He jumped down off the chair, sending a cloud of stuffing up into the air as he rushed to greet us. His excitement turned into an emergency stop as he got close, whining at us as he stood at arm's length. He stalked down the hall and then turned about in indecision before coming back to sniff at us again. We were both covered in thrall. I'm sure we smelled lovely. We had another set of clothes to burn.

"You going to beat him?" Justine asked, amused as Dog ran back and forth in the hall, wanting to say hello but unable to get past his sense of self-preservation as he smelled thrall.

"I don't think I can," I admitted. Seeing him run around neurotically blunted my anger. I just couldn't watch his display of indecisive craziness and still be mad.

"Guess we shouldn't have used all the water up in the bathroom last night," Justine said, raising her eyebrows in apology as she handed me back my shades. Her eyes were her own again.

"We still have the gym shower," I said, taking the cross bar off the guest bedroom door so we could get out to the gym roof.

Dog followed us onto the roof without worry, not seeming to mind the height as he walked across the gang plank. As soon as he was on the roof, he started a circuit of the outside edge of the building, sniffing about madly then peeing every few feet as he marked his territory. I didn't have the heart to tell him there weren't likely to be any other dogs sniffing about.

"Half and half, water hog," I told Justine as she rushed to beat me to the shower.

"Of course," she said with surprised humor, the look on her face asking how I could even suggest she'd use more than her half. "Now turn around. I know how excitable you get," she told me, motioning for me to spin around with her hand.

"I need to make sure you don't use more than your half of the water," I pleaded.

She raised her eyebrows at me but wouldn't give in. Make a girl turn into a clawed monster just once and she won't even let you sneak a peek.

I stood there, facing away as she complained about how cold the water was, scrubbing clean before rinsing off with a last squirt of water. I made a mental note to wash the roof off when the sun came up, not liking the idea of all the blood and whatever else ran off us baking on the roof.

When Justine was finished, she wrapped herself in her robe and finally told me it was my turn. The funny thing was, she didn't seem to have the same restriction about watching me shower. She sat on one of the workout benches, watching me scrub down as she talked about the attack.

It was the first time the undead had really tried to get into New Dover. She asked me if I thought we'd really pushed them back. I didn't answer. I understood what she meant. If the undead had really wanted to get over the wall, they could have just swarmed the outside of the buses until they had a ramp of bodies. The attack hadn't been well planned; it was almost as if a few grays and their hordes had decided to make a go at us on their own.

I didn't really want to talk about it. It was easy to get stuck dwelling on the unknowns, and my thoughts and feelings weren't going to make anyone feel warm and fuzzy, including myself. I ignored her and did my best to change the subject, complaining that she got to watch while I'd been forced to turn around.

That's when Justine revealed just how much of a chauvinist she was. She informed me that as part of the superior sex, seeing me naked wasn't going to result in her losing control and jumping on top of me. I acted shocked, but she was probably right.

I refused to be self-conscious as I took my shower. If she wanted to watch, I wasn't going to blush for her. "I'm just amazed that it can look so innocent," she blurted out as I washed my hair. My eyes popped open to look at her as she smiled wickedly back at me. I was forced to use a jet of water to clear the soap from my eyes as Justine giggled quietly.

She handed me a towel when I was done, slapping my butt affectionately as she snuggled against me in her fluffy robe. We made it to the edge of the roof leading down into the spare room before we realized Dog wasn't with us.

I called him a few times, whistling at him to come. "Damn dog is going to make me chase him," I told Justine. We saw him sitting at the far corner of the gym looking at us, not moving. Of course he'd pick the dark corner on the far side of the gym, past the port-o-potty looking building where the stairs came up from below. It was about as far from us as he could get and still be on the roof.

"I'm going to go get some clothes on," Justine said, standing on tiptoes to kiss me on the cheek.

I was high as a kite as I walked across the green outdoor carpeting onto the black tar and pebbles of the roof. Dog could be a pain in the ass tonight, and I wasn't going to care. I half expected him to bolt as I got closer, but he just sat there, looking at me with huge doggy eyes.

I got ten feet from him before I realized his eyes were wide with fear, his fur jumping in little twitches as the muscles underneath fired off in spasms of terror. I understood his fear as an ice-cold arm slipped around my neck and the sharp edge of a blade pricked the flesh at my side.

I was screwed. The knife was positioned to slide between my ribs; I'd be lucky to get out a loud whisper before I was dead.

"Tell the dog to get," a hoarse voice scratched at my eardrum. The arm around my neck loosened just a fraction so I could speak in a whisper.

"Go, Dog. Go," I begged. Thankfully the words broke whatever spell Dog was under, and he ran to the gangplank, pissing the whole way.

"Thank you," the voice whispered, this time a little easier. The arm around my neck straightened and disappeared behind me as the tip of the knife left my side. "You can turn around," my ambusher said, a touch of amusement in his words.

"Haeslig," I said when I saw him. "Did you take a wrong turn?" I asked, trying to sound calm. He smiled back at me, rocking onto his heels, completely unconcerned that he was in the heart of enemy territory. I tried to look equally relaxed, but I had a gray in front of me and a thirty foot drop all around—and nothing on but a towel.

"It seems you overheard more than I thought," the gray said, surprised I knew his name. He stepped back into the shadows. For just a split second, I thought he was going to evaporate off the roof, but he was just grabbing something hidden in the darkness.

I shivered as I realized how easily the gray faded into the night. He could have been there the whole time I was showering, buck naked, with all my weapons left down in the apartment. The chill went to my stomach, turning to anger as I thought about him watching Justine shower as well.

She would have sensed him, though, wouldn't she? She'd been hypersensitive to the presence of the undead since the first time she'd shifted. Either Haeslig hadn't been on the roof until she'd left or she'd been so tired she'd missed him.

Haeslig slid his knife into its sheath, the shiny blade disappearing as if being swallowed by the dark. I tensed, wanting to attack while his weapon was no longer in his hand.

"Relax. I'm not here to hurt you," Haeslig said in an eerie approximation of a soothing voice.

"You seem to keep popping up. What do you want?" I said bluntly.

"I could say the same about you. Everywhere I look, you and your little friend keep turning up as well."

At the mention of Justine, I took an involuntary step forward.

Haeslig put his hands up, the whites of his palms floating in the darkness. "I could have killed you before you knew I was here. Please remember that," he said.

"So I'm supposed to trust you? After what you did to Mr. Deringer?" I spat at him. He'd taken the old man's life as I lay hidden in the rain, too wounded to stop him. It had been on the second or third day after the end began.

"Maybe trust is too strong of a word, but I've saved you more trouble than you know," he said. "I could have told Sam about the others who went to the marina. He would have torn apart your little town to find you."

I hesitated. I'd been so sure we'd just gotten lucky that night. Billy and Tara had died at the marina, and Haeslig had let Sam and the others believe it had been Justine and I who had fallen. I'd assumed whatever memories he stole from old Mr. Deringer had been muddied, but I'd been wrong.

"Why?" was all I could get out.

"Sometimes we are forced to follow those who are unworthy, and Sam would have been twice the devil if he'd been elevated by our master." The words hung in the air. I wasn't sure what to say. "But those days are past. I didn't come here to talk. I came to give you a gift," Haeslig said, pushing something out of the dark with his foot until it was directly in front of me.

A black PVC storage case, four feet long and six inches deep, sat on the roof at my feet. I kicked it with my foot but kept my eyes on him.

"I really would have done it already if that was why I was here," he told me frankly.

"Reading my mind?" I asked, bending over to pry open the metal clasps.

"No. I can only do that by tasting you," Haeslig offered,

his voice slippery and suggestive. I shivered at the thought.

I opened the case to find a military issue M25 sniper rifle, four clips, and at least ten boxes of ammunition. "What kind of gift is this?" I asked. It didn't make any sense.

"My master was left in a bad state after you destroyed his portal across the river. His brothers know he is weakened and came hunting for him, so he puts me out here on the edge of the battle while he hides. I don't think I'm meant to survive." Haeslig said the last part very pointedly.

"So you want me to shoot him?" I asked, wondering if I was being recruited to be his Oswald.

"Oh, no. I don't think you could do that," Haeslig replied without even trying to hide his smugness. "Your job is to help draw him out. All you need is a little more exposure, and the right words to get back to him, and he will come forth. Once he knows who you are, and that you're killing his lieutenants, he won't be able to stay in the shadows."

"Ah, I understand. You want me to be the bait. And why would I want to do that for you?" I asked, standing back up to look him in the eyes.

"Because of her," Haeslig replied, pointing a long pale finger toward the apartment.

Half naked or not, I was going to kill him. I stepped forward, driving my fist into his jaw. It felt like punching a slab of frozen beef.

"She feels it pulling at her, doesn't she?" he said, taking a step sideways, dodging my second roundhouse with ease. The words stopped me in my tracks.

"What does she feel?" I demanded. He knew.

"I tracked her when she went running last night. She was heading north, but my master told me he was moving south," Haeslig confided, as if I'd understand what he meant.

"And why does this matter?" I demanded. I was scared and confused, and my damn dog had run pissing himself instead of staying with me.

"He doesn't know she's alive, but he is looking for another who can unlock a portal for him. She's still linked to him because of what was begun at the power plant, and every time he searches, she is pulled to him like a magnet. Eventually she won't be able to resist, and she will turn and go to him." The last was a promise.

"He's doing this to her?" I asked, swallowing hard.

"He needs to find another key to open a portal before his brothers hunt him down and kill him. Every gray he loses is one he cannot replace until he has a new gateway. You draw him out, and I will see to the rest. Then your Justine will be free of his will pulling at her."

"And all I have to do is kill your brothers?" I asked grimly.

Haeslig made a grunting affirmation and pulled back into the darkness, disappearing from view. He was getting ready to bolt.

"One more question," I demanded.

"Yes?" Haeslig responded, his voice quiet and just audible.

"Why are their eyes cut up?"

"Odd, that you would ask me about them, but if you must, I will grant you this second gift: Ravi is their master, and he takes their eyes. The Ravens are hunters, bred to walk in the light to hunt your kind as well as mine, while we are weaker. Their night eyes are no good for this, so Ravi cuts them out and uses…replacements." His voice was fading. "Oh, one last word of advice: be careful with the dog. If the wind had been blowing the wrong way, you might have had a hundred brutes tearing down your gate." Then he was gone.

I didn't have to ask where the replacement eyes came from. I was sure the donors weren't willing participants. And I didn't even want to think about what could have happened if the wind had been blowing the wrong way. What was I supposed to do with Dog? Toss him over the side of the outer wall and let him get torn to pieces?

Chapter 10

I felt like I'd just done a huge hit of psychedelics as I walked back into the apartment, the world spinning around me in unbelievable distortions. A gray had just given me the same weapon I'd carried as a Marine Scout in order to hunt his own kind.

My steps slowed as I made my way into the spare room. I expected Justine to be waiting for me, fully dressed and aiming her MP5K at the door as I came through, but she was already in bed, rubbing Dog's stomach as his hind legs twitched and fluttered in scratchy happiness.

I leaned the gun case against the wall and slipped inside the room, shutting the door behind me, feeling like I'd somehow dodged a bullet.

"Come to bed," Justine said, pushing Dog out of my spot. He gave me a look as he circled and lay down on his blanket in the corner.

My stomach was turning over as I thought about what had just happened. What would Justine do if she knew I'd talked to a gray? At the least she'd be pissed; at worst, she'd think I'd turned traitor. Of course, the discussion hadn't exactly been optional.

Justine brought my speeding mind to a complete halt as she slid a hand across my belly, not stopping when she reached the edge of my towel. I stuttered out her name and tried to roll toward her, but she told me to stay still, teasing that if I touched her, she'd make me sleep on the floor.

Everything else slipped away as she caressed me. The feel of her warm leg against mine and the smell of her hair melded into a single intense feeling as my legs began to tense. Justine started to move her hips against my leg, a faint moan escaping her lips as her mouth brushed across the skin of my shoulder.

I was inching closer and closer to climax, my legs tensing as Justine kissed my shoulder, her breath heavy in my ear. I felt her teeth touch my skin, then felt them sharpen, piercing my flesh with ease. I froze, not sure what to do. She pulled back, kissing the small wounds with warm lips.

I heard her swallow hard and gritted my teeth as she tightened her grip ever so slightly on a very delicate part of my body. I was afraid we'd crossed the line again, even more so that she was going take an important part of me with her if she lost control. A hiss of breath escaped my lips as I felt her grip loosen, but I didn't breathe again until she told me she was OK.

"Why don't we just cuddle," I said, trying to roll toward her again. She shushed me, pinning me to the bed with a hand.

"I just can't get too excited, but you can," she whispered in my ear, caressing me faster.

I cried out her name when I came, and then begged her to stop as I reached the painful post orgasm stage. She rolled away from me with a contented sigh, letting me put my hand on her side. I caressed her flank gently, but she slapped me when my stroke lingered too long on her rear, warning me to behave.

I kissed the side of her neck, feeling guilty that the pleasure was one sided, but we were both afraid of what would happen if she let go. She told me drowsily that she loved me, which meant everything to me, and then fell quietly to sleep.

I thought the guy was supposed to fall asleep after sex? Not the girl. I guess she had done all the work, though.

Justine was up and about the next morning before me. I could hear her moving about the kitchen, but I was just so comfortable I didn't want to get out of bed—right up until Dog pulled my covers off and proceeded to get into a wrestling match with them on the floor.

She smiled at me as I entered the living room. I sat down on the couch and played with Dog as Justine opened several MREs and debated out loud with herself over which one would give Dog the least amount of gas. What can I say? She's a special girl.

She decided on beef stew, which made me question the soundness of her selection criteria, and then laid out our breakfast. We had juice and vegetable rice with the ever-present peanut butter and crackers; the MRE crackers were a bit hard, but the peanut butter was first class.

"I think you should stay in today," I told her, spreading peanut butter onto a cracker as I watched her reaction.

She stopped chewing and looked at me as if I'd just called her ugly. I'd meant to work it into the conversation smoothly, but I was nervous and just blurted it out.

"Really?" she asked, narrowing her eyes.

"We need to earn tickets today, but I'm afraid what happened last night is related to Dog," I told her, waving to the mutt as he pushed his bowl around the kitchen floor, licking every last molecule of stew off it.

"What do you mean?"

"Which way was the wind blowing last night?" I asked. "I'd bet my ass it was blowing to the east. I think there is a reason there aren't any dogs left."

It sounded nuts, but we'd both seen the shredded corpses of several canines back in Jersey. Dog was the first living specimen we'd seen since before.

"So what do you want me to do?" she asked, clearly not agreeing to stay inside the compound while I went out on my own but wanting to hear what I had to say and see where it ranked on the stupidity meter.

"You need to shave Dog and bathe him. Maybe hang some car fresheners from his collar," I suggested.

Dog stopped nosing his bowl around and barked at me when I said his name. She gave me a hard stare, but I kept my face carefully neutral.

"If you get hurt out there, I'll be really pissed," she said, tacitly agreeing to stay inside the walls.

"I'll be real careful," I promised.

I finished eating and waited until she went into the bathroom to grab my things and rush out the door. I snagged the long gun case as I slipped out, amazed and relieved she hadn't noticed it. The stairs almost claimed me as I fumbled with everything, trying to keep from dropping my gear and tripping over it at the same time.

I hated leaving her behind, even for a few hours, but I didn't want her to know what I was doing, or why. I grabbed my scavenging cart from under the stairs, dumping everything in before rolling away in a hurry. It was time to go hunting.

The streets were fairly empty as I pushed my cart along the sidewalk, but I saw people peeking out of partially boarded up windows, nervously looking out at the world. The previous day's attack at the gate had soured the mood inside New Dover.

I found a moldy couch sitting outside a garage door on a side street and paused to settle in my gear. I sat the gun case across the top of my cart, hesitating before I flipped the latches. Part of me expected the case to be empty, maybe wanted it to be empty, but when I threw the lid open, the gun lay safely nestled inside. No chance it was a dream.

I unpacked the M25 carefully, taking apart the bolt and making sure everything was in good working order. The gun appeared to be new. I loaded several clips and slid them into my cargo pockets before slinging the weapon over my shoulder.

I hid the gun case under the couch, looking around to see if anyone was nearby, and then rolled back out onto the main street. I'd spent a lot of time walking around New Dover when I was recovering from my back injury, but since then, I'd stuck mostly to our side of town. The majority of people were now living around the center of New Dover, where the lights were strung, giving the less populated streets an empty, haunted feeling.

I walked up to the western gate without being noticed and could have walked through if I'd been able to open it from street level. The exit was obstructed by a large mail delivery truck on one side, and a semi trailer on the other. I had to call up to get the attention of the guards on top of the mail truck; they were so focused on watching the other side of the street they were oblivious to what was behind them.

They let me out with a grumble about having to open the gate and shut it behind me with a bang the moment I was through. I didn't say anything to them about leaving their backs exposed. They were amped up after the night before and wouldn't have listened anyway.

I waited until I was out of sight of the gate and picked up my pace until I reached a slow run. I kept to the center of the streets and made a beeline for the quickie mart. If I was going to accomplish the goals I'd set for myself for the first day of hunting season, I was going to have to hurry.

The store was about the same as we'd left it, except for evidence of a raccoon or maybe some rats that had gotten into the racks of candy. I cleared the store quickly, scanning the aisles and the back room with my flashlight before loading up my cart. I stocked up on dry goods. It looked like a decent amount of volume, but it was light, which was what I wanted.

My back was slick with sweat and my shirt soaked through when I slowed to a walk, coming into sight of the west gate. "You running from something?" one of the soldiers yelled when I was closer, my running making him nervous.

"Tickets," I told him. "Just tickets. I'll be back this way as soon as I drop this stuff off," I warned him. Let him think what he would. After the night we'd had, scavengers could probably ask for double rates. The same soldier told me he needed more chew when he let me back out. I told him I'd do what I could and slipped out the gate. It was like anything else: a little grease kept the wheels moving.

I followed my same route back to the quickie mart, not something I would have done if I hadn't been in a rush, and quickly repeated my earlier performance. I cleared the store and loaded my cart up with the last bit of valuables from inside, being sure to take several tins of chew from over the register before heading out.

When I was just out of sight of the west gate, I found a minivan and hid my cart inside. I'd completed the easiest part of the day; it was time to move on to the hard part. I headed north, moving fast, keeping a pistol in my hands as I crossed into the territory where the Ravens and the other grays had warred.

The streets looked different in the daylight, but I could easily tell where the battle had taken place. Blood and bits of bone stained the ground, and small chunks of unidentifiable meat littered the ground for several blocks. I moved up onto the sidewalk to keep from running through the worst of it. I was getting tired of burning my clothes.

I was glad to put the battleground behind me and put my feet on streets not stained with blood. I pushed on and found what I was looking for just a little further north.

The store was named "Gently Used." It sounded like a bad Internet dating site to me. It was actually a sporting goods store specializing in selling and trading used equipment. I'd passed it the other night on my way to find Justine without really thinking about it. There wasn't much need for soccer balls or hockey sticks at the moment, but I'd remembered it the moment I started to formulate my plans.

Finding the door of the dark store locked tight, I picked up a rock, more worried about being quick than being quiet. Justine would've been mad. I always told her to take the quiet route.

I expected the rock to go through the door in a nice explosion of glass. It surprised me by bouncing off and flying back past my head. I checked the door: barely a mark where the rock had hit.

Rock one was about the size of my hand. I found rock two in the parking lot: half a cinder block with nice pointed edges. I did one full turn and let go of the chunk of concrete, launching it at the door. The glass shattered with a loud pop, shards flying inward to spill across the floor in front of the cash registers.

I flicked on my flashlight and climbed in. I wandered around the store, picking up a few rolls of cloth tape but not finding what I'd truly come for until I reached the last aisle. I grabbed two cans and stuffed them into the cargo pocket on my hip.

After peeking outside the door to make sure the noise hadn't attracted anything, I climbed out. I moved out at a fast run, feeling like the day was flying by too quickly. It was before lunch, but I wasn't sure how long it was going to take me to get back to camp after it went down, and I wanted as many hours of daylight as I could get.

I headed east and then south, slowing several times to survey the area before I found suitable ground: a nice two-story house with steep gables overlooking several open lots, giving me a clear view of the self-serve gas station and mini mart one street over.

The house was divided into two apartments, a set of pressure-treated stairs leading up to the second story unit. I took the steps two at a time, trying not to pay attention to the squeaking as I went up. The door at the top of the landing stood open about an inch.

Small, bloody fingerprints were lightly outlined on the edge of the door, as if a bloody little hand had reached out and pulled the door partially closed. I was reaching for my machete when I heard the sound of bare feet slapping on the floor.

I had just enough time to step away from the door before it slammed open and a body came crashing through. The mailman's outfit had just enough time to register before he hit the railing and flipped over, falling head first. When he hit, it sounded like an overripe watermelon exploding.

I'd planned on cleaning the room out with my machete, not wanting to draw attention to myself with any gunfire. The thrall had taken care of it himself though, crashing through the door and over the railing before I could even draw my blade.

I peered over the edge, disgusted but unable to keep myself from taking a look at the way the mailman's head was now spread over a three-by-five-foot area. So my back was turned when something jumped on me, carrying me off balance. I caught myself against the railing as fingers scraped at my skull, trying to get a hold of my hair.

Fortunately, I'm a firm believer in short, low-maintenance haircuts, even after two years of being out of the Marines. I highly advise a buzz cut—it makes it harder for anyone or anything to get a good grip.

Whatever was on my back shimmied up to wrap its legs around my neck, cold flesh slapping into my face as it fought to complete a scissor lock around my airway. Little fingers groped around my forehead, searching for my eyes. I grabbed an ankle and threw my body into a spin, flinging the form on my back into the door jamb with a thud. I kicked its body into the apartment as I stepped through the threshold. The little thrall rolled to a stop against the couch as I whipped my machete free and looked around the apartment.

Sleeping bags covered the floor of the living room, and cases of water stood stacked against the wall by the television. A gas lantern sat on a small end table by the couch.

I amaze myself with what I am able to remember, especially since there were a half dozen ten-year-old thralls looking at me with dead eyes and bared teeth from just inside
the kitchenette. Brown rust covered them from head to toe,
their clothing stiff with dried blood.

I'd been really hoping to find the house was empty. In
my mind the hardest part of the day was still to come, which
was probably my mistake. I should have taken the stairs
quietly and backed off the moment I saw bloody fingerprints
on the door. Rushing will get you killed.

I kicked the door closed behind me and threw the dead
bolt. I didn't want to have to worry about anything else coming at my back. Then I stepped forward, giving me just
enough room to swing my machete. The thralls in the kitch-
en were staring at me, waking up from whatever lethargy
came over them during the day. The first one broke free like
a shot, bounding onto the counter and diving at me, dirty
little hands outstretched.

My blade hesitated for just a split second as my mind
dealt with the cartoon pajama bottoms. Then I swung hard,
taking off the top of the thrall's skull before stepping quickly
to the side. The top of its head hit the vinyl floor at the entry
and slid to a halt while its body crashed into the drywall.

Like sharks, the other thralls reacted to the movement
and the blood, all of them pouring out of the kitchen toward
me at once. It's hard for the mind to adjust to fighting the
undead. Human enemies can be pushed back with wild
swings or even a scream. The undead just press forward,
not caring if you're hacking at them, screaming, or pissing
yourself.

The swarm hit me from two directions, half of them coming over the counter while the other half ran around the
kitchen island in a frontal assault. The bodies coming over
the island got to my blade first, pushing me back against the
door. I cut three small forms down just as the second wave
hit me.

A fat little kid with a round face charged head first, his
hands at his sides as he came in like a bull at the perfect
height to nail me in the crotch. It took me off guard when he
jumped at the last moment, hands flying up to wrap around

my machete arm and scurry up my body. His legs wrapped around my arm like a vice as hands pulled at my shirt collar, trying to get to my neck.

The fat kid was quick. I grabbed him by his hair, holding his teeth away from my flesh as I kicked out, catching the next thrall in the face. I let go of the fat kid's hair, punching him hard. Teeth broke and fell inward, his head bending back with a crunch from the force of the blows.

The thrall I kicked tumbled backwards, carrying the one behind him to the ground as I twisted to the side, ramming my shoulder into the door, trying to crush the fat kid. Foul-smelling liquid squirted out of the kid's rear as I rammed him against the jamb, a jet of brown and red squirting down the wall. I grabbed him by the back of his shirt as his grip loosened, flinging him off me and across the room. He sailed over the kitchen counter to hit the cabinets with a bang, rattling the dishes inside before falling onto the stove on his way to the floor.

The two I'd taken down like bowling pins were back up, but they came straight for me in single file, letting me cut down one and then the other in rapid succession. The fat kid I'd thrown into the kitchen came waddling back out into the main room. His leg or pelvis must have been shattered because his hips moved in a funny way each time he took a step. I took his head off at the neck.

I looked around the living room and the bodies strewn about, stepping over them to check out the rest of the apartment. The scene was horrific. The adults in the main bedroom had been eaten alive. Blood covered the bed, and a thick trail led into the bathroom. Someone had tried to crawl away, but they hadn't made it. A woman's body was lying in front of the tub, most of her lower half missing. Maggots and other things moved inside her open abdomen.

Of course what I was looking for was in the middle of the master bedroom, on the ceiling. I grabbed cushions off the couch and threw them into the bedroom so I could get to the pull-down staircase to the attic without stepping on the bed. I went up the pull-down stairs with a Glock at the ready. There wouldn't be enough room to mess with the machete up there, and I wasn't going to risk getting pinned if someone had managed to escape into the attic after getting bit.

The attic was clear, full of nothing but Christmas decorations and bags of old clothes. I passed by the carefully stored and labeled remnants of holidays past and went to the storm window under the closest gables.

I slid the window open and climbed outside, moving carefully up the slope until I reached the valley where two of the rooflines met. It wasn't too steep, and it would give me some cover from any angle but right in front of the house. I pulled the rifle strap off my chest and checked my field of fire.

A tree on my left partially blocked my line of sight, but I could see the front of the gas station across the way without an issue. Even with iron sights, there was no way I was missing from such short range.

I checked the time and knew I had to move quicker. I still needed to kill my targets and get back inside the wall with my cart before dark. After what had happened the night before, I wasn't about to approach the gate at night, I'd be shot, and no one on guard duty would care one way or another. I left the rifle resting on the roof and climbed back into the house.

The gas station had two pumps and a small office next to its single garage bay. It looked like it had been built when the development was new, twenty years ago, probably constructed on the outside edge of town so people could get gas coming into and out of the community. Then it had been swallowed up as more and more houses went up around it.

I half expected the pumps to have the old numeric displays with moving tiles, but they were the modern kind, complete with credit card swipers. A sign hung over the garage door declared that they worked on all cars, foreign and domestic.

A bundle of newspapers sat on a plastic milk crate next to the office door. The printing was illegible; the whole bundle had turned into a disfigured block of paper after being left out in the elements for so long.

I knocked the papers onto the ground, grabbing the milk carton as I tried the office door. It was unlocked. Beat-up wood paneling covered the office walls, and boxes of motor oil and windshield washer fluid stood stacked up against the front window. I set the milk crate on the desk and set two bottles of windshield washer fluid in before moving to the back of the office.

I tipped one of the shelves clinging to the rear wall, sending manuals and automotive parts books spilling onto the floor. I took my shelf and the milk crate outside, then hurried back to grab the wastebasket from next to the desk.

I took the cloth tape I'd liberated from the sporting goods store and looped it around the milk crate, taping the shelf to it, making myself a little diving board. The milk crate wasn't the perfect height, but when I put the can with its orange top on the concrete curb around the pumps, it all fit together quite nicely. The shelf taped to the milk crate jutted out over the top of the air horn, separated from the activation button by just a few millimeters.

I set the wastebasket on top of the shelf and opened the first bottle of windshield fluid. The button on the air horn didn't start to move until I'd poured half the first gallon into the wastebasket. I set the full bottle on top of the pump over my contraption and drew my machete. It wasn't pretty, but I was reasonably sure it would work.

I took a deep breath and then used the tip of my blade to puncture a slit in the side of the full container. I waited just a moment to make sure a thin but solid stream of blue flowed out of the bottle into the wastebasket before taking off at full speed.

I'd been worried about getting enough pressure on top of the air horn to activate it and misjudged the weight I preloaded in the waste bin. The horn began blowing a continuous, annoying cry before I reached the door at the top of the stairs leading into the apartment. I pushed the door shut behind me and leapt over the bodies strewn through the living room to get to the attic.

My foot slipped on the shingles when I was halfway out the window, causing me to do a painful split. I ignored the pain and pulled myself through, trying not to slide off the roof as I hurried to where my rifle lay resting between the gables.

I settled into the valley, watching as movement resolved into thralls coming from up and down the street. The air horn continued to blare as I searched. Dozens of thralls were already in sight, moving toward the noise at a confused walk, some of them veering off for a few steps then correcting as the sun blinded them.

I waited. Two minutes passed with the horn still shrieking before it began to weaken, its tone taking on a squeaky quality that gradually faded as the horn ran out of air. At least a hundred thralls stood around the pumps, pushed tight up against one another as those behind pressed forward blindly.

I was doing my best Justine impression under my breath, cursing as I searched the thralls for the target I wanted. They were nothing but dead meat. It was a gray I needed.

I didn't trust Haeslig, but I believed part of what he was saying. If I wanted to free Justine, I was going to need to kill whatever connection they still had to her, and to do that, I needed to get to the boss. I was sure Haeslig was using me, and Justine, but that didn't mean I couldn't use him right back.

One of the thralls pressed up against the gas station office held something up over his head. The bright orange plastic on top of the horn was clearly visible even without optics. I wondered what the thrall was doing until I saw a hand reach down from behind the sheet metal sign on the roof and take the horn.

I was a little disappointed in myself. I'd been looking for a gray to come walking directly into my trap, to play by my rules. I should have known they would be smarter than that.

I sighted on the sign on the roof and took my shot. A loud twang filled the air as the bullet punched through the sheet metal, and then a gray stood up. He dropped the air horn and clutched his chest, pulling his hand away to look at it. My second shot hit him at the base of his neck, directly in his suprasternal notch.

The gray dropped off the side of the building and out of sight. I watched, expecting the thralls to go berserk, but they continued to mill about aimlessly. I knew grays were tough, but there was no way it could have survived the second shot.

I watched, wondering if maybe the gray was somehow hanging onto life as it bled out. The thralls continued milling about as I waited for them to go mad. I almost ignored the movement off to my left, but it drew my eye back just in time to see a shadow disappear behind the large tree bordering the empty lot.

I tried to sink into the roof as I watched. The thralls at the gas station were slowly spreading out, seemingly at random, but I kept my eye on the tree, positive I'd seen something move at its base. A flicker of movement behind the tree settled it for me. Something was definitely there, searching, just like I was. The head of a gray slowly poked around the tree, scanning the line of houses around me. He knew there was a shooter, but he hadn't been able to locate me—yet.

I watched and waited as the gray played peek-a-boo behind the tree. His head would appear for a moment, then move just before I could squeeze the trigger. I had my attention focused on the gray, trying to decide if I should risk taking the shot at the corner of his head or continue to wait, when my brain registered what was on the periphery of my vision.

The thralls had started to disperse like random particles from the gas station, but more than half were moving across the empty lot in my direction. And their body language had changed. That was one of the creepy things about thralls. They moved like they were half drunk when they were on their own, but the moment their gray gave them an order, they moved with purpose, their spines straightening and their heads lifting to look at something other than the ground.

I lifted my eyes to take a closer look at the wave of thralls crossing the open lot. The moment I did, the cohesiveness of the group fell apart. The thralls' heads fell and they started moving in a more random pattern, no longer crossing the lot in a generally straight path.

I sighted in quickly on the tree, taking the only shot the gray hiding there had left me. I cursed myself for an idiot as I shattered his kneecap, letting go of my rifle. The curse turned into a scream as I rolled onto my back, not caring if the rifle slid down the roof.

My arms crossed as I drew my pistols and fired blindly up the angle of the roof, knowing he had to be very close. When I'd lifted my head to look at the thralls, they'd immediately stopped moving. There was no way the gray behind the tree could have seen such a small movement. Someone had to be much closer, nearly on top of me.

My first wild rounds passed over the gray's shoulder as he leapt through the air, his teeth bared and his clawed fingers outstretched. I corrected as his shadow crossed above me, the .40 caliber slugs tearing into each of his shoulders and working their way down his torso as I emptied both my Glocks. The last rounds punched into him just before his body collided with mine.

He landed on top of me hard, his weight driving the air out of my lungs. I punched at him with my pistols, trying to fight my way from under his weight, forcing us both onto the main slope of the roof. We began sliding head first toward the roof's edge.

The gray's mouth was next to my ear, his breath wet and heavy as he exhaled. I pistol whipped him from behind, our bodies continuing to slide down the slope as I pummeled him. The back of his skull was shattered bone held together by ragged skin by the time I realized he was dead. We came to a precarious halt at the bottom of the slope, the back of my head resting against the aluminum gutter.

I slid my pistols into my cargo pockets, flattening against the shingles to get all the traction I could. I lifted the gray's head as I tilted him off me, looking at his face. He was a standard gray; no one had modified his eyes.

He looked like a geeky twenty-year-old who had been sitting in front of a computer monitor all summer, avoiding the sun. With his mouth closed, he wouldn't have looked out of place on any number of city streets throughout the world. It made me wonder how long they'd been lurking among us.

He might have passed for human at a distance, but pushing him off me, I could feel the difference. The son of a bitch was heavy. He hit the ground with a nice thud.

Getting back up the roof was not easy. I rolled onto my stomach and did odd pushups to get myself far enough up the roof so I could spin around and get my feet facing down slope. I'm sure it looked very graceful.

I grabbed my rifle on my way back up the roof, stopping next to the window to look out over the lot, expecting to see a wall of undead coming my way. I was surprised by what I saw. They weren't coming for me; they were running.

The gray I'd wounded at the tree was trying to get away. He was still standing, but barely. I could see the top of his head bob up and down as he hopped along, struggling to escape with the help of a protective ring of thralls.

I smiled as I snugged the rifle against my shoulder and aimed directly into the rear of the undead formation. Three thralls dropped to the ground as my first rounds passed through them. Two of them struggled to get up, but I ignored them as the primary mass of undead continued on, the formation collapsing in to fill the empty space. I put more rounds into the group, dropping multiple thralls with each bullet, taking out bodies faster than the remaining undead could fill the gaps.

There are days when work is so much fun.

I ejected the clip and slammed a new one home, being careful not to lose my empty magazine so I could reload it later. The thralls had re-formed around the gray, but their numbers were thinned. I sighted back in on my target. Thralls obscured most of his body, leaving me fleeting glimpses as he hobbled along. I shifted my aim slightly, tracking the gray's right arm where it hung draped over a thrall's shoulder. I took careful aim and took my shot.

The bullet struck the gray's elbow, passing through it in a little explosion of meat and bone before hitting the thrall in the back of the neck. The thrall collapsed as if a switch had been thrown, taking the gray down in the process. The gray rolled off the thrall's body, landing on his back. The stump of his arm waved in the air as he screamed, blood spurting in jets.

The gray continued to scream as he tried to clamp his hand over the end of his stump, his legs thrashing and kicking. Thralls circled around him, trying to shield him as they reached down to pick him up. Either their coordination sucked or his control over them was slipping because they couldn't quite keep a hold on him. They'd get him halfway off the ground and then drop him.

Up and down the street, doors and windows slammed opened or shattered as thralls stumbled from their daytime rest. The gray was calling for help.

It wasn't going to do him any good. He should have called his horde before he was wounded in the middle of open ground.

The thralls almost had the gray back to his feet. He was gripping a thrall so tightly with his remaining hand that I could see where rotten flesh had squeezed between his fingers.

I sighted in again and took two rapid shots. It had been fun, but it was time to go. The first round hit the gray at the base of the neck; the second, in the back of his head. A distinct feeling of accomplishment came over me as he crumpled to the ground.

As the gray fell, the thralls around him paused, frozen as whatever linked them to him unraveled. It was the moment I had been waiting for. Another second, and the thralls were free. They tore into each other and everything around them in a berserk rage.

Several things struck me as I watched the enraged thralls tear into each other. The first was the number of thralls the gray was linked to—the carnage extended for blocks around me. The second was the tight ball of thralls fighting their way clear of the chaos to the far right of my vision. Another gray had to be out there, hiding in their midst. I slung my rifle over my shoulder as I crept back to the window. The escaping gray didn't matter, without a scope, there was no way I was going to even find him in their midst. Besides, I'd bagged my limit for the day. It was time to get back to New Dover.

I came out of the apartment to find a female thrall on all fours, handfuls of the rotten mailman in her mouth and more of him smeared across her face. I came down the stairs with my machete in one hand and a Glock in the other, watching as she gorged herself. I was halfway down when I hit a squeaky step. Her head popped up, her eyes locking onto me. Suddenly she was on her feet and leaping onto the stairs in a frightening flash of speed. I put a bullet in her head before I had time to stop myself.

She moved so fast, I shot her without thinking about it. It was reflex. She'd moved so quickly. I took a second look at her. Her clothes looked like she'd lived in them for weeks, but her flesh was intact and firm, not rotting and sloughing off like the older thralls. I tried not to think about what it meant as I ran.

I got back to my cart drenched and sore, but I was in one piece—and I was a step closer to achieving my goal. The only thing left to do was face Justine and come up with a good explanation for why it took me all day to get two cart-loads back to town.

Chapter 11

The town was still in shock from the attack on the east gate, and the streets had already begun to empty with the sun just beginning its decline in the west. I used my scavenging tickets to buy a few gallons of water and some canned goods. I would have preferred a few MREs, but they were getting harder to find.

I lollygagged after leaving the supply depot, trying to hold off on going back to the apartment, afraid Justine was going to smell the blood on me. I'd tossed my long-sleeve shirt, but I was still worried.

I was thinking about how to distract her long enough to get up to the gym and shower when my boots crunched on broken glass. Someone had thrown beer bottles against the side of our apartment, covering the ground and our stairs in shards of glass.

I spun around, grinding glass into the concrete beneath me, drawing a Glock from under my left armpit as I turned. The large, potbellied man creeping up on me stopped in mid stride, a glare on his face. The top of his head was bald and sun burned the color of his orange-red beard.

"You with that bitch," the man spit at me, his eyes locked on my gun. He held a two-foot length of weathered hardwood in one hand, its end covered in a band of solid steel. Its intended purpose was to fit into a floor jack, but I doubted the man holding it saw it as anything more than a mace.

"You really shouldn't talk about a lady like that," I told him, sliding the Glock back into its holster before slipping the rifle sling off my shoulder and leaning the weapon against the building.

Red smiled at me, revealing several missing teeth and a few more black with decay. His hand flexed on his club as I faced off with him. It wasn't until I took a step in his direction that his look of steadfast anger wavered. I was coming at him bare handed even though I had a machete strapped to my leg and a pistol under each armpit.

"You, your dog, and that woman are going to find yourselves on the other side of the wall," he threatened, his courage wavering.

I drew my machete so he could see the thin ribbon of sharpened steel not hidden by the matte black paint covering the rest of the blade. "Where were you when they broke through the east gate?" I asked.

"I was on the south wall," he said defensively.

"Well, I was standing between them and you, with this," I said, twisting the blade so the edge glinted in the fading daylight. "And the lady was standing on top of the gate killing a gray while you were listening to the fight from a quarter mile away."

Red tried to process the data, matching up the stories he'd heard with what he saw standing in front of him. "Be careful," he warned, trying to sound menacing before hurrying away. I let him go.

The door to the apartment opened when I hit the top stair and Justine looked me over, a neutral expression on her face. I pecked her on the cheek before sliding past her like I was coming home from the office after a normal day's work.

She followed me into the living room and then the bedroom as I hung up my weapons and put the rifle in the corner. Her eyes followed the gun as I set it down. "That's new," she said, watching me with sharp eyes.

"Some of the soldiers gave it to me after what we did yesterday," I blurted out, not really thinking about whether it would hold water or not.

"Good thing you got your reward before they found out about Dog."

"It that what happened here?" I asked quickly. I'd been so nervous about her seeing through me I'd forgotten to ask what should have been my first question.

"Just about. The day started out OK. WC came over to see if you would give him a shooting lesson and ended up helping me give Dog a bath," she said, watching me. She could tell I was holding something back, and she intended to torture me for it. I could see it in her eyes.

"That was very nice of him," I said, trying not to give her an easy win.

Dog slunk into the bedroom as we talked with his tail

tucked between his legs looking very sad, which, given the way he looked, was completely understandable. Someone had taken scissors to him and done a very poor job trimming most of his fur off.

"Poor Dog," I told him, rubbing his head as he came over to me for support, his tail barely lifting from between his legs. "What did she do to you?" I asked him, rubbing the bony spot on the top of his skull. As I scratched his noggin, the scent of cinnamon filled my nose.

"I'm glad WC was around. Dog really didn't want to be groomed. It was almost a wrestling match," Justine said cheerfully, her eyes narrowing just a bit as she watched me, gauging my reaction. I hate it when my response is a fore-gone conclusion.

I forced myself not to react, but I felt my jaw muscle twitching as I fought the heat building inside. She was wear-ing a pair of light cotton pants and a tight T-shirt. I could eas-ily see the dark circles of her small nipples, and the thought of WC seeing her dressed like that created an instant burn-ing behind my ears that ran into my neck as jealousy flared. I refused to completely give in, though.

"That was very nice of him," I replied stiffly. "So what happened after that?"

"I guess by the time we were done washing and trim-ming Dog, the rumors had spread into the Fort. The religious wackos wanted me to put him over the wall." She stopped, thinking about what to say next. "I told them no."

I nodded, sensing there was more she wasn't telling me. Now we were both keeping secrets. "Did you have to shoot anyone?"

Justine laughed at me. "No, I didn't have to shoot any-one, but there may have been a few bruises. It happened after we were done clipping the mongrel. We were going to go get a six-pack when a few of them stopped us on the street. You would have thought it was funny; they thought WC was the one they had to worry about."

"I'm sure I would have been laughing," I said dryly.

"Yeah," she agreed. "The glass didn't start flying until later. I figured I'd let them get some of their aggression out. But enough about my day; how was yours?"

"I made us a few tickets," I told her as she sniffed lightly in my direction. "I stumbled on a few thralls, but they didn't put up much of a fight."

She nodded slowly. "Tomorrow we should hit the Acme on North Dupont. WC told me there were four semis parked at the loading docks, just waiting to be emptied out."

"Is it safe to leave Dog here alone?" I asked her.

She paused, watching me and thinking about her words before she replied. "You're probably right, and WC said he'd come over anytime if I needed company."

Touché. I wanted to say something else, but she disappeared into the kitchen before I could come up with anything. I grabbed a bottle of water and an MRE and headed out onto the gym roof. My head hurt from lying to her, and my mind was full of evil visions about her afternoon with WC. What the hell did WC stand for anyway? I would have to ask him before I pulled his fingernails out one by one.

Metal slammed on metal as I worked away my frustration on the gym equipment, night closing around me. My experience with women was so limited I'd never really had a chance to feel jealousy. It put me on edge.

I knew Justine was just torturing me, but WC clearly liked her, and he would get to spend some time with her again the next day. There was nothing I could do to stop it—not if I wanted to keep Justine safe.

"You were very impressive today," Haeslig's raspy voice called from the shadows. I jumped up, reaching for a Glock before I remembered we were being friendly. After all, I was sort of working for him at the moment. I settled on slipping the shoulder holsters over my arms before moving closer to the dark side of the roof.

"I can't tell if you're yanking my chain or being honest," I said, trying to focus on him.

"Oh, I am being honest. I thought I'd lost you when the third gray made it onto the roof behind you. How did you know he was there?"

"If I told you, it wouldn't be my secret anymore," I said childishly. I didn't want to tell him it was something as simple as seeing how the thralls moved. Maybe if he thought I could sense his kind, he'd be a little off balance around me. I didn't like the way he kept creeping up on me in the dark. It made me feel as if he held too many of the cards.

"Very well," Haeslig sighed. "I come bearing more gifts."

His foot pushed a satchel out from behind the outbuilding. "There is a decent-sized nest at each of the circles on the enclosed map. Getting close to them will be dangerous, but I am sure you will be able to work around that."

"I'm sure," I echoed glibly.

"There are blocks of C4 and detonators in here with the map. You are familiar with this explosive and how to use it?" Haeslig almost sounded eager, which I found very interesting—and just a bit worrying.

"Yes, I know how to use it, and when this is done, you're going to give me something else," I said. When he didn't reply, I continued. "The rifle will be a lot more accurate, with a decent scope."

"Let's see how well you complete your assigned task first," Haeslig replied quietly.

The noncommittal answer made me mad. Why give me a rifle and then refuse to give me a scope? "You seem like a very dangerous and capable fellow, why don't you just go work for Ravi and be done with it?"

"Oh, Daniel, you really do keep surprising me."

"I'm trying to figure out if I should continue with our bargain," I told him pointedly. "Why does this Ravi want you so badly when you clearly have so much loyalty to your current master?"

I thought I might have been talking to the night after the silence stretched on, but finally Haeslig answered. "If Ravi could bring me to his side, it would give him a huge advantage, not to mention the political value of stealing one of Han-su's inner circle away from him."

"And yet your own master leaves you out on the frontlines when you are so valuable," I taunted him.

"I guess he's afraid I have ambitions that might impact his well-being," Haeslig said sweetly. The gray laughed, the noise fading as he fled into the night.

I carried the bag of explosives into the spare room, wondering what I was doing. And on top of that, I couldn't stop thinking about how easily Haeslig came to visit. If he had no trouble getting over the wall and onto the gym roof, I surely others could do it as well. I made sure the cross bar locking off the spare room was tightly in place before I walked into our bathroom.

I'd intended to shower on the gym roof, but after my little visit from Haeslig, it didn't seem like such a good idea. I lit a candle and used a gallon of bottled water to shower: a little bit of water to soap up and scrub and the rest to rinse off.

Justine sat on the couch reading by lantern light when I walked back into the living room. The book was thin and could have been any work of short fiction, but I knew it with just a single glimpse of the cover. She was reading *The Art of War* (孫子兵法) by Sun-Tzu, a personal favorite. It was also on the required reading list for those in the special warfare school at Fort Benning. I'd read the book at least ten times since the day I'd had to write a summary of the values of each of the thirteen chapters.

"What chapter are you on?" I asked.

"Nine." She must have been reading it on and off throughout the day. The whole thing is only a little over a hundred pages, but I hadn't seen her with it before, so I assumed she'd burnt through most of it that afternoon.

"The Army on the March or Moving the Force?"

"What?" she asked, looking at me with puzzled eyebrows.

"The ninth chapter was translated into two popular titles, depending on who published the text. What's the name of your chapter nine?"

"You really scare me sometimes," she said, flicking back a few pages to find the chapter heading. "Neither. It's Movement and Development of Troops," she said, a touch smugly.

"The first two I mentioned were translated by non-Chinese. I bet your copy is different?"

"Damn," she said, flipping the book over so we could both see the back cover. It was translated by Chow-Hou Wee.

"Does it make sense?" I asked, sitting next to her with my hands between my legs, slowly relaxing until our knees touched.

"Some of it makes sense, but some of it doesn't," she said honestly. "What is he trying to say with verse seven?" she asked, letting one of her hands fall onto my leg as she leaned over to show me the passage.

I didn't tell her I didn't need to see it; I'd written each chapter and verse up before, arguing the merits of the statements in the context of the modern world.

"When this was written, it had two meanings. Sun-Tzu stated you should get off the salt marshes without delay for dual reasons. The first was simply because of the inability to get fresh water and food. The second reason was topographical. Salt marshes tended to be low and flat—not the best place to defend if you're attacked."

"You didn't even have to think about that."

"No," I agreed. "I've read it a few times and had to write it up when I was in training. You'd be surprised how a book written six hundred years before Christ still has a lot of military merit."

"Some of it seems pretty basic," she thought out loud, flipping back a few pages and repositioning herself so she was leaning against me.

"Now it is, but how many action movies have you seen where some basic principle came from this book? Think about how many times the good guys have known where the bad guys were because of birds or animals giving away their position."

She scanned the pages until she found it. "Verse twenty-two," she said triumphantly.

"You got it," I told her, putting my arm around her.

I relaxed, the feel of her next to me draining the anxiety out of me. I needed to be close to her that night.

We talked about Sun-Tzu for another hour, her reading and explaining verses while I asked a critical question or two to guide her in the right direction. When she started to slow down and yawned twice in a row, I picked her up against her mild protests and carried her to the bedroom.

Justine was already asleep when I climbed into bed next to her, the book still held loosely in one of her hands. I put it on the nightstand and pulled her body tight to mine as we drifted off to sleep. It was easy to pretend everything was right with the world when she was in my arms.

She was still asleep when I woke up the next morning. I rolled over, stuffing the pillow under my head as I opened my eyes, coming face to face with Dog. He whined gently and went to the door, scratching at it with a paw.

It was early, before most people would be waking up, so I risked taking him out for a walk. I kept it short, letting him do his business and then leading him back inside. Justine was still asleep when we returned.

I packed up a few things quietly, torn between wanting to give her a hug before I headed out and knowing it would be easier if she didn't wake up until I'd left. I wrote her a note telling her Dog had been walked and that I loved her, promising I'd be back by midafternoon. Then I stuffed the satchel of explosives in my backpack with my other gear and headed out.

The gate guards let me through without comment. Waiting for the morning watch to take over, they were only half awake.

I hated leaving Justine in the apartment without talking to her, it felt like a bad way to start the day, but lying to her face about what I was doing felt worse. I told myself it was for the best, it was the way things had to be. She was going to wake up alone, and I was going to go kill some grays.

Chapter 12

My nerves were shot by the time I made it back to New Dover. I'd run out of ammunition for my pistols, and my rifle was down to three rounds. Things had started out well, then gone downhill fast. The guards at the gate spent a bit more time with me than when I left, shining their lights into my eyes and asking me if I'd been bit.

I'm sure I looked horrible, soaked in sweat without any supplies in tow, and the sun was setting.

"I've been running and hiding all day, and all I want to do is get behind the wall. There's some type of gang war going on out there, and I almost got killed by some very pissed off grays when I stumbled between them."

They backed off a little after I barked at them but didn't let me pass until I started to curse at them, unbuttoning my shirt and pulling it down to show my bare chest and shoulders. Thralls and grays naturally went for the neck and upper body.

"Does it look like they're coming this way?" a teenager with a shotgun asked, his voice quivering a little as I pulled up my shirt and slid through the gate as they cracked it open.

"No. It looks like they're concentrating on each at the moment." The teenager looked a bit surer of himself until I added, "But maybe they're fighting over who gets to take downtown." It was a mean thing to say, but I was in a black mood.

By the time I walked into downtown, the big diesel generator was humming and the lights were blazing up and down the street. It was only just getting dark, but the lights made people feel safer.

Justine slammed the door open as I reached the base of the stairs, taking two steps down before she realized I was in front of her. She was dressed from head to toe in black, her combat vest fully loaded with extra mags and her MP5K resting against her chest from its bungee sling. The way she looked would have given any reasonable man pause before messing with her, and that was before I saw her face.

Her eyes were cloudy and discolored like a stormy sky.

And even from a few feet away, I could see the way her fingernails appeared painted black and filed to points. She snarled, but I couldn't tell if she was just pissed or trying to say something. The further she changed, the harder it became for her to speak.

I rushed up the stairs as fast as I could and turned her about, pushing her back inside before anyone could see. The moment the door shut behind us, she turned on me, propelling me against the wall and lifting my feet off the floor. I grunted as the drywall sagged behind me and brought my hands up to grip her forearms, trying to get her to release the two fistfuls of my shirt she was holding me by.

"Don't ever do that again," she growled into my face. "Where the hell were you all day?"

"I got stuck between some Ravens and the others. Spent most of the day running and hiding. Took me this long just to get back here in one piece," I said, trying to shrug out of her grip.

"You smell like gunpowder," she said thickly, her nostrils flaring.

"It got close a few times. There's a war brewing out there," I told her, wincing as the discomfort of being hoisted against the wall grew. She saw the way I was gritting my teeth and let go of me, letting me drop to my feet. She took several slow breaths, standing so close I was pinned between her and the wall, her breath hitting my face with a strange sensation of coolness.

"I'm sorry," she said, rubbing her eyes. Her voice was almost completely hers again. "I got scared when you weren't back by dinner time, and then a few other scavengers came in. One of them was bitten."

"How bad?" I asked quietly.

"They had to shoot him, and then one of the soldiers killed the man's girlfriend when she started to draw on them." She looked away as she said it, and I saw her thinking that it could have been the two of us. I put my arms around her, and we collapsed a little into each other.

"I'm pretty hard to kill," I said, trying to comfort her. She clutched me hard for a moment before letting me go. She walked into the living room and sank heavily into the couch, giving me a look I couldn't read before putting her head in her hands as if she had a headache.

"Let me get cleaned up and we'll talk," I called to Justine as I went into the bedroom, grabbing our blue backpack of medical supplies. A wave of lightheadedness made me clutch the dresser until it passed. I made my way up to the gym room as quickly as I could, wondering how much time I had before Justine came to check on me.

I set the medical bag on the end of the table and unzipped it, pulling half its contents out to find what I was looking for. I set a bottle of betadine, packs of gauze, and a disposable surgical stapler to the side.

Then came the fun part: I pulled my arms out of the sleeves of my shirt and started to tear the duct tape off until only the clotted blood held my shirt to my right side. I'd been lucky at the gate; if they'd pushed just a little harder or asked me to take my shirt completely off, I would have been screwed.

I worked my boots off with my feet and grunted as I unclasped my belt with my left hand, shimmying out of my pants until I was standing in my boxers with the shirt hanging off my side. I grabbed the plastic tubing off the shower bag and unclamped the fitting, soaking my shirt, trying to soften the blood clot enough to pull the fabric free without too much pain.

The brute's spear had grazed my side, the tip cutting a deep slice into my flank where my love handles would be if I had any. The brute had caught me from behind as I fled, his projectile moving so fast I didn't realize I was hit until I felt the wetness creeping down my side half a block later. I might have bled to death if it weren't for duct tape.

The water running down my side turned a deep red as I pulled the edges of my shirt free of the wound, dropping it to the ground with a wet thud when I'd worked it completely free. Another wave of dizziness washed over me as a line of blood welled along the cut and then spilled down my side. I clamped the water off and opened a pack of gauze with my teeth and one hand as I tried to slow my blood loss with the other. The gauze turned bright red when I clamped it against my side.

I grabbed the betadine and the stapler and took two steps to the closest workout bench to straddle it. I set my supplies on the bench in front of me and took a deep breath before doing the deed. I pulled the top of the gauze away from the wound and poured betadine over the gash.

Everything around me spun. I leaned back into the steel of the workout equipment as liquid fire ate across my side. I forced myself to keep my hand clenched down on the wound, fighting the urge to pass out.

When I could sit up again, I grabbed the stapler. A label on the front of the packaging said in block letters, "SINGLE USE ONLY—30 STAPLES."

Besides performing self-dentistry, I can't think of anything less fun than stapling yourself closed. The actual device looked easy to operate; I'd seen one used in a field hospital in Somalia years ago. Pull the edges of meat together and squeeze the stapler until it clicks.

I pulled the gauze away and let it fall. The blood and betadine were making it hard to get a good grip on my skin. A sound that might have been a whimper escaped my throat as I leaned to my side and pinched the edges of my skin together. The first staple felt like a bee sting. Three staples in, my head started to feel fuzzy, but I kept going. I'd been planning on getting the wound closed before Justine found out I'd been hurt, but my goals lowered somewhat as I continued. Now I just wanted to close the wound before I passed out.

When I got the tenth and final staple set, I leaned back, resting my eyes. My stomach was churning, and the rooftop felt as if it were tilting and rolling under me. I breathed slowly, telling myself I wasn't going to vomit. The worst was over. Even if the line of staples wasn't exactly straight, and the edges of the cut were puckered here and there, it would do.

"You failed," Haeslig hissed at me, stepping out of the darkness as I opened my eyes. He was really mad, his hand resting on the hilt of his bowie knife.

"Fuck you," I told him, struggling to stand. My machete lay on the ground with my pants.

"You may have slipped away from me today in the madness, but don't think you can be so rude when you're right in front of me." Haeslig took a step forward, his lips twitching in anger, his incisors clearly visible.

The metallic sound of a charging handle being released clicked loudly in the night, stopping Haeslig cold. I couldn't see her, but I knew she was out there, hiding in the shadows.

"Don't shoot," I begged, watching Haeslig as he moved his head very slowly, his eyes searching. He didn't know where she was either—until the tip of her weapon touched the base of his skull.

Her eyes were solid slate, and her upper lip was pushed out around her elongated incisors. "Oh, I wouldn't dweam of it," she said around her teeth. It would have been funny if she wasn't holding a loaded submachine gun. "At least until after I find out why he's here…and what you failed at." Her voice was an octave deeper than normal, making her sound very threatening—well, except for the way she said "dream."

"What time is it?" I asked.

"Does it matter?" Haeslig asked calmly, leaning forward so the tip of Justine's weapon wasn't directly against his skin. He looked longingly at the darkness on the other side of the gym roof.

"Yes," I told him as Justine snarled, warning him to be still.

"Do you think you can escape me in the dark?" she asked the gray, sounding almost like she wanted him to try.

"No, I don't think I could," Haeslig said thoughtfully.

"What time is it?" I asked again, more urgently.

"Almost eight," the gray replied, his nostrils flaring.

"Perfect," I told him, getting an evil look from Justine. She wasn't in a mood to play games.

"If they caught you and you told them my name…" Haeslig began before a fireball roared into the night several miles to the north, interrupting him. The sound from the first blast struck us as two more explosions rocked the ground, sending smaller fireballs into the sky.

"I didn't fail," I said to Haeslig as I let myself fall back on-to the bench. People were crying and yelling on the streets below us, trying to figure out what was going on outside New Dover.

The gray looked at me hard before his face broke into a

broad, toothy smile. Then he bowed with a flourish.

Justine snarled at him and then me, her eyes darting between us, angry and confused. "You do his bidding like a
dog," she spit at me, rage and betrayal rank in her voice.

"You dishonor him," Haeslig barked back at her before I
could say anything. "He is enslaved against his will." He said
the last with deep satisfaction.

Justine moved so quickly it was a blur. One second she
was a step behind the gray; the next, she had her arm
around his neck, pulling his head back as she pressed the
creature's own blade to his flesh. She'd taken his bowie
knife so quickly it was barely noticeable. "Then you will release him or die," she said.

"I am not the one who can release him," Haeslig said, a
bit less confident with his own knife pressed to his throat.
"He seeks to free you of the being tugging at you: my master.
Dear Daniel here is helping to draw him out, then we will
break the bond between you and Han-su."

Justine pressed with the blade, the gray's skin about to
rupture.

"You are the one who holds him enslaved, Justine. He is
doing this to free you," Haeslig said in a muted voice, careful
not to move his head for fear he'd cut his own throat.

Justine paused, looking at me. She could see the truth
on my face. She let the blade go from Haeslig's throat, ramming it into the sheath at his waist so quickly I wasn't sure if
she'd gutted him at first. "Be gone," she commanded, shoving the gray away hard enough to make him fall to his hands
and knees.

"Of course," Haeslig said, standing slowly, rubbing his
throat. "For your service today," he said to me, putting a box
on the end of the table and then dropping a handful of scavenger tickets on top of it. Justine lifted her lip to show him
her fangs, and he darted into the darkness, leaping into the
protective folds of the night.

Justine turned on me, her face full of disappointment.
"You should not have done this without me," she said.

"I know," I told her weakly, unable to meet her eyes.

"You're wounded. You need to rest, and we need to
talk," she told me, softening just a little. She grabbed the box

and the tickets off the table and stood next to me, her nostrils flaring as thin streaks of blood leaked from between my staples.

Getting down the ramp to the balcony and into our apartment took more effort than it should have. Every time I moved, the staples pulled at my flesh. Justine helped to steady me, but that didn't stop the pain.

She led me into the living room and took my hands to help lower me onto the couch. I fidgeted, trying to find a position where my breathing wouldn't cause the staples to pull. The whole time Justine paced back and forth. I tried not to wince each time she passed.

"Do you know how hard it is to fight this?" she blurted out angrily.

"I'm trying to stop whatever has a hold on you," I pleaded.

"I'm not talking about that. I mean this," she yelled, her face suddenly an inch from mine, her teeth glistening as she let them protrude from her mouth.

I raised my hand, touching her face gently.

"This is who you are, Justine. You don't need to fight it." She really was beautiful, even now, like a magnificent hunter, every bit of her designed for the fight. Something in it resonated with me, drew me closer to her. I craned my neck up to her, but she just snorted at me angrily.

"You would kiss me, and my nostrils are so full of the smell of your blood I can hardly think," she said with disgust.

"Do you really want...want my blood?" I asked her, my hand going to my side without thinking.

"Yes," she snarled, putting a hand on my chest and pushing me back into the cushions as I felt her hot breath on my side, her nose at my wound. Her body lay spread out across me on the couch.

"I am yours," I whispered to her, pushing the back of her head down so her lips were just millimeters off my skin. She sucked in a long breath through her nose, her back shivering as she savored the scent of my blood.

I wasn't ready for it when the warmth of her tongue slid over the edge of the wound. Each time her tongue touched a staple, electricity shot through me, slowly turning into a hot flush. The heat flooded through me, every muscle in my body relaxing, my vision blurring as a narcotic euphoria overcame me.

A hoarse sigh of pleasure escaped my lips as a new heat circled my wound, her tongue tracing the gaps between the staples and lapping up the red wetness of my blood. I caressed the back of her head clumsily through a narcotic haze.

At some point, she climbed onto my lap, her face coming nose to nose with mine. I tried to tell her I loved her, but she didn't let me get the words out. She was kissing and sucking at my lips, trying not to cut me with her fangs.

I kissed back sloppily, cutting my tongue. I didn't care. I wanted her, all of her. I wanted to make love to her, and would have except I couldn't keep my eyes open or make my hands work the way I wanted them to. She felt the lethargy come over me and held my head tight to her chest, humming to me in contentment.

I fell into a deep, dreamless sleep.

When I woke up, my neck hurt, my legs felt numb, and my bladder was painfully full. I had to pee, urgently. It wasn't until I tried to get up that I realized Justine was still sitting astride my lap.

I laid her down sideways on the couch, looking at her skin through the dim morning light as I felt the tips of her fingers. Her nails were their normal, chewed-off nubs. She murmured something to me in her sleep as I ran to the bathroom.

When I came back, Dog was lying on the floor next to the couch, his tail thudding into the floor gently as Justine scratched his head. I ran a finger over the small box Haeslig had left me as I passed the end of the kitchen counter, looking at the graphic on its side. I'd done the job, and he'd come through with the scope.

"You're a fool," Justine mumbled to me as I grabbed two bottles of water from the kitchen counter. She sat up and took a bottle, smiling at me with a look of contentment on her face.

"Just for you," I said as she drank a sip of water. I stretched out, almost fully extending my hands over my head before I felt a twinge at my side. As I lowered my arms, something small fell to the floor with a metallic sound.

Justine sat forward on the couch and grabbed me, pulling me close and staring at my side. The open gash that had poured blood the day before was an angry red welt interrupted by gleaming silver staples. When I'd stretched, I'd popped one free to fall to the ground. The wound looked like it was weeks old instead of hours.

"Wow," Justine said, touching the welt with her fingertip. "How is that possible?" she asked, her mouth hanging open as she traced a zigzag between the staples with her finger.

"I had to pee so bad I didn't even realize I wasn't hurting," I told her, craning my neck down, not quite sure if I was believing what I was seeing.

"Have you always healed so quickly?" She didn't find it very funny when I started to laugh at her. She grabbed a staple and plucked it free.

"Motherfucker!" I yelled, pulling away.

"This is not funny," she said, flicking the staple at me.

"It's not me; it was you," I told her, rubbing my side. It still stung. "You're a predator. When you…" I struggled with the right words. Kiss was the wrong word, and fed would bother her, even though I didn't care what we called it. I settled on what seemed the safest choice.

"When you cleaned my wound, I thought you'd given me morphine. If you were a predator, what better way to subdue your prey than to get him high as a kite? And take Dog here. He licks his wounds but doesn't have a clue why." He looked up at me when I said his name. "Well, he probably doesn't have a clue," I amended, afraid I'd insulted him.

"I guess me and Dog are in the same camp," Justine said, looking from me to Dog, clearly not getting it.

"Dogs have natural antibacterial and healing properties in their saliva that help them heal."

"Great. I'm a drug-dealing predator with healing spit," she said sarcastically.

"Yeah, well, help me finish the job. These staples should have come out a week ago," I said to her with a smile.

We didn't have the special tool they use in hospitals to remove the staples. The medical kit assumes you're going to go to a real doctor to have the things removed. We found out together that needle-nose pliers worked, but it hurt. Justine had to pull one side out and then the other, which stung like a bitch.

"Did last night really happen?" she asked as she knelt at my side, prying the little silver bastards out of my skin.

"It was good for you too, right?" I asked with mock sheepishness. She shook her head in exasperation and ripped the next staple out without even trying to wiggle the edges free smoothly.

"Thank you for trying to make me laugh, but I remember, and it scares me. It felt like I was dying of thirst, and the calling was so strong. I wanted to go to the north, and then the smell of your blood was in my nostrils, and the two became all confused." She dropped the last staple onto the floor, wrapping her arms around my waist, her contentment replaced with fear and concern.

"Justine," I said, tilting her head up so I could look at her beautiful face. "I'd give myself to you freely if it would free you from them. I saw what they did to you back at the power plant, and even for the minute they had you, it was enough for me to know I'd do anything to keep you free."

"I don't want to be the reason you get hurt," she said into my side.

"It's not like you hurt me," I said, rubbing my wound.

"Thank you," she said, standing up and hugging me hard.

We stood in our living room next to Dog and held each other for a long while, each of us enjoying the simple comfort of the other's embrace.

"Promise me something," she said.

"Anything," I vowed, my heart swelling as she squeezed me tighter.

"Don't try to save me alone anymore."

"Deal."

Chapter 13

We spent most of the next day in the apartment. It wasn't planned; it just turned into a pajama day as the morning sun never quite burned through an overcast sky. We spent the morning curled up on the couch under a light blanket, ignoring the world.

Every now and then, my eye would find the pile of tickets on the table. How had a gray come by so many tickets? The thought of using them made me feel dirty, as if I'd been bought.

For lunch we ate canned ravioli and peanut butter crackers. Part of me wanted to go to the roof of the gym and work out, but I settled for sitting on the floor in front of the couch and stretching. My side ached, but it felt good at the same time.

"What did you do out there yesterday?" Justine asked as I touched my toes. The question surprised me. I'd been thinking about how to get in her pants later, not about how I'd gotten myself into such hot water the day before.

"He gave me a map with two marked buildings and ten kilos of high explosives and told me they were nests, which made me think there would be lots of nasties around. I was right.

"It was a banking complex with two buildings separated by a concrete plaza. I've never seen thralls so organized before. Neat ranks of bodies patrolled around the buildings; the smell was horrendous."

"Where were you?"

"Delaware Trust Banking Center." I winced as I said it, knowing it was coming. She slugged my arm hard enough to make me grunt. The banking center was on the other side of no-man's-land. Nobody travelled that far and came back. "That hurt," I whined at her, rubbing my shoulder.

"Sorry. I'll wait to hit you again when you tell me how you got cut."

"The banking towers have a generator complex for its data center. There were two large, ten-thousand-gallon diesel tanks and a five-thousand-gallon propane tank behind the mechanical building. By the looks of the fireworks last night, the tanks weren't empty."

"So you snuck in, planted some explosives, and fought your way out?"

"You really have no patience," I told her, leaning back into the couch. She made amends for punching me by rubbing my shoulders as I continued. "I thought I was being smart. I used some of my cars packed with explosives to drive right under their noses."

She looked around the kitchen, noticing my two big RC cars were gone. "Those were presents," she complained, but she didn't stop rubbing my shoulders.

"I was so busy driving my little toys under the diesel tanks that I didn't notice the gray until he was almost on top of me. Putting ten rounds into a gray a few blocks from their nest was a bad idea," I told her, nodding my head in agreement with myself.

"You need to learn to be quieter," she whispered, tracing the scar on my side with a finger for effect.

All I could say was, "I guess it would be better if I had someone to watch my back."

It was.

Chapter 14

My hip ached something horrible when I woke up, the old injury received at the power plant in Jersey creeping back into my bones through the cool metal I was lying on. I had to think about where I was for a minute to orient myself. After I blew up the nests at the data center, Justine and I had spent the last several weeks hunting and killing grays. One sniper's nest started to feel just like the next after a while.

I let the ache remind me I was alive for a minute and then closed it off, refusing to let it register as I looked through my scope at the center of the burned-out building two hundred meters away and three stories below. I was lying on the top of the heating and cooling equipment on the roof of an old apartment building, waiting for them to come.

It would be soon. Daylight was fading, casting long shadows over the street below. As the sun fled, the inside of the building grew indistinct, clouded in shadows.

The burnt-out building used to be a post office, but only its outer walls remained standing. The roof and contents of the building lay in blackened heaps. Dog whined from the center of the ruined building, his fear growing as night fell. The undead hated man's best friend, and Dog knew it.

Justine was somewhere nearby moving so quietly it was hard to keep track of her, but I felt safe with her watching my back. She would give warning if anything nasty came our way. We were on the outskirts of the city, on the border that made up no-man's-land. Even the craziest scavengers didn't come out this far. The Dupont Highway marked the far edge of where any sane person would want to travel. Beyond that lay uncontested undead territory.

I watched as the still street below us came to life, or at least to motion. Dog's whining drew the thralls from their hiding places. They shambled out of doorways and crawled from under cars, pouring out onto the street as the day fled. They moved with slow determination, surrounding the burnt-out post office.

At least half of the thralls shambling around the post office wore green military fatigues, a statement to how close we were to Dover Air Force Base. They pressed in on the building until they were five deep, forming a wall of dead flesh.

Dog's howling shifted into a high-pitched, panicked cry as the thralls closed in. I searched the darkness surrounding the post office, looking for a gray. They were getting smarter, more wary. Our first hunting trips had been easy. Just the smell of Dog's blanket could pull a gray to us at nightfall. We'd taught them to be more cautious, to fight their urge to rush in.

The thralls flooded into the interior of the post office through the doors and sections of broken down walls. They surrounded a heavy metal security cage, its wheels melted into the floor during the fire. At one point, the rolling cage had been used to lock up valuable packages. At the moment, it housed a plastic dog carrier.

Inside the pet carrier, a black mutt cowered, covered in urine and feces. The thralls rocked the cage back and forth as they pressed in from all sides, but the bars of the security cage were too small to allow them to get to the screaming animal inside. I scanned the writhing mass of bodies, getting frustrated. I could kills thralls whenever I wanted. They were a dime a dozen. It was grays I wanted.

Haeslig had been relatively quiet of late, but the last time he appeared on the gym roof, he said we were close. His master, Han-su, was growing increasingly worried about his losses, and he was getting ready to call together a counsel. It was what Haeslig was waiting for. Han-su was being forced to show himself and prove he was still capable of leading.

I could tell the damage we were doing was having an impact. The grays were being more cautious, even going so far as to send several messages to the people of New Dover in the form of bodies staked outside our gates. Rumors were spreading like wildfire through the town that scavengers were being caught alive so they could be tortured and questioned. The grays wanted to know who had turned the hunters into the hunted.

I didn't trust Haeslig, but it was easy to see Han-su was

getting closer. For the past week, Justine had been jolting awake, covered in cold sweat and breathing hard. It was one of the reasons I'd fallen asleep on the roof. It was hard to rest easy when I knew she was suffering. Both of us were a little worn around the edges. We'd been hunting almost non-stop for the last four weeks.

Below us, Dog's show was almost complete, his whining a constant siren announcing his fear. The thralls were trying to muscle the metal cage apart, but the steel was too strong and the cage itself gave them no good handholds for lever-age. The thralls struggled on, but there was no sign of any grays. I waited, scanning the surrounding buildings.

A grenade popped off in the building just behind the post office, blowing dust and smoke out of the already-smashed third-floor windows. I scanned the building, looking for a tar-get. The grenade wasn't the primary strike; it was really just part of the overall trap. If the grays didn't find anything on their way in, they'd get even more suspicious.

That was why there were seven other grenades scat-tered about the buildings around the post office. Most of the traps were on the upper floors or even the roofs. The grays liked to be above street level when they hunted.

I watched as two shadows fell from a window above and behind the post office, landing on top of the back wall of the burnt-out building. The grays crept forward, watching the thralls as they tried to get into the cage. One of the grays walked along the top of the shattered wall, thinking he was still hidden in the shadows. I saw him crouch to climb down, only to stop himself. He teetered on the edge, fighting to control the urge to go to the cage.

Whatever they had against dogs, it was more than a simple dislike. The smell and sound of a canine was some-thing the undead had a hard time resisting. The thralls around the cage tore their hands apart as they tried in vain to break the steel bars with rotten flesh.

Dog's squeals from inside the cage became a frantic barking, pushing the gray past his limit. He jumped down, pushing thralls out of his way violently to get to the metal framework surrounding Dog. He grabbed the chain I'd looped through the metal door handles of the cage, throwing his body weight back once, then twice. Links went flying. The dog carrier didn't stand a chance once he had the security cage open.

The gray reached into the carrier, his body vibrating with anticipation as he went for his prize. He froze as his hand grabbed the mutt by the back of its neck, the eager pleasure on his face shifting to fear in the moment before the spiked teeth clamped down on his arm.

He jerked about, trying to tear free, but the trap was bolted to a length of chain attached to the bottom of the security cage. The gray panicked. He'd clearly heard the stories. He was stuck, and he knew a bullet couldn't be far behind. He threw his body about, trying to rip free, even if it cost him his arm.

The other gray on top of the wall watched, not sure what to do, but his friend's screaming pulled him in. He jumped down and tried to get his fingers around the trap to free him. Two more grays separated from the mix of thralls surrounding the building, rushing forward to try and help. Four grays: it would have to be enough.

I gave Justine the thumbs-up sign and she smiled at me quickly as she set down the wireless remote controlling the dog sounds and exchanged it for a detonator. She pumped the M57 rapidly as it clicked and clacked.

There was a half-second delay, and then the claymores packed around the inside walls of the post office went off, sending a hailstorm of steel shooting in every direction. We'd set ten claymores around the inside of the building, each containing seven hundred eighth-inch steel ball bearings. You can do the math.

The center of the building became a red haze as bodies evaporated in the storm of flying steel. Everything inside the post office was there one moment and simply not the next.

We watched from our perch, pleased with ourselves. Cinder block walls fell outward in bits of wet concrete slush. The grays were getting smarter, but so were we. They were expecting rifle fire, so we gave them something a little different.

I'd have to give Dog a bone when we got home. He'd been pretty unhappy when I was chasing him around trying to get half a soda bottle under his leg when he peed. I'm sure it was one of those moments when he thought I was losing my mind. Justine had taken the easier job: getting some audio of him snarling and whining.

At first it had been enough to play a tape of Dog to lure grays into the street, but they'd figured out pretty quickly that running into the open was a bad idea when a former Scout Sniper was looking at them down the sights of an M25 rifle. We'd been forced to add to our little shows bit by bit to keep the grays stimulated. The trap under the stuffed animal had been Justine's idea, and it had paid off, pulling three more into the kill zone.

Overall, not a bad hunting trip.

We watched with satisfaction as thralls went mad in the streets, the ground around the post office turning into a battlefield. A fifth gray had been lurking in the mass of thralls out on the street, but he found himself surrounded by the enraged instead of safe in their midst once those inside the post office were killed.

We watched as reinforcements flooded in from the surrounding streets. Two more grays led the assault into the heart of the enraged, trying to get to their surviving comrade who was fighting for his life beneath a squirming pile of bodies.

A gray was a formidable foe, but there are only so many bodies you can have piled on top of you before the weight of your enemy carries you down. We watched…and waited.

We were well into territory no humans ventured into. Getting in and setting up had made for an anxious, tense couple of hours. Our doggy decoy had been stuffed into a plastic container, taped shut, bagged, and then washed in bleach to make sure the outside of the container wasn't carrying the scent.

It had seemed like a reasonable amount of precaution, but watching the undead fill the street in front of the post office for a block in each direction made me question myself. We'd walked by hundreds, if not thousands, of undead, and just a little slipup could have brought it all down on us. It was a sobering thought.

We watched as thralls still linked to grays surrounded

the enraged. It turned into a rugby scrum. An inner ring of enraged were being slowly chewed to bits as a greater number of controlled thralls ate away at their border. The gray pinned at the center of the scrum managed to get to his feet as the numbers of enraged thinned. He swung about wildly with one arm, his other hanging at an odd angle as he battled to stay on his feet. He was lucky his fellows weren't just leaving him to fend for himself.

If we'd been closer to New Dover, the grays would have pulled back and let the enraged run amuck. We'd seen them do it before, but this was well within their territory, and they weren't about to leave a maddened horde running around in their own backyard.

I could almost feel the sigh of relief from the wounded gray as his two rescuers reached him, pulling him out of the clutches of the enraged. It brought a warm feeling to my heart as I watched—from behind my scope.

I breathed out, my sight picture stabilizing as I exhaled. My first round went two inches wide, thrown off just a fraction by the two-liter bottle taped over the barrel. Haeslig seemed to have an unlimited supply of explosives and bullets, but when I'd asked him for a silencer and an M4 assault rifle, he had balked. I think he was afraid it might have given us too much of an advantage. The shot hit my target in the cheek, enough to take down a normal man, but the gray only fell to his knees. My second shot was flying as he reached up, pulling a thrall in front of his body.

It didn't stop the round. The bullet passed through the thrall's body and hit the gray somewhere between his nose and the top of his head. It was hard to tell for sure. My third round flew true and straight, catching my second target on the bridge of his nose.

The rescued gray turned about, not sure what was going on. One moment he had one of his brothers at either shoulder, and then they were both falling to the ground. I watched with a wicked smile on my face as the wounded thrall realized he wasn't saved. A third of the thralls crowding the street paused as their link failed, and then the chaos began anew.

The wounded gray made half a turn, watching as the

thralls around him changed from slaves to berserkers. His head fell to his chest in defeat as the thralls collapsed in, pulling him down under a pile of ravaging teeth and clutching hands.

Justine tapped my shoulder, pointing down into the sea of bodies squirming over each other in the streets. I followed her finger, my eyes locking on the forms moving against the flow.

From the east, a mass of brutes came into view, marching into the fray and not slowing as they tore into the enraged. They left the road behind them covered in bodies.

Justine climbed off the air exchanger and waited for me to pass her my rifle. It was time to get out of Dodge. We jumped over the trip wire in the stairs, descending as fast as we could. We reached street level and slipped outside into the alley by a set of Dumpsters. Justine led the way to the street, peeking around the corner before turning back to me. She held up a finger for me to be quiet as a group of enraged thralls ran by the mouth of the alley.

I tried to sneak a kiss when she turned back to me, but she pulled away. The change still shamed her, filled her with fear. I grabbed her before she could move away and pulled her against me suddenly, causing her to gasp.

"I could hurt you by accident," she whispered in a deep voice, flexing her fingers on my back and making sure I felt the sharp points extending from each. Even partially changed, her fingertips were sharp enough to score leather.

"But never on purpose," I whispered back, kissing the corner of her mouth. She resisted for half a heartbeat then melted into me, her lips moving against mine, a light moan escaping her.

"You're playing with fire, boy," she said as she separated gently.

I smiled at her, hoping she could see how much I needed her.

"Now let's see if you can keep up."

Justine made sure I paid for the kiss with sore legs and a dose of humility. Even though she carried my rifle, and a backpack with our leftover supplies, she ran me into the ground.

When we got closer to New Dover, Justine angled us away from the east gate. The guards on the east gate were high strung. They'd already shot one scavenger coming back from a regular run, and rumor had it one of the "thralls" they'd shot a week before had screamed when they shot him. The guards on the other gates were more alert than they used to be, but at least they weren't shooting scavengers yet.

Of course, I wasn't sure how long that was going to last. The atmosphere inside the town grew tenser each day. Even Big John was starting to have trouble keeping everyone under control.

People were going missing every night, and Big John was in a bad position. People wanted him to do something, but he already had as many men as he could muster on the walls. Every day the headcount showed one or two more gone, and not a sign of where they went.

What really scared me was what Big John was telling his men. No one was to kill any grays until they were coming at the walls. He was telling people we were being punished for something happening outside, and people were starting to look at each other sideways, trying to figure out who was causing the unrest.

We made a point of listening to him like everyone else when he came around, but we were more interested in just getting close enough to let Justine get a feeling. Unfortunately, if the grays had a way to influence him, it wasn't something she could sense. Every now and then, she'd catch the scent of a gray inside the walls, but it was so quick and fleeting that she was never able to get eyes on the intruder.

Worst of all, twice in the last three weeks, the undead had raided New Dover, and both times they'd hit someplace we were weak, pushing through buildings everyone thought were sealed up tight. The cleanup crews, wearing their plastic suits and face shields, stayed busy shoveling up the remains of the thralls and washing the streets with bleach and water.

The attacks really didn't make much sense. The grays could have taken New Dover in a single night if they wanted to. It felt more like they were toying with us, breaking down a door or a few walls to send in some thralls to scare us and remind us where we stood on the food chain.

And then, after one of the undead raids, a shopping cart full of food turned up and two families got into a gunfight across the hallway separating their apartments. No one was left alive to question, but everyone saw the shopping cart when it was hurled out the front door. The closest Shop-A-Lot was on the other side of Dupont Highway. Well into no-man's-land.

It left a cloud over everyone. Had someone given us up for a cart full of groceries? Things got tighter every day, but no one was starving.

The social unrest caused the factions already present to coalesce into ever-tighter groups. The soldiers kept to themselves, leaving the Fort people and the religious nuts to fight for the title of most dangerous armed civilian group.

The Fort people were true to their name, taking every board and nail they could get their hands on until there was only one way in or out of their apartment building. The religious nuts met every morning to listen to Big John, believing he was chosen by God to lead them to safety. I'm not really sure what was more concerning: that they believed it or that Big John did.

"We'll walk to the west side," I told Justine, forestalling her from trying to talk me into sneaking over the wall.

"Dog's going to be mad at you if he knows you made him wait an extra twenty for us to get home," she told me, changing course to take a wide arc around New Dover toward the west entrance. It was the farthest, but we'd scored some whiskey and other items of value for several of the guards there in the past, making them slightly more friendly than most.

"I'll give him extra belly rubs; he'll forgive me."

"I'll have to try that the next time you're mad at me," she teased. I shook my head, wishing she would.

With the nightmares waking her up half changed every night and us spending our days hunting, she was so afraid to lose herself completely to the other side that she wouldn't let me do more than cop a feel and sneak a kiss. Just one more reason to find Han-su and put a bullet in his head.

Chapter 15

Dog went crazy when he heard us on the other side of the door, his feet tapping the floor in a rapid staccato as he waited impatiently for us to enter. When Justine fumbled with the key, he lost all control, scratching away as if that might help us get through the door faster.

Once we made it inside, he circled us, sniffing intensely, his tail high and wagging as he checked us out, making sure we passed inspection. After doing his security check, he moved on to the next critical task and headed to the kitchen to stretch in front of his food bowl.

Justine stowed our weapons and gear as I went to get our mutt some food. "I bet WC fed you before he left for the day, didn't he?" I asked Dog as he wagged his tail patiently, waiting for what was quite likely his second dinner. WC had become our go-to dog sitter when we were hunting. When Dog was done eating, we all headed up to the gym roof.

We had a fairly regular nighttime routine when we were in New Dover. We would watch the sun set from our private rooftop and eat our dinner, watching the stars get brighter and brighter every night.

Justine thought it was because we were heading toward the end of summer, but I argued it was because all the jets were out of the air and the streets were never going to be clogged with cars burning fossil fuels again. She told me to shut up; it was more romantic to think it was because of the seasons. I shut up.

We sat there, staring at the sky and talking quietly. She spoiled it just a little by talking about WC. He was bouncing between a room in the Fort and a bunk with some of the old soldiers. He liked to listen to their stories and didn't mind doing chores for them, but WC didn't want to piss either side off, so he spent a night here and a night there, floating around like a lost child.

I mostly kept my mouth shut. WC was a good kid; he'd been helping us with Dog on a regular basis, which gave him points in my book. I just wished he didn't turn into a wide-eyed teenager whenever Justine was around. We'd offered to help him set up in one of the empty apartments nearby, but he'd refused. I couldn't make the kid move if he didn't want to.

Justine rambled a bit longer before giving up on trying to solve WC's housing problems. She whistled for Dog, and a short struggle ensued. Dog ran in frantic circles when she got the tennis ball away from him, whining until she tossed it at the outbuilding so it bounced back toward us.

We took turns throwing the ball and seeing how high we could get Dog to jump. Eventually the generator switched on and the lights circling the center of New Dover flickered to life. Dog decided he wasn't going to give up the tennis ball anymore, and he and Justine got into a fight. She was batting his head around as he growled and wagged his tail.

Justine smiled at me as she played. I smiled back, but it was a fragile happiness. While we were secluded on the gym roof, the rest of the world seemed far away, but we both knew it was a very delicate illusion.

My eyes drifted closed as I listened to Justine and Dog play. I was exhausted after the last few days of hunting. You would think that lying on a roof hiding wouldn't leave you exhausted, but it's impossible to get any real sleep when you're out there, surrounded by vacant buildings, twitching with each new sound that reaches your ears.

I woke up with Justine lying next to me, crammed between the armrest and my body. A blanket half covered us, and Dog lay on the ground at our feet, the tennis ball touching the tip of his nose.

Justine's hand moved under my shirt, rubbing the space just beneath my belly button. I tried to relax, to will her hand to continue its small circles, but she heard my breathing change or felt me start to respond to her. She slapped my belly and sighed against my neck before nipping me with her teeth. It was both a warning and an invitation at the same time. I could feel her need just as easily as she could feel mine. She just wasn't going to give into it.

"Time to get some dinner," Justine said to me, slapping my belly harder before she got up and left me lying there by myself. I got up and followed her into our apartment.

"Beef stew or clam chowder?" I asked as I looked in the

pantry.

Justine didn't answer. I was about to repeat myself when I glanced over and saw her, leaning on the table with one hand while the other rubbed the bridge of her nose as her eyes scrunched up.

She changed slowly, her eyes and teeth shedding their humanity as she transformed into her other self. Seeing her change always had a strange effect on me. On one hand, it was strange and beautiful, but it was something that appeared to cause Justine a good bit of pain. I watched as her fingernails changed color and elongated, forming fine points. The surface of her claws was shiny and black, almost as if they were covered in black mother of pearl.

She groaned and shuddered as her teeth slipped past her lips. I started to go to her and then checked myself. My emotions always got a little out of whack when I saw her in pain, but I knew from previous experience that the last thing she wanted at that moment was to be touched.

Justine shivered, standing up on her tiptoes as she balled her fists at her sides, clenching her teeth as she pinched her eyes closed. She slowly relaxed her fists and opened her eyes. When she lifted her head to look at me, I was happy to see the deep brown of her eyes looking back at me—even if they were filled with pain. She'd pushed the change back, but it had cost her.

"It's got to be soon, or we have to get away from here. I can almost feel him," she told me, wiping tears away.

I went to her, pulling her close, letting her tears wet my shirt. I made a silent vow to myself for the hundredth time to see Han-su dead.

"It will be soon; I promise," I told her, rubbing her back through her shirt. Dog rubbed against our legs, feeling left out.

"I hope so," she said tiredly.

"Oh, we're almost there," I told her.

Dog froze in his tracks, his eyes locked on the door to the guest room. He always knew Haeslig was here before we did. I found it odd that Justine could sense other grays, but never Haeslig. It was one more thing about him I didn't like.

"Joy," she said dryly as she looked toward our spare room. "I'm gonna stay here if you're OK."

"Yeah. I'll start shooting if I need you," I told her, sliding a Glock into my waistband.

"Don't shoot off anything important," she mumbled to me as I unlocked the guest room.

I went to the center of the roof and faced the darkness. Haeslig was fairly predictable when he came to visit; he hated to let us get a good look at him.

"You'll have to tell me how you sneak in and out so easily someday," I said to break the silence.

"If I told you, it wouldn't be my secret anymore," he said back to me, parroting my words from a few weeks earlier. I had to laugh despite myself.

"I'm guessing you come in from the west," I hypothesized. The guards there relied too much on their spotlights and seemed to think standing in a pool of light would protect them from the nasty things that go bump in the night.

"That was nice work you did yesterday," Haeslig said, ignoring my guess. "One of Han-su's senior captains was injured in the chaos. The captain's anger is nearly uncontrollable; he is demanding Han-su command the destruction of every human within a hundred miles."

Very interesting. It was the first time Haeslig had ever said anything about other humans.

"Really?" I said, trying to keep him talking.

"Han-su's convinced Ravi has recruited several of your old military units to fight for him. Some of your scavengers have been carrying some heavy arms of late, which is actually helping you. Han-su thinks he's picking apart the apparatus piece by piece." Smug amusement filled Haeslig's voice.

"So will Han-su have us all overrun then?" I couldn't help myself from sounding interested this time. There are always unintended consequences. My efforts to free Justine might lead to the destruction of New Dover. The idea put a knot in my stomach, but it wasn't going to change my plans.

"Eventually he may," Haeslig said. "But he's lost too much face to command without being seen. He will have to have a council, make a show of strength. The time is very near."

"When?" I asked.

"I'll send you word at dusk on the night of the meeting."

"And our job is to…" I wondered aloud. He'd already told me we'd stand no chance against his master directly.

"You will have two tasks. The first is to take out his guards, and the second is a product of the first: to be a distraction while I slip the knife into his heart," Haeslig replied bluntly. I couldn't tell if the last was figurative or literal.

"How heavily guarded is he?" I asked.

"There will be two whisperers with Han-su. They will be close by; they can't protect him from any great distance. You will kill the whisperers so I can do what must be done."

"And once it's done, what happens to Justine and me?"

"After I take out Han-su, you will have safe passage back to downtown."

"Very funny," I said to Haeslig.

"I presumed that is where you would want to go," the gray purred back to me.

I grunted something that may have been a curse his way.

"I promise you safe passage away from the fight. You have my word on it," Haeslig said, the normally teasing, jibing tone completely absent from his voice. It almost sounded like he meant it.

"Why do you let these people think they're holding you at bay?" I wondered, scanning the darkness where his voice was coming from.

"Oh, what a grand buffet this is. The fear, the anger, and, of course, the livestock," Haeslig said tauntingly, his moment of seriousness gone.

"Asshole," I said to the darkness. They thought of us as cows to be herded and slaughtered.

Haeslig ignored the insult. "When the time is right, I'll send you word. I may not be able to come myself; my absence would be noted, so please be polite to any friends I may send with the message." Haeslig was enjoying his moment.

"I'll try to keep from putting a bullet in your courier," I said to the emptiness.

Haeslig was already gone.

Chapter 16

Justine was lying on the couch when I came back in. Her eyes were closed, but I could tell she was awake, trying to ignore the gnawing at the back of her head. She held up one finger to me, letting me know to give her another second. She sat up slowly and opened her eyes, squinting against the dim light of the one bulb spanning the kitchen and living room.

I watched as the whites of her eyes changed from gray back to milky white. She was getting hit hard.

"He's so close. I feel like someone's got a dental drill against my skull."

"Haeslig said it was going to be soon. Do you need a fix?" I asked her cautiously. Sometimes it was better if she just let herself change and gave into the hunger, if only a little.

"No," she said, but she didn't sound so sure of herself. "I feel like there are bugs crawling on my skin. I'm afraid if I start, I won't be able to stop."

Not a good day to get sucked on by your girl.

"Do you want to be alone?"

"No. Tell me what Haeslig said."

"It won't be much longer. He thinks it will be any day now. He'll send word with the location, but after that, it is up to us to take out Han-su's bodyguards. He called them whisperers," I told her, remembering the strange grays we'd encountered at the power plant back in Jersey. "They need to be put down before he can perform his little act of regicide."

"Suicide mission," Justine said bluntly.

"Only the best for us, babe," I replied quietly.

"It's not too late to run," she offered. I knew she meant from her just as much as from the mission.

"No. We can't let them have a string tied to you," I told her, stressing the word "we."

Justine lay on the couch with her eyes closed as I spread out maps of Dover on our table, jotting little notes down on the papers with a finely sharpened pencil. I didn't know if we'd ever be going back to the area around the burnt-out post office, but updating the maps gave me something to do.

"Waiting sucks," Justine said at some point, not lifting her head up or opening her eyes.

"Yep," was all I could say. Waiting before the mission was always hard.

When it was time for bed, Justine tossed and turned all night, moaning in her sleep. I tried to get some rest, but it was hard.

Sometime in the early hours, just after the sun began to creep into the sky, an air horn went off once, paused, and then repeated two more times. Justine's eyes popped open as I scurried out of bed, her irises completely gone.

"Stay here; I'll go have a look" was all I said to her. Three blasts meant the grays had left another present outside. She swallowed and nodded her head in agreement. It was hard for her to talk when she was past a certain point.

I made it to the west gate to find a small mass of people standing on top of the gatehouse. Several scavengers who'd gone missing had turned up.

Their bodies were in the middle of the intersection a block away. Two of them lay on the ground, but one was duct taped to a wooden desk chair, wide bands of tape holding his chest against the seat back. His head was rolling around, but no one on the wall made any motion to go out.

"Open the gate!" I yelled, drawing one of my pistols. A guard started to argue, but I asked him very intensely what he would want someone to do if he were out there. Several of the other men looked at each other, feeling a touch of shame, and lined up behind me.

I told them they could turn around if they wanted when we were halfway to the bodies. From the wall, it had been hard to tell what was going on. The closer we got, the more obvious it became.

The man taped to the chair jerked his head about, trying to follow the sounds of our approach with empty eye sockets. It looked like his eyes had been sucked out of his head, violently. His eyelids and the flesh around his orbits were frayed and chewed on. The white of his skull was visible around his eyes and along his cheekbones. The rest of him wasn't in any better shape. His legs were gone from just above the knee.

As we got closer, he started to thrash in his chair, the stumps of his thighs wiggling in the air as he struggled. Jagged edges of bone stuck out from the meat of his thighs. The ends of the bones had been gnawed on, and every exposed surface of his skin showed evidence of bite marks.

Lying in relative peace on either side of the chair were two more bodies, their necks disjointed from being broken. It wasn't what killed them, though—not the first time at least. Each of them had bite marks on their necks. I tried not to think about what the two dead thralls had done to their friend after being turned. Blood covered their upper bodies, and their bellies were distended and full.

I put a bullet in the thrall's head. He'd suffered enough.

"Can we get out of here?" The three men with me were looking around at the empty buildings and cars, spooked.

"Go get something that will burn," I told them flatly. They rushed back to the gate.

I raided a few nearby cars until I had four spare tires and a mound of other flammable crap. Of the three men who'd gone back inside the wall, only one of them came back out, carrying two bottles of rubbing alcohol. He told me sheepishly his buddies were covering us from the wall.

I poured the alcohol over the pile and lit it before it could evaporate off. The scavengers deserved better, but a smoky pyre was the best they were going to get.

My helper rushed back to the gate ahead of me, leaving me to take up the rear, lost in thought. Big John was standing inside when I came through, his eyes watching the fire until the closing gate shut it out. I tried to slip past him, but he stepped in front of me. "What changed?" he asked me, his voice was full of emotion. He looked exhausted.

"The world ended, I guess," I told him, not sure what to say.

"Not that, Daniel. What changed here? The devil children have been around since we staked our claim on New Dover, but they seem to have taken a very strong interest in us of late."

"The lights, the generator, too many people gathered together, take your pick," I said quietly, sadly, not sure what to say.

Big John leaned closer, putting his mouth to my ear so I could hear what he said. "There was a note on one of the bodies last week. My people took it before anyone else could see it."

"And?" I asked, not sure where Big John was going.

"It was very strange. You carry yourself like a military man, both you and that girl of yours. You've served in combat together I would bet," he said, looking from the machete strapped to my thigh to the Glocks under my armpits.

"And?" I asked again. I made a mental note to tell Justine what he'd said. She would get a kick out of his comment. She'd been in high school while I was fighting in Afghanistan.

"The note," he said, his eyes locking on mine. "It said we were to put anyone who was helping the military killers outside the wall. Do you know anything about that?"

"You think some of the soldier boys are responsible for stirring up the grays?" I asked him.

He shrugged his shoulders, looking twenty years older than he had the first time I met him. "You let me know if you hear anything, Daniel; the price we are paying may be too high." Big John walked away to join up with several of his foremen who were waiting for him.

The walk back to the apartment seemed a lot longer than it normally did. I was so distracted I didn't notice WC until he was falling into me. I turned a corner to take a side street back to our place, and he stepped out of a doorway, grabbing me with his hands and carrying us both off balance. I was already going for a pistol when our eyes met, which was lucky for him. I might have shot him first and realized he wasn't a thrall too late if he hadn't made eye contact.

His face was a mess. His right eye was swollen closed, and the rest of him was all bruises and cuts. Whoever beat the hell out of him must have had at least one good-sized ring on.

"What happened to you?" I asked him. He opened his mouth to say something, but all he could do was blubber a little and spit up a mouthful of blood as his eyes rolled backwards.

I caught him as he started to fall, hiking him up by his shirt so I could get him over my shoulder. He was only a few inches shorter than me, but he weighed less than Justine. The kid was all legs and baggy clothes.

I got him back to the apartment without a problem. Whoever had beat on him must have been spooked when the horns went off. It probably saved WC's life.

I kicked at the door until Justine opened it, putting the barrel of her MP5K in my face until she realized it was me. "Sorry," she said, happy to see I was safe and upset to see I was carrying a body. She lifted WC's head by his hair as I walked down the hall to the couch. "Please tell me you didn't do this to him."

"He's just a kid," I growled at her, pissed and a little hurt she could even think I would have beat WC down so cruelly.

I got him onto the couch as Justine ran to get the medical bag from the bathroom. As she spread the first-aid kit onto the coffee table, I checked to make sure he was breathing and then pulled back his swollen eyelids, making sure his pupils reacted equally to the light. He'd taken enough blows to the head to make me concerned about serious trauma.

"You see who did this?" she asked as I let her take over, swabbing cuts and cleaning out the deeper gashes on his face. Her eyes fluttered from the deep lustrous brown to slate and back again, moment by moment, showing how easily her emotions were unsettling her.

"No, I found him like this when I was almost home. He must have been trying to get to us."

"A few more hits and they would have cracked his head open," she said, feeling the back of his skull for fractures.

"Gun's gone," I said, lifting his baggy shirt. He always kept his big chrome automatic under his belt.

"Hope he got a few of them."

"Yeah, but I don't think so," I told her. "He wasn't on the street that long. I think the spectacle outside the gates saved him."

"How bad?"

"Three more," I told her. "And Big John spilled some strange news after. The grays think there is a military unit

hunting them. They left a warning to put anyone who sup-
ported the military outside the wall."

"We have them on edge," Justine said with a smile.

"Yes, we do," I agreed, wondering how we were going to
spend the day, and the next, until we got word from Haeslig.
Having the undead on edge wasn't doing much for my
nerves.

I told her what Big John had said about us serving together in the military, which earned me one of her amazing
smiles in response. The only thing that ruined it was that she
was squeezing antibiotics into a gash on WC's forehead at
the time.

When Justine was done cleaning WC up, she settled
down on the chair next to the couch with a book to keep
watch over him. The cover featured a bare-chested man
clutching a half-naked woman. I raised an eyebrow, but she
just gave me the finger.

Dog sat between them, putting his head on Justine's lap
for comfort before licking WC's limp hand, puzzled why he
wasn't getting any attention from that direction.

WC woke up around lunchtime, moaning as conscious-
ness came back to him painfully. His arms flailed for a second until he heard our voices, telling him he was OK.

"Who did this to you?" Justine asked.

"Don't know," he mumbled through plump, split lips.
"They kicked down my door this morning; everything after
that is blank."

"You owe anyone?" Justine asked.

"You hit on anyone's girl?" I chimed in, getting a dirty
look from Justine for it.

"Just yours," he said, smiling until he moved his face too
much, cracking open his bottom lip in the process. He talked
slowly, the words coming out thickly from between his fat lips.
"I was in my room at the Fort. I think it was one of the guys
from the firehouse."

"You cool here?" I asked Justine, my voice cold and
steely. Instead of coming after me, they'd taken down the kid.
I wasn't going to let that stand.

She thought about it for a moment, struggling with her
desire to do the job herself. I placed one of my fingers under

my eye, pointing at it. She got the message.

"Yeah. I can take care of one wounded kid," she told me, making WC grimace again with a different kind of pain.

"You have anything you want from your flat?" I asked him. I hoped I'd find something there that told me who had beaten him. Even in chaos, there had to be some accountability.

"If it's still there, a set of dog tags should be hanging from the corkboard by my bed. It's the last room on the left, second floor," he croaked.

"OK," I said, picturing a set of gold dog tags with diamonds around their edges.

Justine ran to the door when I was about to leave. "Be careful," she told me, standing on her toes to kiss me quickly.

"Always," I said, kissing her back.

I'd seen so much violence in my life, but I would never understand it. WC was a human, a member of our team. And yet they'd beaten him down hard. If a few more punches had been thrown, he might never have woken up. He actually looked worse when I left than when I'd found him that morning. His bruises had been given time to bloom.

I walked out the door, wondering how far I was going to have to go to get my vengeance. Halfway down the street, a rough-looking fellow with a scraggily beard kicked off the wall and started to trail me. It was Billy from the firehouse, looking leaner and more dangerous than before.

I headed for the Fort, expecting him to close on me as we walked through empty streets, but he just kept his distance, trailing behind me. I paused opposite Building C, which they'd turned into the Fort, looking at the two men guarding the front door—and their shotguns.

I pulled out the olive drab scarf I used when the bodies got thick, covering my face from my nose down as I crossed the street to the Fort entrance. Between the scarf and my sunglasses, most of my face was hidden.

The two bouncers looked up at me as I got closer, their shotguns held a little tighter. I walked right up to them with my arms held loosely at my sides, trying to look as non-threatening as I could.

"Billy wants me to get something out of the apartment.

Big John is on his way over," I told them bluntly, assuming they knew what had happened to WC. The two looked at each other as my heart pounded in my chest and I wondered whether I'd gambled and lost.

"Don't know what you're talking about," the larger of the two men said, stepping aside to let me in. I brushed by them without saying another word, expecting to hear Billy start screaming behind me.

It hit me the moment I made it through the door. The air was thick with the smell of people living too closely together. The odor was sickening, making my stomach want to empty itself. I told myself the bandana was keeping the worst out. The doors to most of the first-floor rooms were closed, but the few that stood open revealed trash and garbage piled high up onto the walls. They were filling the empty rooms with garbage.

A plastic tarp was hung at the top of the stairway to the second floor, giving me a half second of pause before I brushed through the cut down its middle. The smell in the second floor hallway was horrible by normal standards, but after walking through the first floor, it came as a welcome relief.

I was three-quarters of the way down the hall when I heard people coming up the stairs, cursing. I slipped into WC's apartment just as bodies pushed through the plastic drape at the far end of the hall.

Between the kicked-in door and crap spread across the floor, it looked like a cyclone had touched down in the room. Stacks of graphic novels and comics hid most of the floor. The corkboard was screwed to the wall by the bed, adorned with some crude pencil drawings of thralls as well as some choice images from "AssFreak" magazine.

He may have been a kid, but he was definitely into advanced porn. The dog tags hung from a pushpin in the center of the corkboard. I took them in my palm and looked at them, surprised. They were simple metal tags stamped with a few words. I finally knew his real name, even if I had no clue where the WC had come from. From a distance, they might even pass for the real thing.

Tyler

&

Anna Sophia

I guessed Anna Sophia was his girlfriend from before. I put the tags into my pocket and turned around—just in time to say hello to Billy and another man standing in the door. Billy smiled back, pulling a hunting knife out as his friend leveled a snub-nosed .38 at me.

"All this over a disagreement at the firehouse?" I asked, taking a half step closer to the door.

"And he was hanging out with your slut and the dog," Billy reminded me, bringing his arm back but keeping the knife low, ready to strike.

"Go for the guns and I'll pop you," the other man said in a thick southern drawl.

"No worries," I said quietly, calm filling me.

"Maybe once we throw your bodies outside the wall with that dog, they'll stop hunting us," Billy said.

"You never know until you try," I encouraged him.

The words barely left my lips before Billy started to move, bringing the hunting knife in hard and fast, driving it toward my gut. I let him come to me, using my left arm to sweep the weapon away from my body as I stepped in close.

I'd meant to try and take control of the weapon, but I'd hit his arm with so much force he let go of it, sending it flying to sink into the drywall up to its hilt.

Billy tried to step to the side to give his buddy a shot at me, but I managed to get a hand on his arm and spin him about, pulling him close to my chest. His buddy didn't hesitate. He was already pulling the trigger as I pinned Billy to my body. The first round hit Billy in the chest, causing him to stiffen in shock. I tightened my left arm around his neck as I slid my hand between us to draw a Glock, bringing it up under Billy's armpit.

The second two rounds from the .38 hit Billy in the upper left chest and shoulder, spinning him out of my grasp as his legs buckled. He fell away from me, carrying my shot low and to the side as his body slid down my arm.

The round hit the southern man's thigh, dropping him to one knee as he pulled the trigger without aiming, his shot going high and to my right. He grabbed the gun with both hands, trying to steady himself as we looked at each other down the barrels of our guns.

I got my shot off before he did. The round hit him center mass, shattering his breastbone. My next shot was overkill, hitting him between the eyes as he fell backwards.

I stepped over the bodies and out into the hall, grabbing the blond girl standing there before she could react. I pushed her against the far wall, looking to see if anyone else was coming. Her eyes were wide. She didn't even go for the gun at her waist; she just looked at the bodies on the floor in shock.

"You killed them," Blondie said in disbelief. "You fucking killed them!"

"Why are you here?"

"Billy told me they were just going to scare the kid, make him leave. He said he didn't want him in the same building as the rest of us." Her voice was rising to hysterics.

I looked back into WC's room and then put the Glock against her temple before she could register what was going on, taking her life with a single shot.

A woman started to scream midway down the hall as she peeked out to see what was going on. She started to scream, "Gray!" and it took me a moment to realize she was looking at me. From a distance, in the gloomy hallway, I guess I looked scary enough.

I screamed back at her, and she slammed her door shut.

There wasn't a stairwell at this end of the building, and there was no way I was making it out the main door. I could hear her screaming inside her apartment, and it sounded like a herd of buffalo were charging through the hall below me. It wouldn't be long before they reached the second floor.

I saw a dead elevator at WC's end of the hall but no stairs, just a large window letting murky light in from outside. I put two rounds into the heavy sheet of glass and hit it at a run, bursting through the weakened section of glass.

The sudden transition from dimly lit hall to morning light sent a stabbing pain into my eyes, even with my shades down. I hit the ground blind, the impact racing up my legs to my hips as I let myself collapse and roll, trying to convert the downward force into a less harmful lateral movement.

I stumbled to me feet, the old injury to my right hip burning as I hobbled away, forcing myself to move through the pain. I made it to the corner just as gunfire erupted from the second floor, rounds hitting the ground behind me just as I made it to cover.

Air horns were blaring by the time I got a block away, my scarf tucked into a pocket, the sound of the Fort bell on the roof clanging between blasts of the horns. I ignored the alarms, forcing myself to walk normally, if slowly, as I circled back to the apartment, trying to look unhurried as other people rushed around, trying to figure out what was going on.

As I got further from the Fort, my heart rate slowed, the events in WC's room replaying themselves as I got further from the crime scene. Billy and the other dead fellow had attacked me and gotten what they deserved.

As for Blondie, her fate had been sealed the moment I saw her hands. She wore a massive diamond, and her knuckles were raw and busted up. WC was going to have scars from that ring for the rest of his life. He was lucky to have both his eyes and the ability to wipe his own ass to boot. A few more taps and she might have broken his skull open and killed him. As it was, his face would be covered in little scars.

I climbed the stairs to our apartment, relieved to be home.

"What happened out there?" Justine asked, slamming the door and locking it behind us.

"The kettle's getting ready to boil over. They were going to kill WC for what happened at the firehouse—and for hanging out with you and Dog."

"For helping me shampoo a dog?"

"Yep."

"Good thing I didn't blow him," she said sarcastically as she walked down the hall.

"Thanks," I said to her back, shaking my head. "Is he awake?"

"No. He's sleeping now. Did they see you? Will we be having company soon?" She said it almost casually, but she had our "Get out of Dodge" packs leaning against the island separating the living room and kitchen.

"Nobody saw me. Right now they think a gray got inside the wall."

"And none of them will ever mess with WC again?"

"Never," I told her, a note of finality in my voice.

She nodded, satisfied.

After the morning's excitement, the rest of the day dragged. We took turns watching WC and talking about what was next. Not with Haeslig; we pretended he didn't exist. We talked about where we were going to head after New Dover, as if the world were still a rationale, sane place.

Justine talked about the vacation she and her brother went on that always seemed to be part of her happiest memories. She was sure it had been just before Sam adopted them because the memories were so pure and full of happiness for her.

I told her about my mother, of what little I remembered about her from before she passed. My eyes had been really bad then. I could remember the way she smelled and the way it felt when she held me, but there was so little imagery to describe. It was all remembered sensations and emotions.

How do you describe what it feels like to have electricity pulsing through your raw corneas and the feel of your mother's skin, her hand sliding across your back, slowly taking the pain away? I can't do it justice.

Justine listened to me try, holding me tight at the end, having no idea how much she meant to me. Talking about my mother was like pulling open my chest and leaving my heart beating in the open air. They were sacred memories.

Around us, New Dover went about its day without noticing our absence. The alarms eventually stopping blaring, but we heard several patrols pass below our windows.

It was a long day.

Chapter 17

Two more days passed in grinding boredom. We hid in the apartment as downtown deteriorated into a riot of anger and fear that didn't quiet until the night forced everyone into their holes.

Late on the second night, Dog started to freak out, and WC, who was now conscious and able to open both his eyes well enough to see, almost unloaded a revolver into the drywall separating us from the spare room. I'd told Justine it was bad idea to let him have a gun.

"Something's out there," he said, forcing his voice to sound steady despite his shaking hands.

Justine looked at me and crossed the distance to WC, putting a calming hand on his shoulder and suggesting I go take a look as she pushed the revolver's tip slowly downward until it pointed at the floor.

"I'm sure it's nothing; the pigeons drive Dog crazy," I told him as I unlocked the door to the spare bedroom.

"Fuck that! Trust the dog," he said, the revolver clutched on his lap.

It was probably a good suggestion, but one I couldn't take. This was it; I could feel it: the culmination of a deadly game of chess was drawing near. I knew that Haeslig only saw us as pawns, but it only mattered for a little while longer. I was only planning on playing by his rules for so long.

The gym roof was especially dark that night. Normally the front of the building got a little light from the lamps strung up along downtown, but the diesel generator had been struggling to stay running since nightfall. The lights would flicker and come on, then fade as the generator started to die, then surge back to life as someone revved the diesel, trying to keep it going.

The effect was eerie, a slow strobe that made you feel like you were about to fall even though you were on solid ground, or roof, as it were. I held a Glock at my side and walked to the middle of the roof, waiting.

"Peace," a voice said from the bottom of a well. The sound was so deep, so lacking in any higher tones, that it

sounded fake. "Hay…slig sent me," the voice said, having trouble making the name understandable.

I scanned the darkness around the small, raised building on the roof and realized the voice was coming from above it. The brute's head and shoulders were above the outbuilding. I waited for the brute to say something else, but he just stood there, waiting.

"What did he send you for?" I asked.

"Oh," the brute said slowly, his arm coming up over the cubby to throw a satchel at my feet. I jumped back with a start. "You have?" he asked, standing like a lump in the dark.

"Ah, sure," I told him, picking up the satchel. Clearly the brute wasn't going to be giving any detailed instructions.

I saw the darker shape of his head and shoulders disappear and heard the faint slap as his feet hit the pavement on the other side of the gym when he stepped off the roof. It was an impressively quiet sound given his size and how far he'd just fallen.

I grabbed the satchel and headed back to the apartment, feeling uneasy. It was one thing for Haeslig to slip in and out, but the brute was five times his size and he'd made it in— and would no doubt make it back out—without raising the alarm.

"Don't shoot me," I yelled into the apartment as I came through the spare room.

"You're good," Justine called back. I still poked my head around the door to be sure. They stood in the kitchen, drinking warm cokes, WC's new revolver sitting on the counter between them.

"What's going on?" WC asked.

"Dover isn't going to be safe for much longer," I told him, setting the satchel on the island. It was made of old, worn leather and had a nametag clipped to the shoulder strap. I could imagine a middle-aged professor stuffing his papers into it at the end of the day, or a businessman filling it with contracts and memos.

"You're freaking me out," WC said, looking from me, to Justine, to the satchel, picking up on how we were both fixated on it.

"Sorry," I told him. "This place isn't going to last. It's not safe here."

He didn't want to hear it. Even after getting beat nearly to death by his own kind, he wanted to believe New Dover could survive.

"You're the ones giving the army guys information, aren't you?" WC blurted out. A moment after he said it, his eyes went to his revolver, his throat working up and down in fear as he wondered if he'd just gone too far.

"Dude, we are the good guys," Justine told him, sliding his revolver toward him on the counter so he could take it if he wanted.

"Yeah, yeah. You are the good guys," WC repeated, looking at his hand and how close it was to the butt of the gun but not moving to take it.

"This place isn't safe. They move in and out whenever they want," I told him. There could be no doubt who "they" were. "This town is going to be destroyed. It's just a matter of time." I couldn't help but look at the satchel when I said it. I wasn't trying to scare WC, but I felt like he deserved the truth.

"Something big is about to go down?" he half asked, half accused.

"I don't believe in sitting around waiting for them to come for us. We fight or we die." It was as simple as I could make it.

WC fell silent as he thought about it. "So what are you going to do?" he asked me, a bit of mischievousness creeping into his voice.

"The grays have a hierarchy. They have leaders, and we are going to try and kill one of them."

Justine winced when I said it, still not sure which side of the fence WC was on.

"What can I do?" WC asked.

"If we don't come back, you should get out of Dover." I paused. The next bit was going to hurt. "Let Dog go outside the wall—and then run for it."

"But…" WC started before Justine cut him off.

"It sucks. Delaware sucks. This whole thing sucks, but Dog's going to drag every gray, brute, and thrall to him like a magnet."

Hearing his name, Dog came out to sit between us all, looking at each of us, trying to decide where his highest likelihood of a belly rub was going to come from. He decided on Justine and plopped down so she could get to work. She bent down and scratched his belly slowly, her eyes welling up as his tail thudded happily on the floor.

"And where do I run?" WC asked, his voice quivering.

"West and then north. There are some maps on the table. Try to get into the mountains in Pennsylvania, away from the population centers."

"And…" Justine said, standing up from her belly scratching duties to go into our room. She came back out with a pack very similar to ours. "We got you a present."

"There is enough food for two weeks, three if you ration it, a nine millimeter pistol, and a nice, lightweight parka, which should hold you over into fall," I told him, showing him the pistol and a box of ammunition in a side pouch of the backpack.

"You think I'll live that long?" Sadly, it was an honest question.

"If you can make it out of Dover before it all falls apart, and you move during the day, maybe get a little luck in the mix, and don't decide to sleep in a nest full of thralls—yeah. I think you have a shot," I told him. If I'd met him before all this, I would have said not a chance, but he'd survived this far and that was proof enough he was capable.

"OK," he said, picking up a map of Delaware and plopping onto the couch to study it, trying not to look like he was watching us as he sat there in shock.

Justine crowded close to me, both of us staring at the leather bag on the island. I hesitated as I reached for it, but she was nodding, urging me to open it. I undid the clasps on the flap and flipped it back, reaching inside.

We were both a bit surprised as several eight-by-ten glossy photos spilled onto the counter. They showed a tall form draped in black, his face hidden from view by a cowl. Haeslig had taken a black grease pencil and circled the tall figure, writing "Han-su" beneath it.

Thanks, Haeslig. I never would have figured that out.

In each of the photos, two grays followed close behind

him wearing loose vests that showed different parts of their arms and sides in each shot. The same scribbling we'd first seen on the old men back at the power plant covered their bodies, but where those grays had been old and wrinkled, stooped over with age, these two glowed with strength and vitality.

Under the photos was a brochure for the State College Amphitheater and a seating map, adorned with a bit more of Haeslig's artwork. Justine stared at the drawing, her eye color shifting rapidly. I put a hand over hers, not sure if she was OK.

"I'm good," she said. "It just feels so unreal."

"It's almost done," I promised her, spinning the seating diagram around so I could get a better look at it.

Han-su was drawn in dark ink on the stage with his two bodyguards next to him. A stick figure with a long rifle was positioned in the lighting control booth, and another stick figure in a dress had been drawn with a small machine gun in the banks of lights and speakers along the upper lip of the theater. I guess the dress was Haeslig's idea of a joke.

Dotted lines traced out of each of the stick figures' guns to collide with the back of a bodyguard's head. The words "*Tomorrow Night*" were scrawled on the bottom of the map in a clipped, oddly flowing script.

"Creeps me out," Justine commented. There was something playful and evil in the way the diagram was drawn.

"Has to be done," I told her quietly, pulling out a local map to look at routes to the theater.

"What if it's a trap?"

"Haeslig has slipped in and out of here two dozen times. If he wanted us dead, I think he could have managed something less elaborate." I was careful to keep my voice low so that WC couldn't overhear.

"If he wanted us dead," Justine agreed, looking at the black and white photo of Han-su.

Chapter 18

The west gate was barely manned when we slipped through it early the next morning, our packs strapped to our backs. The guards were locked up tight in their pillbox and either didn't care that we were leaving or didn't even see us as we pushed the gate open wide enough to slip out.

Saying good-bye had been tough. Dog was happy we were awake so early, prancing around and tripping us up as we dressed and did a final check of our gear. In sharp contrast, WC looked at us with dead, flat eyes. He reeked of uncertainty and fear. I don't which of the two of them it was harder to walk away from.

Justine cried quietly most of the way to the gate, wiping her eyes with the back of her hand as she walked in front me, not wanting me to see. She had gotten pretty close to Dog.

Outside the wall, we picked up the pace, swinging west before turning north toward the amphitheater. When we were inside the mile marker, we slowed down, Justine stopping every now and then to clutch her forehead.

"Go slow. He's very close, and they are everywhere," she whispered to me.

"You OK?" This wasn't going to work out real well if she wasn't able to keep her head clear.

"Yeah. It feels like the worst PMS headache I've ever had."

She rubbed her forehead again and then tapped her finger in the air to the right, her eyes going a little wider, their whites swirling with hints of slate as I watched her, transfixed by the change. Her canines slid past her lips, her fingernails sliding out of her flesh to form dangerous black claws. It was the fastest I'd ever seen her turn so completely.

She pointed at the nearest cross street, darting away from me so quickly I didn't have time to follow. She was back on me before I could catch up, grabbing me by my backpack and dragging me after her.

My feet raced to keep up with my body as she propelled me forward, rushing me across the street and past several townhomes. She dragged me past two doors, slowing just a hair in front of each before jerking me forward again. At the third door, she kept moving, kicking it in without slowing her pace before pushing me roughly into the darkness of the house.

I skittered across the floor, barely keeping my feet as I ran into the far wall, spinning around just in time to see her slam the door shut in a strange display of quiet as she checked her motion just before the door made contact with the frame.

I waited as Justine hovered at the front of the house, peeking through the dirty windows. She held up a finger for me to be extra quiet as shapes moved through the street in front of us. A stream of shadows passed by as Justine hid behind the door, shaking her head at me as I put a hand on the butt of one of my pistols.

I paused, my eyes locked on the cloudy window panes. Justine held a finger up to me, telling me to be patient. A moment later, the street was empty again. I breathed a little easier.

"Kl-eer," Justine struggled to say, opening the door a crack to get a better look down the street.

"How much farther?" I asked as I stopped next to her, running my hand down her side to the top of her rear. She made a sound very much like a purr in response and shot me a warning look.

She slipped the city map out of her front pocket, letting the door open a little further for more light. We still had six or seven block to go, and she didn't look happy about it.

I put my thumb and forefinger down on the map, holding them two inches apart as I picked them up to show her with a smile: it wasn't that far. She gave me the finger and turned to the door, stuffing the map into her pocket as she went.

She punished me by picking up the pace, running to the end of the next block where she hunkered down behind a line of burnt out cars to let me catch up. The street was a parking lot as far north and south as we could see, burnt out cars extending from one side of the street to the other, jammed so tightly together most of them wouldn't have been able to open their car doors when the fire started.

Justine pulled me low as I scanned the burnt-out husks

and pointed at the roofline off to our left, her eyes locked on something I couldn't see. I knelt down to get a better look up through the skeleton of the car we crouched behind, but I still couldn't see anything.

She nodded very slightly up to the roof again just as a shape separated from an attic window and darted over the roofline to disappear. The gray must have been sitting in the shade of the dormer window, nearly invisible—to me.

I gave Justine a thumbs-up when she turned back to me. It was hard to interpret her expressions when she was changed, but she gave me a nod of her head before leading the way off. She found a narrow path between the burnt-out cars and then cut down a less congested side street to get us off the main thoroughfare.

As we got closer to the amphitheater, the air began to get heavy and wet with the stench of rotting flesh—a stark contrast to the neighborhood, which was all new construction. The houses had been part of the urban renewal projects kicked off a few years ago, built after the theater renovation.

When we turned the next corner, we could see the curved wall of the theater rising above the trees, its exterior covered in patterned concrete designed to mimic the appearance of an ancient coliseum. I'm sure it looked very nice when the stench of death wasn't overpowering your nostrils and the grass wasn't thigh high.

Justine kept a hand on my pack, urging me to go faster as we ran to the end of the block, crossing the final street as quickly as we could. She propelled me forward until we were running between the trees circling the outside of the theater, not stopping until we hid inside the shadow of the closest decorative arch.

My legs burned as I struggled to catch my breath. Sweat ran down my arms and dripped onto the ground as I crouched, leaning my back on the concrete as I let the tall grass swallow me up to my neck.

Justine slid out of her pack, setting it next to me on the ground as we both searched the street we'd just come down for signs of movement. We'd just run down a street of beautiful new houses—filled with thralls.

We were halfway down the street when we both realized just how close the thralls were. At first it looked like the insides of the houses were empty, and then the subtle lines of different shapes in the windows became clear as bodies shuffled about. Luckily it was nearly noon, and the thralls were jostling each other to get away from the windows, trying to hide from the sun.

I spent a few minutes catching my breath before my heart stopped pounding. Justine waited impatiently, her eyes darting about. When I was breathing normally, she pointed to herself and then motioned with the blade of her hand around the edge of the building. I nodded, starting to stand up, but she shook her head in the negative, touching my chest carefully before pointing to the ground. She wanted me to stay put.

I stared at her, not wanting to let her go by herself, but she tapped my chest again, using her knuckles this time and pointed at the ground forcefully. I rubbed my breastbone and nodded agreement. I wasn't going to win the argument. She moved to the edge of the arch before looking back one more time to make sure I was sitting tight, and then she was gone.

I watched the street, counting the seconds in my head, telling myself this was exactly what I'd been trained for as I passed a pistol from hand to hand, wiping the sweat off my palms every now and then. Of course, I'd never been so poorly restrained in the field before. I just couldn't seem to control the nervous energy flooding into me.

It wasn't fear, at least not for myself. I could have sat there until my water ran out if it was just me, but Justine was out there, and I had no way of knowing where she was. Even in her changed state, knowing she was faster and stronger than me, it felt wrong to let her go scouting alone. The watch on my wrist seemed to shake my arm each time the second hand moved forward, reminding me Justine still wasn't at my side.

To cap it off, I almost pulled the trigger when she popped into the space under the arch to my left. One moment there was nothing there, and the next, something moved through the grass so quickly my brain couldn't define friend or foe before I was swinging the pistol around.

Her hand caught my wrist gently but firmly, keeping the tip of the weapon well away from her. She slipped inside my arm the moment I relaxed, pressing her body tight against me as she put her head into the space between my neck and my shoulder.

It tickled, especially when she shivered against me. "How's it look?" I breathed into her ear, pulling her tighter to me as she growled deep and low in her chest. I squeezed harder, enjoying the coolness of her flesh against my burning skin. I listened as she swallowed hard several times, fighting to push back the change far enough to regain her voice.

"I don't scare you," she said thickly into my neck, still not believing it.

"Not even a little," I told her, my free hand stroking her flank. She tried to say something back, but I was already kissing her neck, working my way up to her chin and around her lips, trying not to cut myself. Even in the between state, her incisors were to be respected.

I got a jab in the ribs for distracting her with kisses. "You weren't kidding about the PMS," I groaned, rubbing my side as if she'd done some damage.

"You're an ass," she struggled to get out, pulling a black marker out of her breast pocket and turning to the wall.

main entrance
quarter around the building
shitload of brutes

I guess they don't train teenage girls how to give tactical summaries in school these days.

"At least I came prepared," I told her, pulling a bundle of blue and green climbing rope out of my pack.

She nodded in agreement as she took the bundle, clipping it to her belt. She moved like a panther, running out of our cover to place one foot on the closest tree, pushing off it and flying upward with her arms outstretched, catching the lowest branch. She pulled herself into the greenery and disappeared into the tree. Only a faint tremor of leaves revealed her movements as she climbed.

A shadow crossed the open ground between me and the tree as Justine leapt to the amphitheater wall. I caught one glimpse of her beautiful ass above me as she climbed and had to shake it off, telling myself to focus. I waited as she moved out of sight, listening for any sound of alarm, half expecting bodies to come crashing down from above.

I grabbed the end of the rope when it tumbled down next to me and tied the free end to our packs. Then I took hold of the line and leaned back, making sure it was secure before taking the first few meters hand over hand. When I got above the arch, I steadied myself with my feet, climbing as fast as I could.

Justine grabbed my hand when I reached the top, pulling me over the ledge to stable ground. She had our packs up before I rubbed the cramps out of my arms. We were on an open walkway behind a huge array of lights, looking down into the open-air theater.

We jogged along the service walk until we reached the center of the building, where a multi-story structure formed the spine of the theater. The door into the building was unlocked. Justine went through first, leading the way into the dark interior. I came in behind her, slowing to lift my shades and let my eyes adjust to the darkness.

On our left, a short stairway led down. A sign by the stairs proclaimed the control booth and private boxes were both below us. We descended to the next landing. Halls split off to the left and right, leading to the private boxes. The control booth stood directly in front of us.

Light spilled into the hallway as Justine slipped through the door into the control room, crouching to stay below the control panels built against the large windows.

The view was impressive. The stadium seating descended to the stage level below us, while massive lighting and speaker pods circled the upper rim of the amphitheater. Justine turned to me and smiled toothily as we looked down on the stage.

"Let's get dis done," she said slowly, taking her time to pronounce each word.

"I couldn't agree more," I said, grabbing her pack so she could slip out of the straps.

Chapter 19

Waiting is a highly tuned skill. People think it's a passive process, an exercise in controlling boredom, and while that's certainly a part of it, the bigger challenge is training to stay alert and not slip into a daydream. It sounds so simple, but when you're sitting in enemy territory, the odd mix of adrenaline and fear can act like the midday heat on a summer day, urging you to shut your eyes for just a minute to rest.

We sat in the darkness, watching the light trace lines of brightness across the floor as the sun moved above us. The waiting was hard on both of us. Twice I'd had to shush Justine. I couldn't quite reach her from where I was, but she was close enough to hear me.

It must have been especially hard for her. Before we hid, she'd told me she could feel them coming—from all around us. My concern grew as the last beam of sunlight crept across the floor and faded. Justine couldn't sit still; she kept moving and fidgeting.

The time was upon us. The undead began marching through the orchestra entrance in pairs, a gray next to a brute, each pair perfectly spaced from those in front and behind. I shushed Justine one last time, tracking the undead with my rifle as they marched around the curve of the orchestra pit and turned to face the stage as a single entity.

The undead stood facing the stage as the temperature dropped. Goose bumps broke out all over my arms. Absolute silence reigned—until a pitiful noise escaped Justine. She mewled off to my right, the sound sending a spike of fear through me. I couldn't lose her now; it was almost go time.

The heavy canvas curtains at the rear of the stage split apart as two grays pulled the fabric back, their heads bowed slightly in respect as an obscenely tall, thin gray stepped through onto the stage. The grays arranged around the stage opened their voices in unison, a harsh, unknown language coming off their lips.

I couldn't understand what they were saying, but it sounded like they'd said it many times before. I zoomed in and focused on Han-su's long, alien-looking face. Thin strands of hair fell sparsely across the top of his head like clear silk threads.

The grays holding the curtains released them and took their places on either side of their master. I focused on the gray to the right of Han-su, looking at his pale face and exposed incisors, watching as his lips moved in a never-ending chant. I couldn't stop looking at his arms, at the flowing script covering his exposed skin, the bluish ink pulsing from within.

Justine was pulling in air as if she were about to drown, hyperventilating in short, gasping breaths. I didn't have a choice: I had to reach out and touch her. I couldn't sit there looking down my scope listening to her suffer, not knowing if she was OK.

I stretched out slowly, moving as quietly as I could. I reached out across the cramped space between us, creeping my hand across the floor, pulling my upper body closer to her. My side was pressed painfully into a metal strut, my fingers reaching out into the black. I shifted my butt and pressed harder into the obstructing metal, my fingers just brushing up against the fabric of her clothes.

I pushed harder, the strut pressing painfully between my ribs as I got a finger curled in the cloth of her pant leg, pulling her foot toward me until I could grab her ankle. Her skin was cold, and I felt her breath hitching in her chest with just a hand on her leg. The honorific mantra was winding down. We didn't have much time, and I couldn't do this without her.

I shook her leg, trying to get her to snap out of whatever paralysis held her, my own fear growing with each second. One of the whisperers was looking around, sensing something wasn't right.

"Brothers," Han-su said, his voice echoing through the amphitheater. "We find ourselves under attack from all sides," he continued, his voice cutting through the air. I could just see the whisperer through the scope, stepping forward to get his master's attention.

I pinched Justine's leg hard, digging my fingernails into her flesh. Our presence was about to be discovered. Justine yelped, pulling her leg away from me. She shook her head and turned to me with blazing eyes, her upper lip was pushed out, fangs fully extended. I matched her stare for stare until she smiled, and I knew she was still mine.

I turned back to my rifle. I fought a brief urge to take a shot at Han-su and then pushed it away. We had a plan, and although I didn't trust Haeslig, I believed him when he said trying to take out his master with a rifle would lead to failure.

For the first time in my life, it felt strange to pull the trigger. The grip was plastic, and the trigger felt flimsy, but the rifle went off, taking the head off the brute on the far right of the stage. As the brute's body collapsed, I pulled my head out from the cardboard box taped over the monitor, keeping an eye on the screen as the image shook.

I'd barely had time to pull my head away from the monitor when four brutes ran across the light rigging to dive into the empty seats just below the control booth. They hit the structure at full speed, tearing apart the luxury boxes as they worked their way into the control booth. The image through my scope shook as a brute picked up the shooting platform and then turned to static as the creature snapped the rifle in two and broke apart the camera bolted to its sight rail. It's amazing what you can do with enough time and unlimited access to a few electronics stores.

My screen was already dead by the time the brutes in the control booth tripped their good-bye present. I couldn't see it, but I could hear the popping of grenades as they went off in rapid succession.

I looked to Justine one final time before putting the second part of our plan into action. She was breathing hard but nodding her head in the affirmative. I tucked one arm over my eyes and flipped the trigger with my other hand. It felt like a massive weight was leaning on my chest as the pressure wave rolled over me. Above us, the floor of the stage erupted as detonation cord cut two large holes into the planking, dropping the tattooed grays down into the crawl space where we were hiding. Justine had told me the space under the stage was called the trap room, but it didn't look like much more than a crawl space to me.

My ears were ringing from the concussion, and my eyes were tearing up, but that didn't stop me from aiming and firing. The MP5K's roar was dull in my ears as I unloaded on the whisperer four feet in front of me. The blast and the fall had barely fazed him. He moved like lightning, the blue scrollwork on his arms flashing as he spun around, taking cover behind a concrete support column.

The gun's slide clicked back on empty as the whisperer came smoothly around the other side of the concrete support, a dark smile on his face as he closed the distance between us. I dropped the machine pistol as I grabbed my machete, bringing it around as hard as I could in the confined space.

The whisperer didn't try to dodge or evade, he just raised his arm to take the blow. Blue light flashed and flew through the air like fireflies as the edge of the blade stopped cold, unable to cut his flesh.

I pulled the blade back to hack at the whisperer again, but his hands were already grabbing me, spinning me around violently. He pulled me off my feet and sent me flying through the air. My stomach rose into my throat for a split second as weightlessness overcame me, and then I slammed into the front wall of the crawl space. My back flattened against the wall before my head whipped back with a crack. There was pain, and then everything faded.

The back of my head hurt, and I knew there was something I should be doing, but everything was fuzzy. I blinked, sucking in a breath to try and clear my mind. When my eyes focused, I was looking up through one of the holes we'd cut in the stage with the det cord, watching the control room burn.

I remembered stringing the grenades together with wire. They must have set the control room and the luxury boxes on fire when they went off. I blinked again, shifting my focus to the figure standing on the stage above me.

Han-su wore a strange expression on his face. He looked pleased. That's when it all came back to me: we were here to kill him. I blinked again, knowing the smile on his face meant something bad for me—no, for us. The moment I thought it, the sound of Justine screeching cut through me like a knife. I shifted my view back into the crawlspace, searching for the source of the sound.

Justine was in the middle of a savage battle. I'd never

seen her so lost in the fight before. She moved like liquid between the two whisperers, kicking and punching in a constant whirl of activity, a beautiful grace behind the brutality of it. It took my breath away to see. She was a predator of the highest order.

Which made it even harder to watch as the whisperers slowly ground her to dust. Each time Justine struck a whisperer, their skin would flare blue. Their vests were in tatters, but their skin was unbroken. Justine was not so lucky. A trickle of blood ran down her face, and she had multiple cuts on both arms. As for me, I was left for dead or dying, a mere human to be forgotten. They should have made sure I was dead.

The MP5K was lost somewhere in the darkness under the stage, but I'd managed to keep a hold on the machete when I was thrown. I fumbled it back into its sheath and pulled the Glock from under my left armpit.

Justine screamed and snarled as the whisperers tormented her, tearing her back to shreds one little cut at a time. They were playing with her. As soon as she turned to face one, the other would score a glancing blow from behind. I knew why Han-su was smiling. They weren't trying to take her down, not yet. They were just enjoying the game as they bled her slowly. She was fast and tough, but there was only so much she could do against an enemy she couldn't damage.

I put two fingers in my mouth and whistled. It sounded dull to me, but both the whisperers turned to look. I lifted the Glock at them as they stood waiting, unafraid. Justine stepped toward the distracted grays as I shifted my aim until Han-su was in my sights.

Two rounds thundered from the gun, empty casings spinning through the air. Above me, a blue sphere of light flashed around Han-su as the whisperers threw their hands out, shifting their shields to defend their master.

The air in front of Han-su thrummed with energy, and the bullets formed comet tails as they were caught in the whisperers' shields. As the bullets disintegrated in flashes of blue fire, Justine landed on the back of the closest whisperer, her legs wrapping around his midsection as her fingers closed on his face.

Whatever power they had, they still had limits. Justine's clawed fingers dug into the whisperer's face, the tip of her index finger slipping into the gray's eye a moment before she tore his head savagely to the side so she could rip at the pale flesh of his neck with her teeth. Blood, deep and rich, sprayed from his throat to cover her face as her weight carried them both to the ground.

Blue lightning raced through the tattoos on the downed whisperer's skin, making Justine twitch with each pulse. She bit and tore, spitting out chunks of meat from the gray's throat as the shocking pulses slowed and then ended.

The remaining whisperer stepped back, looking at Justine and his fallen brother with shock. I put a shot into his forehead as he looked up to his master for direction. Blue light flared, keeping the round from penetrating, but the kinetic force snapped his head back, causing him to stumble. I aimed my next series of shots all at Han-su. Either way, one of the bastards was going down.

Training, or maybe compulsion, made the whisperer shield Han-su, and the rounds aimed at the undead lord dissolved in the blue sphere of energy that flashed into being as each round met its edge. Justine was on the second whisperer before my last round left the Glock, punching a hand into the side of his ribcage so she could get her fingers around meat and bone.

The whisperer screamed in agony as she tried to tear out his insides, driving an elbow into her face as he fought to free himself from the pain. She shrugged off the blow, ramming her arm farther into his chest.

The whisperer's screaming increased into a shrill cry of pure anguish. Justine cut it short when she took his throat in her free hand. She looked up to meet Han-su's gaze as she crushed the whisperer's airway with a snarling smile. The whisperer shook and contorted, his eyes bulging. His legs kicked out as he fought to pull air into his lungs, his face turning a deep purple.

"*Enough!*" Han-su bellowed. Justine looked up, showing her teeth as she threw the body of the dead whisperer to the ground. A primal growl escaped her lips as she crouched to leap up onto the stage. Even in his anger, a pleased smile still touched the corners of Han-su's mouth.

I dropped the empty Glock and drew my remaining pistol. Justine was overmatched, but she was too lost in bloodlust to realize it. I brought my arm up as fast as I could, my finger already tensing on the trigger. If I could just get a few shots off, maybe Justine would have a chance to hurt him while he was distracted.

The thought flitted through my mind as an iron bar slammed into my wrist. My pistol flew out of my hand and went skittering away in the darkness beneath the stage. Cold fingers grabbed my arm, whipping me around. I threw an elbow into the gray behind me as I tried to twist away. Concrete would have yielded more. Steel pincers grabbed my arms from behind, pulling my elbows to the middle of my back painfully.

I was immobilized, forced to watch hopelessly as Justine uncoiled. Han-su put out a hand almost casually, catching her by the throat like she was a harmless kitten, not a bundle of muscle and claws trying to tear him to pieces. She wrapped around his arm, trying to use her leg muscles to push free, at the same time scratching and clawing at his flesh.

Han-su looked at her with something close to amusement on his face as she raged. He let her struggle for another moment and then shook her violently. Her body whipped this way and that as she went from a scratching, fighting, hellcat to a pitiful creature just trying to hold on to keep her neck from being broken. Han-su didn't stop shaking her until her legs unlocked from around his arm and her body hung limp.

I kicked and struggled against the figure holding me, trying to get free. The gray was pinning my arms behind me, my elbows almost touching in the center of my back. I raged, ignoring the pain, but was unable to break free.

"Bring him," Han-su commanded.

The hands released me, only to grab me roughly and throw me up onto the stage proper. When I tried to climb to my feet, I was kicked from behind and knocked roughly to my knees.

"Master," a voice whispered from behind me, steel fingers running through my hair to force my chin down in deference, no. Fresh anger welled up in me. I knew that voice.

"I was wrong to doubt you, child," Han-su said, sending another wave of cold washing over me. "She is quite magnificent," he said, mostly to himself, his free hand touching her face.

I surged to my feet only to be punched in the kidney by Haeslig. The gray pushed me away like trash as he took a shallow bow to his lord. I staggered to a stop, helpless as Han-su lifted Justine's face so close I thought he meant to kiss her.

A strangled cry broke from my chest as his face stopped, nose to nose with hers. He pulled back her eyelids, flashes of blue running across his hand as he stared into her eyes. Her body convulsed and her hand came up to grip Han-su's wrist in a feeble gesture. A smile crept across Han-su's face as Justine's hand fell away. In a last flare of defiance, she spit weakly in his face before her body went slack once again.

Anger, quick and absolute, overcame Han-su. "Insolent slave!" he hissed as he threw Justine. I managed to step to my right, catching her body in mine. We tumbled backwards in a tangle of arms and legs. The world was a blur of motion and pain. Justine's augmented weight threatened to crush me as we rolled across the stage floor, coming to a halt against a pile of moldy stage curtains. I came to rest almost in a sitting position, Justine's body lay behind me, her legs on either side of my waist.

The other grays still stood around the edge of the stage, all save Haeslig. "Thank you, Master. I swore I spoke the truth. She is something truly special," Haeslig rasped in his deep, dry voice.

Rage and fear turned my stomach. I'd wanted to believe we had a chance to get out, even if the odds weren't in our favor. To know we were set up from the beginning, and I'd brought Justine directly to them, made me want to vomit.

I wiped blood away from my eyes. My head had been gashed open during the tumble. Blood and sweat ran down my face, mixing with the tears streaming from my eyes as I twisted to get my hands on Justine, trying to see if she was breathing.

The coolness of her skin when she was changed had never bothered me before. I'd always been able to touch her and know the strength of life just beneath the surface, regardless of how cool she felt. Now I pressed a hand to her chest, not feeling a heartbeat, unsure whether the coolness touched was the coldness of death.

My fingers spread out over her chest, tears running down my face. The stillness went on and on, my own heart dying with each passing second. Pain and sadness mingled with shock. It hurt to breathe. My hand was sliding off Justine's chest when the hammer blow of her heartbeat struck. I pressed my hand down, not sure I hadn't imagined it. The next beat struck me like lightning.

She was alive.

My world snapped back into place, the fear of losing Justine turning to a white hot fire. "You bastard!" I yelled at Haeslig, spraying spit as I screamed. Fresh blood ran between my eyes, dripping off the end of my nose.

Haeslig turned his head to look at me. "It was the only way," he said, spitting the words at me with disdain.

"Kill the boy. He will pay for killing my shields," Han-su commanded, apparently willing to forget the more significant part Justine had played in their deaths.

"Yes, Master," Haeslig said, putting his hand on the pommel of his bowie knife.

"Fucker!" I hissed, climbing to my feet as I drew my machete.

Haeslig slid his bowie out, looking at me with a strange smile. The bastard was enjoying the game. Hatred welled up like fire in my veins. I wanted so badly to find out if his blood would quench it. I smiled back at him as he approached. When he was halfway to me, he spun on his heel, leaving his back to me.

"Coward!" I hissed, but Haeslig only held up a hand as if to tell me he'd be with me in a moment. I was about to say something else when the air around us thrummed with energy. I shut up, watching as frost formed up and down the length of my machete and my breath plumed in the air.

"What is this?" Han-su exclaimed, pointing a disturbingly long finger at Haeslig.

"It was the only way," Haeslig repeated, stepping aside as the air next to him shimmered and fell apart in flakes of crystallized ice.

A tall, sinewy form stepped from within the shimmering flakes of snow. He wore dark clothes, and a head full of black hair fell to his shoulders. The newcomer could have passed for an exceptionally tall man except for his hands, which ended in claws almost as long as his digits.

"So my stepson betrays me," Han-su said, straightening out his robes and flattening them to his chest as he looked at Haeslig.

"He offers you redemption," the newcomer intoned, a plume of frozen air leaving his lips as he spoke.

Han-su broke out in nervous laughter. "You will shortly remember that I am your equal, Ravi," he spit. "How dare you call me to open a portal with my own blood?"

Han-su flicked his hand and his grays began to close on the stage. But then the air in front of them shimmered and crystallized, falling away to reveal a dozen grays and an equal number of brutes blocking the way. Ravi's men now stood between Han-su and his lieutenants.

Ravi laughed, enjoying the moment. "Oh, it really isn't me. Your stepson is the one calling out for it. You know he was feeding your pesky little murderers there all the information they needed to hunt."

Han-su sucked in a breath, his chest puffing up in indignation as his eyes bored into Haeslig. The gray shrunk next to Ravi, his posture changing as though he expected Han-su's glare to burn him where he stood.

"You were a fool to come here," Han-su threatened. The sound of hundreds of screaming voices filled the night air. "My brood is coming," Han-su taunted, stepping sideways and taking a slightly crouched position. "To me," he whispered, speaking to his lieutenants.

"You're weak," Ravi said flatly. "If you were strong, your child wouldn't be here to petition for your rank."

"So be it," Han-su spat, pulling two long blades from within the folds of his robes. Each was two feet long and glinted silver in the night.

Han-su's forces attacked without hesitation, almost punching through the wall of Ravi's forces to reach their lord in that first rush. In the end, the numbers were on Ravi's side, and his grays and brutes pressed Han-su's forces away from the stage.

Haeslig and Ravi moved apart so they could come at Han-su from opposing sides.

Han-su snarled in frustration, realizing he was on his own. He edged closer to Haeslig, sliding his two blades lightly over each other, making a metallic rasping noise.

Ravi held back, letting Han-su edge closer to Haeslig. For a moment, it appeared Ravi was just going to watch Han-su and his rival fight it out, but the moment Han-su focused fully on Haeslig, Ravi struck.

Ravi appeared more human looking than his counterpart, right up until he attacked. When he moved, any illusion of humanity fell away. No human had ever moved so fast.

Han-su had taken a slashing wound across his back before he realized Ravi was on him. Han-su spun around, deflecting the next strike with one blade as he pushed Haeslig away from his front with a wild slash. Blades and claws met in sparks of blue fire as Han-su and Ravi fought.

The two masters danced across the front of the stage, elegant and deadly as they fought. Haeslig followed them as best he could, trying to stab at Han-su whenever the opportunity presented. He was a third wheel in a fight that was well over his head.

A cold feeling sunk into my belly as I watched. I'd come to see Justine freed from Han-su's grip, but seeing the two masters battle chilled me. They were too strong. It made me mad and shamed me, but it was time to run, even if Justine wasn't free yet. I sheathed my machete and grabbed Justine by the shoulders of her combat vest, dragging her away.

She weighed a little over a hundred pounds soaking wet, but I only got her a few feet before I was huffing and puffing. When she was half turned, her weight doubled or tripled, and as completely changed as she was, I think her weight must have been multiplied by double that again. Not that I'd ever mention that fact to her—ever.

I pulled her another few feet before having to pause and rest again. The inside of the amphitheater was a raging mess. I was afraid if she didn't wake up, I wasn't going to be able to move her far enough away to get clear. One side or the other would eventually win the fight, and I didn't want to be anywhere close by when that happened.

I stood over her and tilted her head back so the blood dripping off my nose fell on her mouth and chin. It wasn't enough. I put a hand to my scalp, squeezing the edges of the gash until fresh blood flowed freely. A stream of red traced across her cheek until I corrected my aim, letting it flow in a long stream past her lips. Her mouth filled with blood and she swallowed, but it was a slow, lazy motion. Her eyelids were starting to flutter as her mouth opened wider, the blood calling to her.

Haeslig hissed, bringing my attention back to the front of the stage as he stumbled a few steps away from the fight. He staggered and dropped to one knee, pressing an arm to his mid section. Bright red blood spilled over his arm to sprinkle the stage floor. The gray drove the point of his bow-ie into the wood to help push himself back to his feet, his face grim and full of pain.

Han-su glanced at Haeslig with a look of evil delight on his face. Before he could savor it, though, Ravi had closed on him again. The two masters met in a blur of strikes and parries, blue sparks flying between them. When they parted, they each took a step back, panting for breath.

Han-su stood tall for a moment and then his shoulders slumped forward as he pressed a hand to his chest. The front of his dark robes was shredded and wet. He looked around, a touch of panic visible in the way his head darted about, looking for his lieutenants. They weren't going to be any help. They fought in a tight knot, surrounded by Ravi's ambushers, barely able to defend themselves as they were pushed farther and farther up the bleachers. The fire cast the whole scene in flickering orange and red light.

Haeslig sidled up next to Ravi moving stiffly, his wound slowing him. I smiled as I saw the blood dripping off Haeslig's arm. He'd betrayed us, used us as pawns so he could lure Han-su to his death. I'd played right into it, chewing up grays until Han-su finally had no choice but to show his face. If I got lucky, I'd get to see Haeslig's life blood spilled onto the stage floor.

I slapped Justine across her face in frustration, trying to wake her. The only thing I got in return was a faint moan. I grabbed her by her vest again, pulling her away inch by inch. I saw a door at the back of the stage. I had to get to it. I'd worry about what came after that when I got there.

I pulled her a few more feet and paused to breathe; watching the battle in front of me, afraid at any moment someone would remember us. As if called by my thought of trouble, a thunderous boom cut through the other sounds of chaos.

Beneath the burning section of the amphitheater, a wide series of emergency exit doors warped as more blows landed on them. Han-su looked to the doors with hope, his attention taken for just a second. Ravi saw the opening and darted forward, a clawed hand striking in a wide roundhouse.

Han-su saw it coming. He moved with such purposeful grace I thought he may have pretended to be distracted just to goad his enemy into a hasty attack. Han-su caught Ravi's wrist on his blade and flicked the blow aside as he drove his other dagger forward. Ravi turned, the blade meant to spear his heart slicing across his breast instead. The sudden change in posture left him unable to recover in time to dodge the vicious kick Han-su leveled at him. Hit hard, Ravi was propelled into the air, coming down over one of the gaping wounds in the stage to fall into the space below.

Haeslig found himself wounded, standing in front of his old lord, his face a mirror of the fear gripping his gut. I watched, wanting Han-su to cut the bastard down and at the same time afraid he would. Once he cut down Haeslig, I didn't doubt he'd turn his attention on us. It surprised me when Han-su hissed at Haeslig and then bolted off the stage, racing into the bleachers, trying to flee.

Ravi leapt up from beneath the stage, snarling in anger as he stalked passed Haeslig, shouldering him out of the way. Ravi jumped into the first row of bleachers, whipping something off his belt as he gave chase.

Han-su was racing up the bleachers when Ravi whipped

out an arm, a thin cord whistling through the air like a shot. The weighted end of the cord wrapped around Han-su's calf, taking one of his legs out from under him.

The tall gray caught himself on his arms but it was a short-lived save. Ravi jerked down on the cord, dragging his enemy through several rows of bleachers. Before Han-su could do anything, Ravi took the cord in both hands, pulling with all his strength.

Bleachers flew through the air as Han-su came sliding down, scrambling to get a handhold. He was clutching a plastic seat in his hands when he came to a stop at Ravi's feet. The blue plastic fell from his fingers a moment later when Ravi kicked him in the face with enough force to snap his head back at a painful angle. Han-su's head rolled as Ravi picked him up and threw him down onto the concrete in front of the stage. Han-su hit hard, flattening with a thud.

I was almost to the rear of the stage, but I couldn't take my eyes off the battle. Justine's head had fallen back to look up at me, her eyes rolling disturbingly to the back of her head. I kept moving, trying to ignore her vacant stare.

Han-su staggered to his feet, dazed and unsteady. He'd lost his blades somewhere during his tumble through the bleachers. Haeslig was screaming, urging Ravi to finish it. I understood why he was so animated when the emergency doors behind Han-su fell with a squeal of tearing metal a moment later.

A sea of writhing forms spilled through the opening, surging out of the tunnel beneath the bleachers. Ravi tried to get to Han-su before the horde of undead could surround their master, but he was too late. A crush of bodies enveloped Han-su in a protective wave as he stood tall above them, waving them forward. Grays, brutes, and thralls climbed over each other in their eagerness to save their lord.

Ravi met the wave of thralls with a howling scream, his claws sweeping through the first bodies unlucky enough to reach him. Haeslig watched the horde rushing in and paused at the edge of the stage. He leaned forward like he was going to jump down and join Ravi and then backed away from the edge of the stage slowly.

Ravi screamed, "To me, to me!" over and over as he

fought. The grays and brutes who'd been part of his original ambush broke off their attempt to crush Han-su's surviving lieutenants and came crashing back down the bleachers, forming a loose wedge as they descended.

They punched a hole halfway to their master before the sheer numbers pouring in ground their forward momentum to a halt. The area in front of the stage became a blender as Han-su's and Ravi's forces each fought a brutal battle to finish the fight. If either side could kill the other's master, the battle would be more than half won.

Haeslig was caught up in the edge of the maelstrom, his own retreat thwarted by several of his brothers seeking vengeance for his betrayal.

I had almost reached the door at the rear of the stage.

Ravi was surrounded, fighting off the press as best he could. Bodies would surge over him and then he'd reappear as he cut through whatever was on top of him. Haeslig was much closer to the stage but just as occupied as he fought to keep two grays from finishing him off. Ravi was cut off from all sides, and every moment, he looked closer to being overwhelmed.

My butt hit the door. I'd made it to the exit. I grabbed the handle, cursing as it refused to turn. I dragged Justine against the wall and turned back to the door, cursing and kicking the painted steel again and again. Other than scuff marks from my boots, the door was unharmed.

I turned to rest, my back to the door, panting as I wiped the blood off my forehead to keep it from running into my eyes. The split in my head had started running as I kicked at the door. I looked out on the nightmare scene raging in front of the stage and shook my head. It seemed so unfair that we'd survived everything so far only to be slaughtered because I couldn't open a door.

I was about to turn back to the door when I saw a brute come up behind the two grays fighting Haeslig. I was sure the turncoat was about to meet his end. Instead, the brute grabbed the two grays by their heads and crushed them together. Haeslig slumped in weariness as the brute stood over him, battering thralls away as they tried to swarm.

Ravi was tearing through everything that came his way,

but even so, he was disappearing from view moment to moment as bodies surged over him. Ravi's forces had been picked apart and now fought small, desperate battles for survival as wave after wave of thralls crashed upon them.

Han-su stood victorious amidst the chaos, thralls streaming around him in a never-ending flood to pour into the meat grinder that was the last stand of Ravi's remaining forces.

I watched as Han-su urged wave after wave of thralls at Ravi, thinking the fight was coming to an end. Ravi was buried beneath a swarm of thralls, and more pressed in every moment.

I was about to turn back to the door in a panic, feeling like our time was running out, when a ripple rose through the masses around where Ravi had been standing and everything in a twenty-foot circle fell to the ground like blades of cut grass. Ravi stood in the center of the clearing, his arm rotating over his head as he spun a length of cord in the air. The line raced with blue fire, and anything stepping into its path dropped to the ground, severed through and through.

Ravi took a painful step toward Han-su, dragging one leg behind him. A brute and two grays charged in, trying to slide beneath the spinning death above their heads. Ravi adjusted, and even the brute's thickness was no match for the spinning cord and the blue fire racing up and down its length. The smell of burnt meat mingled with the smell of rotten flesh as more thralls crowded in only to be cut down in wisps of steam and smoke. The length of cord was moving so fast it looked like a large blue disc was hovering around Ravi.

Han-su waved his hands as he screamed unintelligible words, trying to direct the mindless crush of bodies pouring into the theater. Ravi stood where he was, the cord moving faster and faster over his head until I could hear the whistling over the sounds of the fire and the battling undead.

A loud pop rang out and then Ravi held his hand straight over his head. The length of cord raced around his arm then wrapped around his body, outlining him in blue flames. A flash of light lit up the theater. When it vanished, the space where Ravi had stood was just a burnt image of light in the back of my eyes.

A second pop sounded, followed by another flash of light. It took my eyes a second to adjust, and then I found him. Ravi had reappeared behind Han-su, his body still draped in cord flashing with blue flames that licked at his clothes.

The fire raging in the center of the amphitheater cast everything in flickering red light as Ravi snaked a loop of cord around Han-su's neck. Ravi pulled the cord tight, spinning Han-su in a tight circle, threatening to kill his captive unless the ring of grays around them backed up. Han-su tried to speak, but the cord cut too deeply into his throat. Ravi put his mouth to his rival's ear, saying words only Han-su could hear.

Whatever was spoken, Han-su was not happy to hear it. His legs kicked out feebly, his eyes wide. The circle of grays edged in, but Ravi forced them back with a snarl, pulling the cord tighter around Han-su's neck.

Han-su made a hand gesture at his grays, but they didn't help him and retreated, disappearing into the mass of thralls. I couldn't help but smile; they were abandoning him. I watched, unable to look away, wanting to see Han-su's life end.

Ravi smiled, thinking he had carried the day—at least until the two brutes pushed their way through the thralls carrying a still form between them. Han-su stretched his fingers out to the brutes, slowly curling them into a fist. Ravi shook his prisoner angrily, not yet understanding.

I did. The grays weren't abandoning their lord. They were running for their lives.

The brutes set their cargo down: a gray, his form so still the brutes each kept a hand on either of his shoulders to keep him from falling. His ashen skin looked like solid stone, and something strange covered his face. It looked like spider eyes had been tattooed all over his exposed skin.

Realization slowly dawned on Ravi. He pulled Han-su's head to his ear, screaming at the other master as he shook him. Han-su's face was turning purple, but his eyes were open as one of the brutes stepped behind the tattooed gray, grabbing his head and twisting it violently.

Ravi was screaming, but both the tattooed gray and

Han-su were already dead. I knew the moment Han-su died because whatever hold he had on Justine was released, and she bolted upright, screaming. She looked around, the scream dying on her lips as she took in the scene around her, uncertain of where she was until I put my hand out for her. Her mouth moved, unable to make the words she was trying to speak, but she took my hand.

The battle in the amphitheater paused, everything quiet but for the crackling flames. The stillness settled and then erupted in a sudden cry as the link to thousands of thralls was severed at once. As chaotic and horrible as the battle had been before, it paled in comparison to the raging hell of thousands of enraged thralls.

Ravi disappeared once more, buried under a sea of enraged. The pile of bodies crawling over him quickly rose until a hill of undead squirmed and writhed where he'd been standing. Justine growled deep in her chest, panting softly as her eyes took in the hell on earth before us.

"Can you open the door?" I asked her. Enraged filled the theater, and the grays and brutes still fighting for survival were only going to keep them occupied for so long.

Justine grabbed the door knob, the muscles in her arms flexing as she twisted it as far as it would go, wrinkles forming around the steel of the handle as the metal bent. The muscles in her arms quivered, straining against the tempered steel until she had to let up, rubbing her hands together to take away the sting. The door still blocked our way.

"Let me know when you have it open," I told her as she took up her grip on the door handle again. She nodded as I readied myself with my machete, shaking out the kinks in my arms. I was useless against the security door, but I could buy her time.

I took the head off the first thrall to reach me, stepping to the side as its body fell. I chanted curse words as I worked, swinging the machete over and over as a constant stream of thralls made it onto the stage and loped toward us. Something slammed into the door behind me, and I spared a glance over my shoulder, hoping to see the door swinging open. It was still closed, Justine's fist resting in a huge dent in the center of the door.

"We have to go!" I screamed at her, as if she didn't understand how bad the situation was.

She nodded, ignoring the pain as she pulled her hand back, leaving the print of her bloody knuckles on the steel. She huffed once and began pummeling the door like it was a punching bag.

I wiped my brow with my forearm as the next wave of thralls came loping across the stage. I didn't try and hold my ground; I moved in a small box around the doorway in front of Justine, flowing around bodies as I cut them down, sliding beside and through them as they came to meet their end.

The thralls were running so fast they were hitting the rear of the stage wall even though they were already dead, their momentum carrying them onward to thud against the concrete, leaving bits and pieces of their putrefying faces stuck to the surface as they fell. Justine ignored the bodies slamming into the wall on either side of her, concentrating on the door.

The sounds of rage and agony filled the building. Rotted, decayed throats raised voice to the song of hell, thousands of undead screams and cries rising into the night.

I took the head off another thrall and slipped on the blood-slick floor, sliding to my knees in the midst of the next oncoming wave of undead. Justine was pounding on the door; she couldn't have heard me if I'd been right next to her.

I pushed myself backward, lashing out at legs with my machete, kicking up a wave of filth as I slid. The mass of thralls in the building began to flood over the stage along its entire edge. We were running out of time.

A brute appeared out of the chaos, kicking and punching the enraged away from him as he charged me like a massive linebacker. I shook my head in disbelief as I climbed wearily back to my feet. The theaterre was burning down around us while crazed thralls surged everywhere, and yet I was squaring off against a brute.

He looked at me with big saucer eyes as he closed the distance, throwing a thrall behind him like a bowling ball, tangling up several more of the enraged as they swarmed up onto the stage. I steadied myself, waiting until he swatted another thrall away from his side to strike.

I leapt forward, my blade high in the air, aiming for his neck. Surprise filled me as Justine slid between me and the brute, a hand flying up to catch my right wrist.

I realized a half second too late that it wasn't Justine. Haeslig had my wrist in an ice cold hand, his fingers pressing into my flesh painfully. "There's no time for this!" he screamed into my face, nodding to the brute, who looked at us both with a puzzled expression.

Justine turned around just in time to have the brute push her out of the way and kick the door in as if it were made of cardboard. She snarled at Haeslig when she saw his hand gripping my wrist, and he let go quickly, looking behind him before darting past her through the door. The time had come to flee or die.

"Fuck," was all I could say as Justine grabbed my shoulder, pulling me past the brute into the darkness behind the door.

I got one last look through the doorway before the brute came through. The bottom of the theater was a writhing mass of arms and legs, interspersed with whirlpools of death where a gray or brute fought to raise the price of their life just a bit higher. Here and there thralls stumbled about in flames, spreading fire to anything that would burn.

Then the brute was squeezing through the door and grabbing everything in the hallway to block the way behind us. It wasn't much, but it would delay the thralls long enough for us to gain some ground.

Haeslig led us through the rear of the building, pausing to let the brute take out the door leading to the staff parking lot. The battle raging on the other side of the theater spilled rapidly around its outside border; enraged thralls fought everywhere. Bodies pressed up against the fence around the staff lot, and several thralls struggled in the barbed wire strung across the top of the fence.

"Lead them away," Haeslig said to the brute as we made it to the gate closing off the lot. The brute nodded, shattering the lock holding the gate closed without any effort.

The big guy stepped out into the open and started to whoop. It was a strange sound, something between a dog barking and a baby with a deep chest infection coughing. He waited until he was sure he had their attention and then ran off to the northeast, clapping his hands together as he went—a final oddity to add to the memory of a bad night.

Haeslig started to jog to the northwest but stopped, pausing to make sure we were following him. I looked at Justine. She shrugged, growling at Haeslig in warning as she nodded for him to move.

Even with Haeslig leaking blood from multiple wounds, I had trouble keeping up. Haeslig would have left me behind, I think, but Justine slowed down every time I had to catch my breath; he in turn would slow down as well, fretting at our pace.

"We are almost there," Haeslig said to us, urging me to keep up.

Behind us, the fire expanded, brightness growing as the flames spread to the surrounding townhomes, tinting the night orange.

I was getting ready to tell Haeslig we were parting ways no matter what when we stopped at the next intersection. He walked up to me, his face only a few inches from mine.

"I keep my bargains," he told me, pressing a set of car keys into my chest. "Keep her safe," he said, his eyes locked on mine. "For me," he mouthed before stepping away. It put a chill in me as he spun about, rapping his knuckles on the hood of the late-model Buick in front of as he walked away. I wanted to do something, to stop Haeslig, but Justine was already collapsing into the backseat, and I was exhausted.

I let Haeslig go and climbed into the Buick. The shade of green was slightly different from the one we'd rolled into Dover in, but it was close enough.

Epilogue

We tried to make our way south the next morning, but the madness from the night before had left most of Dover burning and the streets swarming with enraged thralls.

If anyone downtown was alive, we never got closer than twenty blocks to them. The flames and shambling hordes of thralls kept pushing us farther away until we didn't have a choice. We needed to put ground between us and Dover before the day was spent.

We drove north into Pennsylvania, mostly in silence. Justine spent the most part of the first two days sleeping in the backseat. Bruises circled her neck, and both her hands turned black and blue from where she'd tried to fight her way through the door.

She cried quietly in those first days as her body worked to mend itself, putting her in a black mood. That didn't improve until we were climbing into the mountains of northeastern Pennsylvania. The natural beauty of the land seemed to pick up her spirits as we drove.

I held her hand as we meandered up and down mountain roads, not caring about anything else as long as I had her close. I refused to think about Haeslig's last words to me until there was something I could do about it.

"Stop," she said to me as we meandered along a mountain road. "I think I know this place."

I pulled over and we climbed out of the Buick. "I've been here. I know where I am!" she said, full of astonishment and excitement.

She was right. She knew exactly where we were.

www.ingramcontent.com/pod-product-compliance
Lightning Source LLC
Chambersburg PA
CBHW060800120626
46557CB00001B/42